BLOOM COUNTY®
EPISODE XI
A NEW HOPE

BERKELEY BREATHED

IDW

BLOOM COUNTY EPISODE XI: A NEW HOPE

BERKELEY BREATHED

A WORD ABOUT THE ACCOMPANYING TEXT IN THIS VOLUME:
ALL COMMENTARY COMES FROM THE ORIGINAL FACEBOOK POSTS
AS WRITTEN BY FANS IN REACTION TO BLOOM COUNTY STRIPS.

PUBLISHED BY TED ADAMS
DESIGNED BY SERBAN CRISTESCU
COVER AND LOGO DESIGN BY BERKELEY BREATHED
EDITED BY SCOTT DUNBIER

WWW.IDWPUBLISHING.COM

TED ADAMS: CEO & PUBLISHER
GREG GOLDSTEIN: PRESIDENT & COO
ROBBIE ROBBINS: EVP/SR. GRAPHIC ARTIST
CHRIS RYALL: CHIEF CREATIVE OFFICER/EDITOR-IN-CHIEF
MATTHEW RUZICKA: CPA, CHIEF FINANCIAL OFFICER
DIRK WOOD: VP OF MARKETING
LORELEI BUNJES: VP OF DIGITAL SERVICES
JEFF WEBBER: VP OF LICENSING AND SUBSIDIARY RIGHTS
JERRY BENNINGTON: VP OF NEW PRODUCT DEVELOPMENT

PRINTED IN KOREA

19 18 17 16   2 3 4 5

ISBN: 978-1-63140-788-8 HARDCOVER
ISBN: 978-1-63140-699-7 SOFTCOVER

Dedicated to the anonymous fan that years ago dropped off a box
on my desk at a signing that contained a carefully arranged set of complete
Bloom County strips: the only one to ever exist. We've used it ever since as
a guide. Also dedicated to the wonderful fans who follow *Bloom County* so
loyally on Facebook—your comments inspire me daily.

And, of course, to Milo, Sophie and Heather.

—Berkeley Breathed

THE FIFTH ELEMENT

Over the years since I stopped my daily comic strip, I've oft pondered what was off. I wouldn't have quit 26 years ago if something hadn't been amiss. In those olden days, popular newspaper comics earned millions a year.

Yet, as is part of my dubious legend, I never met a single deadline—not one—in nearly a decade. I was always, always late. I made the mistake of adding up the costs of those missed deadlines, in syndicate fines, and emergency shipping costs. It is a Ferrari-e$que number.

Off. Why couldn't I execute the comic strips in anything but a frenzy of weekly, rushed, and woefully late panic? And why was I ready to depart the hard-earned space in a thousand newspapers after only nine years?

What was *off*?

I wasn't sure, but I very much suspected that whatever it was, it was identical to the magic, unnamed fifth element that had flown from both Gary Larson's creative id as well as Bill Watterson's.

Note that previous to *The Far Side, Calvin and Hobbes,* and my own romp, successful comic strips simply didn't stop. Typically, strippers died with their inky boots on, with ideas scrawled around their studios for strips still yet to draw. Often their children, widows, or their dogs would try to soldier on.

Why did we *not*? What was *off*?

My mind went to this yet again in 2015 when Harper Lee's villainous publisher put to press her exploratory practice notes and called them "Mockingbird's Prequel."

Soon after, Harper—one of *Bloom County's* most unexpected fans—finally departed. She left having abandoned quite a creative universe of characters almost 55 years before—the very ones that had directly inspired my own in 1980.

Why the silence after *Mockingbird*... the hushed void that her vile publisher so desperately tried to fill? What... had been off for Harper?

I mourned Miss Lee and her vanished world. And then thought about my own. Rare, these: Worlds and characters that are more alive for one's readers than they are for their creator. We who stumble upon them are the Blessed Ones... not so much clever as maybe just plain *lucky.* We shouldn't walk away too easily.

So in 2016 I reread the letters that my childhood literary hero had come to write me a generation later, imploring me not to end the characters that meant so much to her. She, the silent and mysteriously invisible ghost of the literary world, the Great Unheard and Unspoken... had signed a letter to me—to Opus really— "Love, Harper."

She let her created universe die. Yet she demanded *mine* to keep going. She ran out of time. I still had some. After 26 years, I considered, and made the decision, to revive *Bloom County* in the time it takes to toast bread.

Look at the picture here. I've just found the old four frames from *Bloom County,* circa 1984... and drawn Opus within one of them for the first time since 1989.

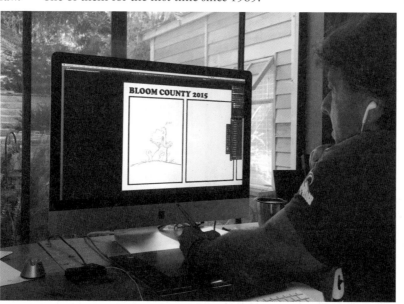

I wasn't entirely sure at all that I could get to panel four with any particular creative purpose.

When I did, my family reports that they heard a noise unique to their experience living in my midst. A noise I myself cannot remember actually uttering during the 30 years previous: I snickered like a kid. I had amused myself.

I had finally found my own audience.

It took a quarter-century, middle age, children and the traumas and triumphs of a life very, very fully lived to deliver the **Fifth Element** so absolutely positively needed for a writer... but one so easily lost.

Not love. That's relegated to life itself. Art and expression needs much more. But it's related:

JOY.

Read the strips in this book with a discerning, jaundiced eye and compare to the *Bloom County* of old. There is plenty of shared DNA. But there is something else. You can see it in the faces of my characters and the attitude of the prose.

I am having as much fun as you are.

No more fatigue-drunk drives to airports at 5:00 A.M. I can't wait to get back to the sketchpad and make myself laugh and get it posted fast. I read all the comments and giggle with all of you on Facebook.

Joyfulishness.

"Don't let Opus die," wrote Harper.

Okay. A bit late. Some things don't change.

Berkeley Breathed
Santa Barbara, California
Spring, 2016

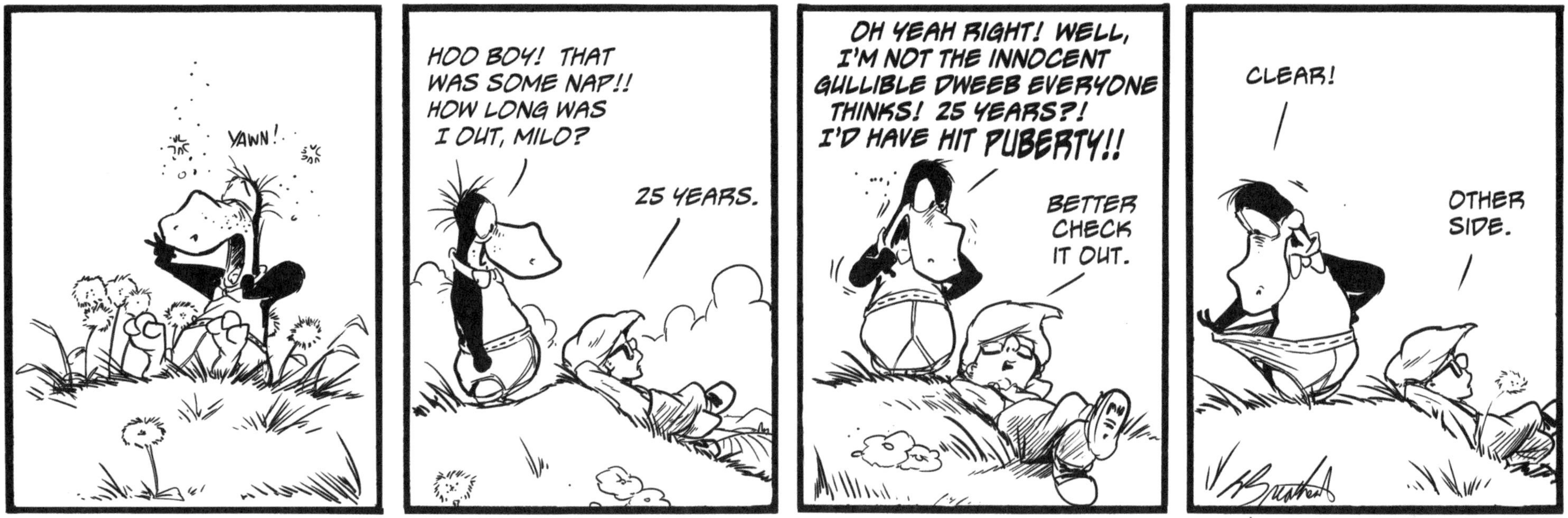
YAWN!
HOO BOY! THAT WAS SOME NAP!! HOW LONG WAS I OUT, MILO?
25 YEARS.
OH YEAH RIGHT! WELL, I'M NOT THE INNOCENT GULLIBLE DWEEB EVERYONE THINKS! 25 YEARS?! I'D HAVE HIT PUBERTY!!
BETTER CHECK IT OUT.
CLEAR!
OTHER SIDE.

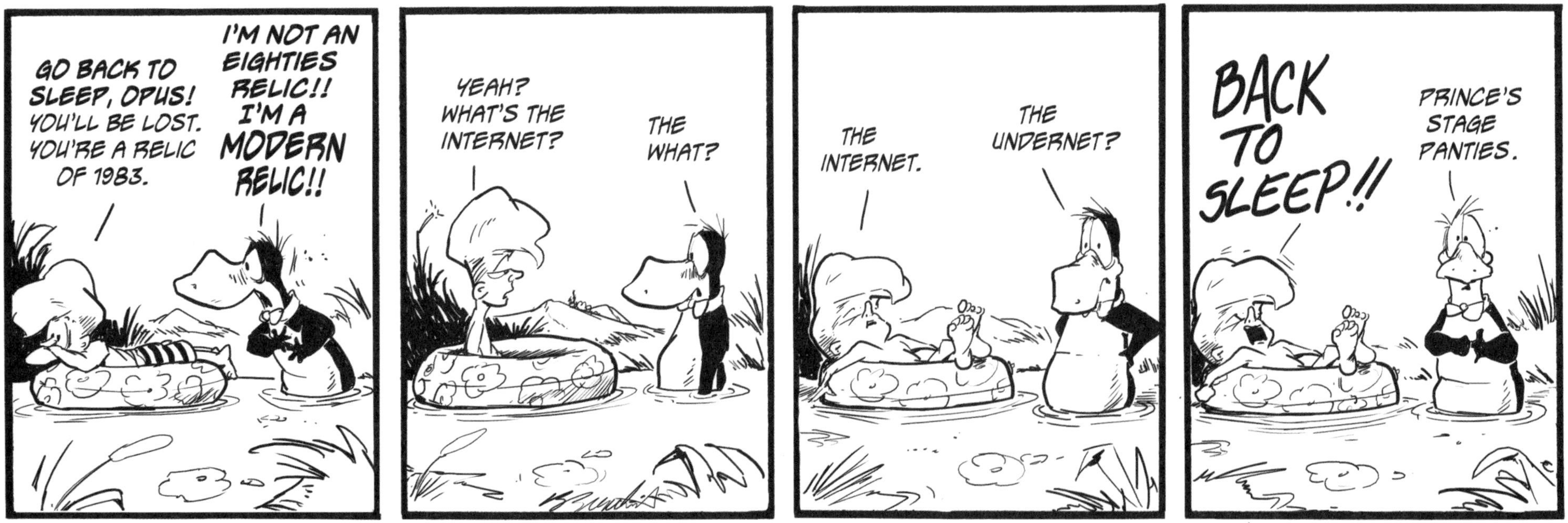
GO BACK TO SLEEP, OPUS! YOU'LL BE LOST. YOU'RE A RELIC OF 1983.
I'M NOT AN EIGHTIES RELIC!! I'M A MODERN RELIC!!
YEAH? WHAT'S THE INTERNET?
THE WHAT?
THE INTERNET.
THE UNDERNET?
BACK TO SLEEP!!
PRINCE'S STAGE PANTIES.

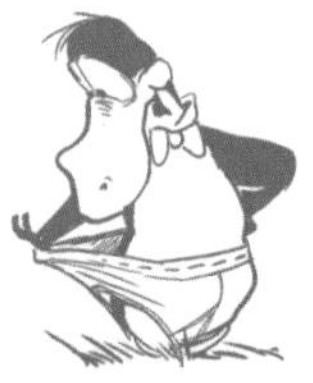

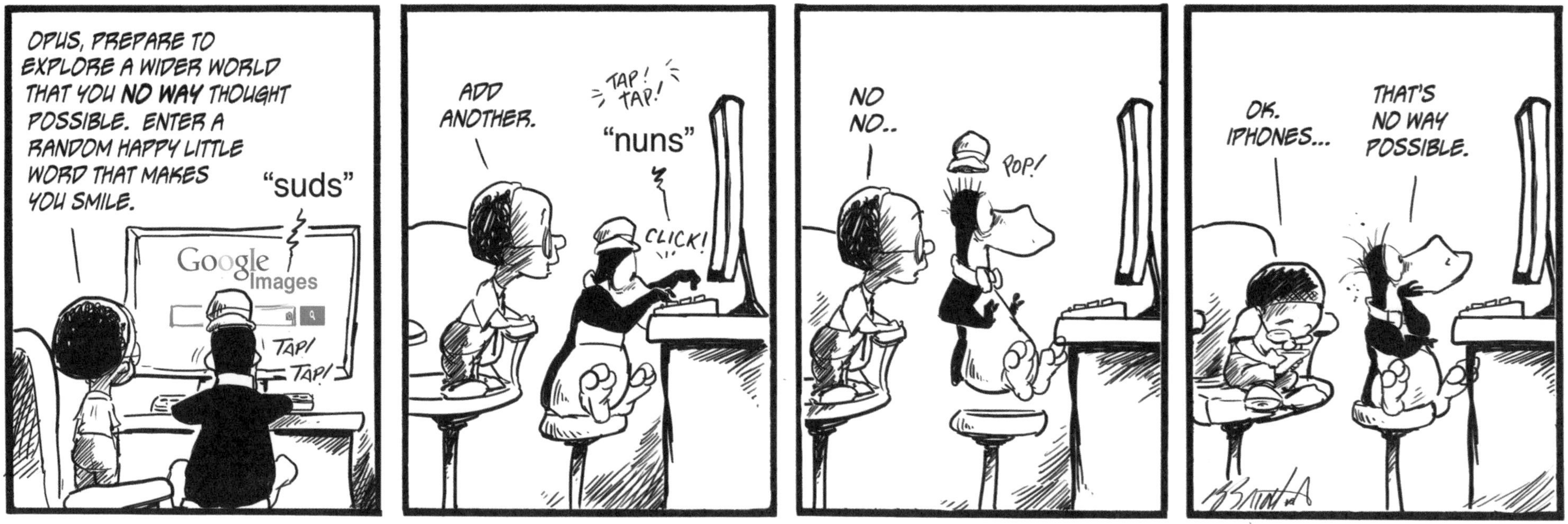
OPUS, PREPARE TO EXPLORE A WIDER WORLD THAT YOU NO WAY THOUGHT POSSIBLE. ENTER A RANDOM HAPPY LITTLE WORD THAT MAKES YOU SMILE.
"suds"
Google Images
TAP! TAP!
ADD ANOTHER.
TAP! TAP!
"nuns"
CLICK!
NO NO..
POP!
OK. IPHONES...
THAT'S NO WAY POSSIBLE.

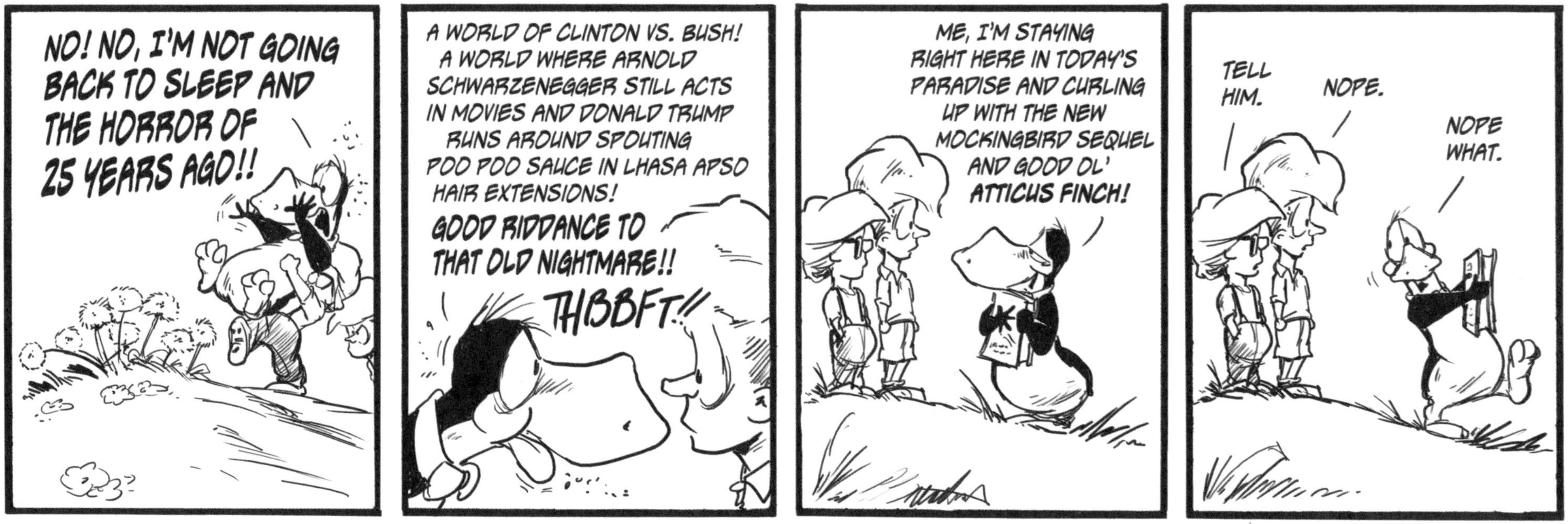
NO! NO, I'M NOT GOING BACK TO SLEEP AND THE HORROR OF 25 YEARS AGO!!
A WORLD OF CLINTON VS. BUSH! A WORLD WHERE ARNOLD SCHWARZENEGGER STILL ACTS IN MOVIES AND DONALD TRUMP RUNS AROUND SPOUTING POO POO SAUCE IN LHASA APSO HAIR EXTENSIONS!
GOOD RIDDANCE TO THAT OLD NIGHTMARE!!
THBBFT!!
ME, I'M STAYING RIGHT HERE IN TODAY'S PARADISE AND CURLING UP WITH THE NEW MOCKINGBIRD SEQUEL AND GOOD OL' ATTICUS FINCH!
TELL HIM.
NOPE.
NOPE WHAT.

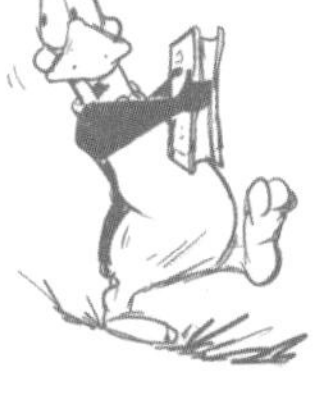

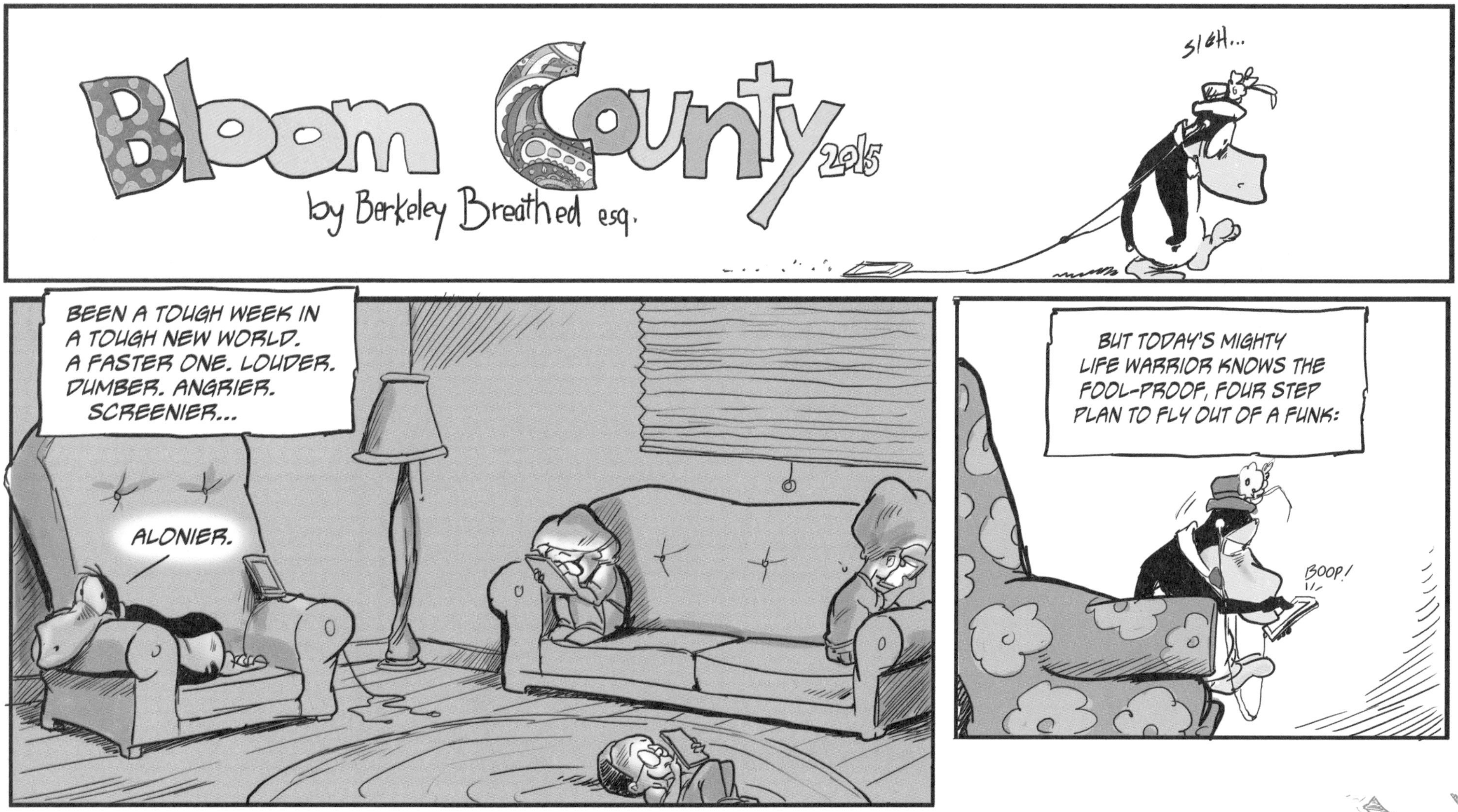
Bloom County 2015
by Berkeley Breathed esq.
SIGH...
BEEN A TOUGH WEEK IN A TOUGH NEW WORLD. A FASTER ONE. LOUDER. DUMBER. ANGRIER. SCREENIER...
ALONIER.
BUT TODAY'S MIGHTY LIFE WARRIOR KNOWS THE FOOL-PROOF, FOUR STEP PLAN TO FLY OUT OF A FUNK:
BOOP!

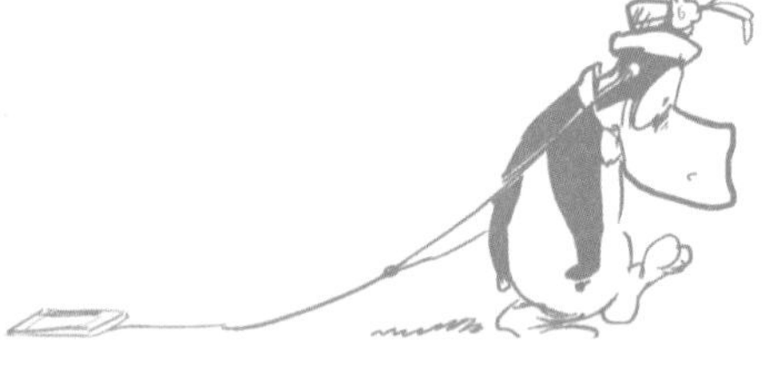

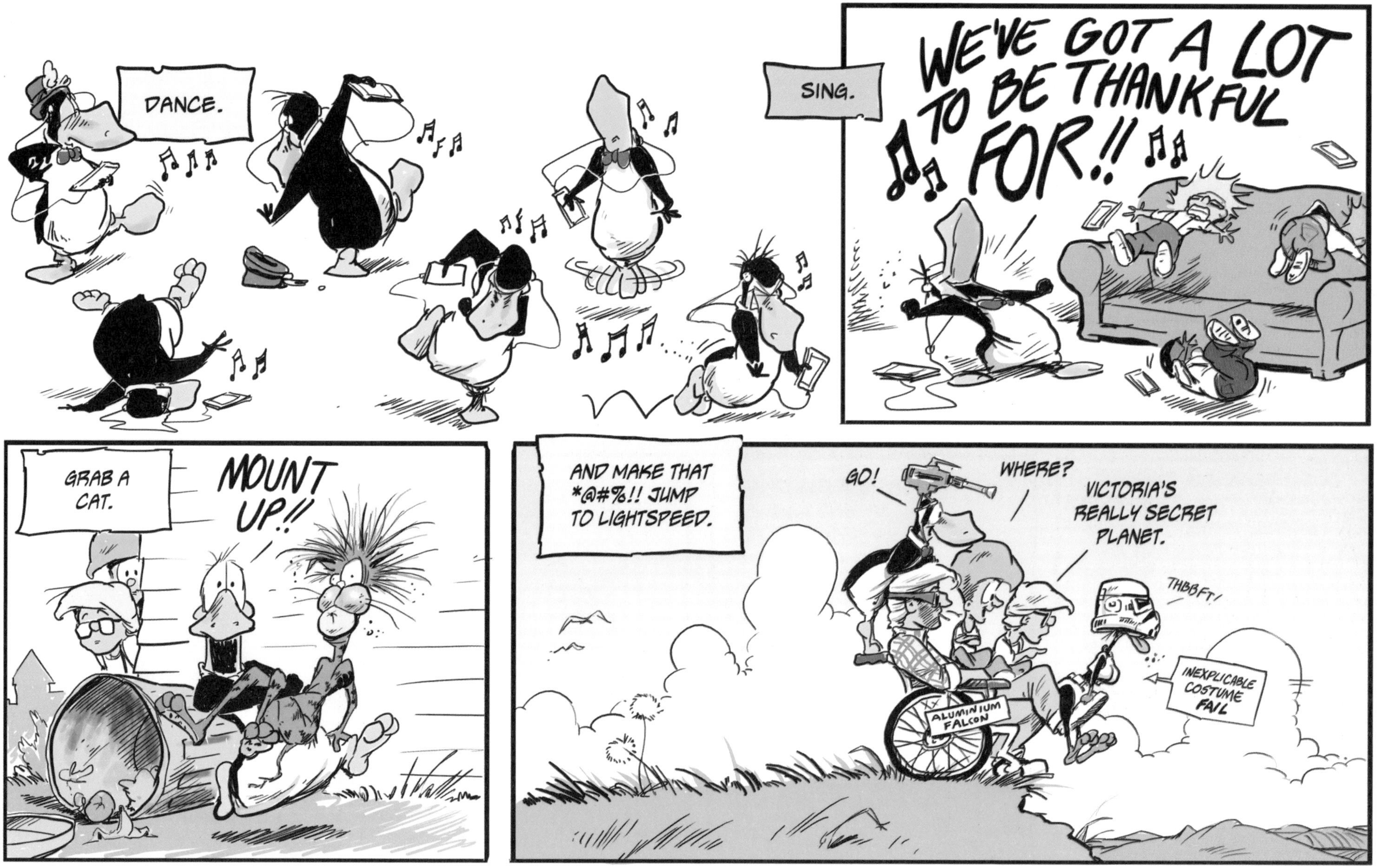
DANCE.
SING.
WE'VE GOT A LOT TO BE THANKFUL FOR!!
GRAB A CAT.
MOUNT UP!!
AND MAKE THAT *@#%!! JUMP TO LIGHTSPEED.
GO!
WHERE?
VICTORIA'S REALLY SECRET PLANET.
THBBFT!
ALUMINIUM FALCON
INEXPLICABLE COSTUME FAIL

In the early '80s I was in 8th grade living with my dad overseas when my dad shared this comic strip that made him laugh. He was a closed off individual and I thought if this *Bloom County* comic strip can provide an opening and maybe a way to connect… I had to give it a try. It worked! Not miracles, but it was something and sometimes that is enough. I also started drawing your characters and still to this day when I am inspired to draw I return to Opus & the gang! My dad has since passed, but I still have all your books and refer to them often. Thank you for being the connection for my dad & I. It was, and still is, greatly appreciated.

Your humble fan forever,
—Nicole Crawford

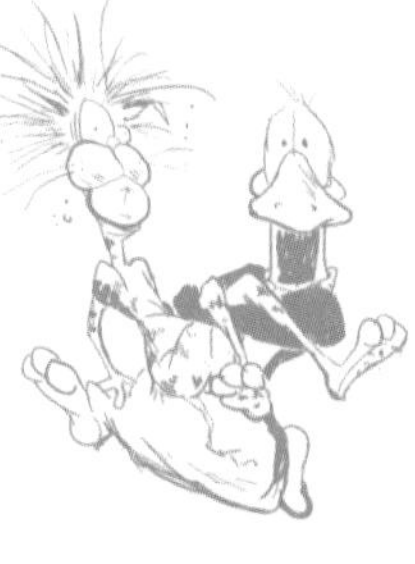

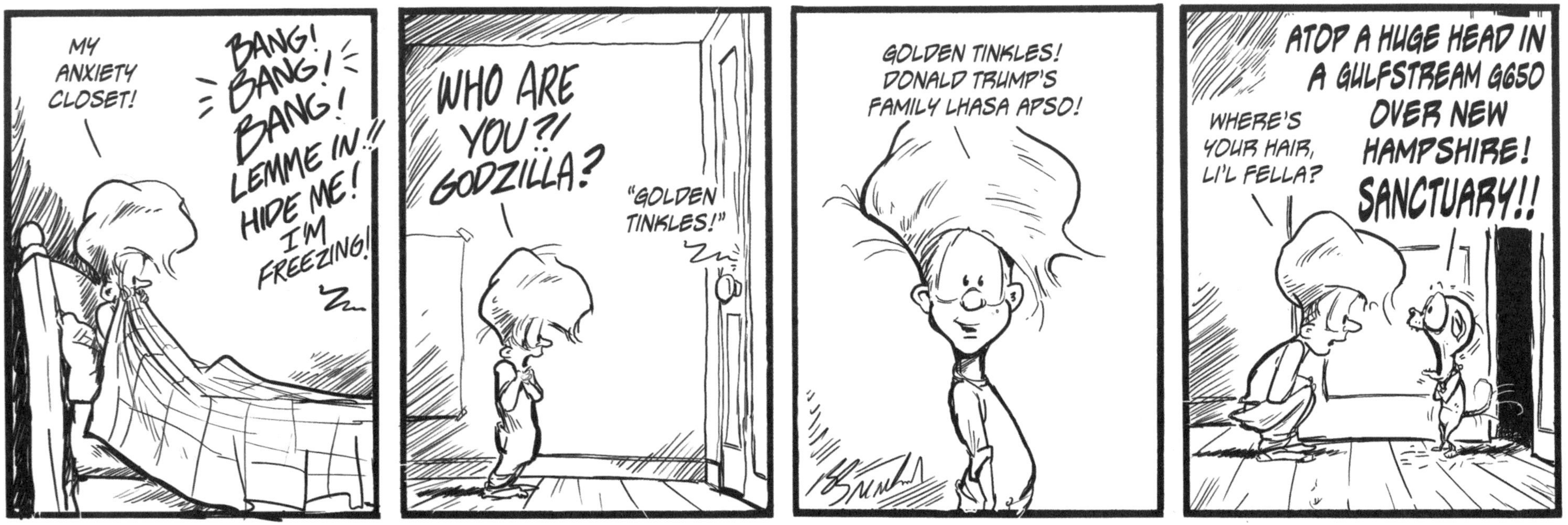
MY ANXIETY CLOSET!
BANG! BANG! BANG! LEMME IN!! HIDE ME! I'M FREEZING!
WHO ARE YOU?! GODZILLA?
"GOLDEN TINKLES!"
GOLDEN TINKLES! DONALD TRUMP'S FAMILY LHASA APSO!
WHERE'S YOUR HAIR, LI'L FELLA?
ATOP A HUGE HEAD IN A GULFSTREAM G650 OVER NEW HAMPSHIRE! SANCTUARY!!

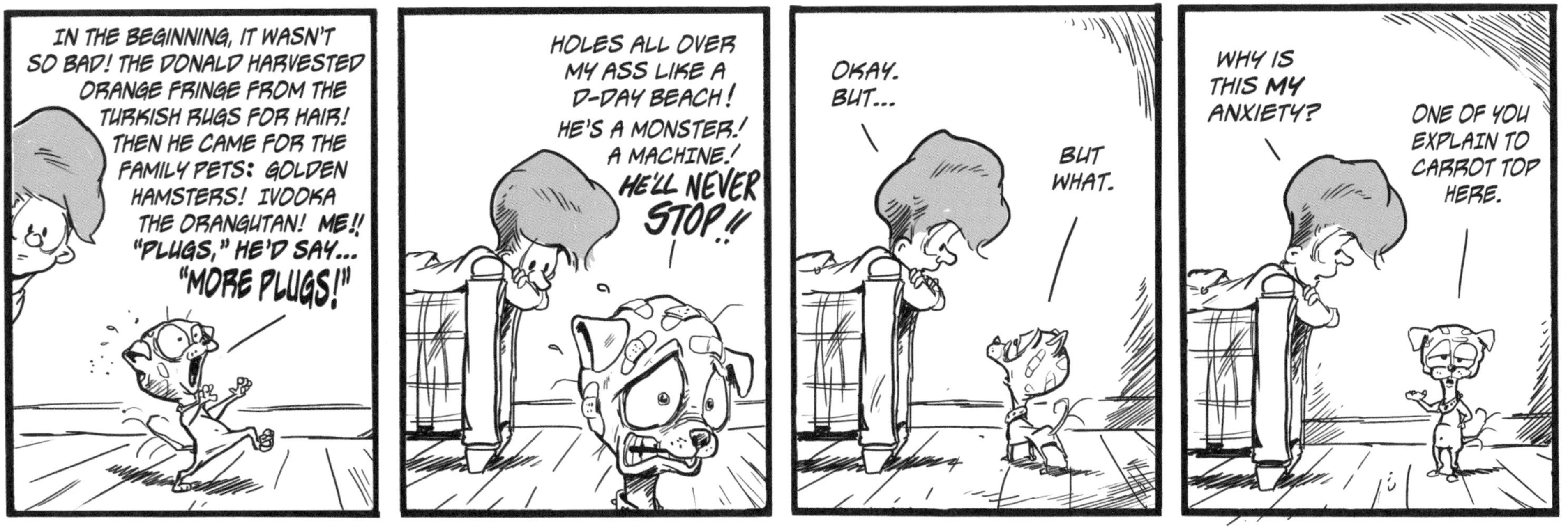
IN THE BEGINNING, IT WASN'T SO BAD! THE DONALD HARVESTED ORANGE FRINGE FROM THE TURKISH RUGS FOR HAIR! THEN HE CAME FOR THE FAMILY PETS: GOLDEN HAMSTERS! IVOOKA THE ORANGUTAN! ME!! "PLUGS," HE'D SAY... "MORE PLUGS!"
HOLES ALL OVER MY ASS LIKE A D-DAY BEACH! HE'S A MONSTER! A MACHINE! HE'LL NEVER STOP!!
OKAY. BUT...
BUT WHAT.
WHY IS THIS MY ANXIETY?
ONE OF YOU EXPLAIN TO CARROT TOP HERE.

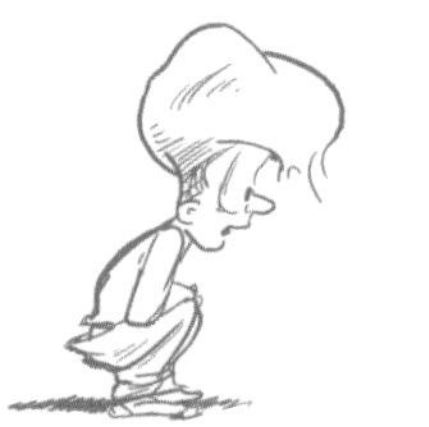

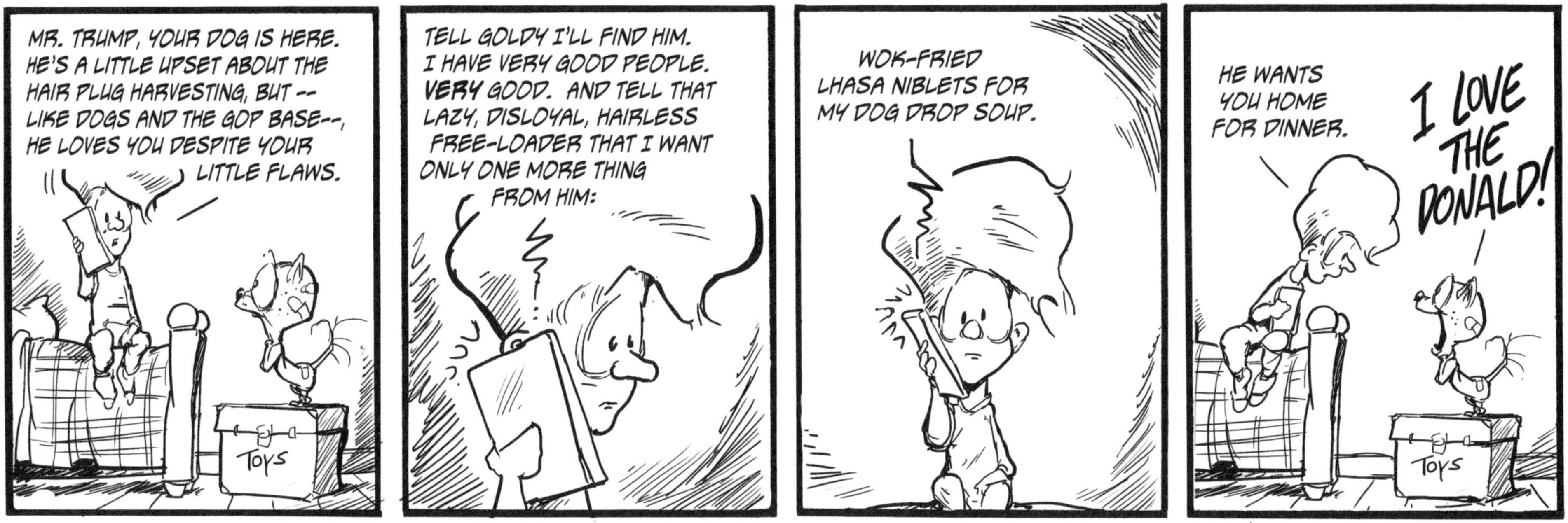
MR. TRUMP, YOUR DOG IS HERE. HE'S A LITTLE UPSET ABOUT THE HAIR PLUG HARVESTING, BUT -- LIKE DOGS AND THE GOP BASE--, HE LOVES YOU DESPITE YOUR LITTLE FLAWS.
TOYS
TELL GOLDY I'LL FIND HIM. I HAVE VERY GOOD PEOPLE. **VERY** GOOD. AND TELL THAT LAZY, DISLOYAL, HAIRLESS FREE-LOADER THAT I WANT ONLY ONE MORE THING FROM HIM:
WOK-FRIED LHASA NIBLETS FOR MY DOG DROP SOUP.
HE WANTS YOU HOME FOR DINNER.
I LOVE THE DONALD!
TOYS

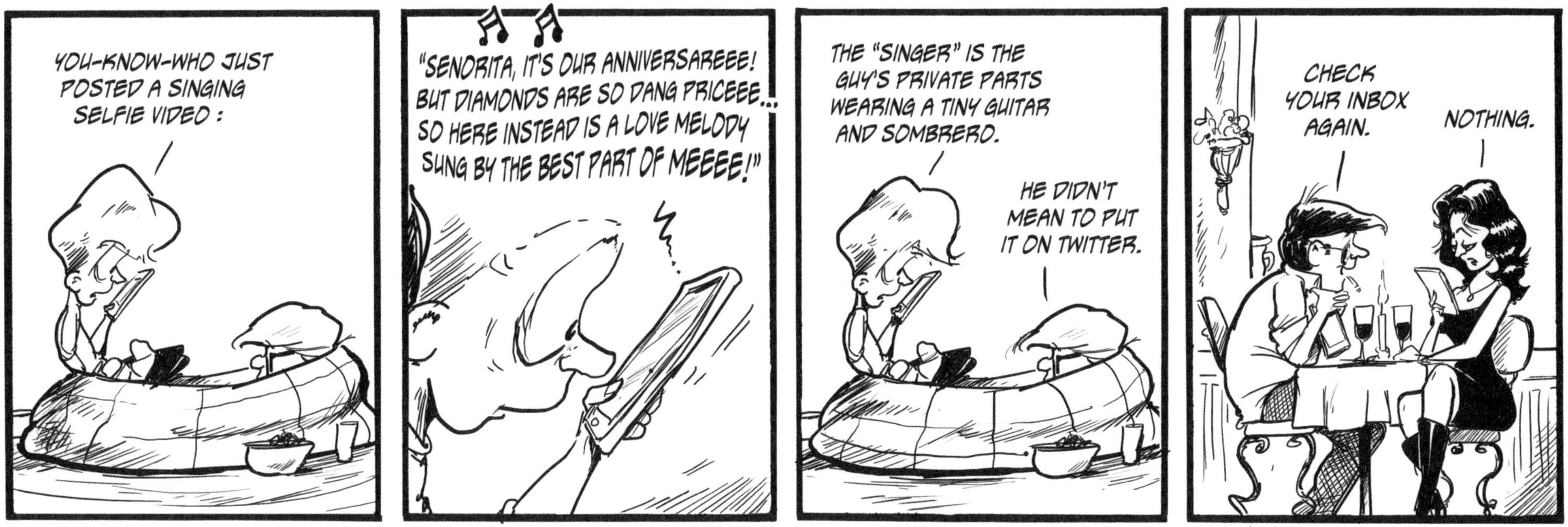
YOU-KNOW-WHO JUST POSTED A SINGING SELFIE VIDEO :
"SENORITA, IT'S OUR ANNIVERSAREEE! BUT DIAMONDS ARE SO DANG PRICEEE... SO HERE INSTEAD IS A LOVE MELODY SUNG BY THE BEST PART OF MEEEE!"
THE "SINGER" IS THE GUY'S PRIVATE PARTS WEARING A TINY GUITAR AND SOMBRERO.
HE DIDN'T MEAN TO PUT IT ON TWITTER.
CHECK YOUR INBOX AGAIN.
NOTHING.

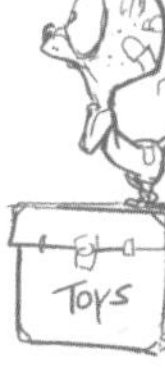
TOYS

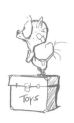

Bloom County 2015
by Berkeley Breathed esq.
SSH! GOLDY! IT'S THE PURPLE SNORKLEWACKER IN MY CLOSET!
CRASH!
AAGH!
THERE'S AN AWFUL MAN IN THERE! BIG HEAD... PINK TIE...
TRUMP!
DONALD!
OO! AWFUL!

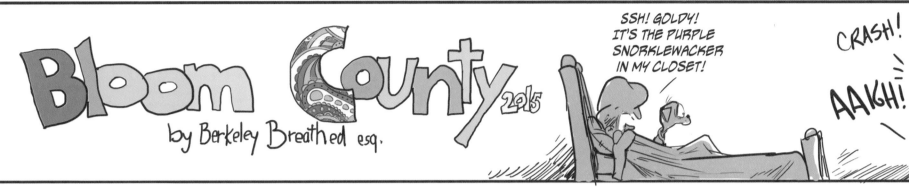

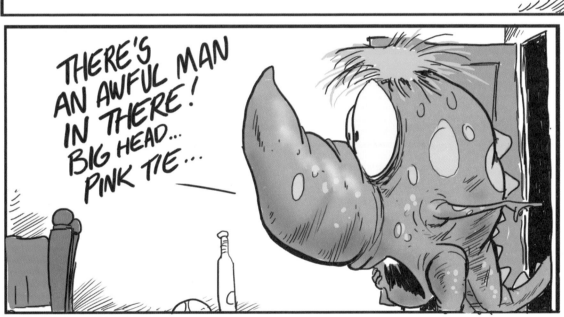

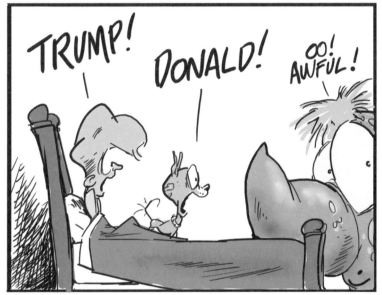

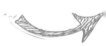

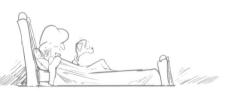

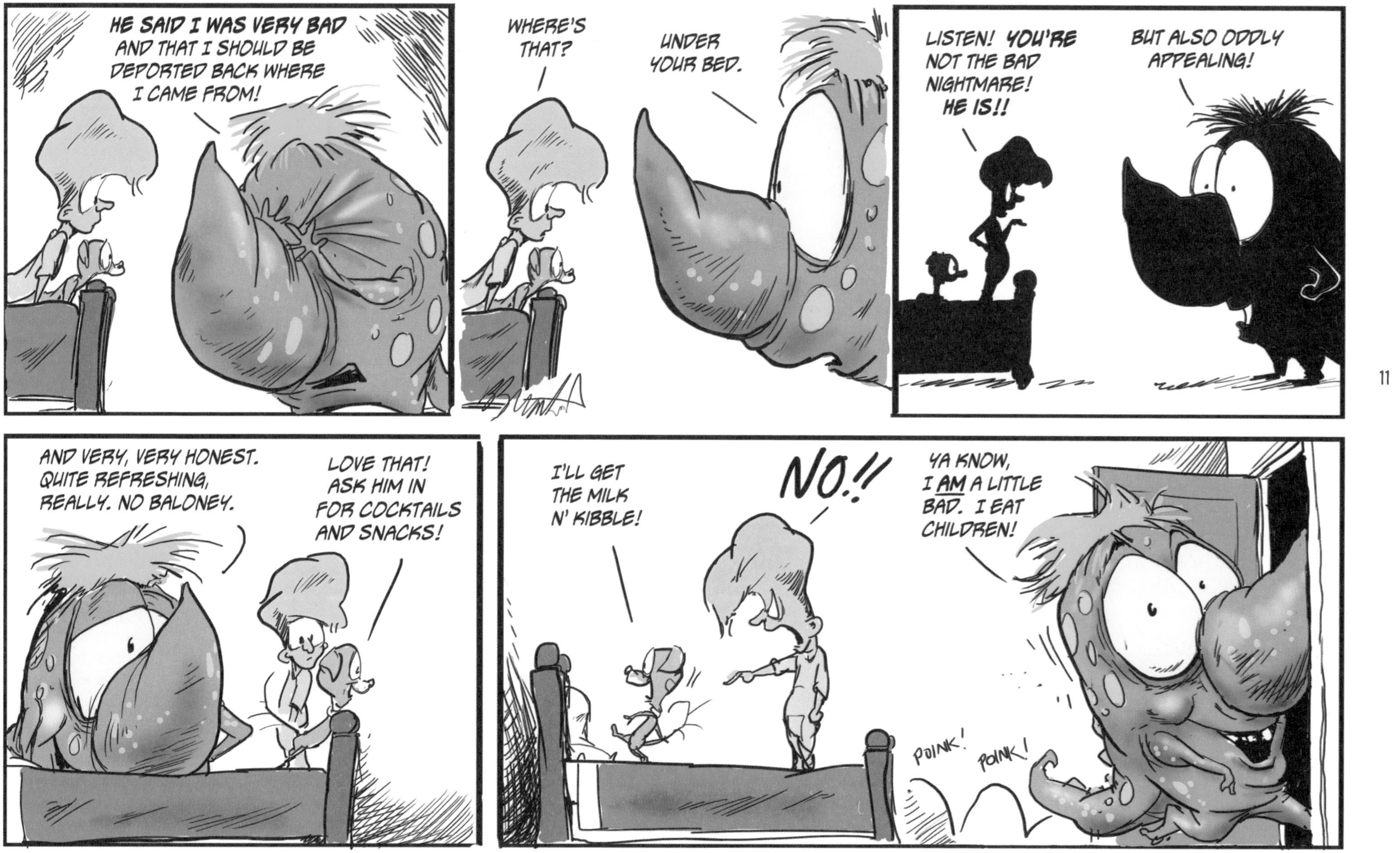
HE SAID I WAS VERY BAD AND THAT I SHOULD BE DEPORTED BACK WHERE I CAME FROM!
WHERE'S THAT?
UNDER YOUR BED.
LISTEN! YOU'RE NOT THE BAD NIGHTMARE! HE IS!!
BUT ALSO ODDLY APPEALING!
AND VERY, VERY HONEST. QUITE REFRESHING, REALLY. NO BALONEY.
LOVE THAT! ASK HIM IN FOR COCKTAILS AND SNACKS!
I'LL GET THE MILK N' KIBBLE!
NO!!
YA KNOW, I AM A LITTLE BAD. I EAT CHILDREN!
POINK!
POINK!

In a world that sometimes feels like it's flying apart, it's beyond perfect that we can again visit *Bloom County* for a welcome dose of lunatic sanity.

—Kerstin Oman

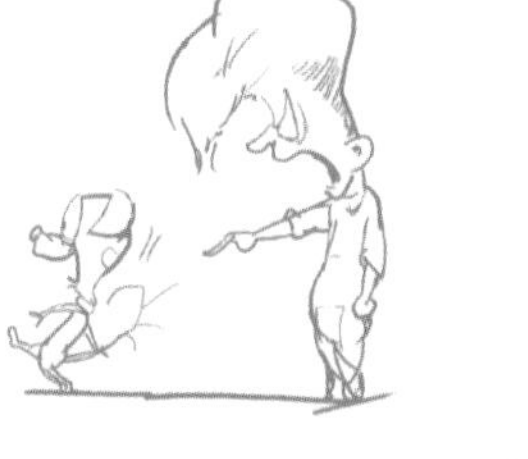

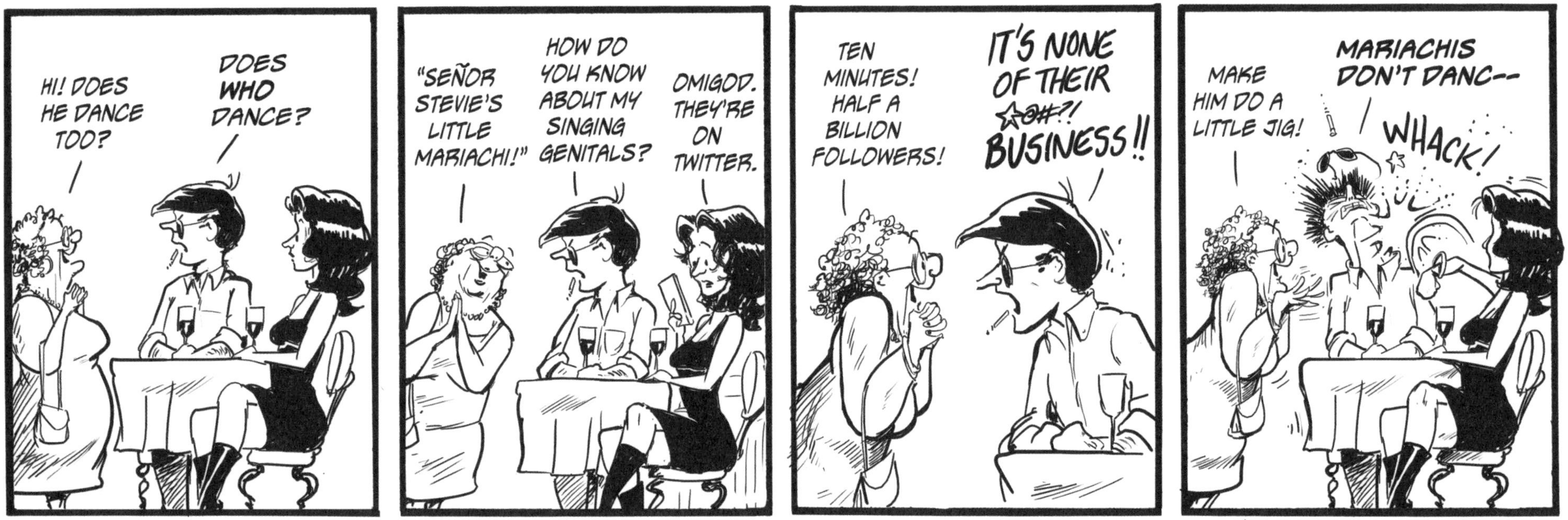
HI! DOES HE DANCE TOO?
DOES **WHO** DANCE?
"SEÑOR STEVIE'S LITTLE MARIACHI!"
HOW DO YOU KNOW ABOUT MY SINGING GENITALS?
OMIGOD. THEY'RE ON TWITTER.
TEN MINUTES! HALF A BILLION FOLLOWERS!
IT'S NONE OF THEIR ☆@#?! BUSINESS!!
MAKE HIM DO A LITTLE JIG!
MARIACHIS DON'T DANC--
WHACK!

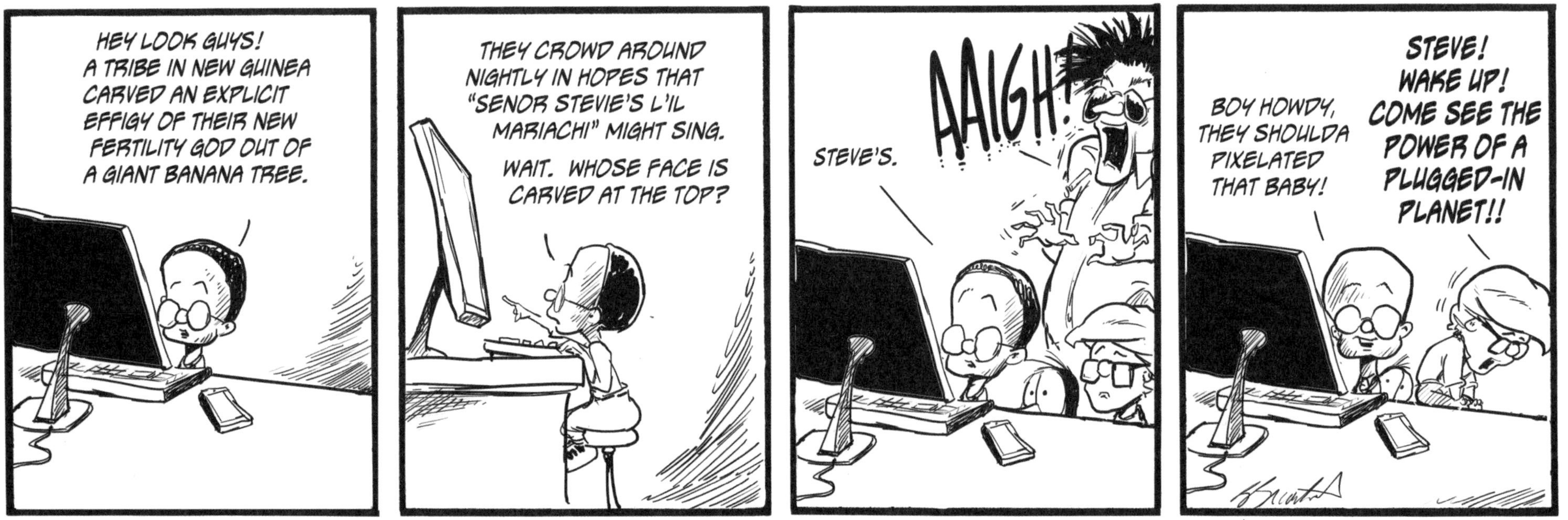
HEY LOOK GUYS! A TRIBE IN NEW GUINEA CARVED AN EXPLICIT EFFIGY OF THEIR NEW FERTILITY GOD OUT OF A GIANT BANANA TREE.
THEY CROWD AROUND NIGHTLY IN HOPES THAT "SENOR STEVIE'S L'IL MARIACHI" MIGHT SING.
WAIT. WHOSE FACE IS CARVED AT THE TOP?
STEVE'S.
AAIGH!
BOY HOWDY, THEY SHOULDA PIXELATED THAT BABY!
STEVE! WAKE UP! COME SEE THE POWER OF A PLUGGED-IN PLANET!!

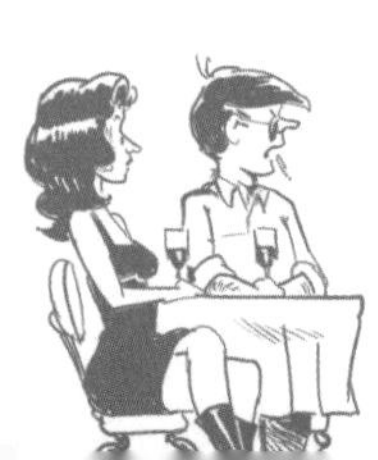

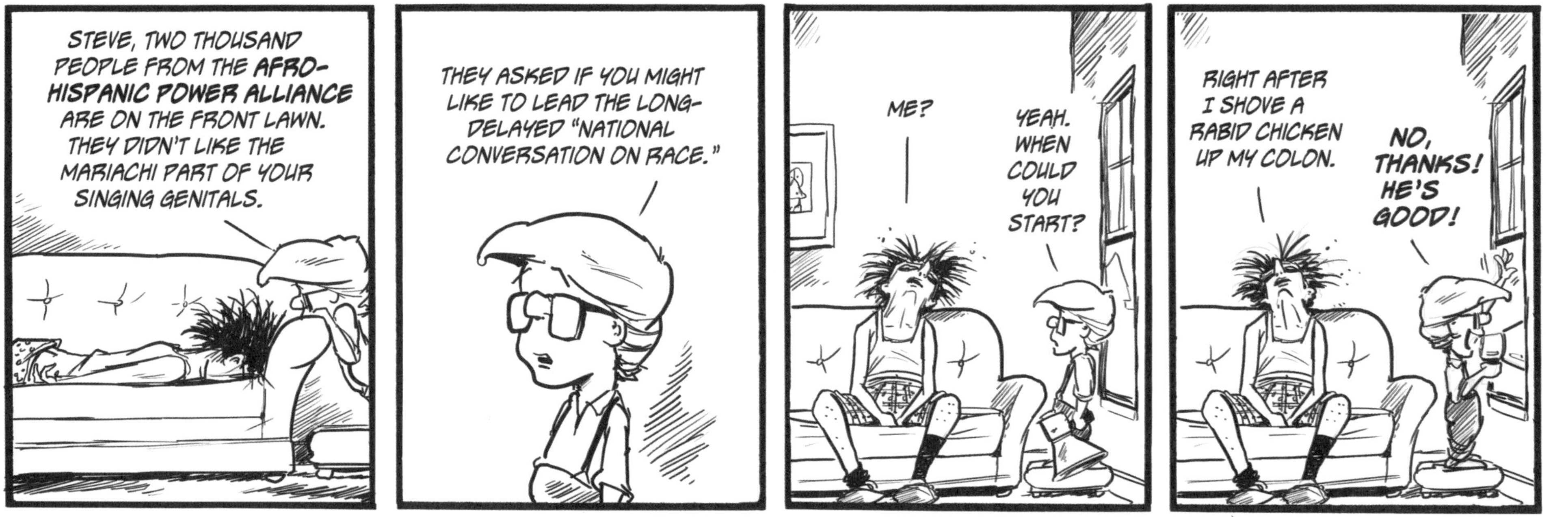
STEVE, TWO THOUSAND PEOPLE FROM THE **AFRO-HISPANIC POWER ALLIANCE** ARE ON THE FRONT LAWN. THEY DIDN'T LIKE THE MARIACHI PART OF YOUR SINGING GENITALS.
THEY ASKED IF YOU MIGHT LIKE TO LEAD THE LONG-DELAYED "NATIONAL CONVERSATION ON RACE."
ME?
YEAH. WHEN COULD YOU START?
RIGHT AFTER I SHOVE A RABID CHICKEN UP MY COLON.
NO, THANKS! HE'S DYING GOOD!

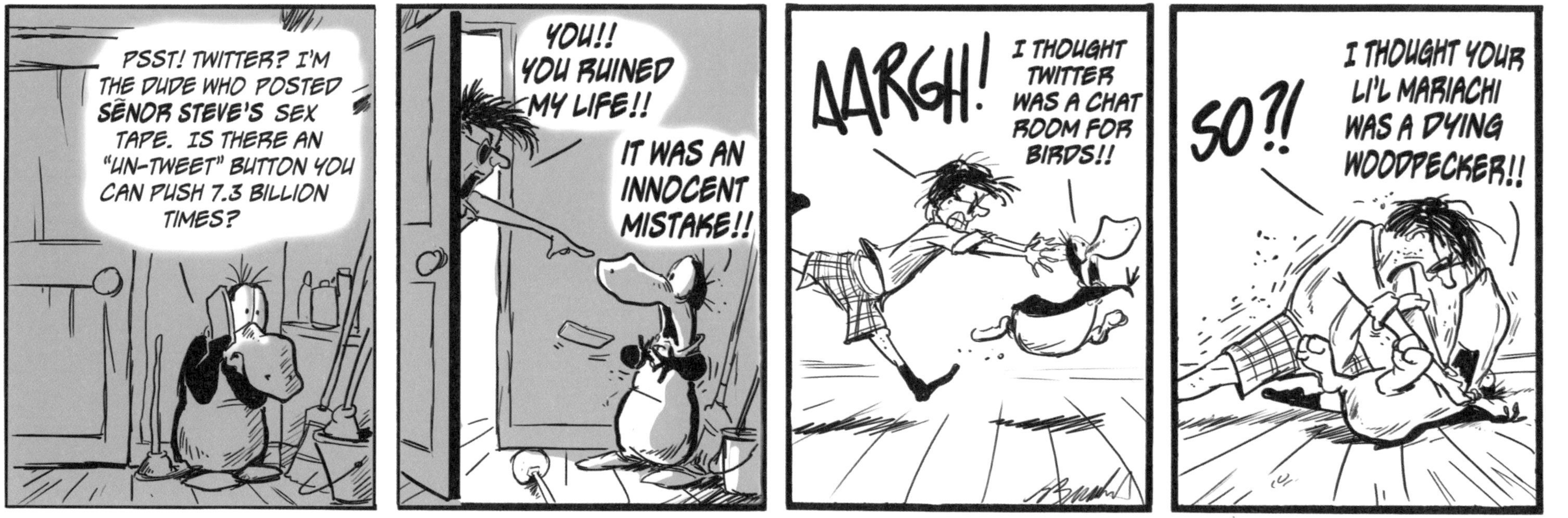
PSST! TWITTER? I'M THE DUDE WHO POSTED **SẼNOR STEVE'S** SEX TAPE. IS THERE AN "UN-TWEET" BUTTON YOU CAN PUSH 7.3 BILLION TIMES?
YOU!! YOU RUINED MY LIFE!!
IT WAS AN INNOCENT MISTAKE!!
AARGH!
I THOUGHT TWITTER WAS A CHAT ROOM FOR BIRDS!!
SO?!
I THOUGHT YOUR LI'L MARIACHI WAS A DYING WOODPECKER!!

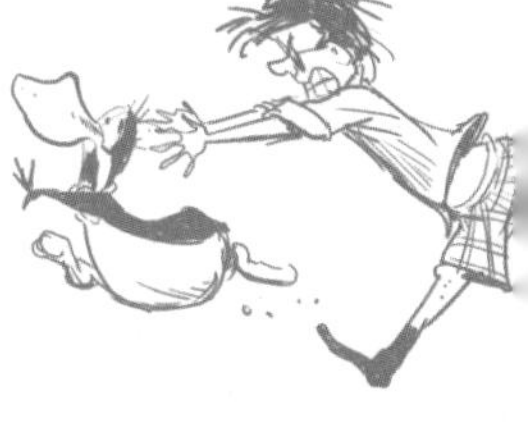

14

Bloom County 2015
by Berkeley Breathed esq.
TUM DEE DUM DUM
WHOA. HELLO.
WHERE'S MY WAIST? THAT'S NOT MY WAIST. THOSE ARE LEGS? THOSE AREN'T LEGS, THEY'RE HOCKEY PUCKS.
WHOA WHOA WHOA...

TUM DEE DUM DUM

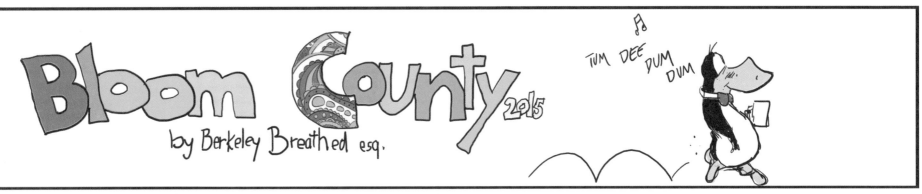

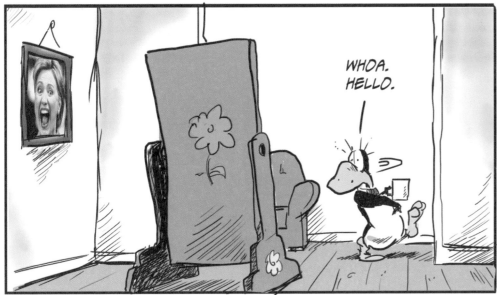

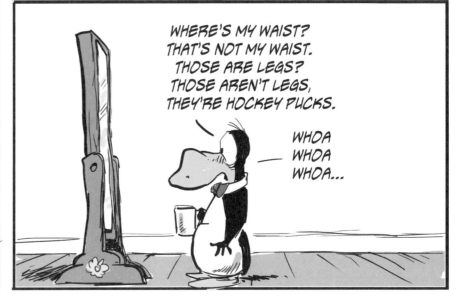

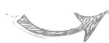

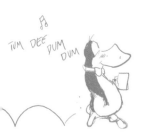

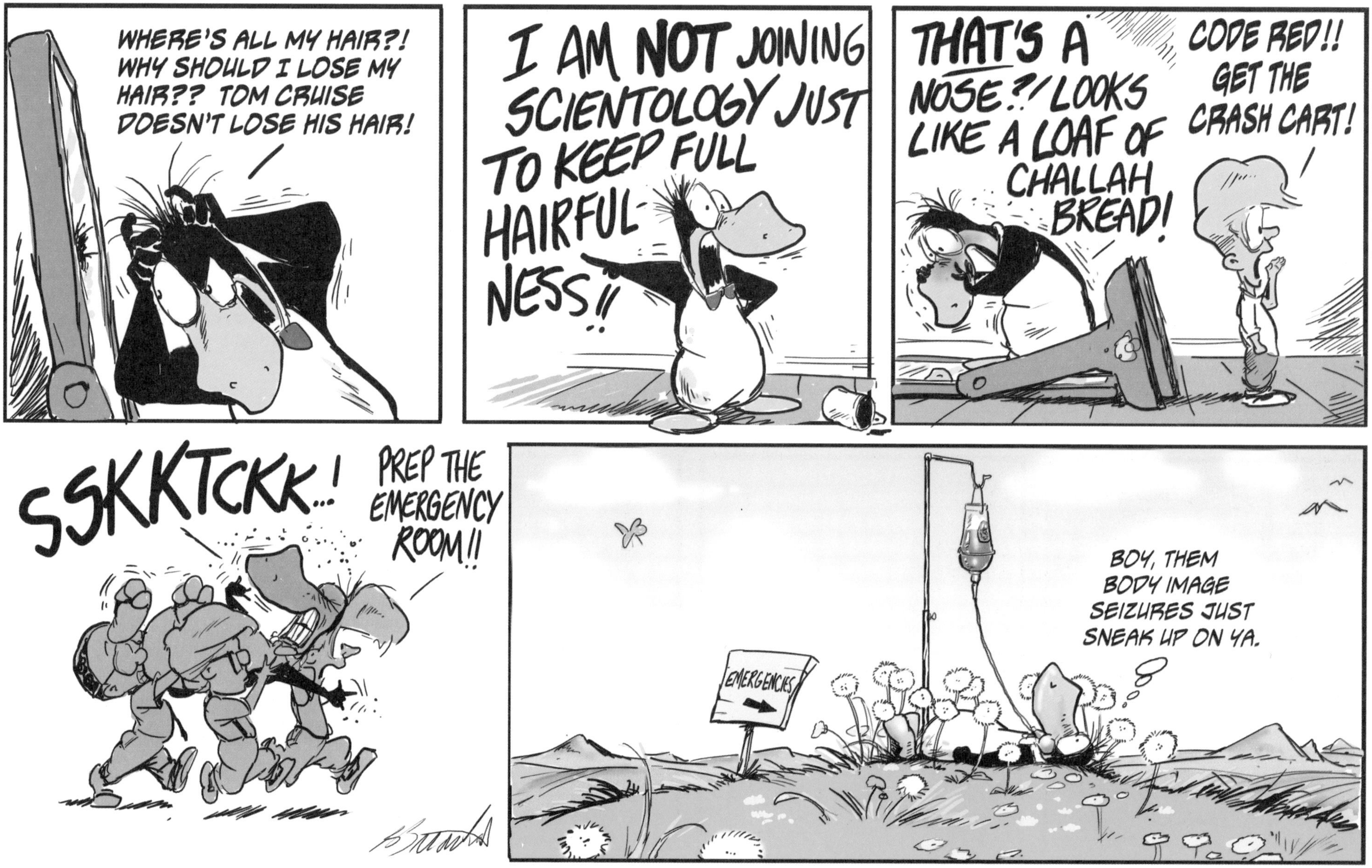
WHERE'S ALL MY HAIR?! WHY SHOULD I LOSE MY HAIR?? TOM CRUISE DOESN'T LOSE HIS HAIR!
I AM NOT JOINING SCIENTOLOGY JUST TO KEEP FULL HAIRFUL NESS!!
THAT'S A NOSE?! LOOKS LIKE A LOAF OF CHALLAH BREAD!
CODE RED!! GET THE CRASH CART!
SSKKTCKK..!
PREP THE EMERGENCY ROOM!!
EMERGENCIES
BOY, THEM BODY IMAGE SEIZURES JUST SNEAK UP ON YA.

Peace and Dandelion Pollen, Mr. Breathed!

—Kate McGonigal

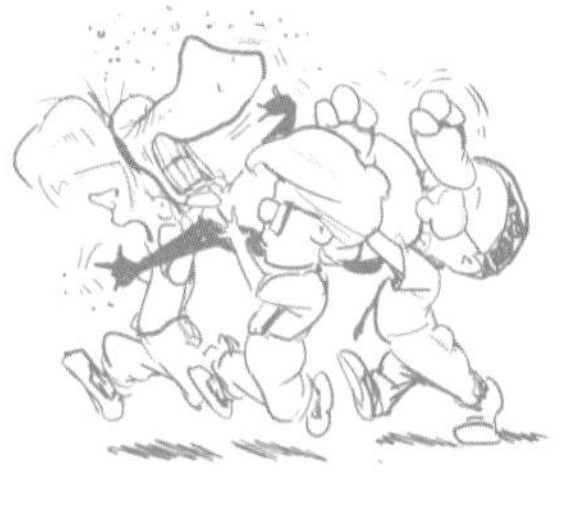

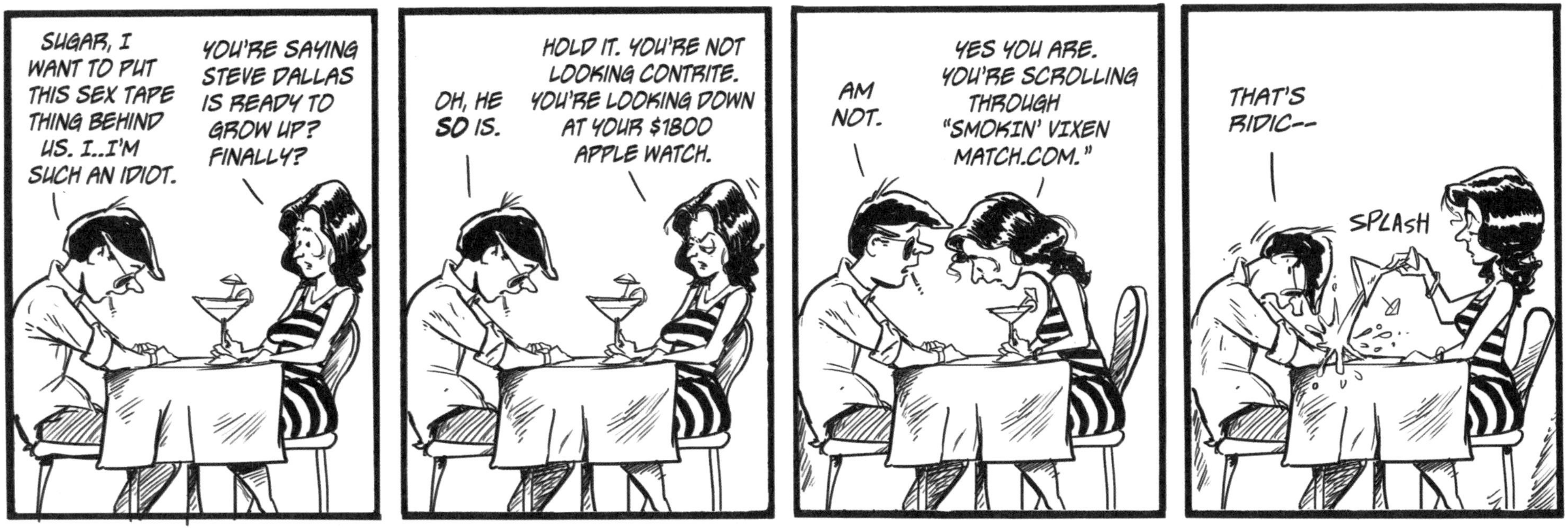
SUGAR, I WANT TO PUT THIS SEX TAPE THING BEHIND US. I..I'M SUCH AN IDIOT.
YOU'RE SAYING STEVE DALLAS IS READY TO GROW UP? FINALLY?
OH, HE **SO** IS.
HOLD IT. YOU'RE NOT LOOKING CONTRITE. YOU'RE LOOKING DOWN AT YOUR $1800 APPLE WATCH.
AM NOT.
YES YOU ARE. YOU'RE SCROLLING THROUGH "SMOKIN' VIXEN MATCH.COM."
THAT'S RIDIC--
SPLASH

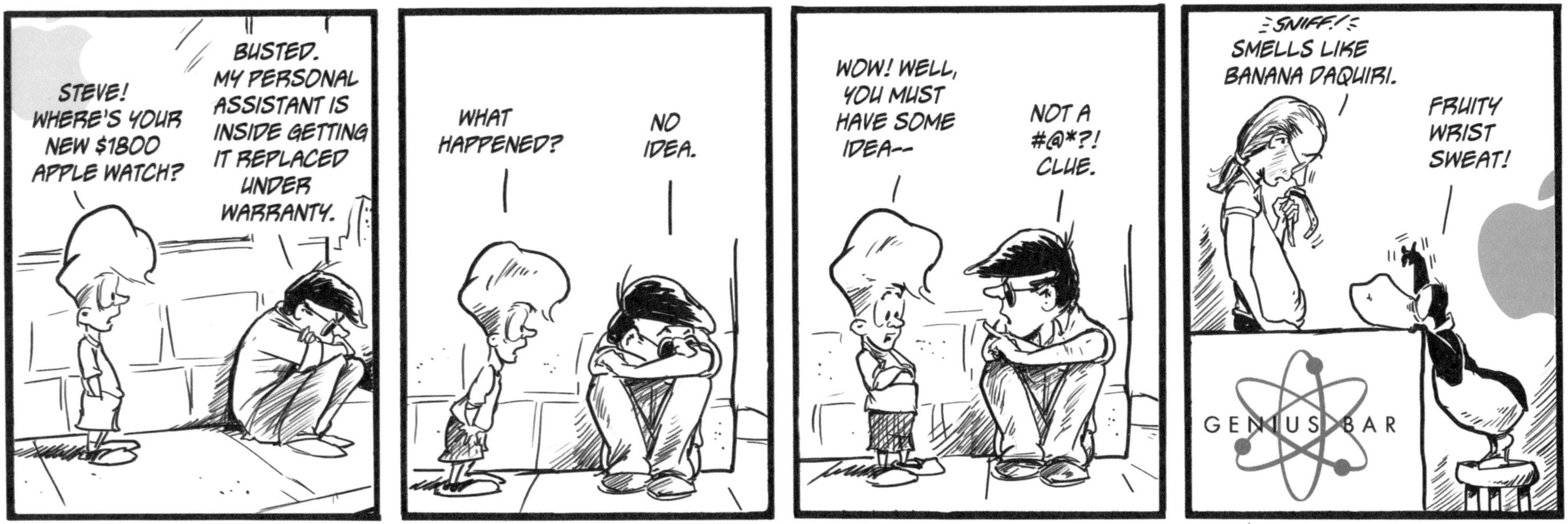
STEVE! WHERE'S YOUR NEW $1800 APPLE WATCH?
BUSTED. MY PERSONAL ASSISTANT IS INSIDE GETTING IT REPLACED UNDER WARRANTY.
WHAT HAPPENED?
NO IDEA.
WOW! WELL, YOU MUST HAVE SOME IDEA--
NOT A #@*?! CLUE.
SNIFF!
SMELLS LIKE BANANA DAQUIRI.
FRUITY WRIST SWEAT!
GENIUS BAR

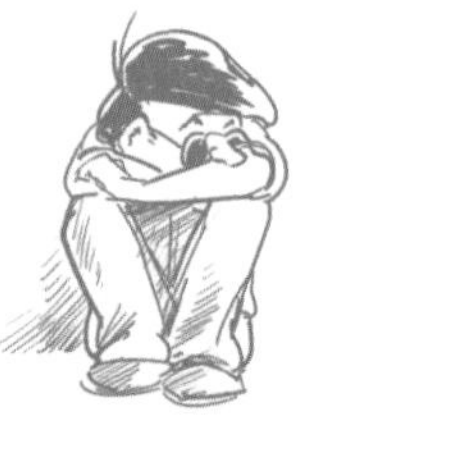

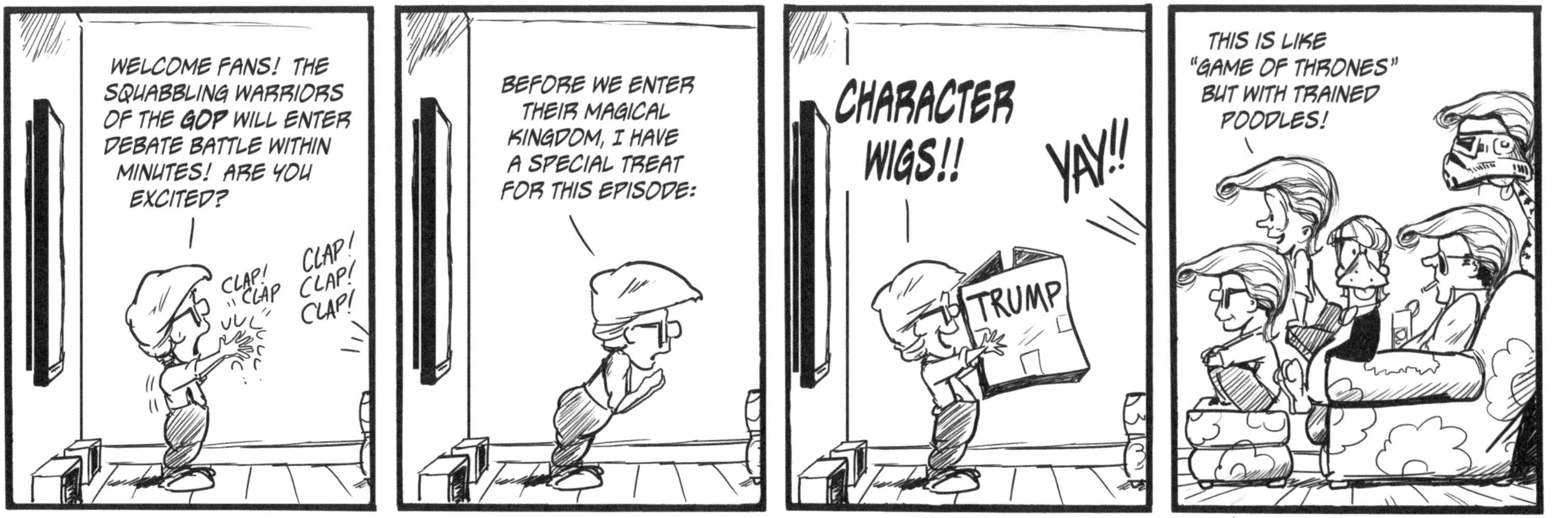
WELCOME FANS! THE SQUABBLING WARRIORS OF THE GOP WILL ENTER DEBATE BATTLE WITHIN MINUTES! ARE YOU EXCITED?
CLAP! CLAP
CLAP! CLAP! CLAP!
BEFORE WE ENTER THEIR MAGICAL KINGDOM, I HAVE A SPECIAL TREAT FOR THIS EPISODE:
CHARACTER WIGS!!
TRUMP
YAY!!
THIS IS LIKE "GAME OF THRONES" BUT WITH TRAINED POODLES!

17

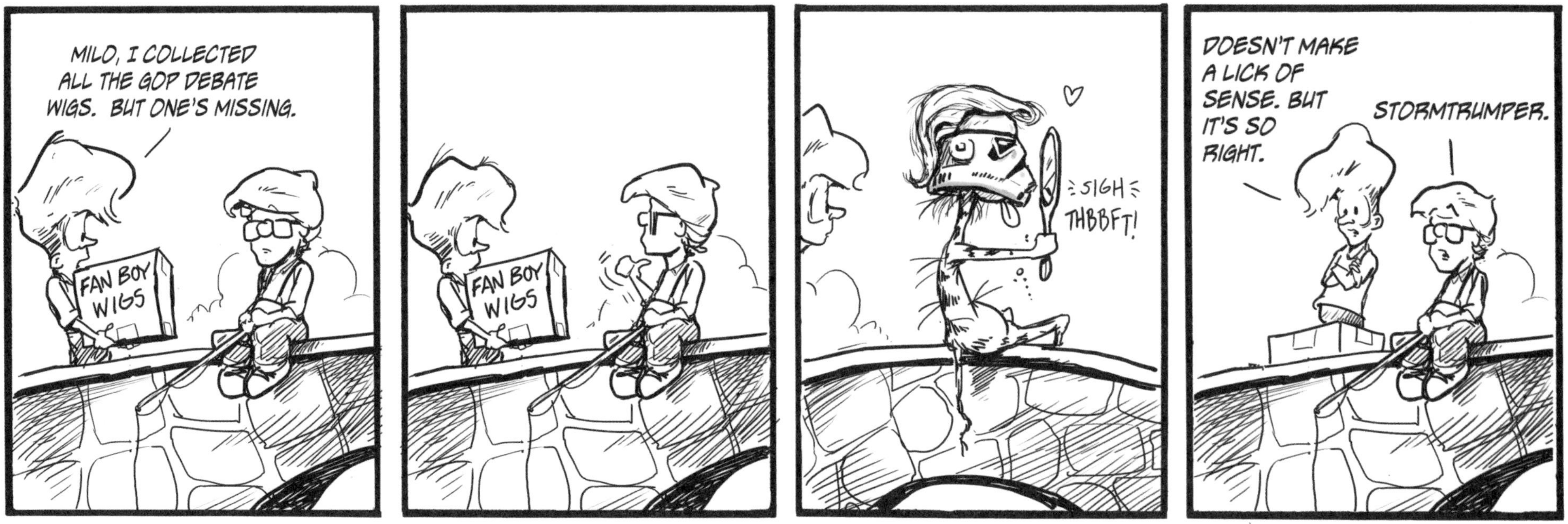
MILO, I COLLECTED ALL THE GOP DEBATE WIGS. BUT ONE'S MISSING.
FAN BOY WIGS
FAN BOY WIGS
SIGH
THBBFT!
DOESN'T MAKE A LICK OF SENSE. BUT IT'S SO RIGHT.
STORMTRUMPER.

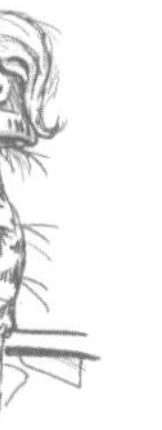

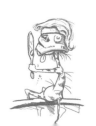

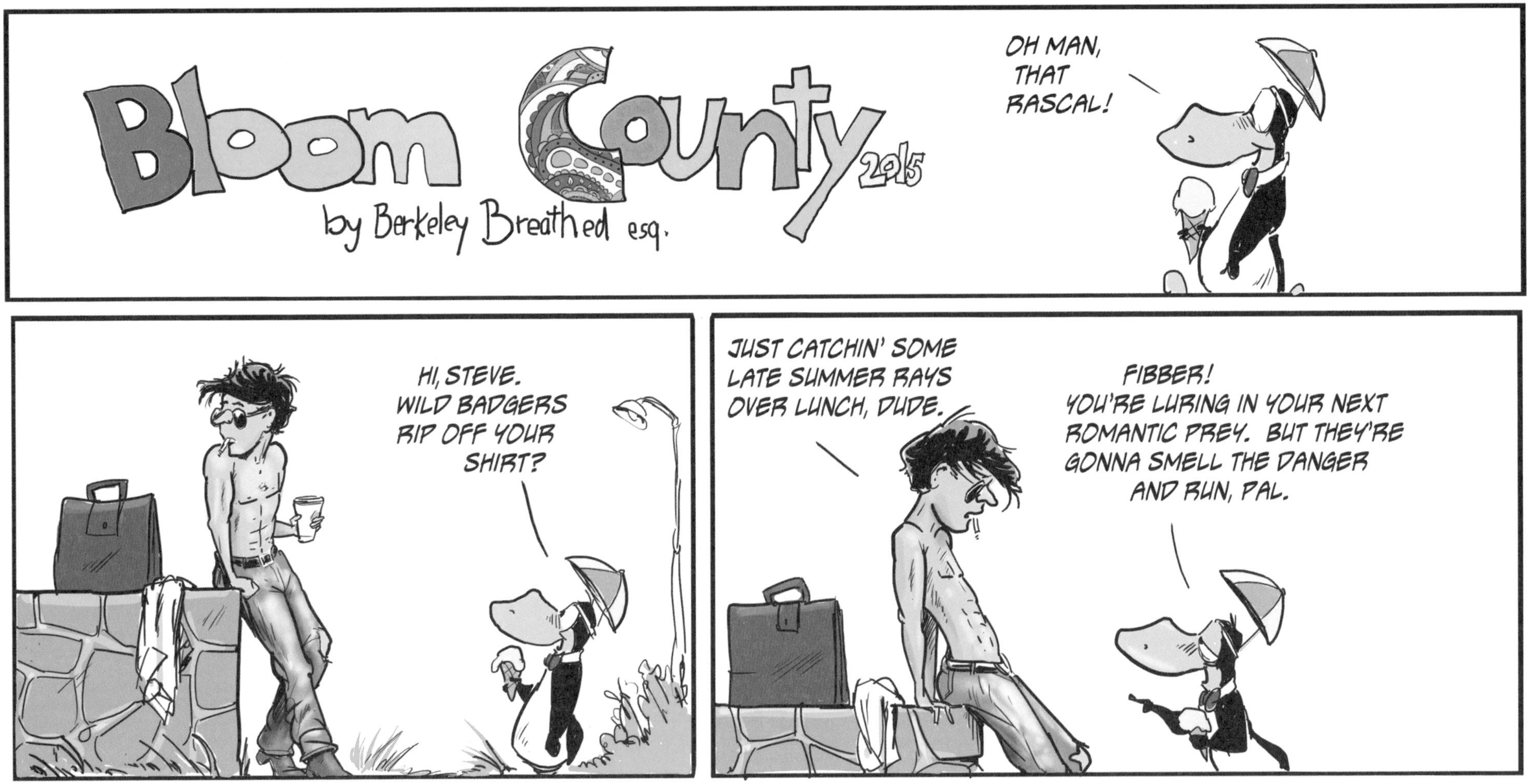
Bloom County 2015
by Berkeley Breathed esq.
OH MAN, THAT RASCAL!
HI, STEVE. WILD BADGERS RIP OFF YOUR SHIRT?
JUST CATCHIN' SOME LATE SUMMER RAYS OVER LUNCH, DUDE.
FIBBER! YOU'RE LURING IN YOUR NEXT ROMANTIC PREY. BUT THEY'RE GONNA SMELL THE DANGER AND RUN, PAL.

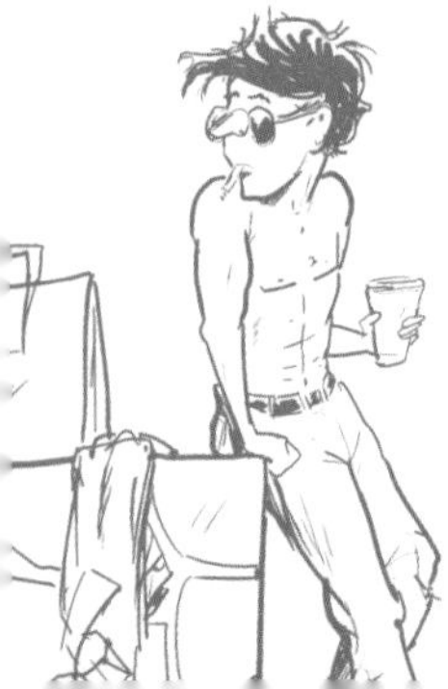

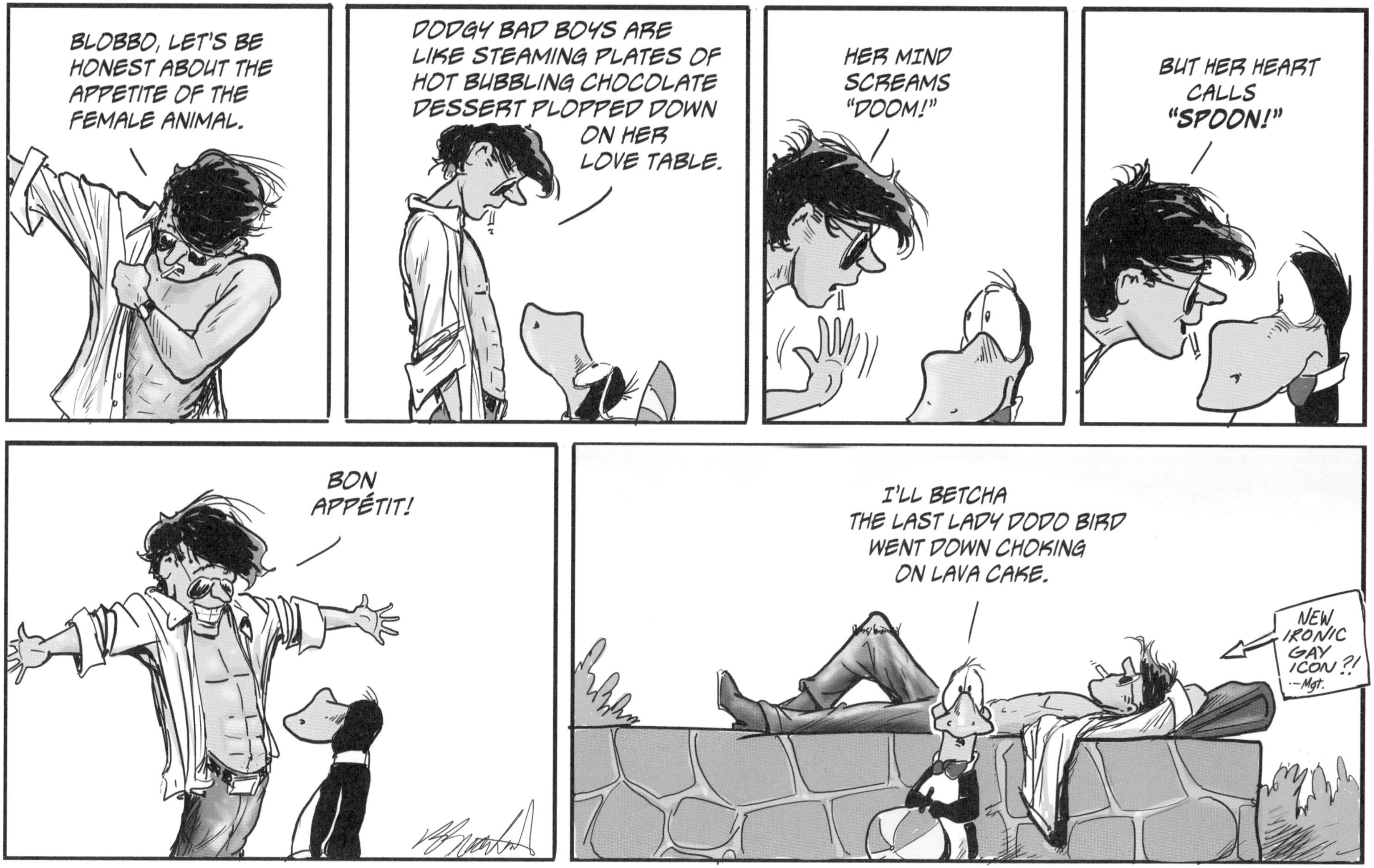
BLOBBO, LET'S BE HONEST ABOUT THE APPETITE OF THE FEMALE ANIMAL.
DODGY BAD BOYS ARE LIKE STEAMING PLATES OF HOT BUBBLING CHOCOLATE DESSERT PLOPPED DOWN ON HER LOVE TABLE.
HER MIND SCREAMS "DOOM!"
BUT HER HEART CALLS **"SPOON!"**
BON APPÉTIT!
I'LL BETCHA THE LAST LADY DODO BIRD WENT DOWN CHOKING ON LAVA CAKE.
NEW IRONIC GAY ICON?! —Mgt.

Today I had an excellent 5km walk around the suburbs, a damned fine cup of coffee with my beloved wife, read a brand-new *Bloom County* cartoon that made me laugh, watched some great TV, scored a terrific hotel-room bargain, laughed with my two daughters, was delighted by the announcement of a new Bruce Springsteen boxed set I've been waiting for for years, and later this evening am going to gently immerse myself in a wonderful whisky from the chilly hills of Hobart. It's been a good day in Australia.

—Jonathan Strahan

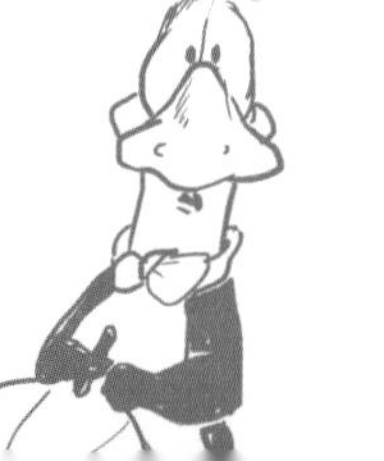

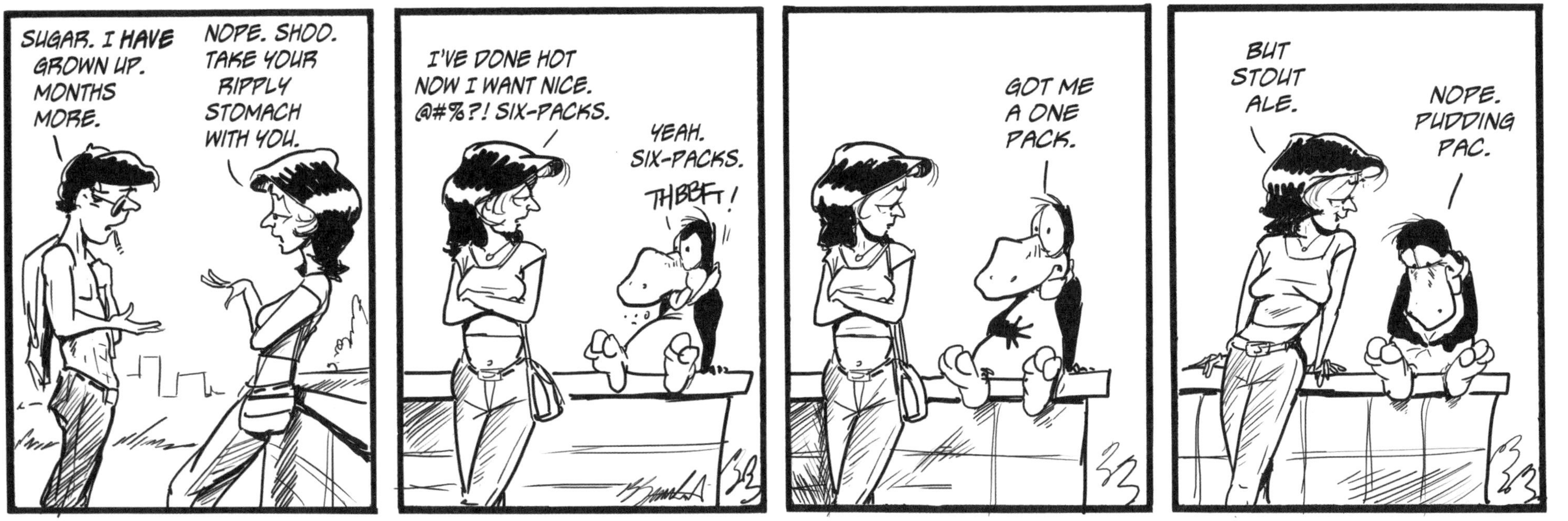
SUGAR. I HAVE GROWN UP. MONTHS MORE.
NOPE. SHOO. TAKE YOUR RIPPLY STOMACH WITH YOU.
I'VE DONE HOT NOW I WANT NICE. @#%?! SIX-PACKS.
YEAH. SIX-PACKS.
THBBFT!
GOT ME A ONE PACK.
BUT STOUT ALE.
NOPE. PUDDING PAC.

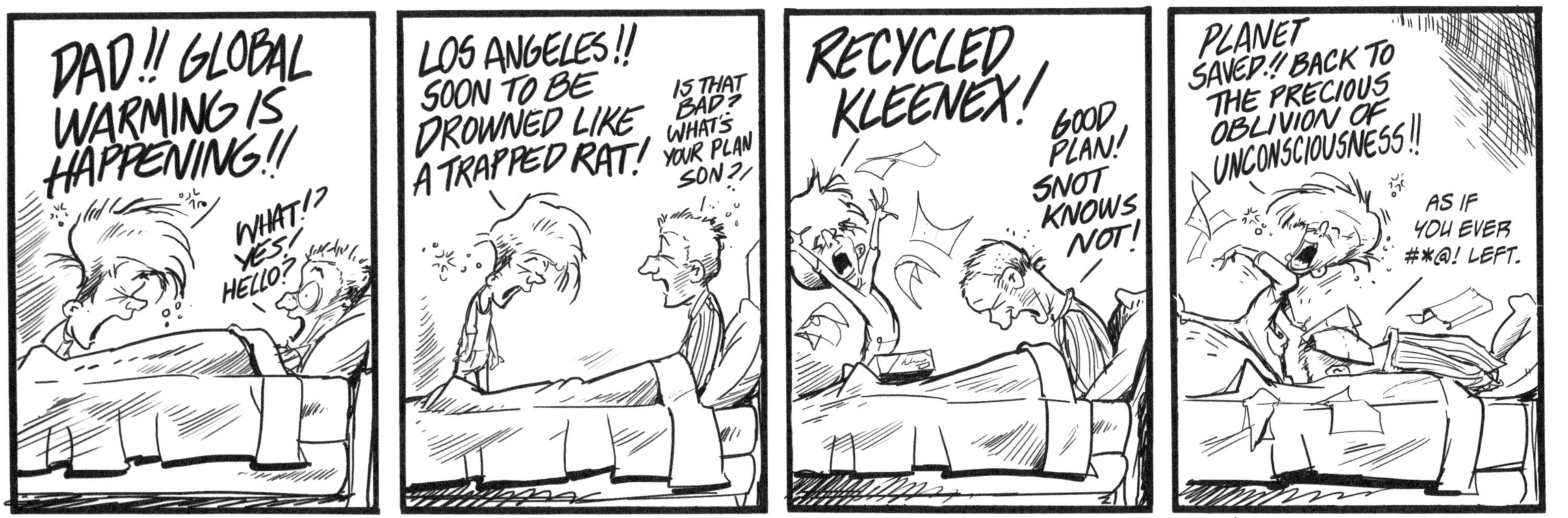
DAD!! GLOBAL WARMING IS HAPPENING!!
WHAT!? YES! HELLO?
LOS ANGELES!! SOON TO BE DROWNED LIKE A TRAPPED RAT!
IS THAT BAD? WHAT'S YOUR PLAN SON?!
RECYCLED KLEENEX!
GOOD PLAN! SNOT KNOWS NOT!
PLANET SAVED!! BACK TO THE PRECIOUS OBLIVION OF UNCONSCIOUSNESS!!
AS IF YOU EVER #*@! LEFT.

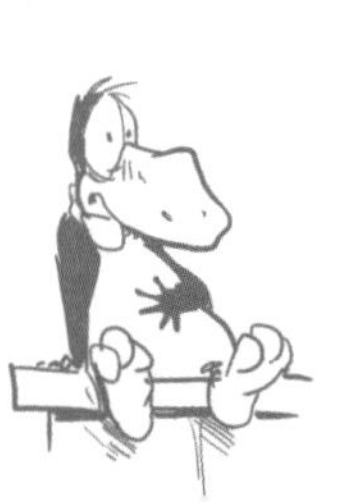

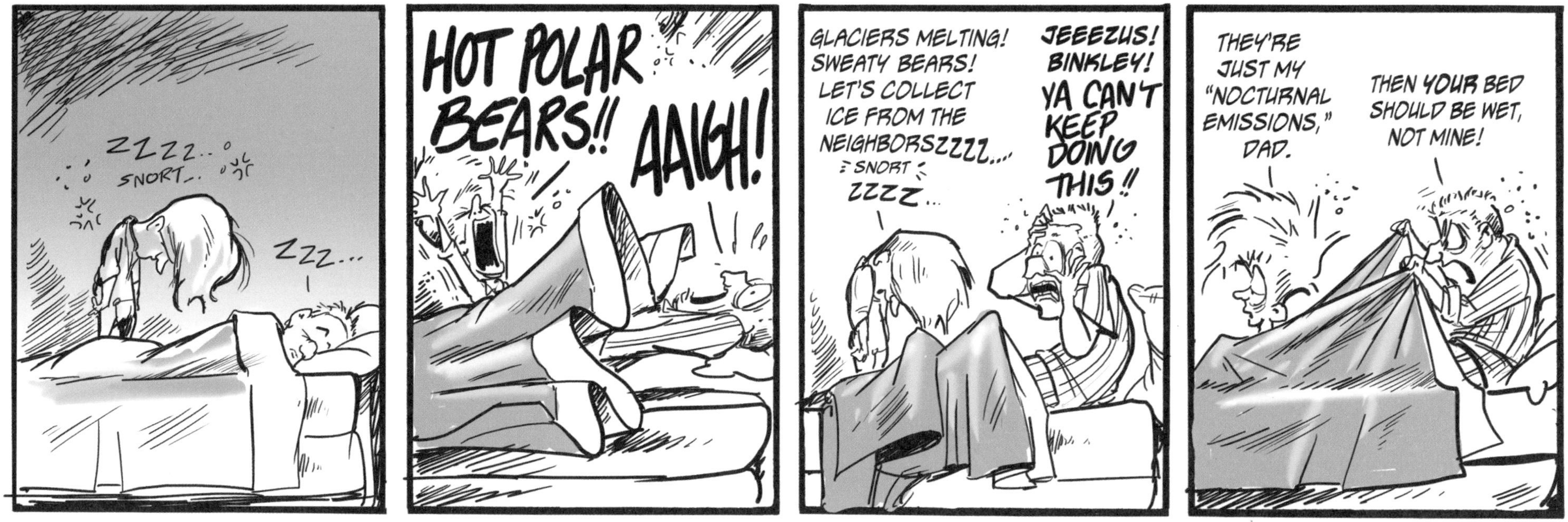
ZZZZ...
SNORT...
ZZZ...
HOT POLAR BEARS!!
AAIGH!
GLACIERS MELTING! SWEATY BEARS! LET'S COLLECT ICE FROM THE NEIGHBORSZZZZ...
SNORT
ZZZZ...
JEEEZUS! BINKLEY! YA CAN'T KEEP DOING THIS!!
THEY'RE JUST MY "NOCTURNAL EMISSIONS," DAD.
THEN YOUR BED SHOULD BE WET, NOT MINE!

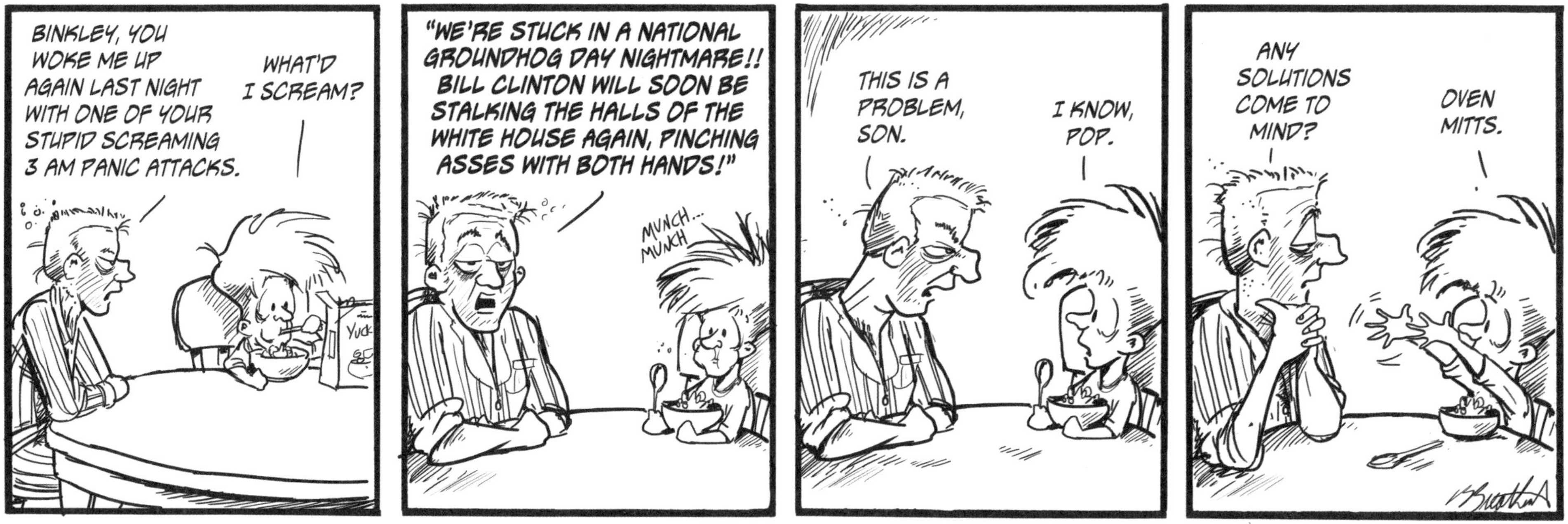
BINKLEY, YOU WOKE ME UP AGAIN LAST NIGHT WITH ONE OF YOUR STUPID SCREAMING 3 AM PANIC ATTACKS.
WHAT'D I SCREAM?
YUCK
"WE'RE STUCK IN A NATIONAL GROUNDHOG DAY NIGHTMARE!! BILL CLINTON WILL SOON BE STALKING THE HALLS OF THE WHITE HOUSE AGAIN, PINCHING ASSES WITH BOTH HANDS!"
MUNCH... MUNCH
THIS IS A PROBLEM, SON.
I KNOW, POP.
ANY SOLUTIONS COME TO MIND?
OVEN MITTS.

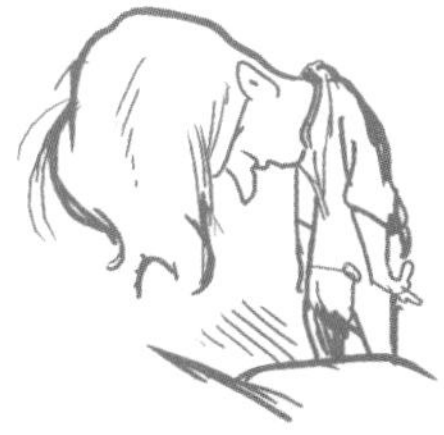

Bloom County 2015
by Berkeley Breathed esq.
ZZZZ... SNORE...
SNORT
3:47 A.M.
ESPECIALLY HIRED LIFE-PANIC PROFESSIONALS READY FOR ACTION.
ZZZ... SNORE SNORT
OH!
MY GOD, EVERY BREATHING MOMENT THREATENS BEING HIT WITH A PLANET-SMASHING METEOR OR ANOTHER KALE SALAD!!

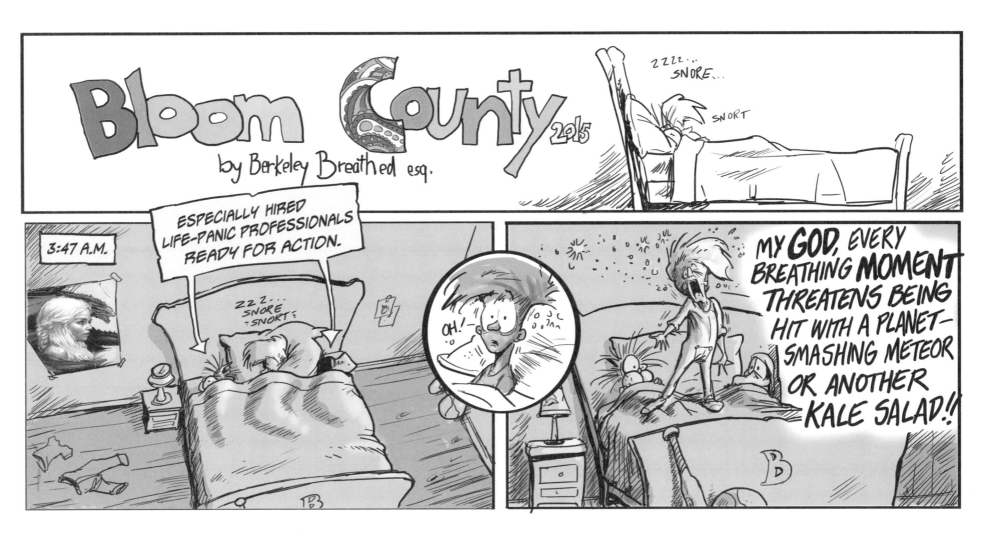

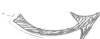

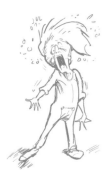

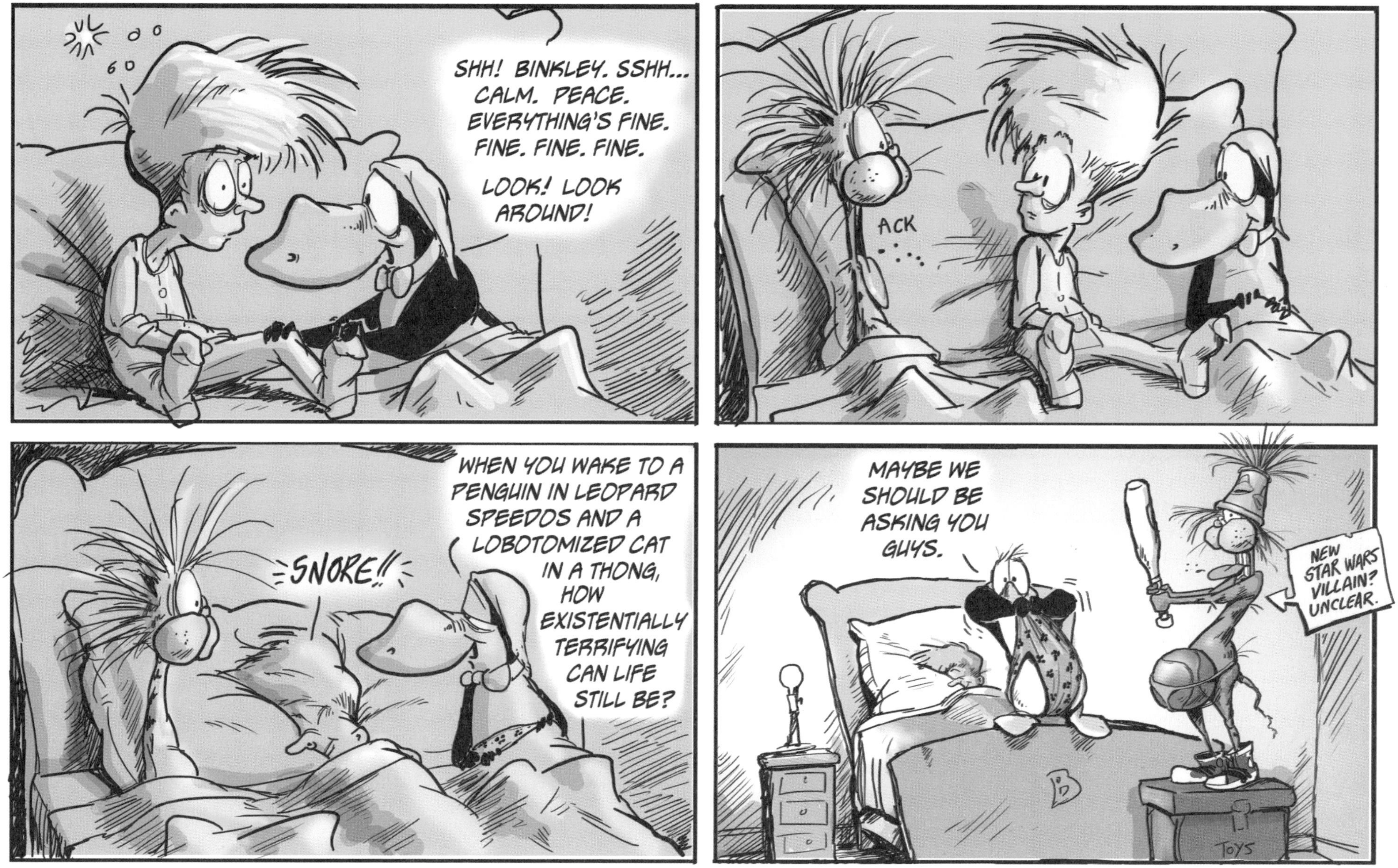
SHH! BINKLEY. SSHH... CALM. PEACE. EVERYTHING'S FINE. FINE. FINE. FINE.
LOOK! LOOK AROUND!
ACK
WHEN YOU WAKE TO A PENGUIN IN LEOPARD SPEEDOS AND A LOBOTOMIZED CAT IN A THONG, HOW EXISTENTIALLY TERRIFYING CAN LIFE STILL BE?
SNORE!!
MAYBE WE SHOULD BE ASKING YOU GUYS.
NEW STAR WARS VILLAIN? UNCLEAR.
TOYS

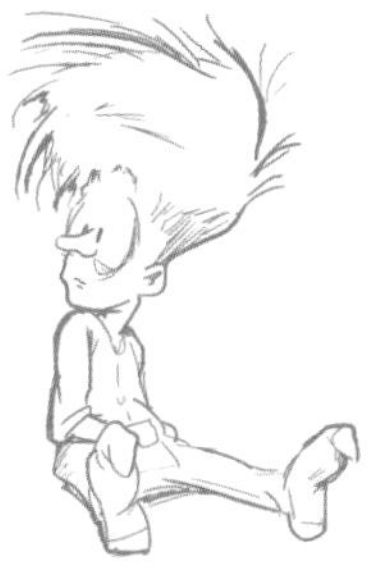

I used to have a stuffed Bill the Cat that was my sole holiday decoration. He was wonderful for baby showers, wedding showers, not just your regular holidays. Does anyone retail a stuffed animal Bill the Cat anymore or is this an exclusively eBay item? I am returning to my minimalist youth. For the disrespectful, he made a nice baby Jesus.

—Bonnie Yantis

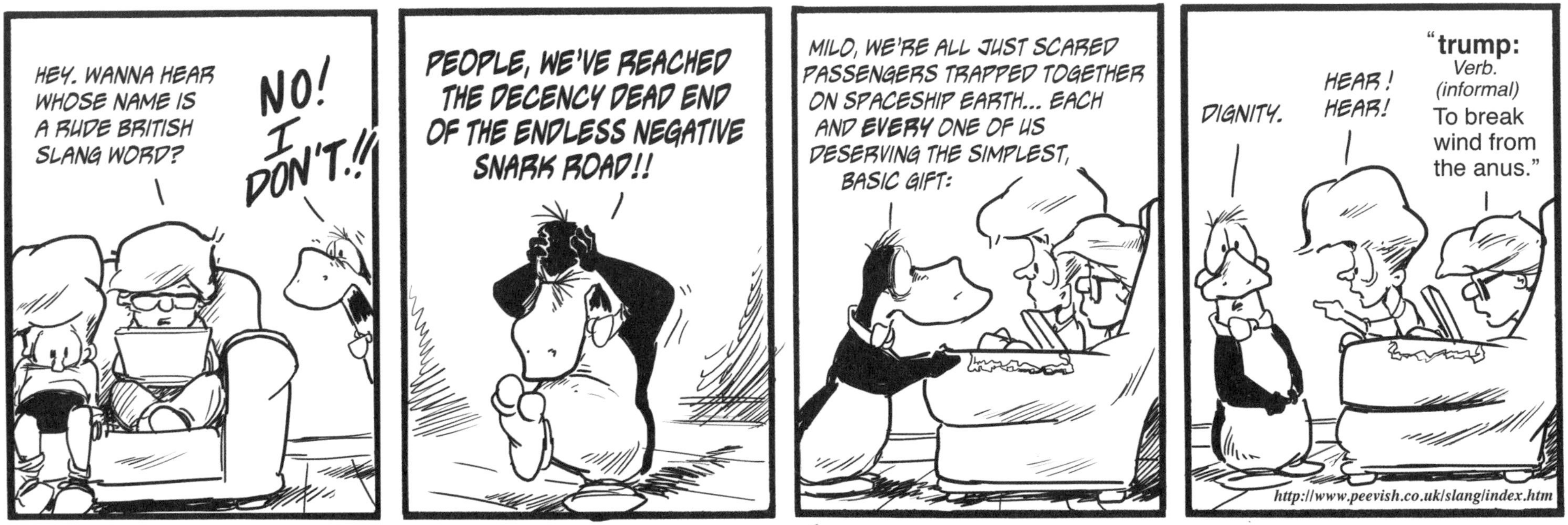
HEY. WANNA HEAR WHOSE NAME IS A RUDE BRITISH SLANG WORD?
NO! I DON'T.!!
PEOPLE, WE'VE REACHED THE DECENCY DEAD END OF THE ENDLESS NEGATIVE SNARK ROAD!!
MILO, WE'RE ALL JUST SCARED PASSENGERS TRAPPED TOGETHER ON SPACESHIP EARTH... EACH AND EVERY ONE OF US DESERVING THE SIMPLEST, BASIC GIFT:
DIGNITY.
HEAR! HEAR!
"trump: Verb. (informal) To break wind from the anus."
http://www.peevish.co.uk/slang/index.htm

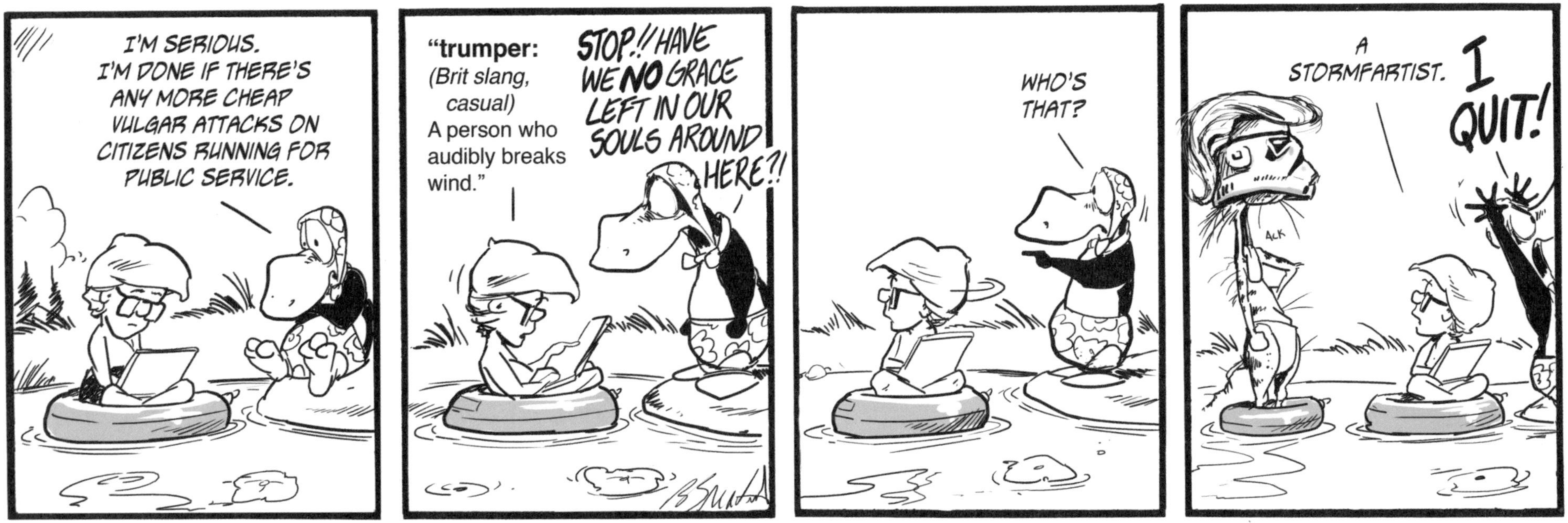
I'M SERIOUS. I'M DONE IF THERE'S ANY MORE CHEAP VULGAR ATTACKS ON CITIZENS RUNNING FOR PUBLIC SERVICE.
"trumper: (Brit slang, casual) A person who audibly breaks wind."
STOP!! HAVE WE NO GRACE LEFT IN OUR SOULS AROUND HERE?!
WHO'S THAT?
A STORMFARTIST.
I QUIT!

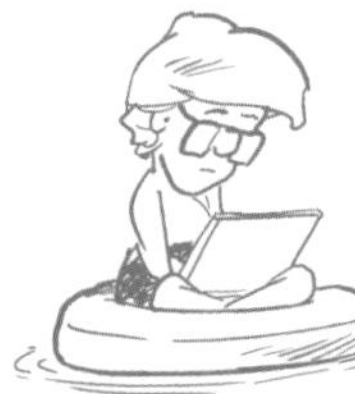

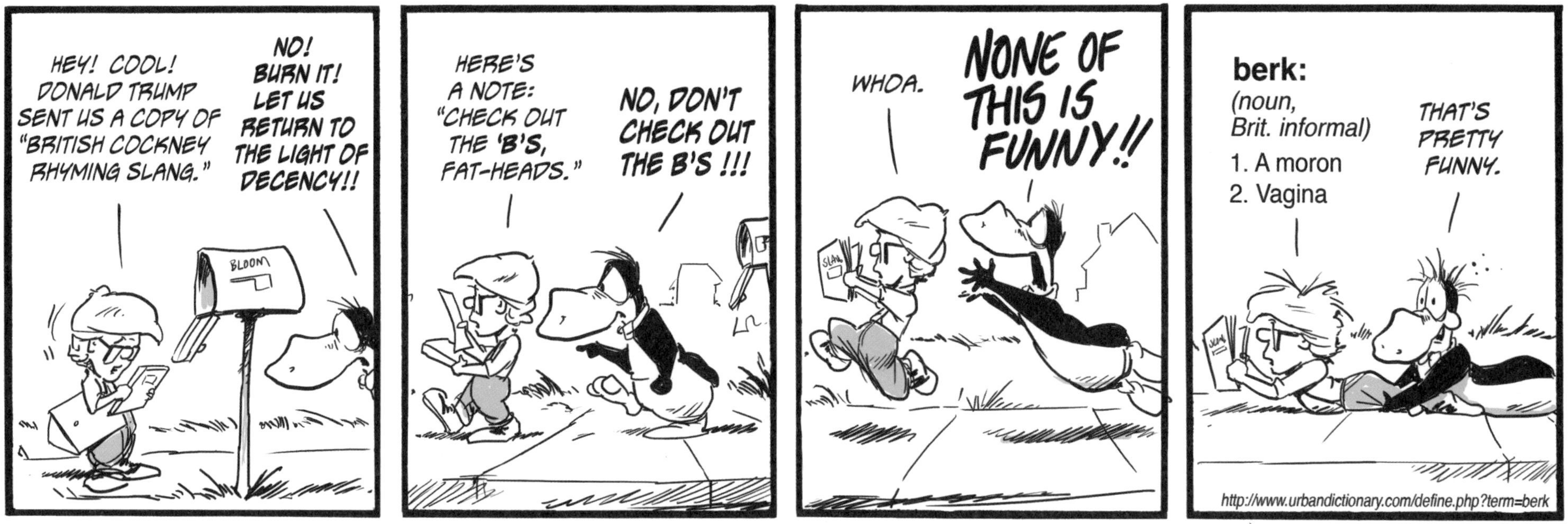
HEY! COOL! DONALD TRUMP SENT US A COPY OF "BRITISH COCKNEY RHYMING SLANG."
NO! BURN IT! LET US RETURN TO THE LIGHT OF DECENCY!!
BLOOM
HERE'S A NOTE: "CHECK OUT THE 'B'S, FAT-HEADS."
NO, DON'T CHECK OUT THE B'S !!!
WHOA.
NONE OF THIS IS FUNNY!!
berk:
(noun, Brit. informal)
1. A moron
2. Vagina
THAT'S PRETTY FUNNY.
http://www.urbandictionary.com/define.php?term=berk

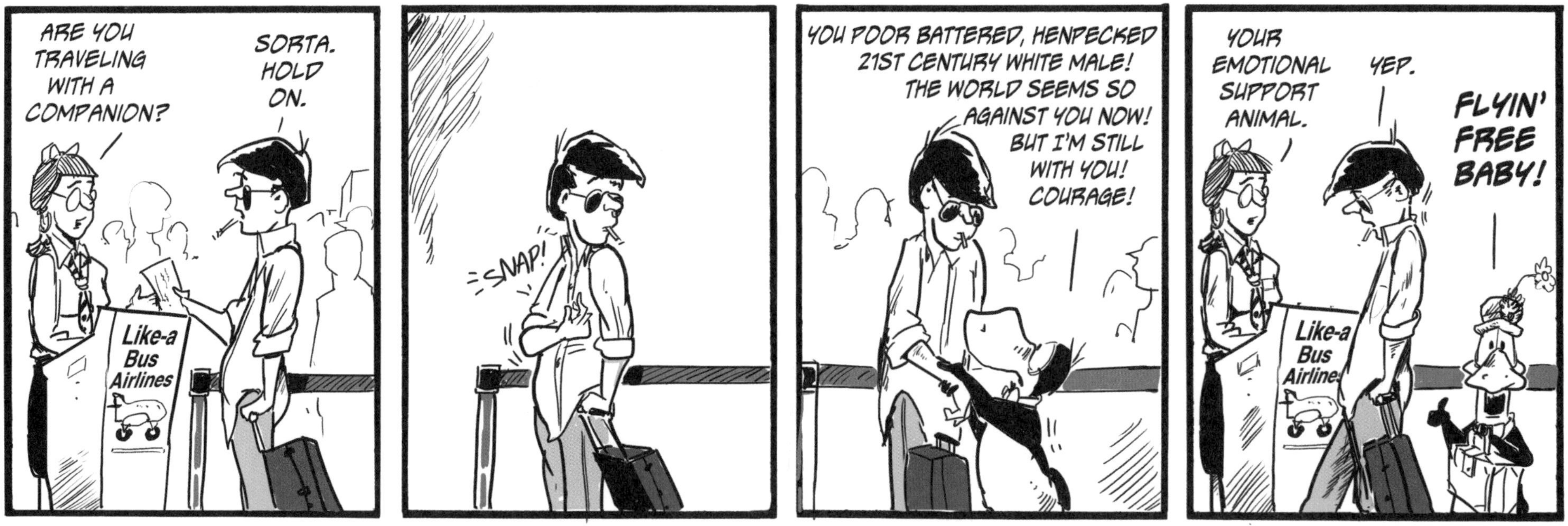
ARE YOU TRAVELING WITH A COMPANION?
SORTA. HOLD ON.
Like-a Bus Airlines
SNAP!
YOU POOR BATTERED, HENPECKED 21ST CENTURY WHITE MALE! THE WORLD SEEMS SO AGAINST YOU NOW! BUT I'M STILL WITH YOU! COURAGE!
YOUR EMOTIONAL SUPPORT ANIMAL.
YEP.
FLYIN' FREE BABY!
Like-a Bus Airlines

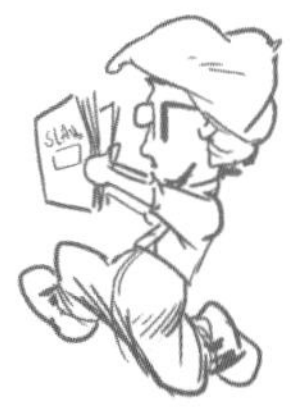

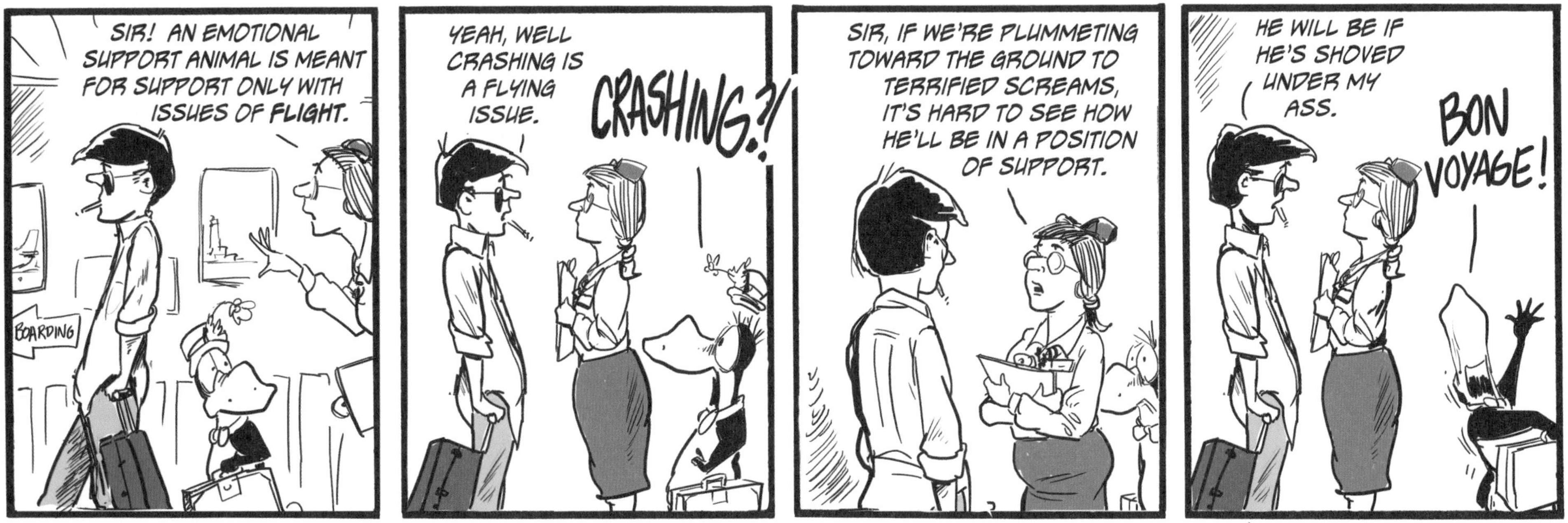
SIR! AN EMOTIONAL SUPPORT ANIMAL IS MEANT FOR SUPPORT ONLY WITH ISSUES OF **FLIGHT**.
BOARDING
YEAH, WELL CRASHING IS A FLYING ISSUE.
CRASHING?!
SIR, IF WE'RE PLUMMETING TOWARD THE GROUND TO TERRIFIED SCREAMS, IT'S HARD TO SEE HOW HE'LL BE IN A POSITION OF SUPPORT.
HE WILL BE IF HE'S SHOVED UNDER MY ASS.
BON VOYAGE!

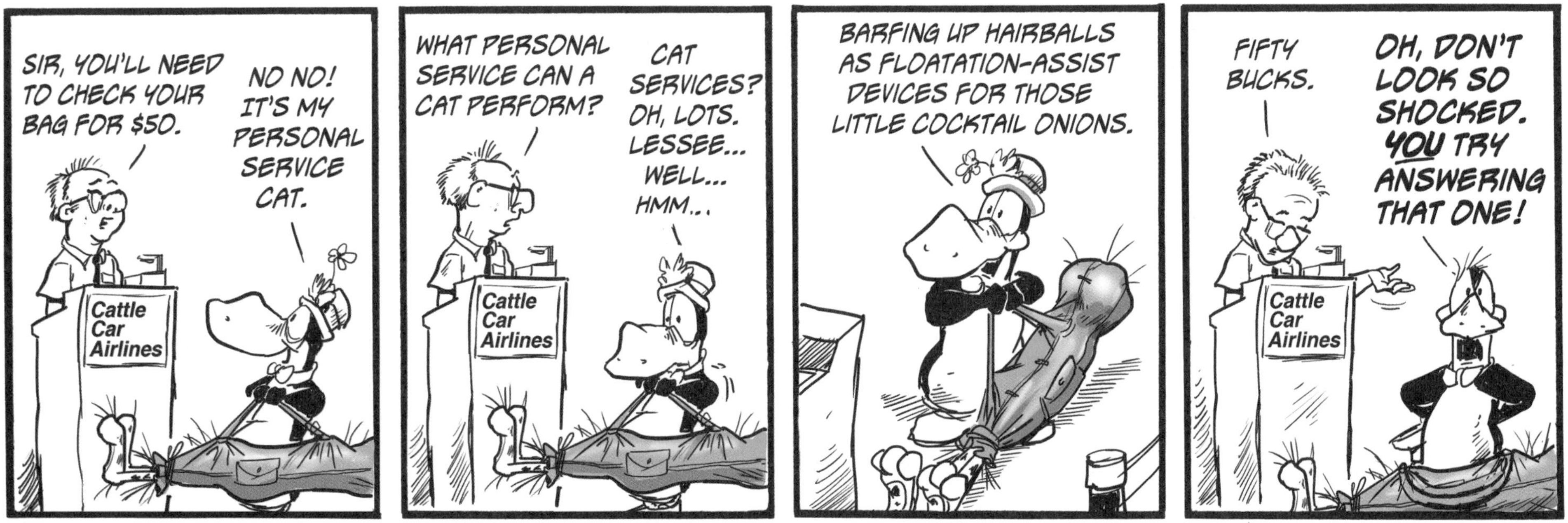
SIR, YOU'LL NEED TO CHECK YOUR BAG FOR $50.
NO NO! IT'S MY PERSONAL SERVICE CAT.
Cattle Car Airlines
WHAT PERSONAL SERVICE CAN A CAT PERFORM?
CAT SERVICES? OH, LOTS. LESSEE... WELL... HMM...
Cattle Car Airlines
BARFING UP HAIRBALLS AS FLOATATION-ASSIST DEVICES FOR THOSE LITTLE COCKTAIL ONIONS.
FIFTY BUCKS.
OH, DON'T LOOK SO SHOCKED. **YOU** TRY ANSWERING THAT ONE!
Cattle Car Airlines

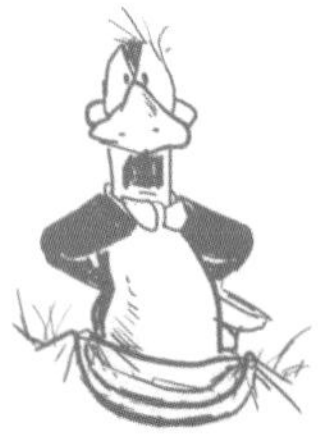

OPUS IS OFF THE RESERVATION. HE'S BEEN HORNSWOGGLED.

NOT THE FIRST TIME.

HE'S STARTED A GRASSROOTS POLITICAL GROUP.

GROUP OF WHAT?

FLIGHTLESS FOWL FOR TRUMP

WELCOME EVERYONE! HOPE EVERYONE HAD A GOOD FLIGHT. NOT. HA!

HA! GOOD ONE!

HILLARY SENT US A TELEGRAM: "WITH YOUR SUPPORT, I'D LIKE TO SEE ALL YOU UNDERCLASS BIRDS GET TAXPAYER-FUNDED SOLAR-POWERED PROPELLORS!"

FLIGHTLESS FOWL FOR TRUMP

FOWL FOR TRUMP

MR. TRUMP SENT A TELEGRAM TOO! "I'D LIKE TO SEE ALL YOUR GIBLETS SERVED WITH GRAVY."

FOWL FOR TRUMP!

WOWZA! HE CERTAINLY IS DARINGLY, SOCIALLY INCORRECT!

ALMOST... SEXY!

YEAH!

FOWL FOR TRUMP!

I TOTALLY WANT TO HAVE THAT MAN'S EGG!

YEAH! WELL, NO.

FOWL FOR TRUMP!

Bloom County 2015
by Berkeley Breathed esq.
HMM. TOO SMALL FOR STEVE DALLAS.
TRUMP!
A TRUMP HAT!! WE HAVE A CLOSETED TRUMPER IN THE HOUSE!
I HAVE HIM TRAPPED IN THE BATHROOM!
HEY, IN THERE! EXPLAIN YOURSELF!
I WANT MY IDENTITY PROTECTED!

TRUMP!

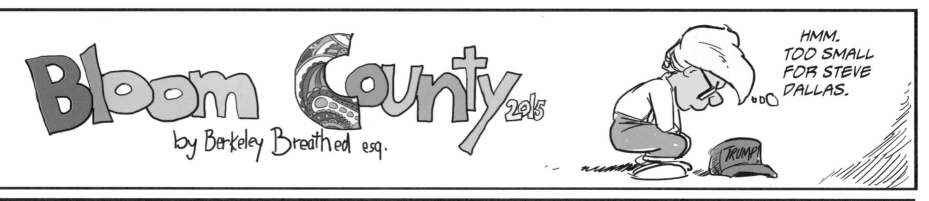

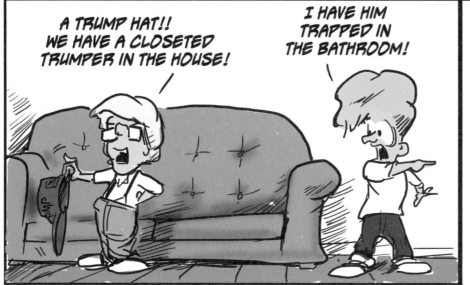

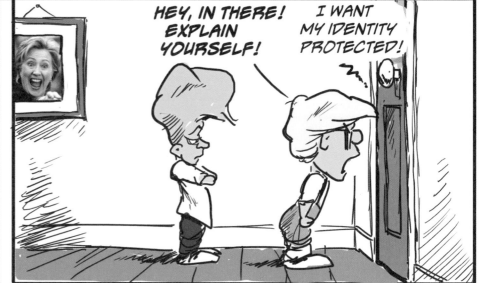

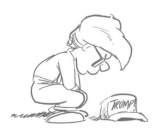

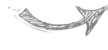

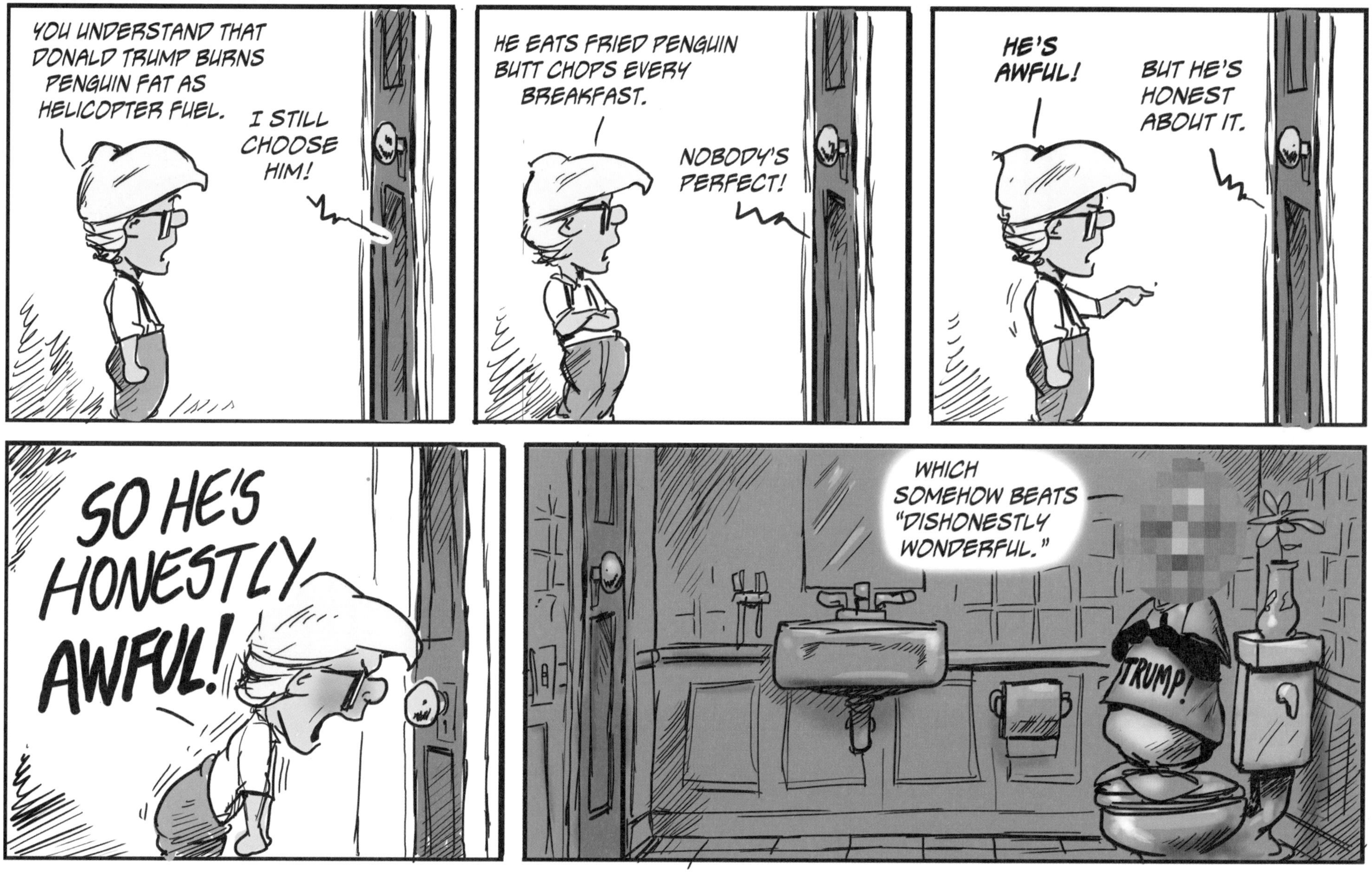
YOU UNDERSTAND THAT DONALD TRUMP BURNS PENGUIN FAT AS HELICOPTER FUEL.
I STILL CHOOSE HIM!
HE EATS FRIED PENGUIN BUTT CHOPS EVERY BREAKFAST.
NOBODY'S PERFECT!
HE'S AWFUL!
BUT HE'S HONEST ABOUT IT.
SO HE'S HONESTLY AWFUL!
WHICH SOMEHOW BEATS "DISHONESTLY WONDERFUL."
TRUMP!

It's funny, some may think this strip is on one side of the political aisle or the other. I don't feel it is slanted either way. I think Mr. Breathed just holds up a mirror to our society. I am absolutely on the conservative side, and I have always found *Bloom County* hilarious. I don't see it as liberal, conservative, or otherwise. If you can learn to laugh at yourself a little, *Bloom County* is for everyone, whatever your political persuasion.

—Jason James

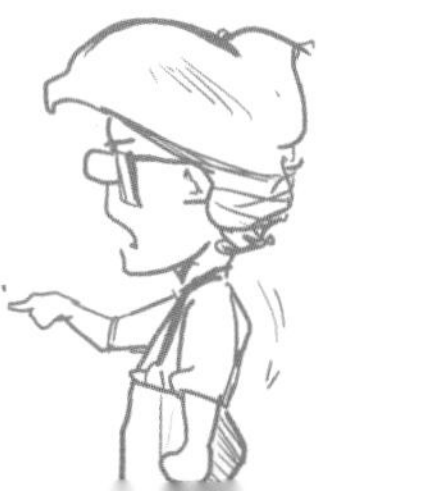

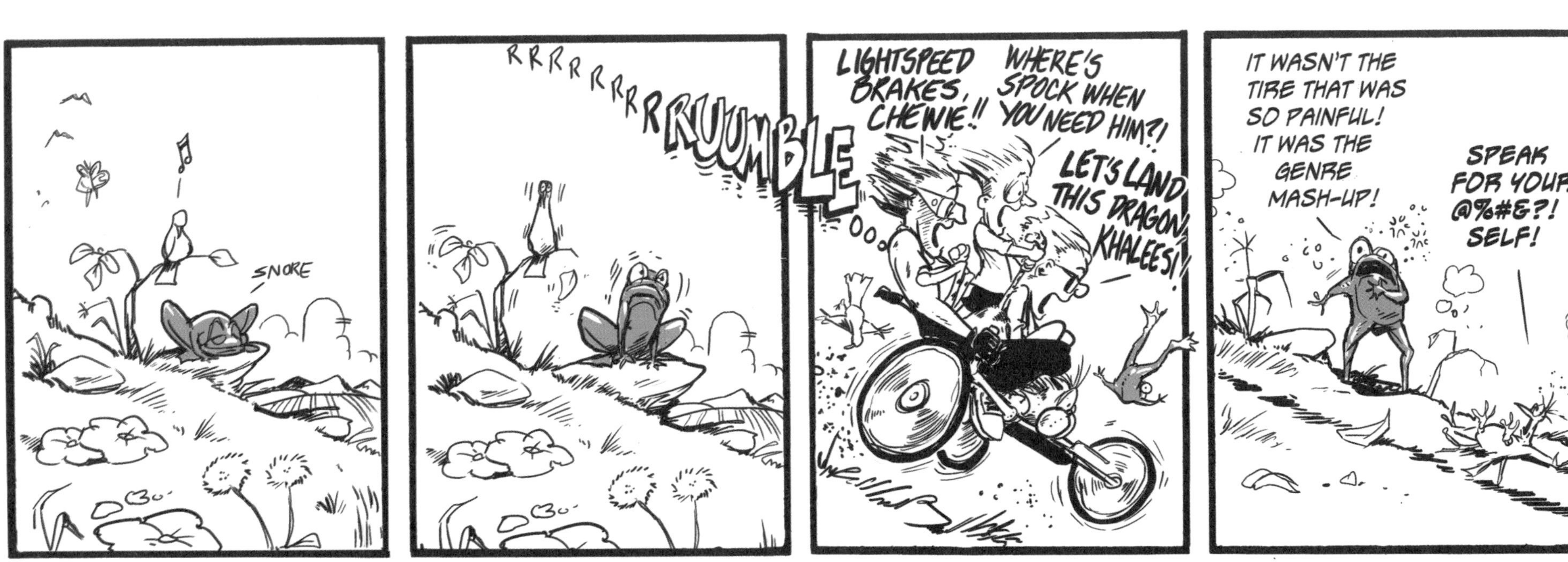
SNORE
RRRRRRRRRRUUMBLE
LIGHTSPEED BRAKES, CHEWIE!!
WHERE'S SPOCK WHEN YOU NEED HIM?!
LET'S LAND THIS DRAGON, KHALEESI!
IT WASN'T THE TIRE THAT WAS SO PAINFUL! IT WAS THE GENRE MASH-UP!
SPEAK FOR YOUR @%#&?! SELF!

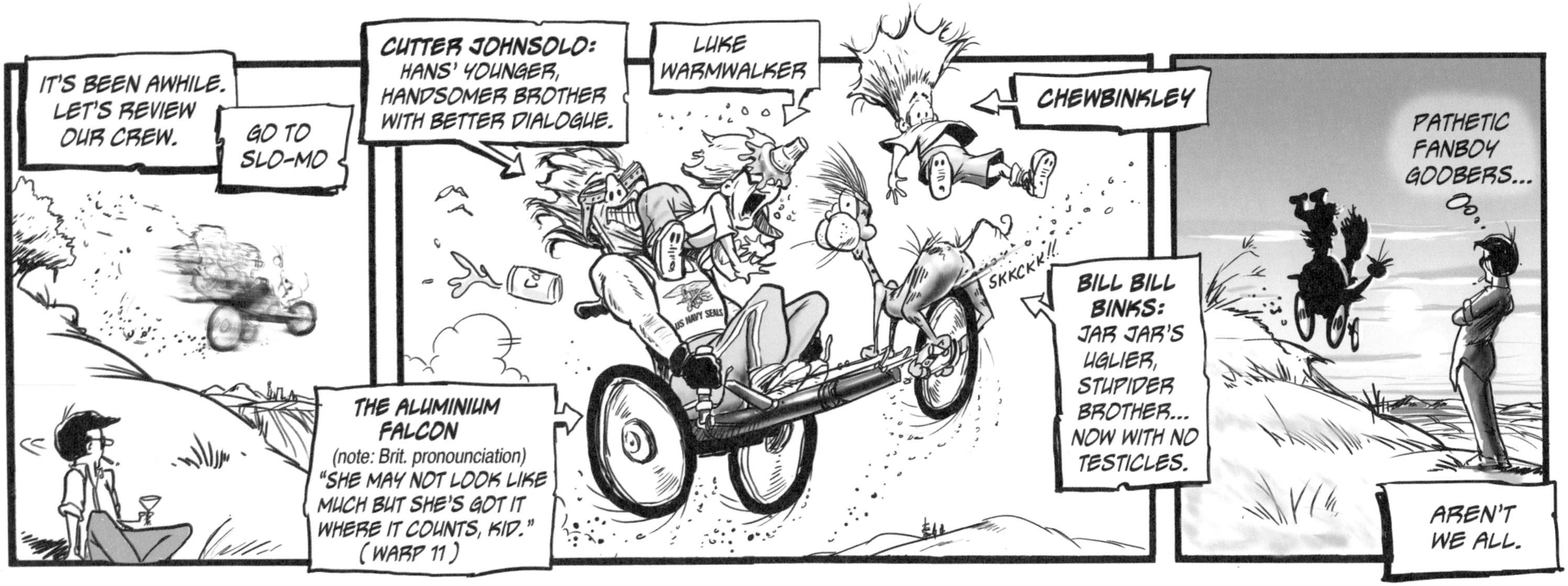
IT'S BEEN AWHILE. LET'S REVIEW OUR CREW.
GO TO SLO-MO
CUTTER JOHNSOLO: HANS' YOUNGER, HANDSOMER BROTHER WITH BETTER DIALOGUE.
LUKE WARMWALKER
CHEWBINKLEY
SKKCKK!!
BILL BILL BINKS: JAR JAR'S UGLIER, STUPIDER BROTHER... NOW WITH NO TESTICLES.
THE ALUMINIUM FALCON
(note: Brit. pronounciation)
"SHE MAY NOT LOOK LIKE MUCH BUT SHE'S GOT IT WHERE IT COUNTS, KID."
(WARP 11)
PATHETIC FANBOY GOOBERS...
AREN'T WE ALL.

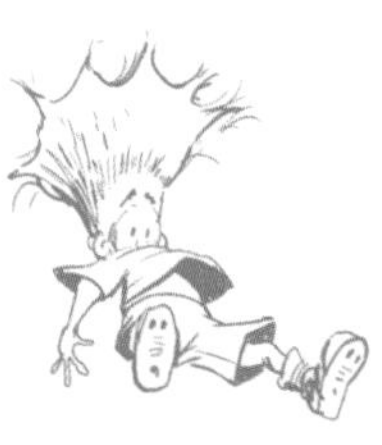

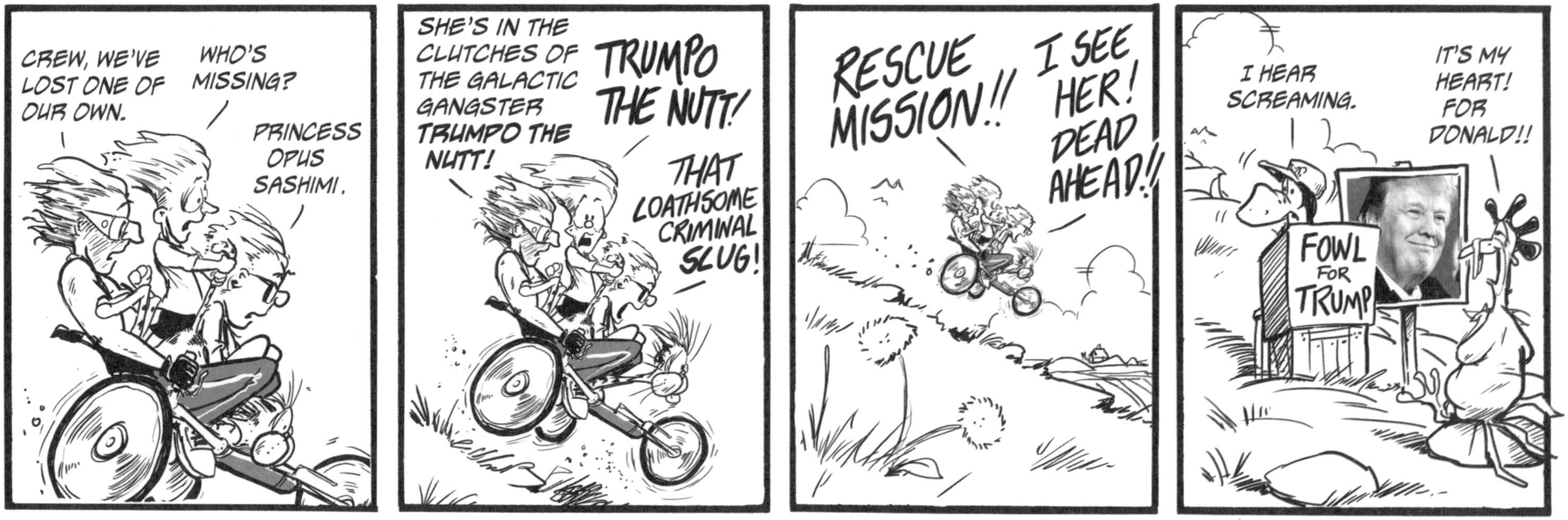
CREW, WE'VE LOST ONE OF OUR OWN.
WHO'S MISSING?
PRINCESS OPUS SASHIMI.
SHE'S IN THE CLUTCHES OF THE GALACTIC GANGSTER TRUMPO THE NUTT!
TRUMPO THE NUTT!
THAT LOATHSOME CRIMINAL SLUG!
RESCUE MISSION!!
I SEE HER! DEAD AHEAD!!
I HEAR SCREAMING.
IT'S MY HEART! FOR DONALD!!
FOWL FOR TRUMP

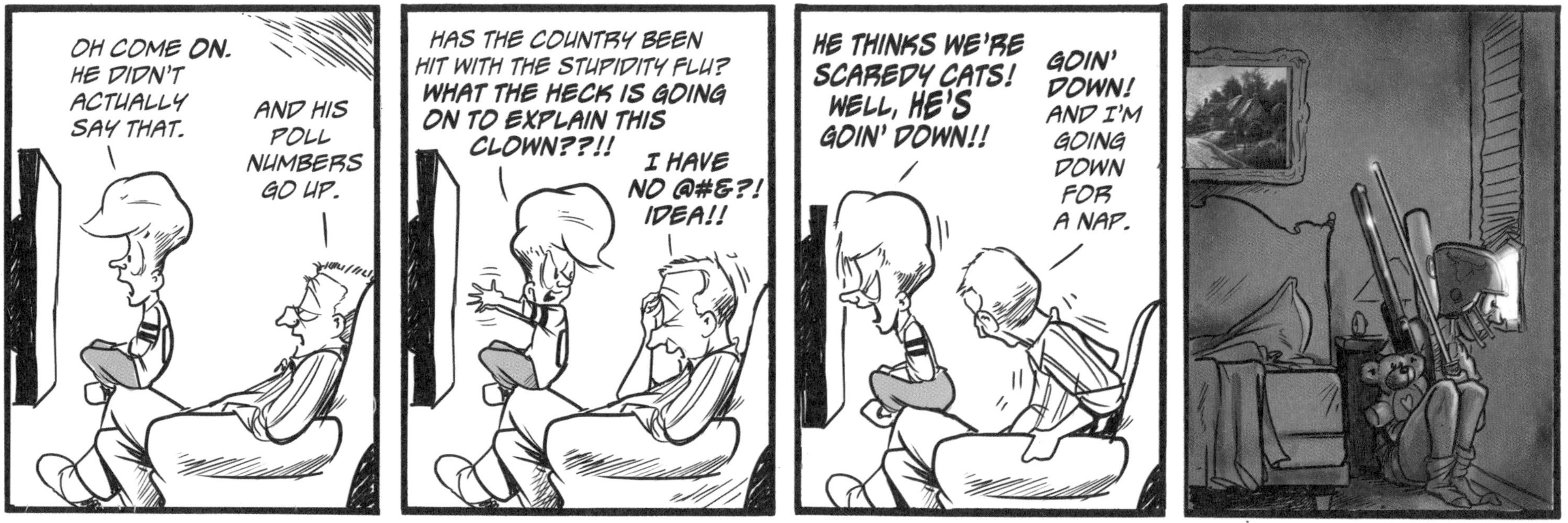
OH COME ON. HE DIDN'T ACTUALLY SAY THAT.
AND HIS POLL NUMBERS GO UP.
HAS THE COUNTRY BEEN HIT WITH THE STUPIDITY FLU? WHAT THE HECK IS GOING ON TO EXPLAIN THIS CLOWN??!!
I HAVE NO @#&?! IDEA!!
HE THINKS WE'RE SCAREDY CATS! WELL, HE'S GOIN' DOWN!!
GOIN' DOWN! AND I'M GOING DOWN FOR A NAP.

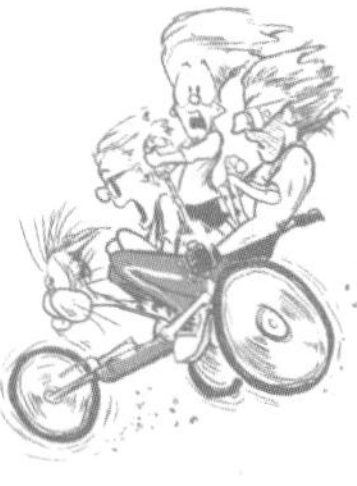

32

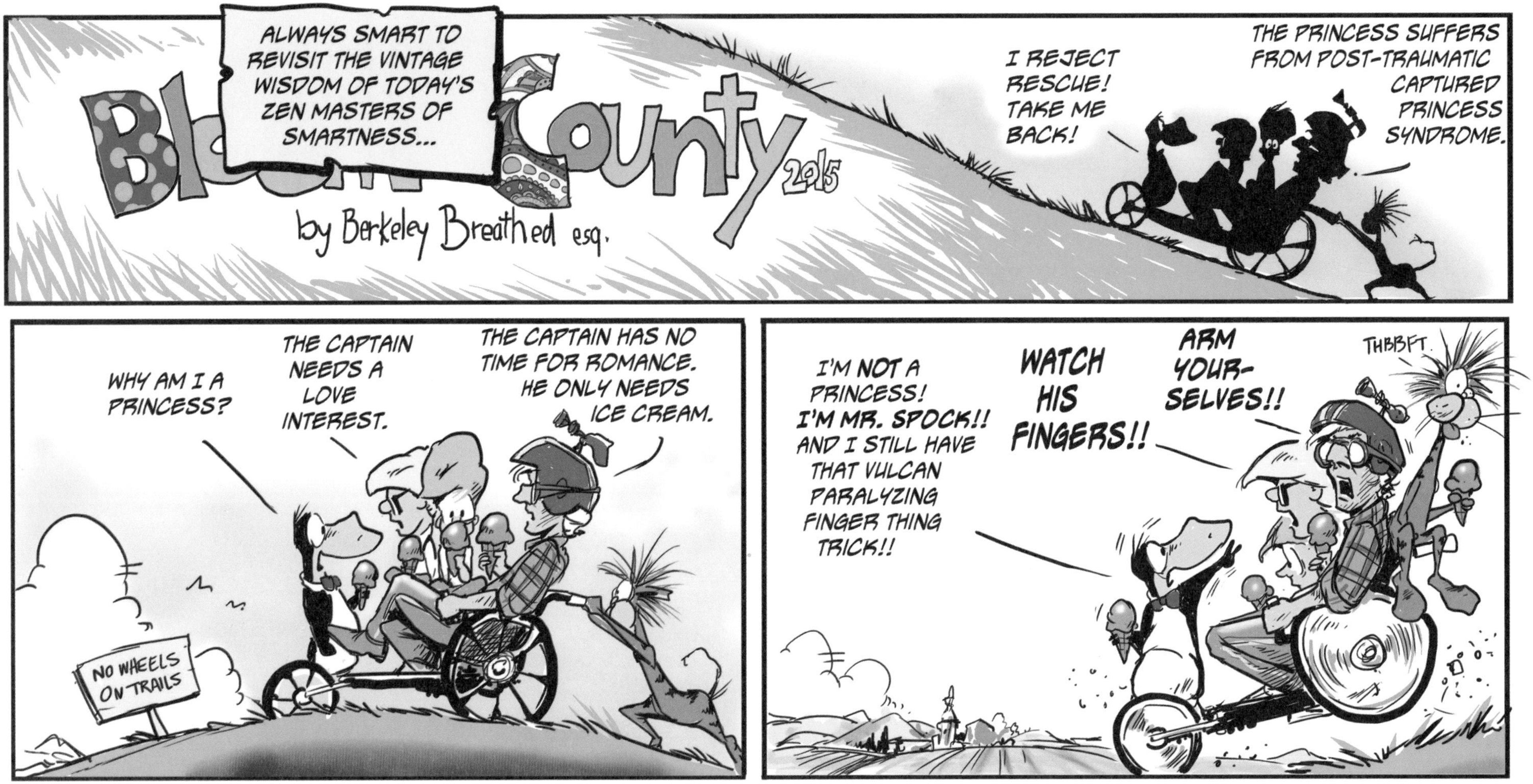

ALWAYS SMART TO REVISIT THE VINTAGE WISDOM OF TODAY'S ZEN MASTERS OF SMARTNESS...
County 2015
by Berkeley Breathed esq.
I REJECT RESCUE! TAKE ME BACK!
THE PRINCESS SUFFERS FROM POST-TRAUMATIC CAPTURED PRINCESS SYNDROME.
WHY AM I A PRINCESS?
THE CAPTAIN NEEDS A LOVE INTEREST.
THE CAPTAIN HAS NO TIME FOR ROMANCE. HE ONLY NEEDS ICE CREAM.
NO WHEELS ON TRAILS
I'M NOT A PRINCESS! I'M MR. SPOCK!! AND I STILL HAVE THAT VULCAN PARALYZING FINGER THING TRICK!!
WATCH HIS FINGERS!!
ARM YOURSELVES!!
THBBFT.

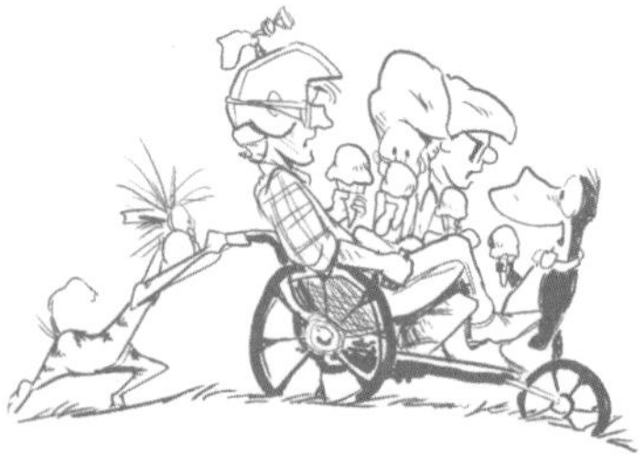

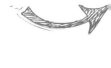

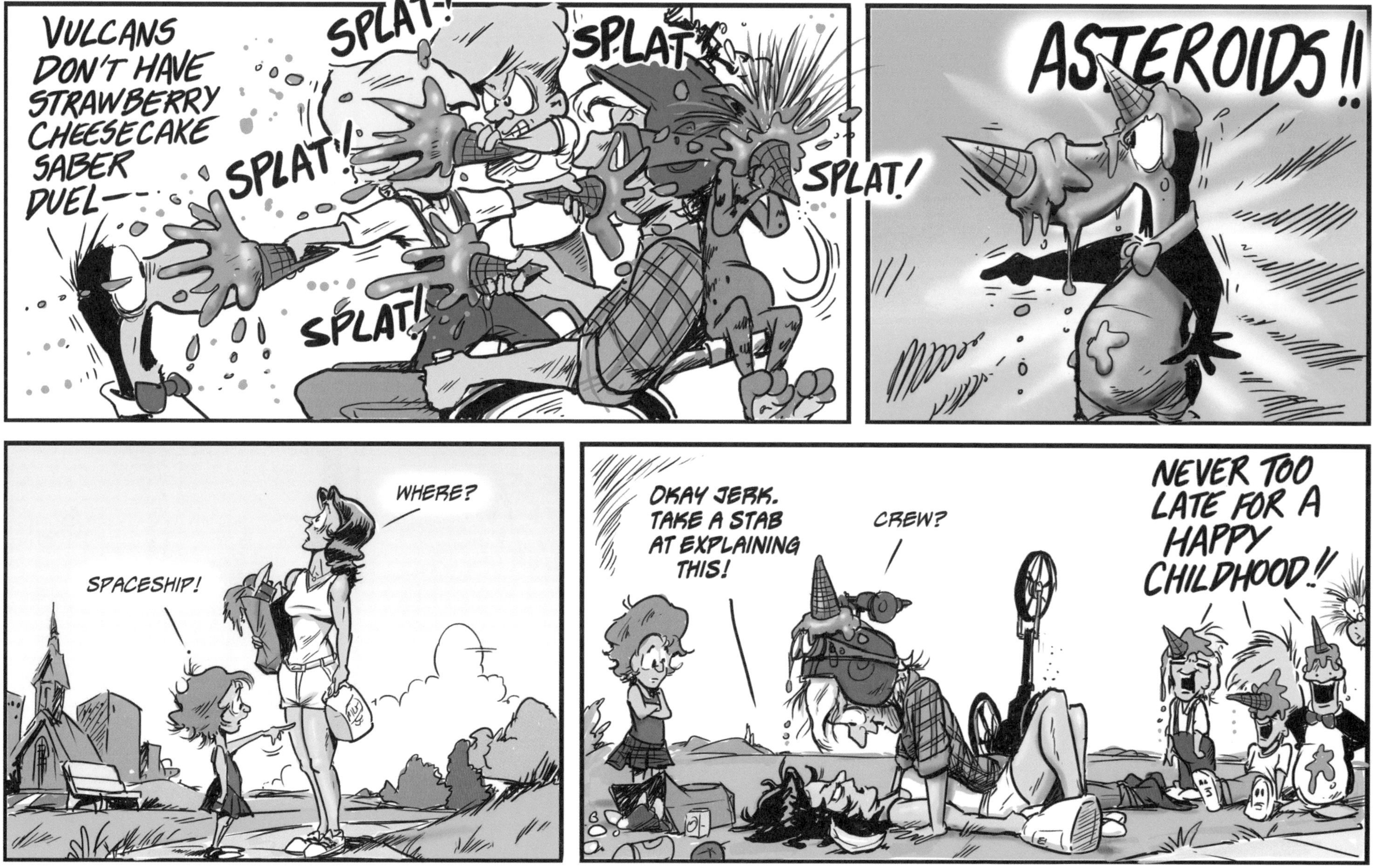
VULCANS DON'T HAVE STRAWBERRY CHEESECAKE SABER DUEL—
SPLAT!
SPLAT!
SPLAT!
SPLAT!
SPLAT!
SPLAT!
ASTEROIDS!!
SPACESHIP!
WHERE?
OKAY JERK. TAKE A STAB AT EXPLAINING THIS!
CREW?
NEVER TOO LATE FOR A HAPPY CHILDHOOD!!

Dear Mr. Breathed, I'm an old man who has lived much and in the end I can't really say what happiness is. I have experienced moments of happiness at different times, but it is, at best transient, and at worst elusive. Perhaps it's a warm puppy, as Mr. Schulz once said, but I tend to think it has something to do with finding something that once was lost, something that was wonderful and special and now has returned.

—Richard Barnard

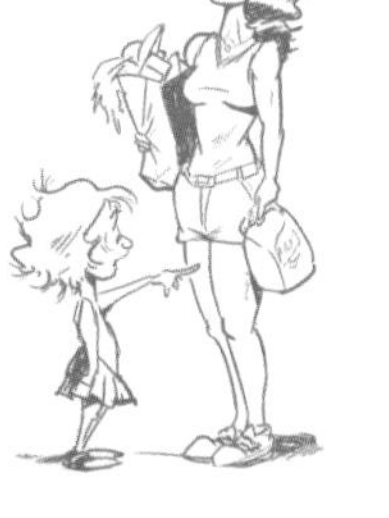

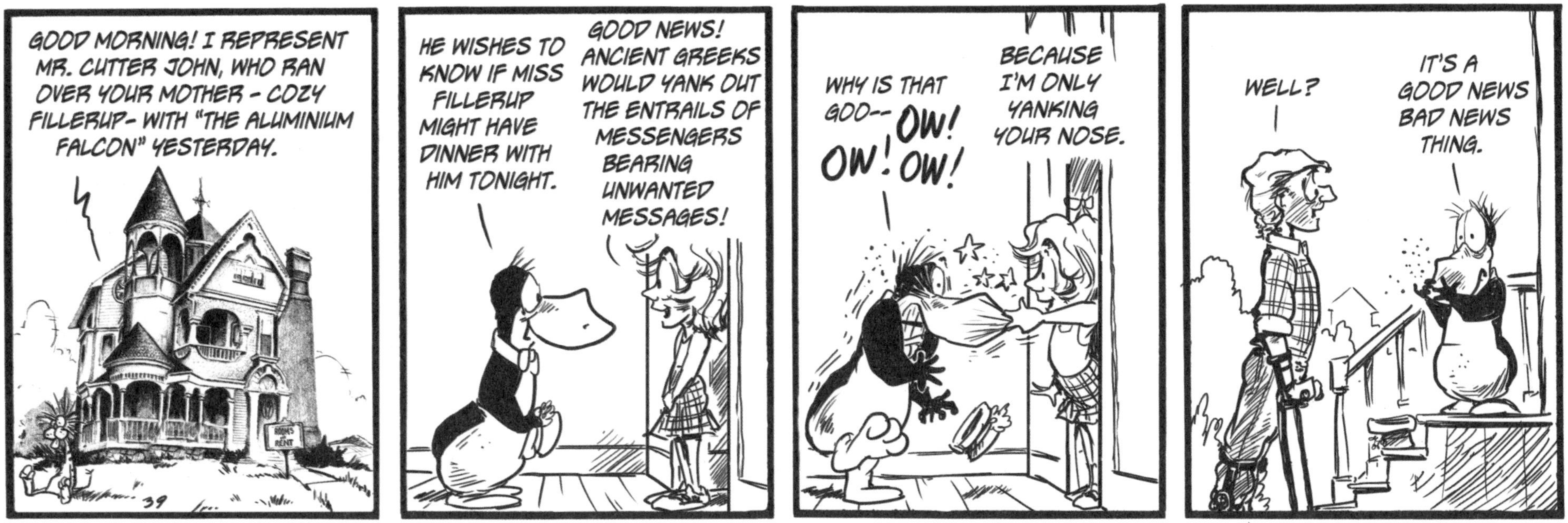
GOOD MORNING! I REPRESENT MR. CUTTER JOHN, WHO RAN OVER YOUR MOTHER - COZY FILLERUP- WITH "THE ALUMINIUM FALCON" YESTERDAY.
HE WISHES TO KNOW IF MISS FILLERUP MIGHT HAVE DINNER WITH HIM TONIGHT.
GOOD NEWS! ANCIENT GREEKS WOULD YANK OUT THE ENTRAILS OF MESSENGERS BEARING UNWANTED MESSAGES!
WHY IS THAT GOO--
OW! OW! OW!
BECAUSE I'M ONLY YANKING YOUR NOSE.
WELL?
IT'S A GOOD NEWS BAD NEWS THING.

34

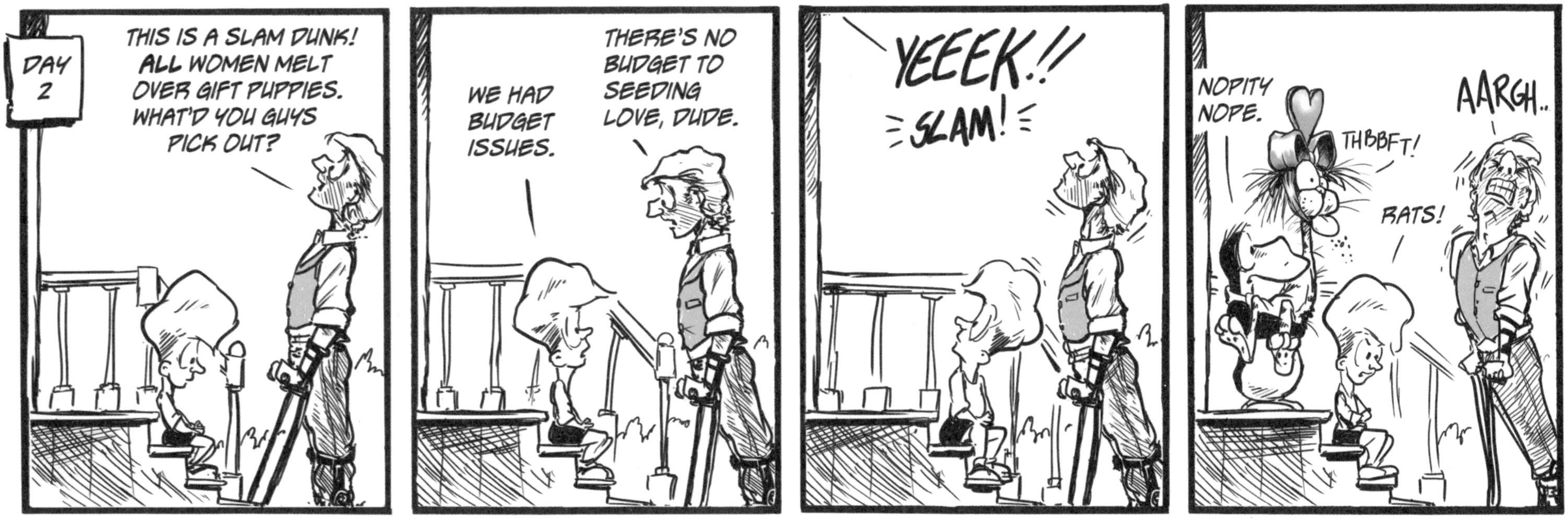
DAY 2
THIS IS A SLAM DUNK! ALL WOMEN MELT OVER GIFT PUPPIES. WHAT'D YOU GUYS PICK OUT?
WE HAD BUDGET ISSUES.
THERE'S NO BUDGET TO SEEDING LOVE, DUDE.
YEEEK.!!
SLAM!
NOPITY NOPE.
THBBFT!
AARGH..
RATS!

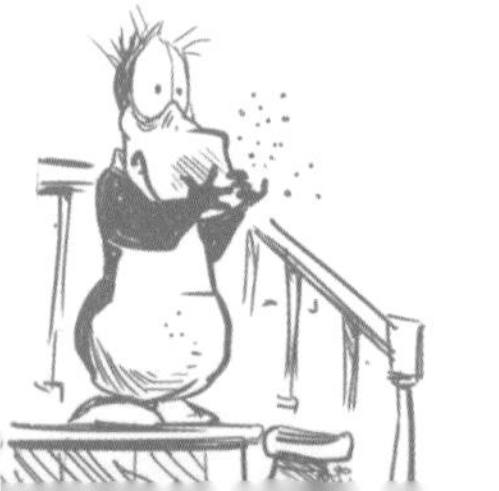

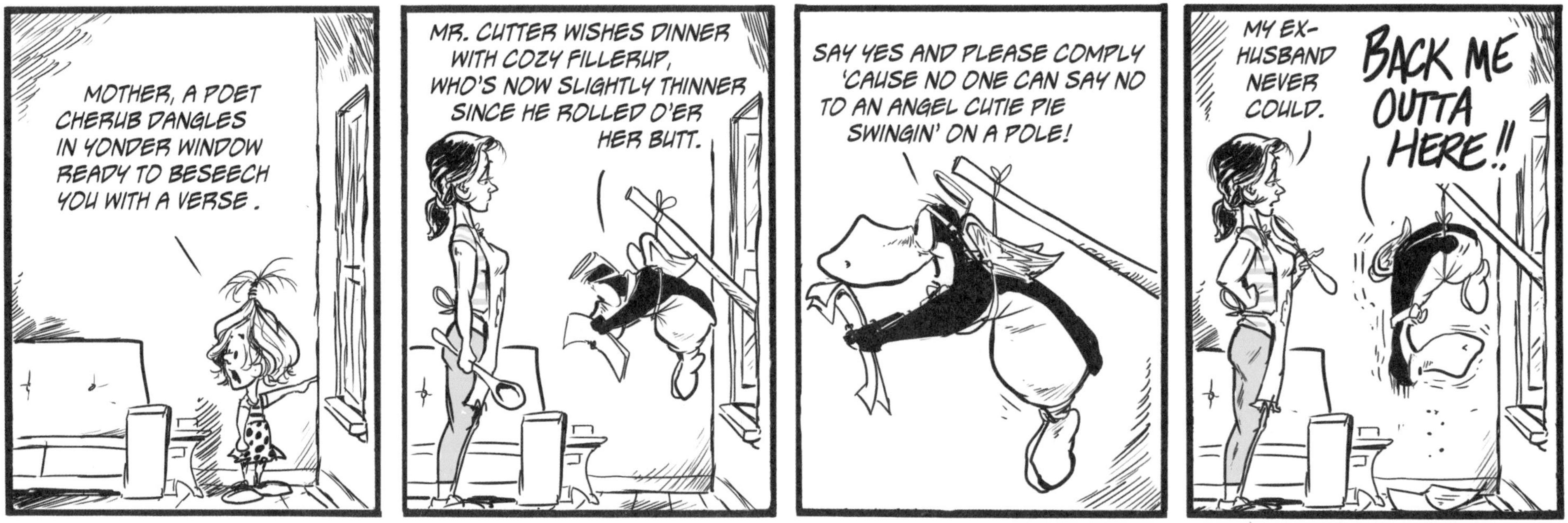
MOTHER, A POET
CHERUB DANGLES
IN YONDER WINDOW
READY TO BESEECH
YOU WITH A VERSE.
MR. CUTTER WISHES DINNER
WITH COZY FILLERUP,
WHO'S NOW SLIGHTLY THINNER
SINCE HE ROLLED O'ER
HER BUTT.
SAY YES AND PLEASE COMPLY
'CAUSE NO ONE CAN SAY NO
TO AN ANGEL CUTIE PIE
SWINGIN' ON A POLE!
MY EX-
HUSBAND
NEVER
COULD.
BACK ME
OUTTA
HERE!!

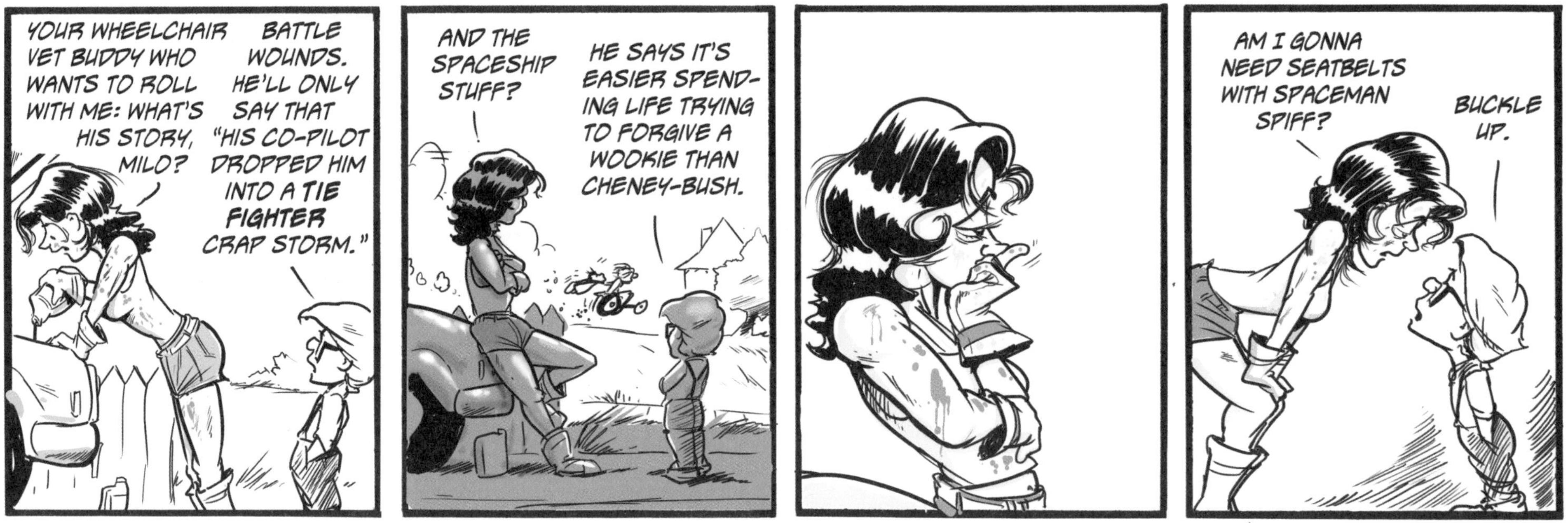
YOUR WHEELCHAIR
VET BUDDY WHO
WANTS TO ROLL
WITH ME: WHAT'S
HIS STORY,
MILO?
BATTLE
WOUNDS.
HE'LL ONLY
SAY THAT
"HIS CO-PILOT
DROPPED HIM
INTO A TIE
FIGHTER
CRAP STORM."
AND THE
SPACESHIP
STUFF?
HE SAYS IT'S
EASIER SPEND-
ING LIFE TRYING
TO FORGIVE A
WOOKIE THAN
CHENEY-BUSH.
AM I GONNA
NEED SEATBELTS
WITH SPACEMAN
SPIFF?
BUCKLE
UP.

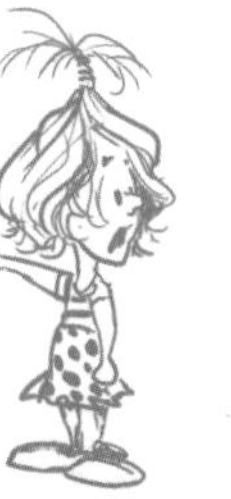

Bloom County 2015
by Berkeley Breathed esq.
KNOCK! KNOCK!
GREETINGS YOUNG FILLERUP!
OH. HELLO. I'M ABBY.
MISS ABBY & COZY FILLERUP
WE'RE HERE TO PRESENT MISS COZY A GIANT BOX OF CHOCOLATE TRUFFLES THAT REPRESENT THE GIANT SWEET AFFECTIONS HELD BY OUR CLIENT TOWARD YOUR MOTHER, WHO HE RECENTLY RAN OVER.

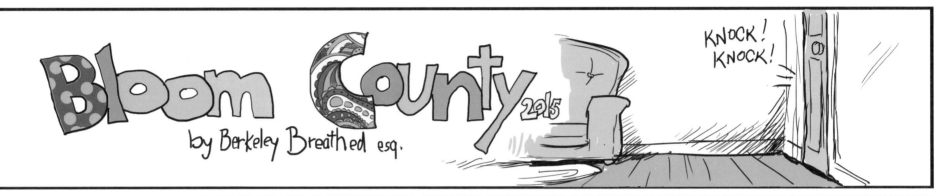

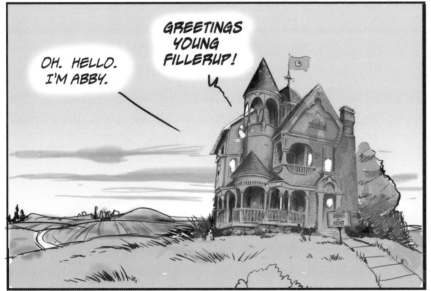

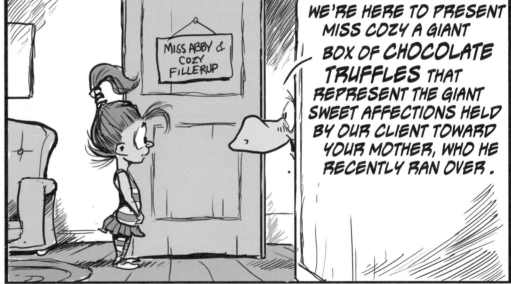

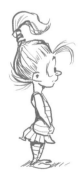

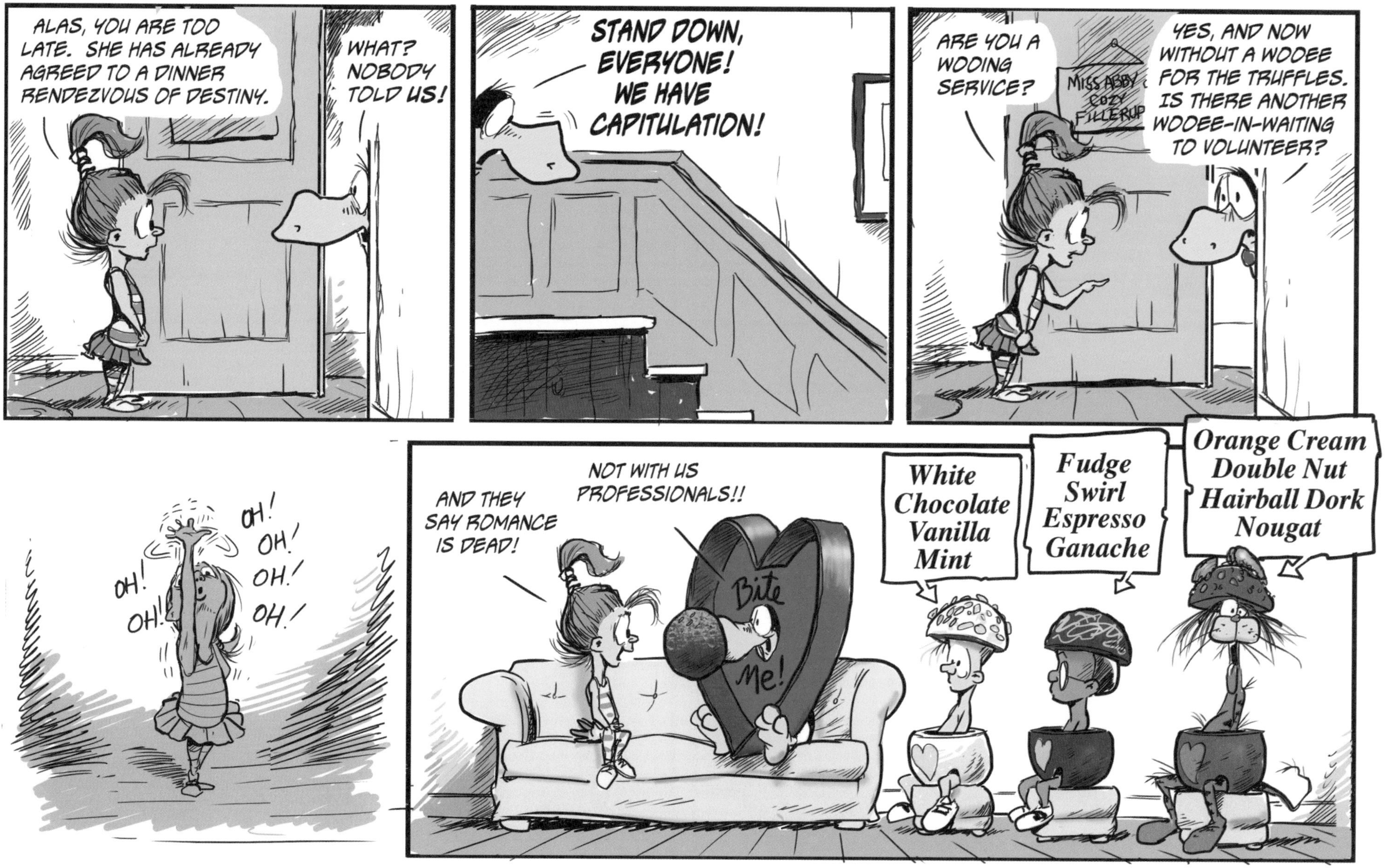
ALAS, YOU ARE TOO LATE. SHE HAS ALREADY AGREED TO A DINNER RENDEZVOUS OF DESTINY.
WHAT? NOBODY TOLD US!
STAND DOWN, EVERYONE! WE HAVE CAPITULATION!
ARE YOU A WOOING SERVICE?
MISS ABBY COZY FILLERUP
YES, AND NOW WITHOUT A WOOEE FOR THE TRUFFLES. IS THERE ANOTHER WOOEE-IN-WAITING TO VOLUNTEER?
OH! OH! OH! OH! OH! OH!
AND THEY SAY ROMANCE IS DEAD!
NOT WITH US PROFESSIONALS!!
Bite Me!
White Chocolate Vanilla Mint
Fudge Swirl Espresso Ganache
Orange Cream Double Nut Hairball Dork Nougat

I told my kids discovering *Bloom County* again on Facebook was like an old friend walking in the bar and sitting at the stool next to you. It is a family tradition every year that we sit together Christmas Eve and read *Red Ranger Calling*. I will mention my kids are 17 and 15 and we still do it.

—Patrick Ford

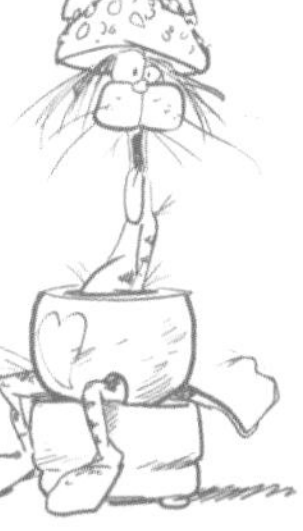

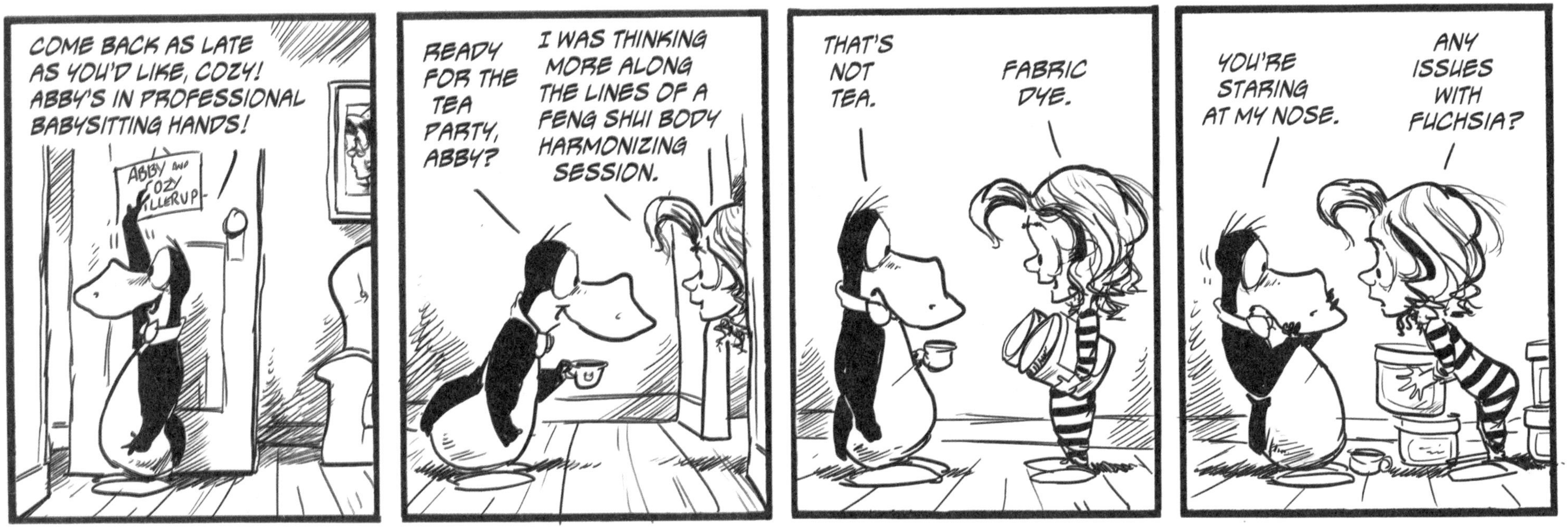
COME BACK AS LATE AS YOU'D LIKE, COZY! ABBY'S IN PROFESSIONAL BABYSITTING HANDS!
ABBY AND COZY ILLERUP
READY FOR THE TEA PARTY, ABBY?
I WAS THINKING MORE ALONG THE LINES OF A FENG SHUI BODY HARMONIZING SESSION.
THAT'S NOT TEA.
FABRIC DYE.
YOU'RE STARING AT MY NOSE.
ANY ISSUES WITH FUCHSIA?

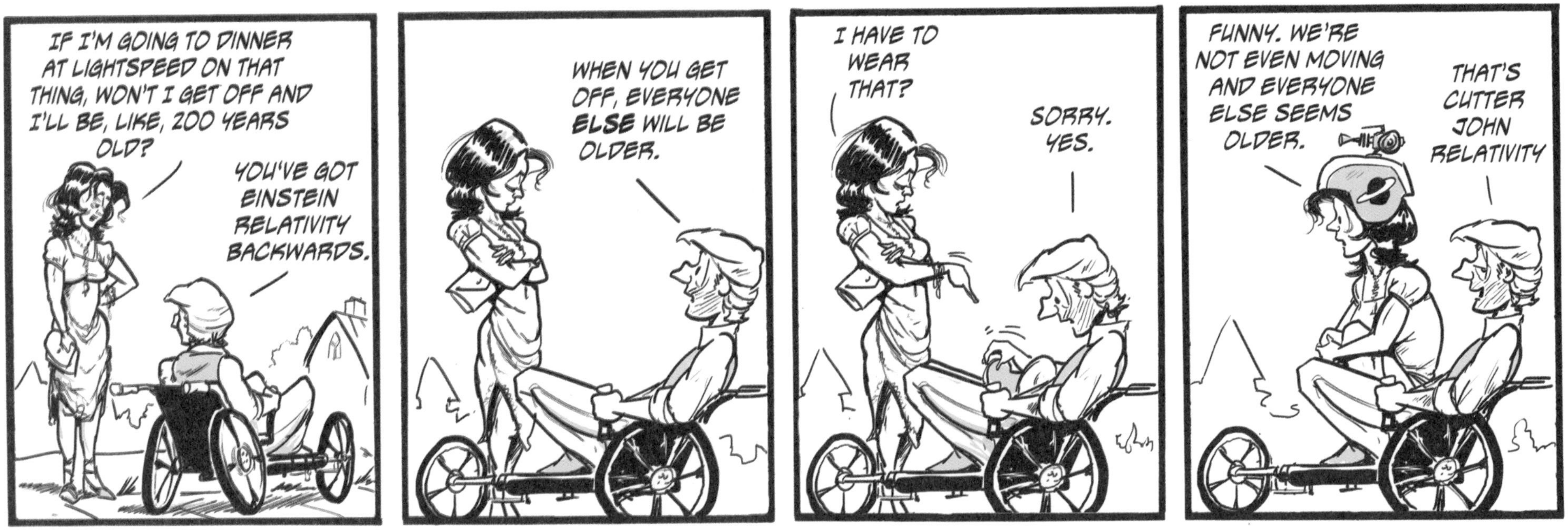
IF I'M GOING TO DINNER AT LIGHTSPEED ON THAT THING, WON'T I GET OFF AND I'LL BE, LIKE, 200 YEARS OLD?
YOU'VE GOT EINSTEIN RELATIVITY BACKWARDS.
WHEN YOU GET OFF, EVERYONE ELSE WILL BE OLDER.
I HAVE TO WEAR THAT?
SORRY. YES.
FUNNY. WE'RE NOT EVEN MOVING AND EVERYONE ELSE SEEMS OLDER.
THAT'S CUTTER JOHN RELATIVITY

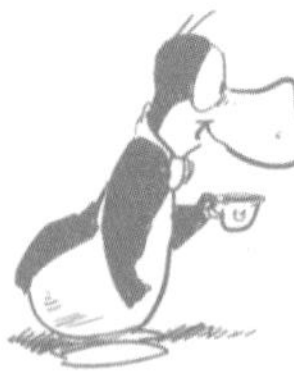

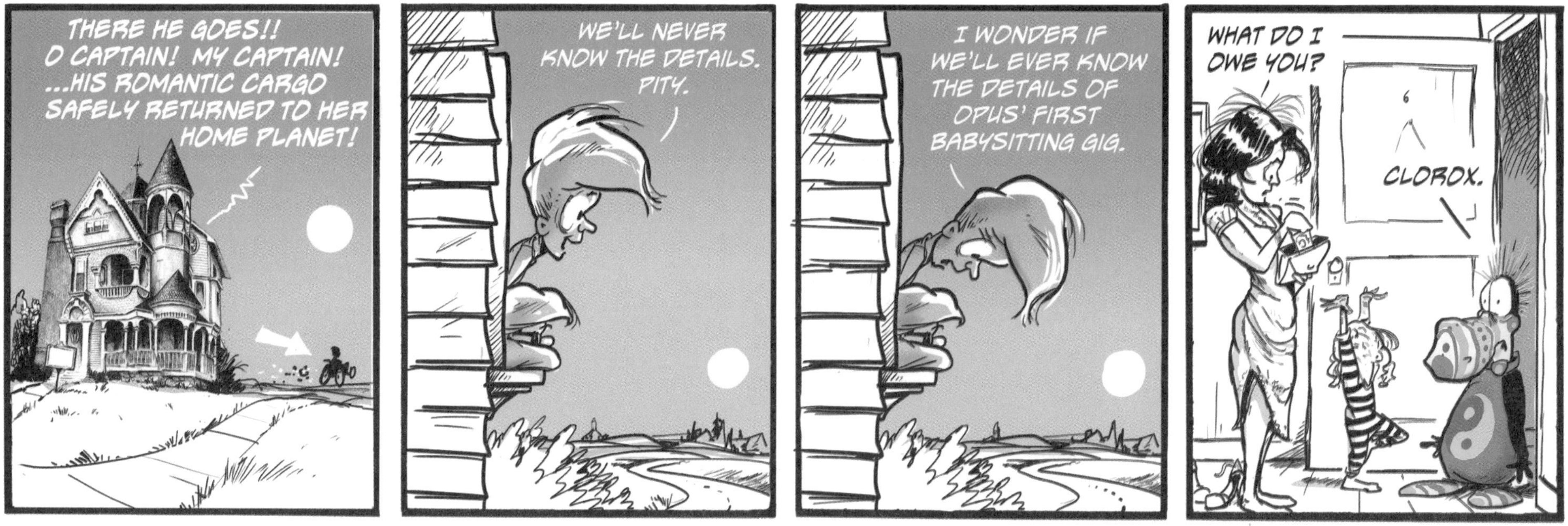
THERE HE GOES!! O CAPTAIN! MY CAPTAIN! ...HIS ROMANTIC CARGO SAFELY RETURNED TO HER HOME PLANET!
WE'LL NEVER KNOW THE DETAILS. PITY.
I WONDER IF WE'LL EVER KNOW THE DETAILS OF OPUS' FIRST BABYSITTING GIG.
WHAT DO I OWE YOU?
CLOROX.

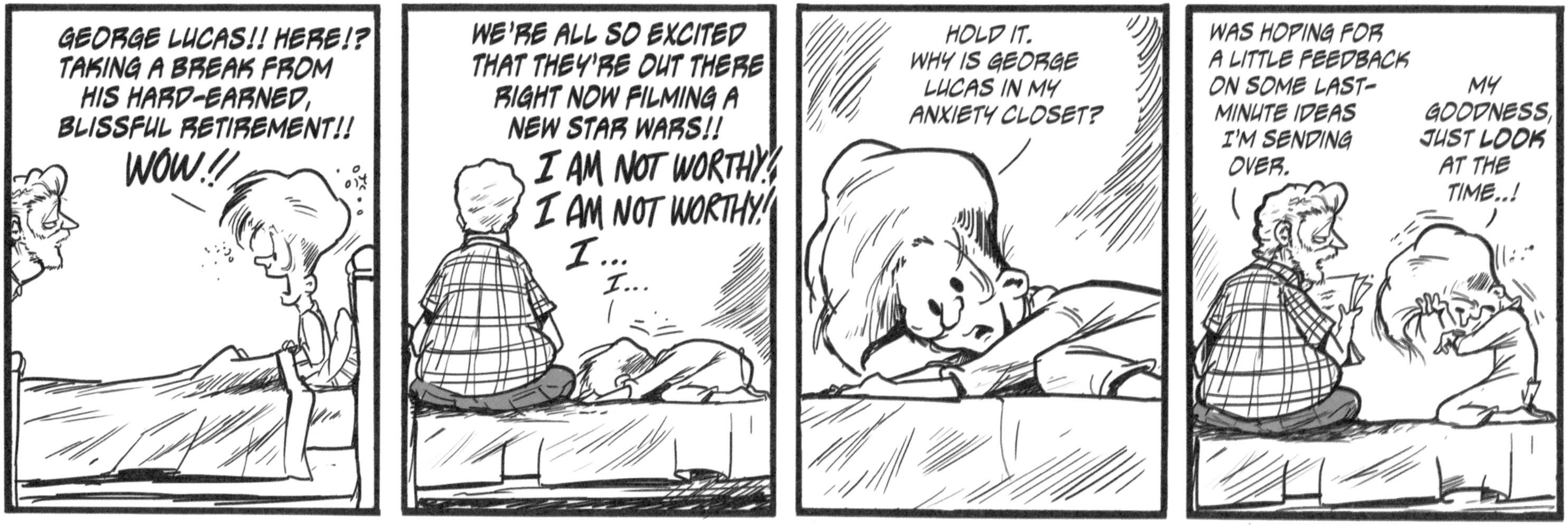
GEORGE LUCAS!! HERE!? TAKING A BREAK FROM HIS HARD-EARNED, BLISSFUL RETIREMENT!!
WOW!!
WE'RE ALL SO EXCITED THAT THEY'RE OUT THERE RIGHT NOW FILMING A NEW STAR WARS!!
I AM NOT WORTHY! I AM NOT WORTHY! I...
I...
HOLD IT. WHY IS GEORGE LUCAS IN MY ANXIETY CLOSET?
WAS HOPING FOR A LITTLE FEEDBACK ON SOME LAST-MINUTE IDEAS I'M SENDING OVER.
MY GOODNESS, JUST LOOK AT THE TIME..!

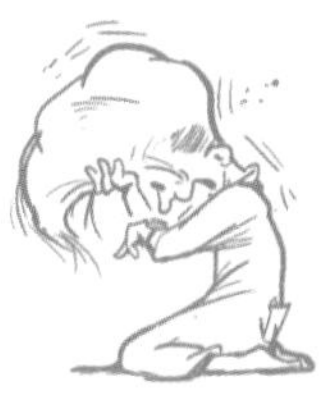

Bloom County 2015
by Berkeley Breathed esq.
BURP
BURP
BURP
MEN'S KOUCH
NO WHIMIN
I WOKE UP WONDERING, THIS MORNING.
I WOKE UP WONDERING... WHY WE **LIVE** FOR MOMENTS TO **DIE** FOR.
MEN'S KOUCH
NO WHIMIN

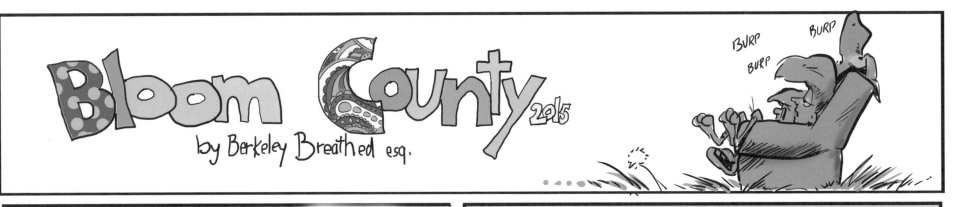

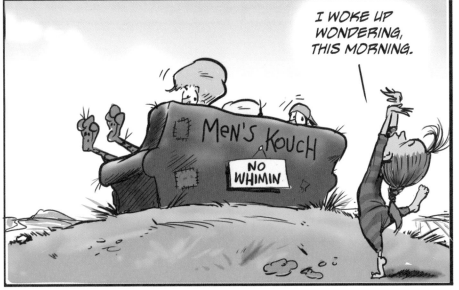

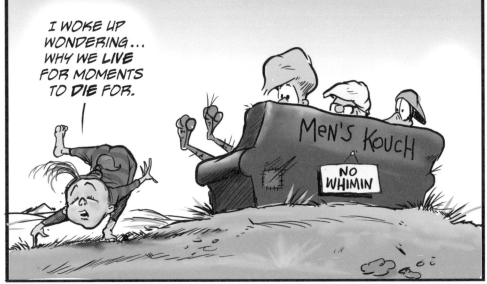

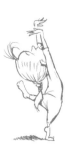

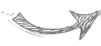

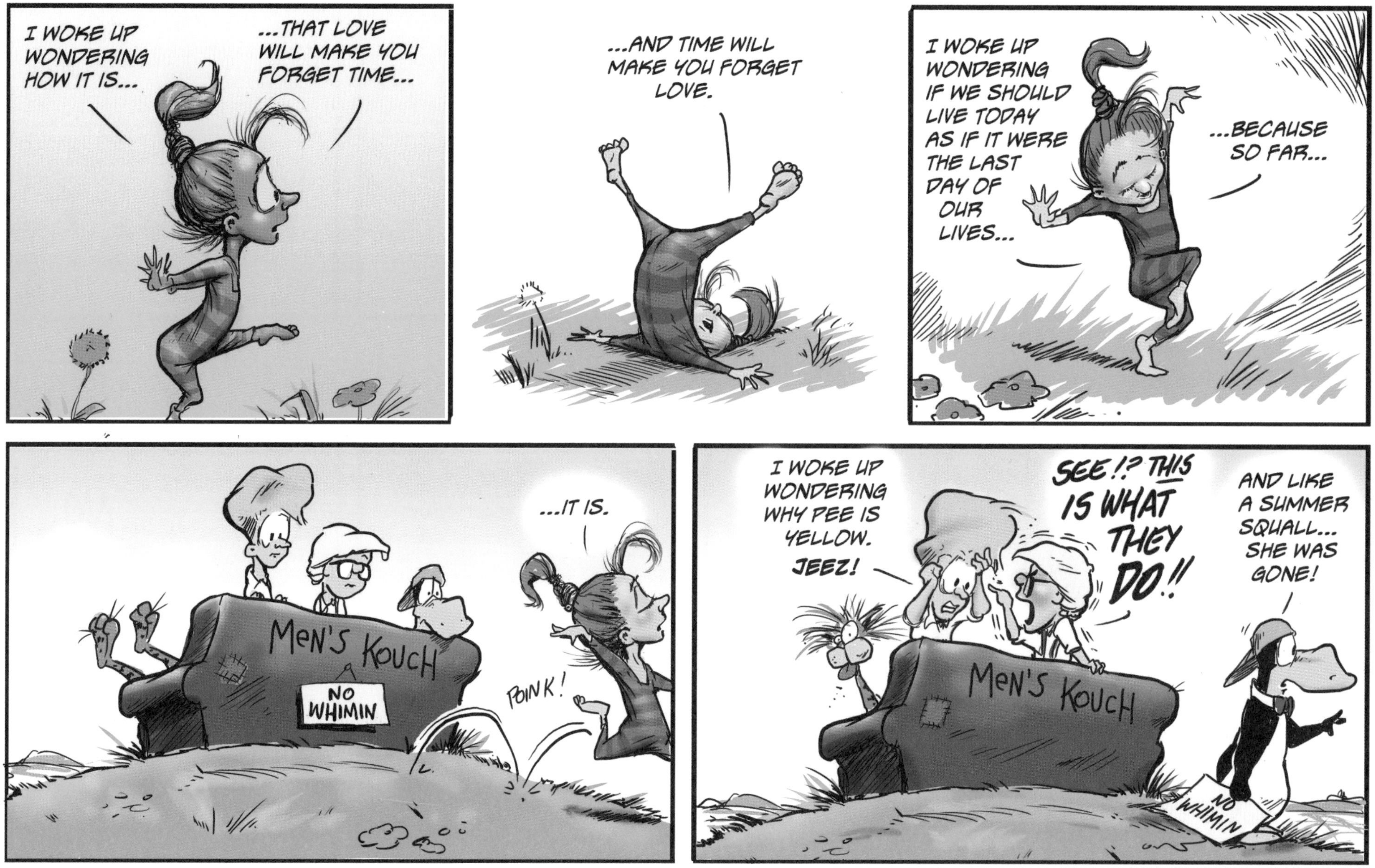
I WOKE UP WONDERING HOW IT IS...
...THAT LOVE WILL MAKE YOU FORGET TIME...
...AND TIME WILL MAKE YOU FORGET LOVE.
I WOKE UP WONDERING IF WE SHOULD LIVE TODAY AS IF IT WERE THE LAST DAY OF OUR LIVES...
...BECAUSE SO FAR...
...IT IS.
MEN'S KOUCH
NO WHIMIN
POINK!
I WOKE UP WONDERING WHY PEE IS YELLOW. JEEZ!
SEE!? THIS IS WHAT THEY DO!!
AND LIKE A SUMMER SQUALL... SHE WAS GONE!
MEN'S KOUCH
NO WHIMIN

I wanted to write to you, something I have never done before, after hearing you on Fresh Air. My husband Raymond M Houston introduced me to your comic strip. Twenty-five years ago when you were in syndication I was well past reading and enjoying comics in my daily work life. Opus and the others have brought back a joy I had long forgotten. Like Atticus Finch, you are a national treasure I am very happy to be introduced to in my adult years. I now enjoy reading *Bloom County* daily with the same zest I did for many old comic strips forty to fifty years ago.

—Arthur Moench

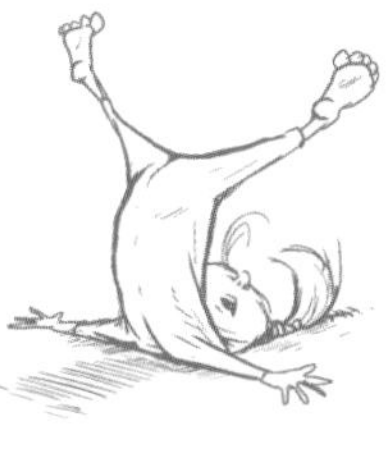

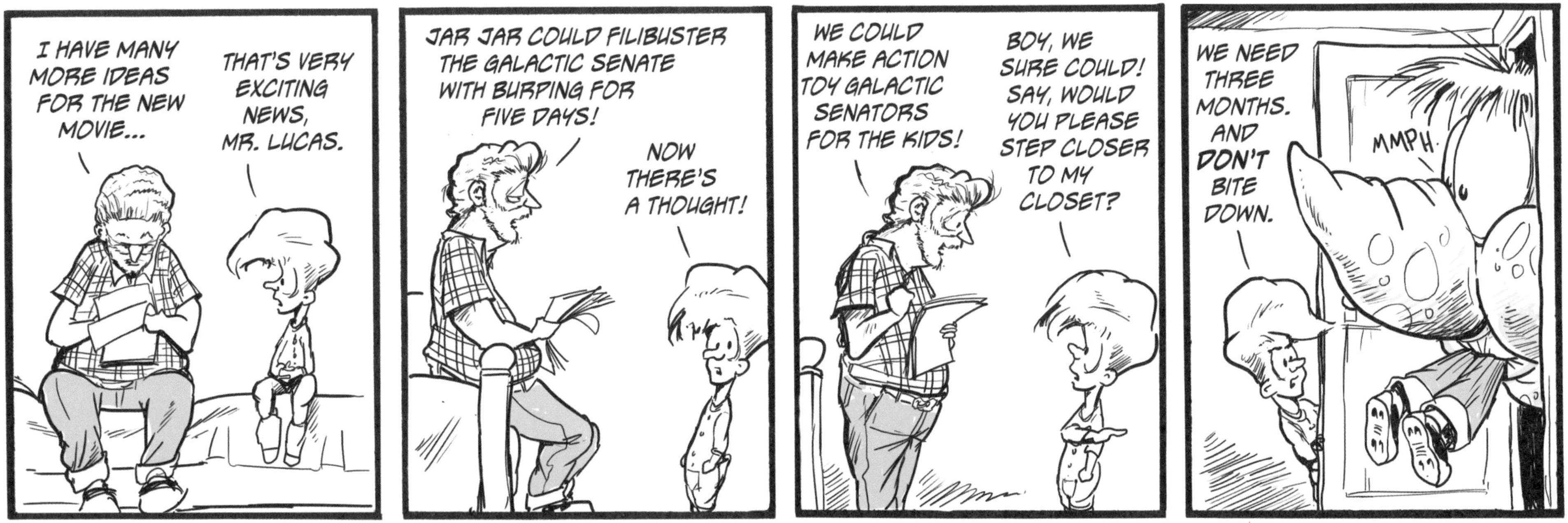
I HAVE MANY MORE IDEAS FOR THE NEW MOVIE...
THAT'S VERY EXCITING NEWS, MR. LUCAS.
JAR JAR COULD FILIBUSTER THE GALACTIC SENATE WITH BURPING FOR FIVE DAYS!
NOW THERE'S A THOUGHT!
WE COULD MAKE ACTION TOY GALACTIC SENATORS FOR THE KIDS!
BOY, WE SURE COULD! SAY, WOULD YOU PLEASE STEP CLOSER TO MY CLOSET?
WE NEED THREE MONTHS. AND DON'T BITE DOWN.
MMPH

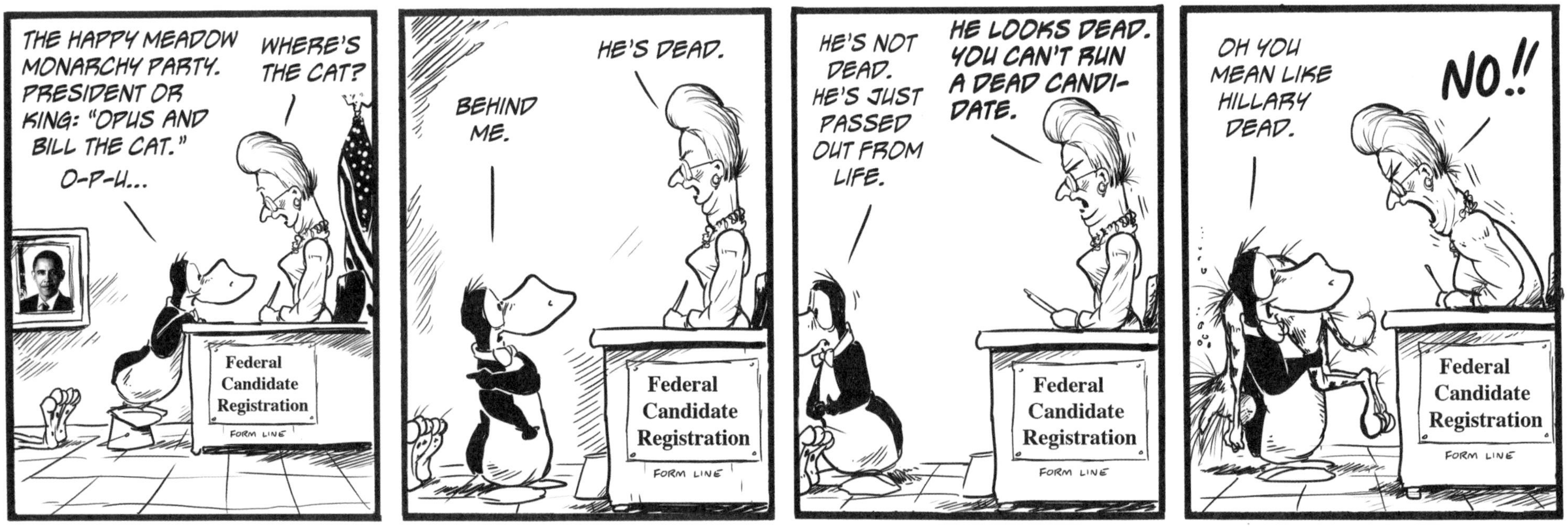
THE HAPPY MEADOW MONARCHY PARTY. PRESIDENT OR KING: "OPUS AND BILL THE CAT."
O-P-U...
WHERE'S THE CAT?
Federal Candidate Registration
FORM LINE
BEHIND ME.
HE'S DEAD.
Federal Candidate Registration
FORM LINE
HE'S NOT DEAD. HE'S JUST PASSED OUT FROM LIFE.
HE LOOKS DEAD. YOU CAN'T RUN A DEAD CANDIDATE.
Federal Candidate Registration
FORM LINE
OH YOU MEAN LIKE HILLARY DEAD.
NO!!
Federal Candidate Registration
FORM LINE

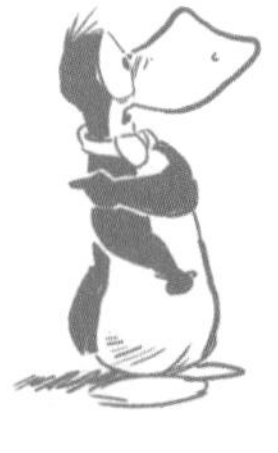

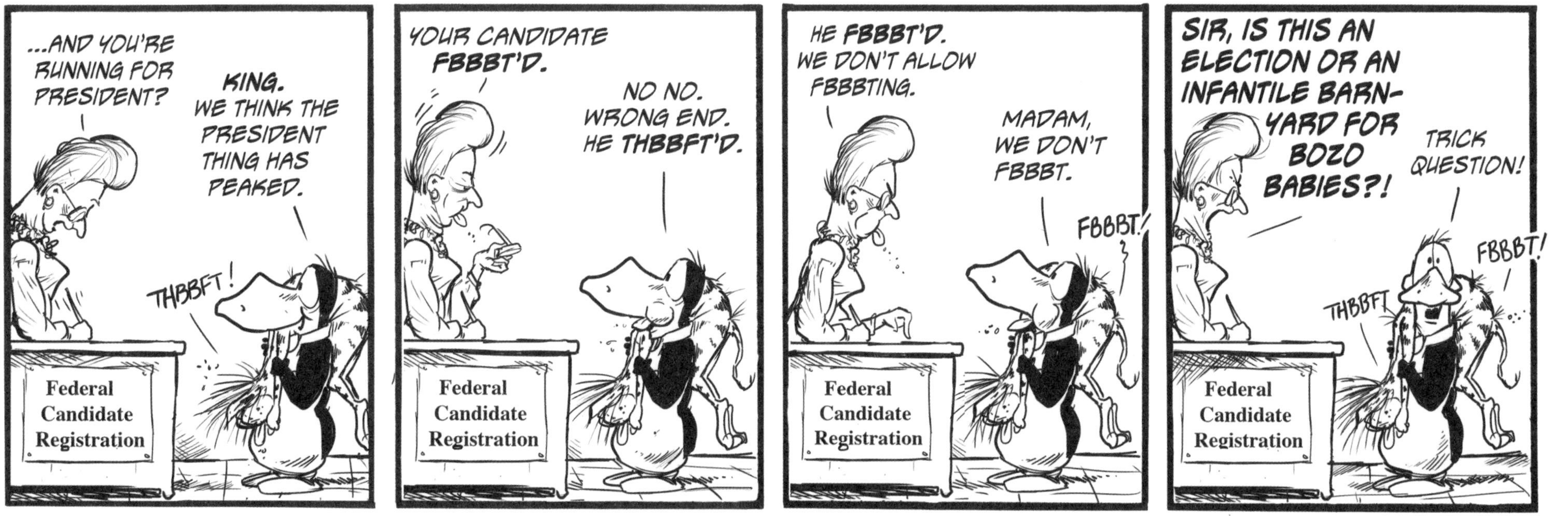
...AND YOU'RE RUNNING FOR PRESIDENT?
KING. WE THINK THE PRESIDENT THING HAS PEAKED.
THBBFT!
Federal Candidate Registration
YOUR CANDIDATE FBBBT'D.
NO NO. WRONG END. HE THBBFT'D.
Federal Candidate Registration
HE FBBBT'D. WE DON'T ALLOW FBBBTING.
MADAM, WE DON'T FBBBT.
FBBBT!
Federal Candidate Registration
SIR, IS THIS AN ELECTION OR AN INFANTILE BARNYARD FOR BOZO BABIES?!
TRICK QUESTION!
THBBFT
FBBBT!
Federal Candidate Registration

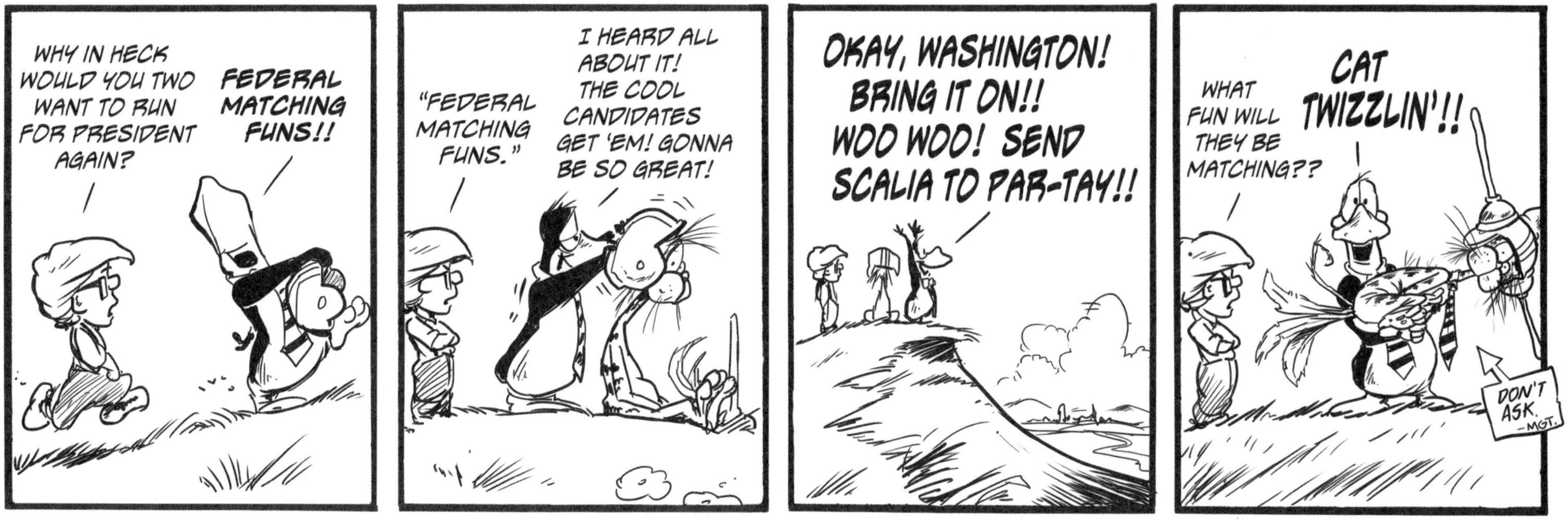
WHY IN HECK WOULD YOU TWO WANT TO RUN FOR PRESIDENT AGAIN?
FEDERAL MATCHING FUNS!!
"FEDERAL MATCHING FUNS."
I HEARD ALL ABOUT IT! THE COOL CANDIDATES GET 'EM! GONNA BE SO GREAT!
OKAY, WASHINGTON! BRING IT ON!! WOO WOO! SEND SCALIA TO PAR-TAY!!
WHAT FUN WILL THEY BE MATCHING??
CAT TWIZZLIN'!!
DON'T ASK. -MGT.

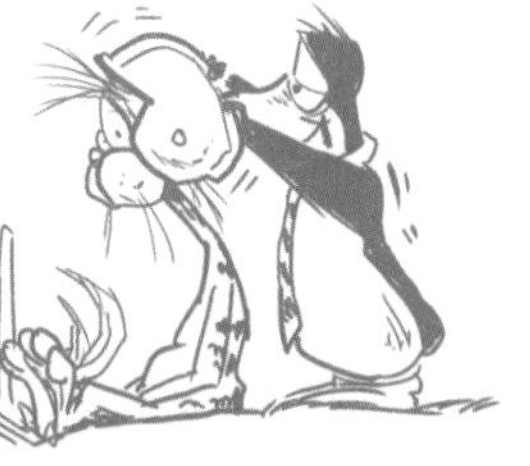

Bloom County 2015

by Berkeley Breathed

POINK   POINK   POINK

WHAT'S THAT TATTOO FROM, MOTHER?

THE FUNNIES.

FUNNIES?

FUNNIES?

COMIC STRIPS.

POINK

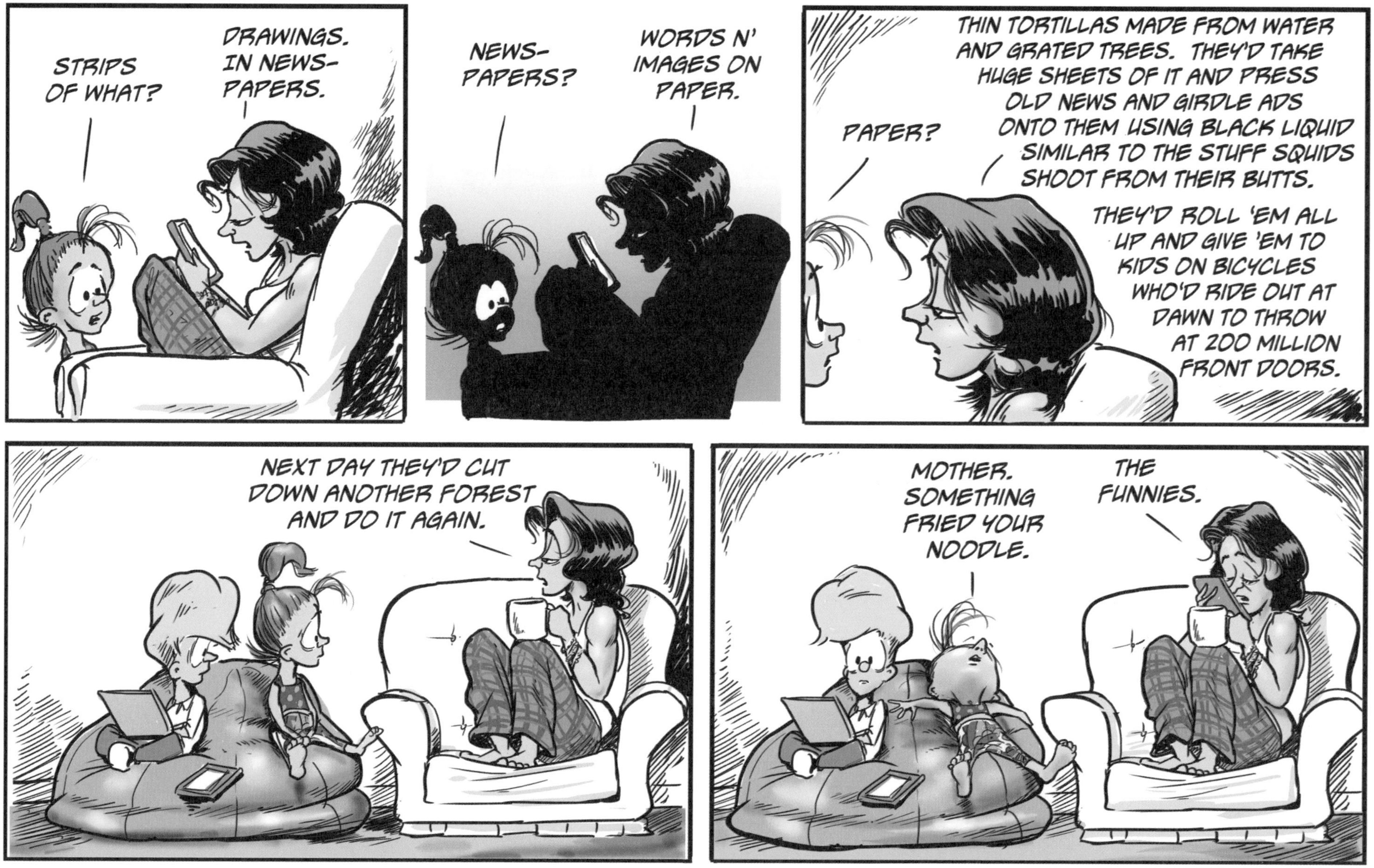
STRIPS OF WHAT?
DRAWINGS. IN NEWS-PAPERS.
NEWS-PAPERS?
WORDS N' IMAGES ON PAPER.
PAPER?
THIN TORTILLAS MADE FROM WATER AND GRATED TREES. THEY'D TAKE HUGE SHEETS OF IT AND PRESS OLD NEWS AND GIRDLE ADS ONTO THEM USING BLACK LIQUID SIMILAR TO THE STUFF SQUIDS SHOOT FROM THEIR BUTTS.
THEY'D ROLL 'EM ALL UP AND GIVE 'EM TO KIDS ON BICYCLES WHO'D RIDE OUT AT DAWN TO THROW AT 200 MILLION FRONT DOORS.
NEXT DAY THEY'D CUT DOWN ANOTHER FOREST AND DO IT AGAIN.
MOTHER. SOMETHING FRIED YOUR NOODLE.
THE FUNNIES.

I thought life had lost its funny…thank you Berkeley Breathed…hitting 60 soon and I now can say there's something to fill that void in today's goofed-up world. Between John Prine's songs, *Bloom County 2015*, a return of *Calvin & Hobbes*, the treasure trove of *Peanuts*…and, of course, Colbert/Stewart…I might just make it.

Long live the Two Spaces Party.

—Lisa Benfield-Edwards

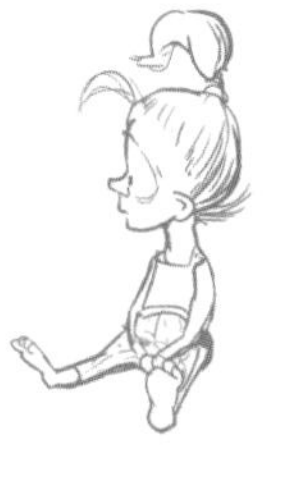

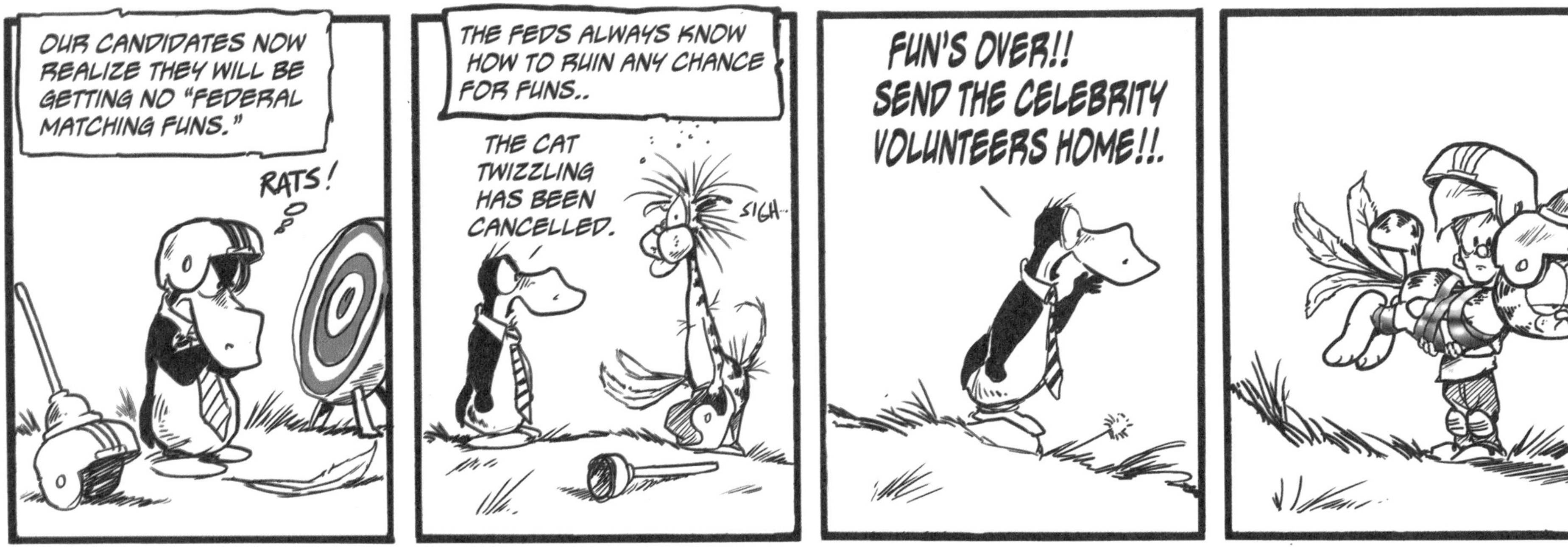

OUR CANDIDATES NOW REALIZE THEY WILL BE GETTING NO "FEDERAL MATCHING FUNS."
RATS!
THE FEDS ALWAYS KNOW HOW TO RUIN ANY CHANCE FOR FUNS..
THE CAT TWIZZLING HAS BEEN CANCELLED.
SIGH...
FUN'S OVER!! SEND THE CELEBRITY VOLUNTEERS HOME!!.

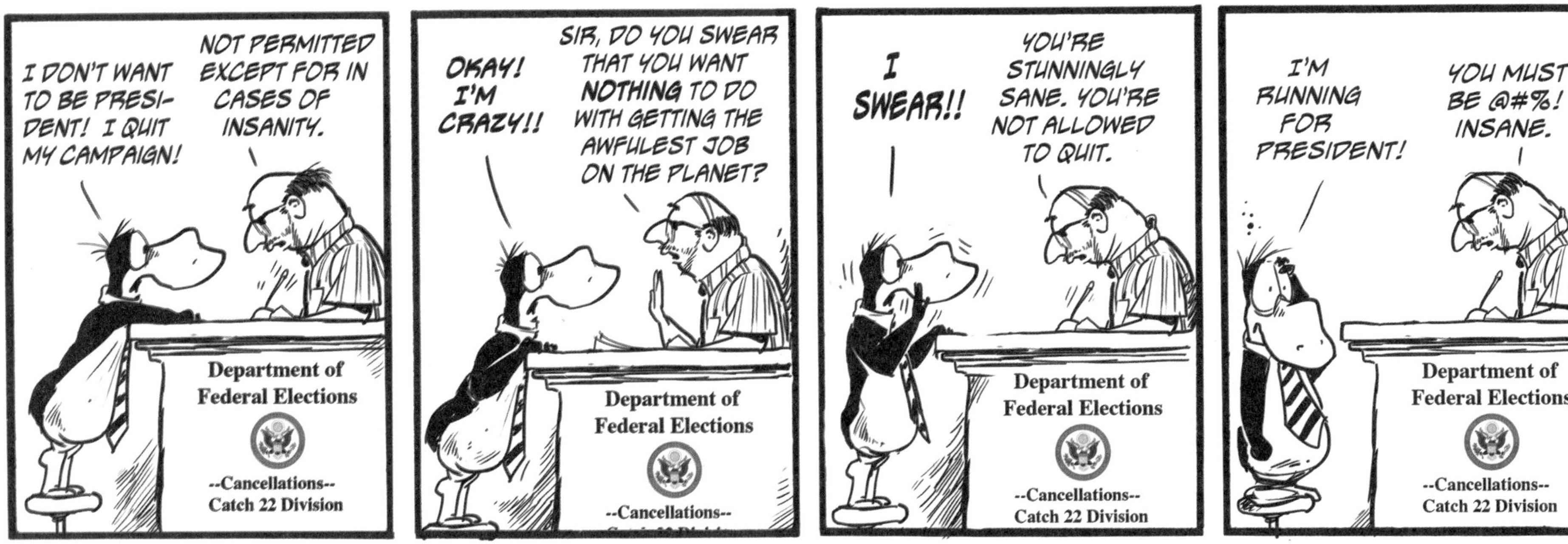

I DON'T WANT TO BE PRESI-DENT! I QUIT MY CAMPAIGN!
NOT PERMITTED EXCEPT FOR IN CASES OF INSANITY.
Department of Federal Elections
--Cancellations--
Catch 22 Division
OKAY! I'M CRAZY!!
SIR, DO YOU SWEAR THAT YOU WANT NOTHING TO DO WITH GETTING THE AWFULEST JOB ON THE PLANET?
Department of Federal Elections
--Cancellations--
I SWEAR!!
YOU'RE STUNNINGLY SANE. YOU'RE NOT ALLOWED TO QUIT.
Department of Federal Elections
--Cancellations--
Catch 22 Division
I'M RUNNING FOR PRESIDENT!
YOU MUST BE @#%! INSANE.
Department of Federal Elections
--Cancellations--
Catch 22 Division

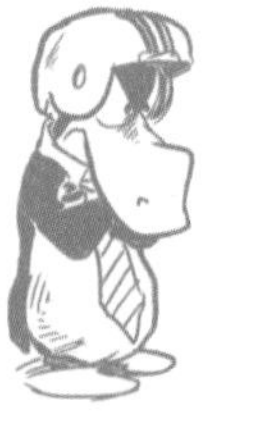

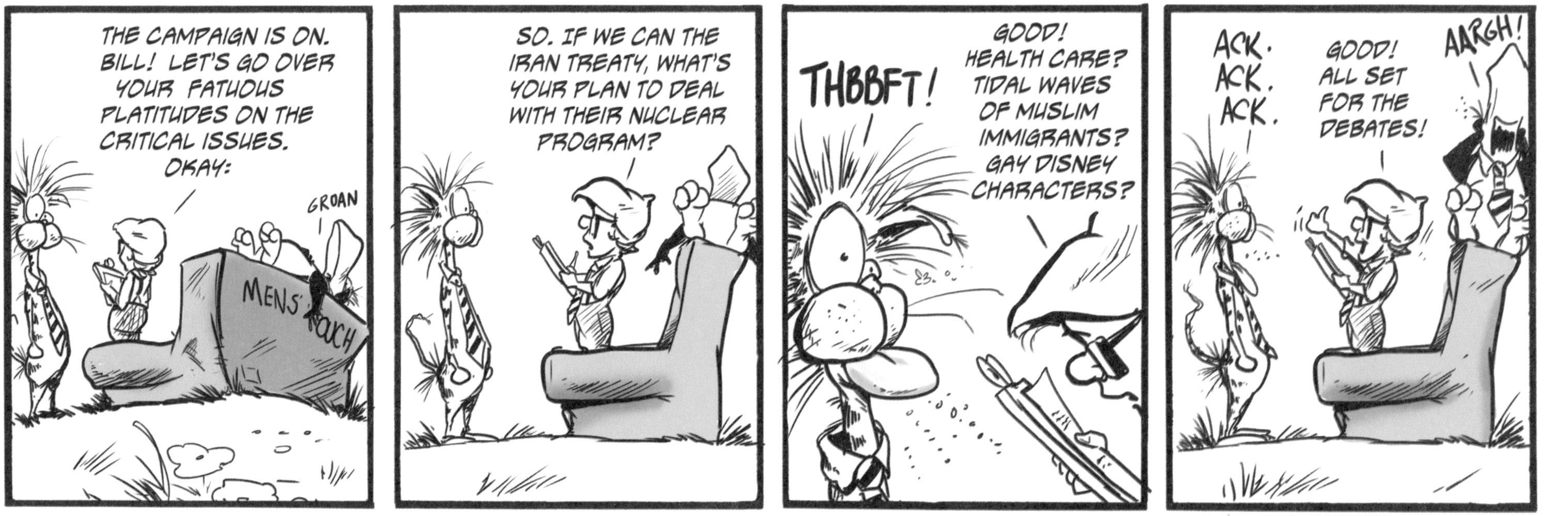
THE CAMPAIGN IS ON. BILL! LET'S GO OVER YOUR FATUOUS PLATITUDES ON THE CRITICAL ISSUES. OKAY:
GROAN
MENS' COUCH
SO. IF WE CAN THE IRAN TREATY, WHAT'S YOUR PLAN TO DEAL WITH THEIR NUCLEAR PROGRAM?
THBBFT!
GOOD! HEALTH CARE? TIDAL WAVES OF MUSLIM IMMIGRANTS? GAY DISNEY CHARACTERS?
ACK. ACK. ACK.
GOOD! ALL SET FOR THE DEBATES!
AARGH!

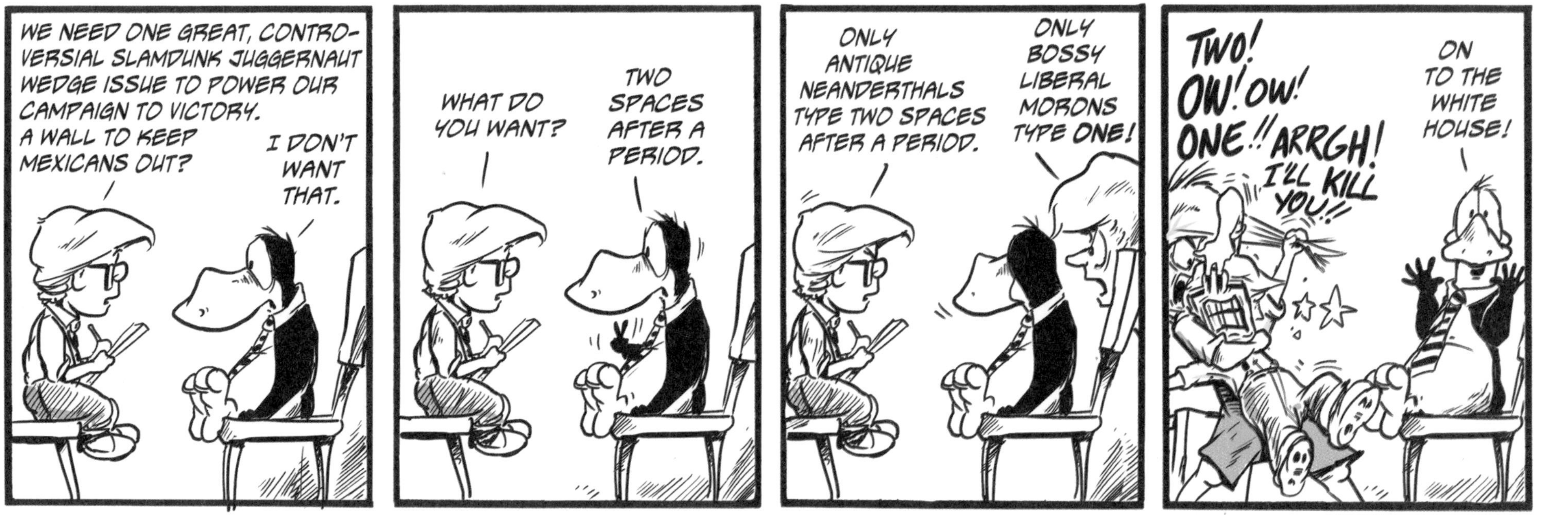
WE NEED ONE GREAT, CONTROVERSIAL SLAMDUNK JUGGERNAUT WEDGE ISSUE TO POWER OUR CAMPAIGN TO VICTORY. A WALL TO KEEP MEXICANS OUT?
I DON'T WANT THAT.
WHAT DO YOU WANT?
TWO SPACES AFTER A PERIOD.
ONLY ANTIQUE NEANDERTHALS TYPE TWO SPACES AFTER A PERIOD.
ONLY BOSSY LIBERAL MORONS TYPE ONE!
TWO! OW! OW! ONE!!
ARRGH! I'LL KILL YOU!!
ON TO THE WHITE HOUSE!

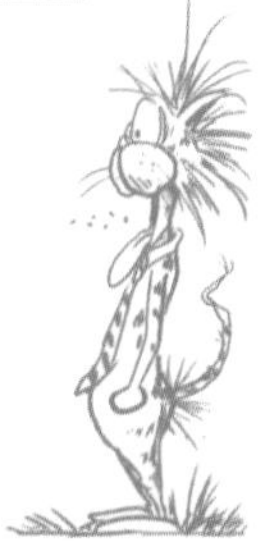

48

Bloom County 2015
by Berkeley Breathed
TUM DE DA DE DE DUM..
GOT ME A WEDGIE ISSUE!
WEDGE!
PUNCTUATION? THAT'S YOUR POWERHOUSE EXPRESS TRAIN TO THE PRESI-DENCY?
YEAH! WHO'S JUMPIN' ABOARD?
2 SPACES
NOT ME. IT'S DUMB.
REALLY? CLARITY TRIUMPHING OVER TYPESETTING BULLIES IS DUMB?!
SPACES

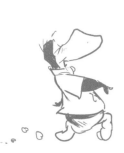

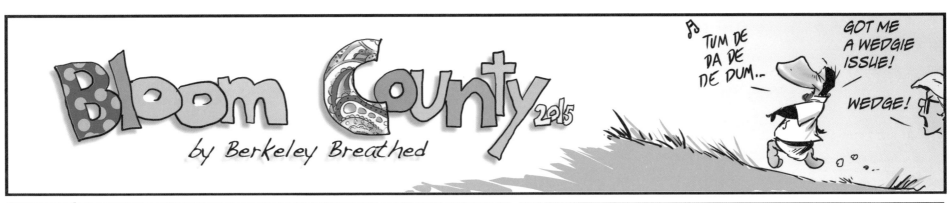

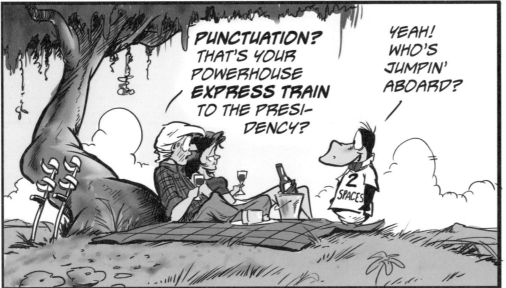

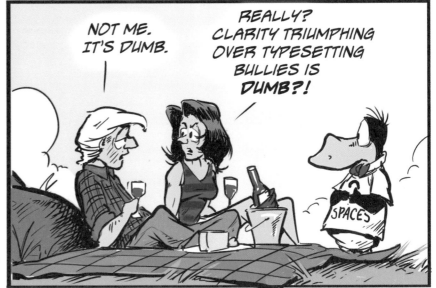

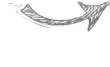

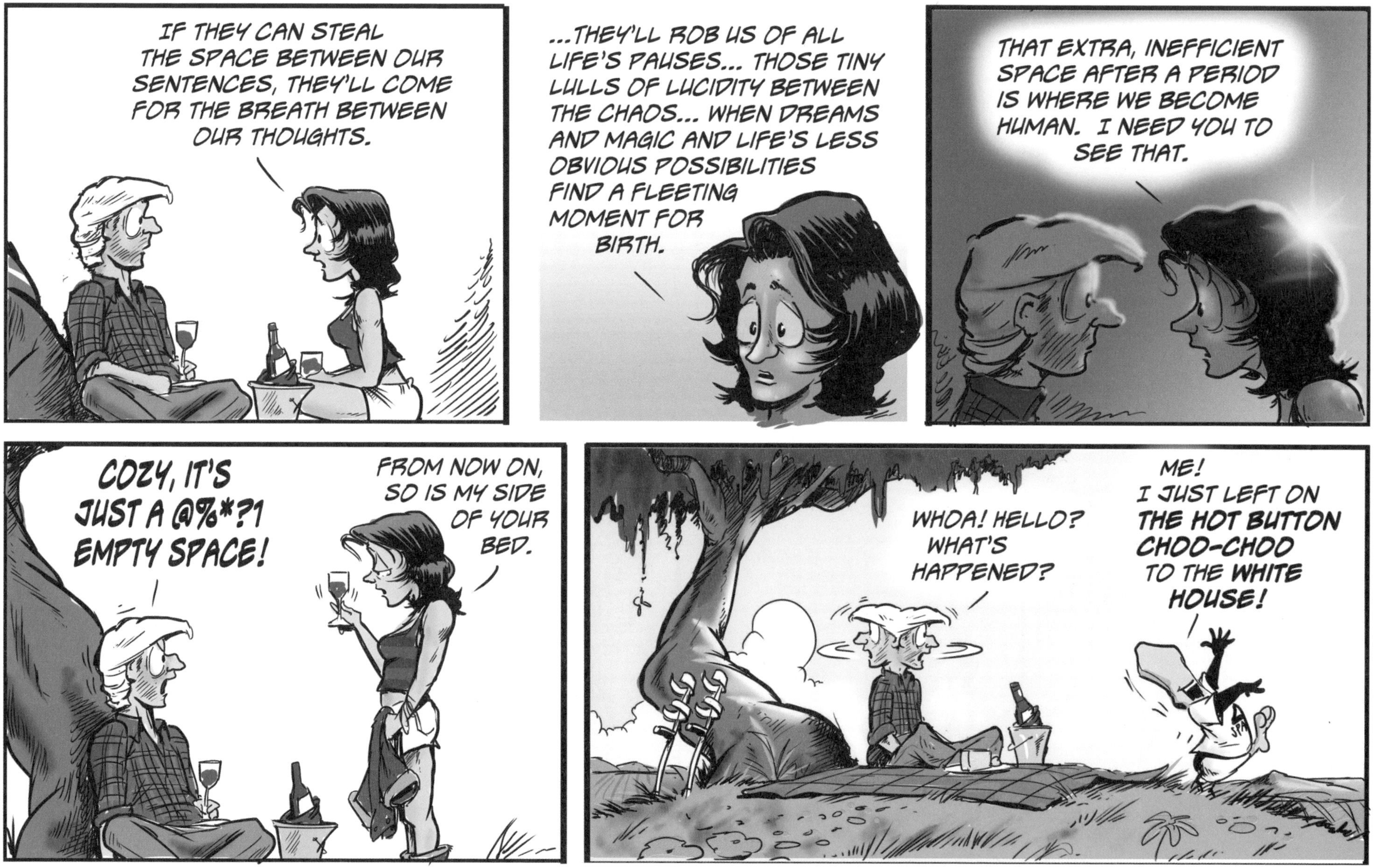
IF THEY CAN STEAL THE SPACE BETWEEN OUR SENTENCES, THEY'LL COME FOR THE BREATH BETWEEN OUR THOUGHTS.
...THEY'LL ROB US OF ALL LIFE'S PAUSES... THOSE TINY LULLS OF LUCIDITY BETWEEN THE CHAOS... WHEN DREAMS AND MAGIC AND LIFE'S LESS OBVIOUS POSSIBILITIES FIND A FLEETING MOMENT FOR BIRTH.
THAT EXTRA, INEFFICIENT SPACE AFTER A PERIOD IS WHERE WE BECOME HUMAN. I NEED YOU TO SEE THAT.
COZY, IT'S JUST A @%*?! EMPTY SPACE!
FROM NOW ON, SO IS MY SIDE OF YOUR BED.
WHOA! HELLO? WHAT'S HAPPENED?
ME! I JUST LEFT ON THE HOT BUTTON CHOO-CHOO TO THE WHITE HOUSE!

Dear Mr. Creator Guy. I imagine, over the last 35 years (or more), one or more people in your life commented to you, "God, you're weird." Speaking for myself, but likely thought daily by the 500,000 plus who stop by daily to see what you're up to, I'd toss out a cheery, "Thank God, you're weird." Who else could so captivate men, women, young, old, happy, sad, fat, skinny, nice, mean, liberal, conservative, odd, mellow, straight, gay or just someone just sitting on a chair wondering about what the cat is thinking and get us all to agree the absurdities you find make the absurdities we all face, share and manage worth at least some of the effort. We're all weird. That may be our best connection.

—Jim Johnson

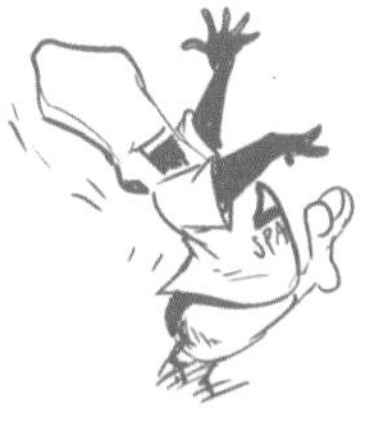

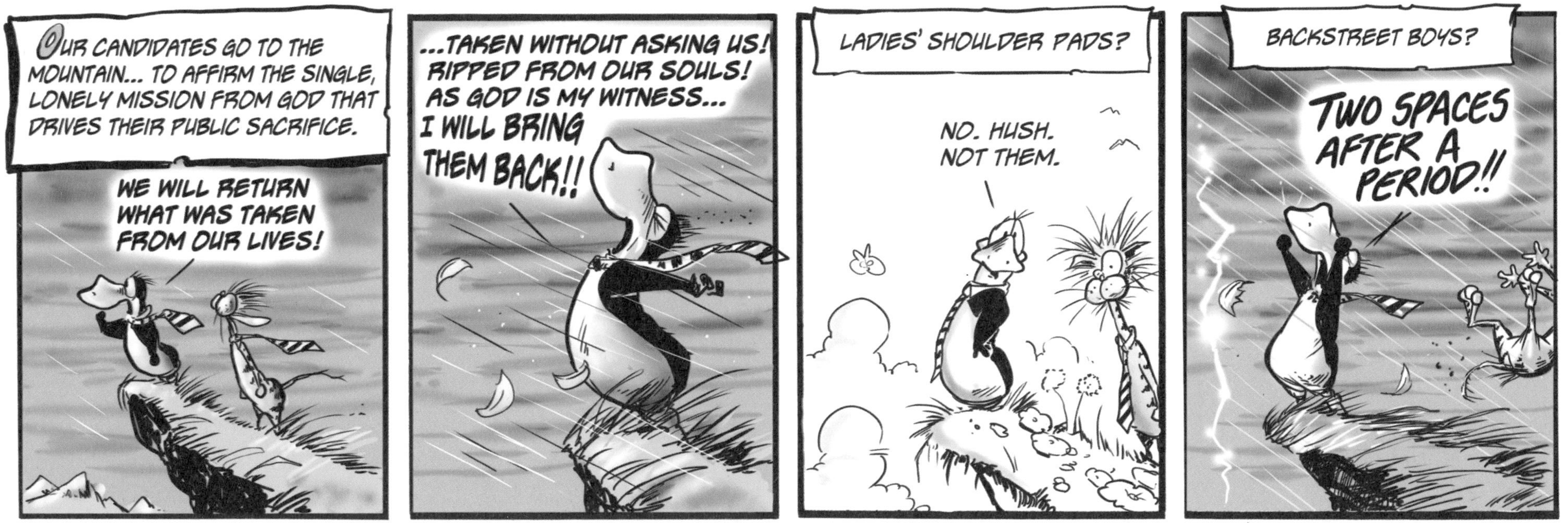
OUR CANDIDATES GO TO THE MOUNTAIN... TO AFFIRM THE SINGLE, LONELY MISSION FROM GOD THAT DRIVES THEIR PUBLIC SACRIFICE.
WE WILL RETURN WHAT WAS TAKEN FROM OUR LIVES!
...TAKEN WITHOUT ASKING US! RIPPED FROM OUR SOULS! AS GOD IS MY WITNESS... I WILL BRING THEM BACK!!
LADIES' SHOULDER PADS?
NO. HUSH. NOT THEM.
BACKSTREET BOYS?
TWO SPACES AFTER A PERIOD!!

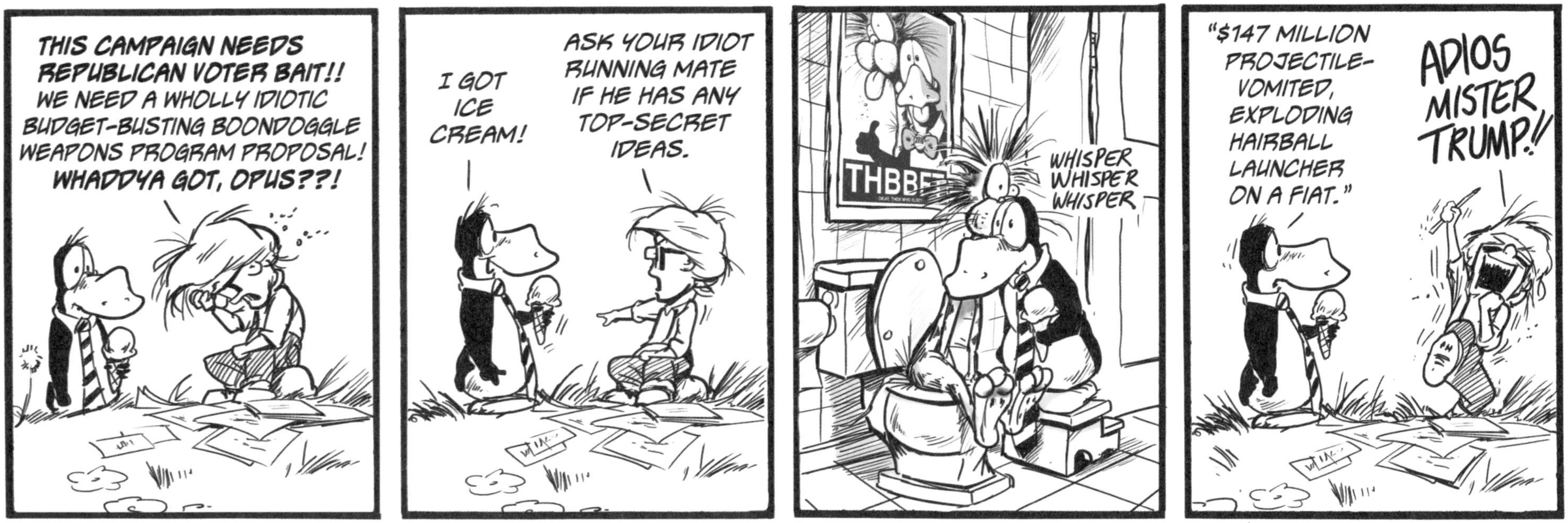
THIS CAMPAIGN NEEDS REPUBLICAN VOTER BAIT!! WE NEED A WHOLLY IDIOTIC BUDGET-BUSTING BOONDOGGLE WEAPONS PROGRAM PROPOSAL! WHADDYA GOT, OPUS??!
I GOT ICE CREAM!
ASK YOUR IDIOT RUNNING MATE IF HE HAS ANY TOP-SECRET IDEAS.
WHISPER WHISPER WHISPER
"$147 MILLION PROJECTILE-VOMITED, EXPLODING HAIRBALL LAUNCHER ON A FIAT."
ADIOS MISTER TRUMP!!

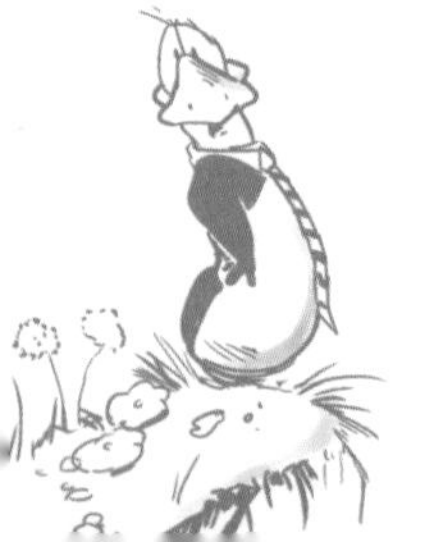

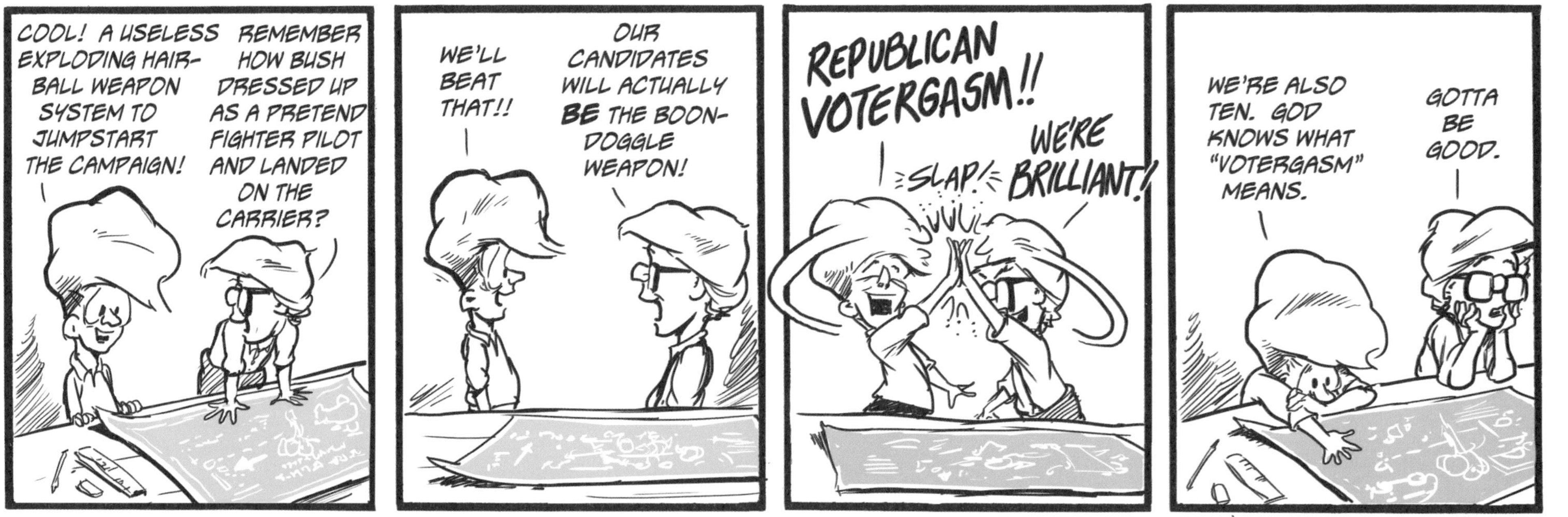
COOL! A USELESS EXPLODING HAIR-BALL WEAPON SYSTEM TO JUMPSTART THE CAMPAIGN!
REMEMBER HOW BUSH DRESSED UP AS A PRETEND FIGHTER PILOT AND LANDED ON THE CARRIER?
WE'LL BEAT THAT!!
OUR CANDIDATES WILL ACTUALLY BE THE BOON-DOGGLE WEAPON!
REPUBLICAN VOTERGASM!!
SLAP!
WE'RE BRILLIANT!
WE'RE ALSO TEN. GOD KNOWS WHAT "VOTERGASM" MEANS.
GOTTA BE GOOD.

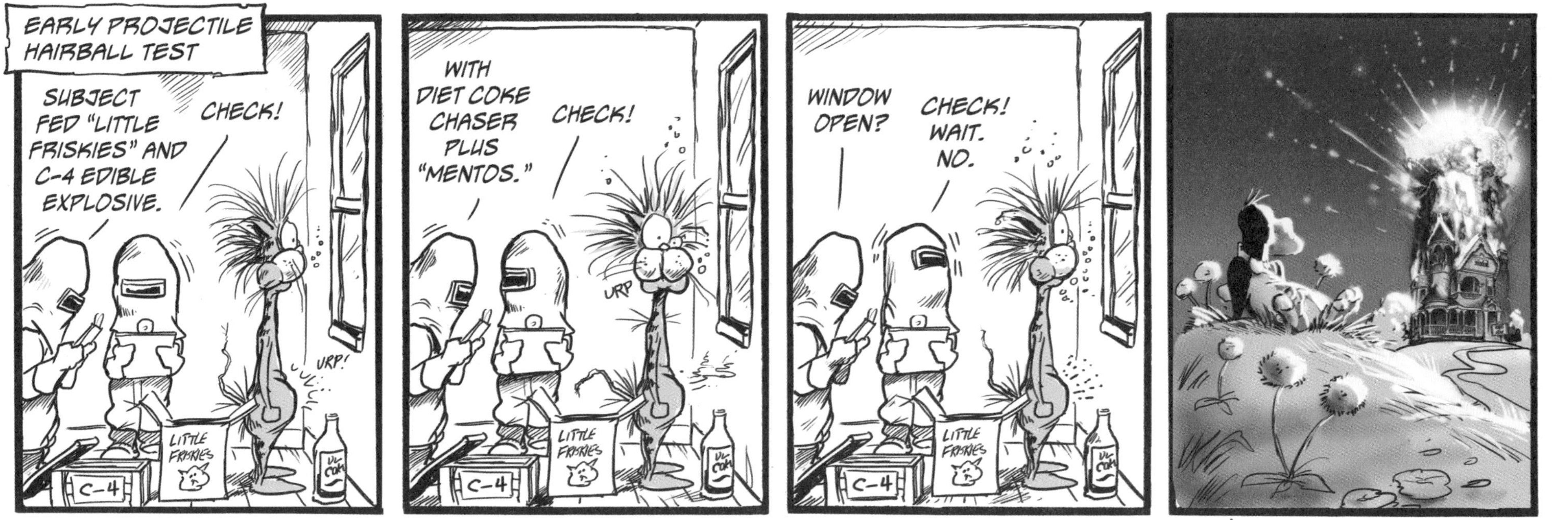
EARLY PROJECTILE HAIRBALL TEST
SUBJECT FED "LITTLE FRISKIES" AND C-4 EDIBLE EXPLOSIVE.
CHECK!
URP!
LITTLE FRISKIES
C-4
WITH DIET COKE CHASER PLUS "MENTOS."
CHECK!
URP
WINDOW OPEN?
CHECK! WAIT. NO.

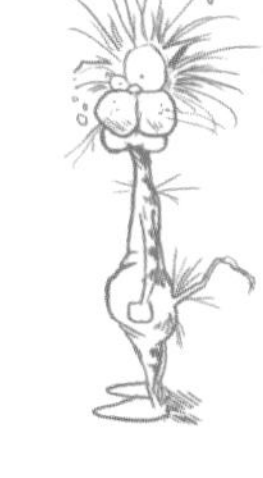

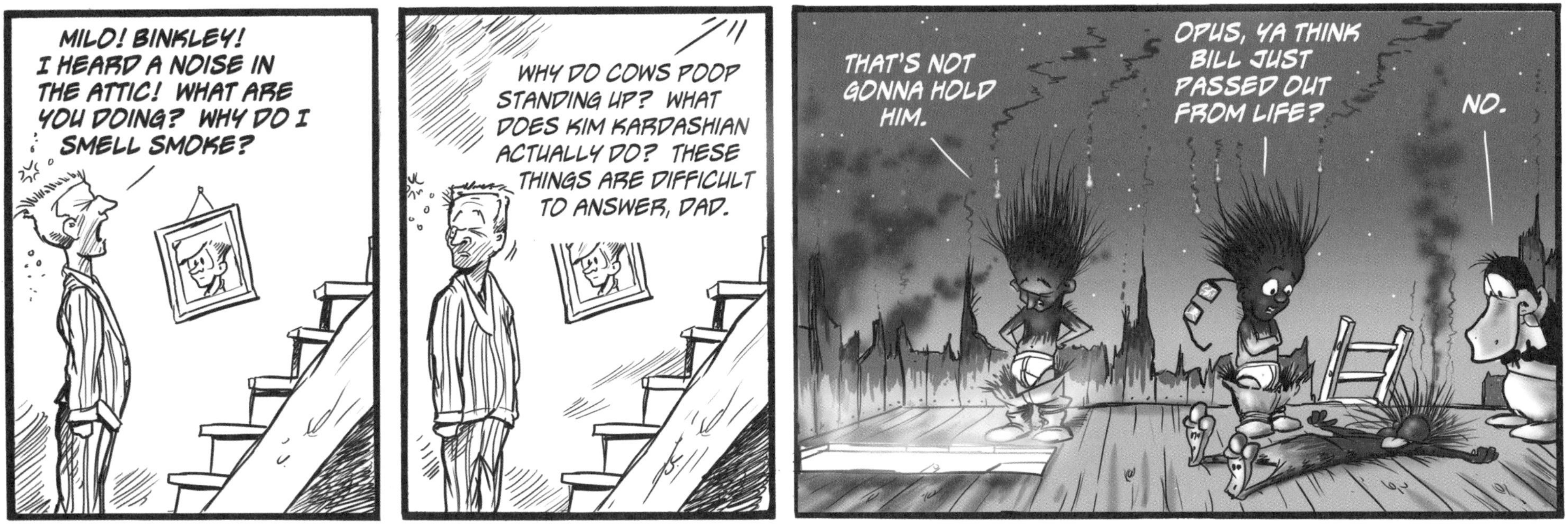
MILO! BINKLEY! I HEARD A NOISE IN THE ATTIC! WHAT ARE YOU DOING? WHY DO I SMELL SMOKE?
WHY DO COWS POOP STANDING UP? WHAT DOES KIM KARDASHIAN ACTUALLY DO? THESE THINGS ARE DIFFICULT TO ANSWER, DAD.
THAT'S NOT GONNA HOLD HIM.
OPUS, YA THINK BILL JUST PASSED OUT FROM LIFE?
NO.

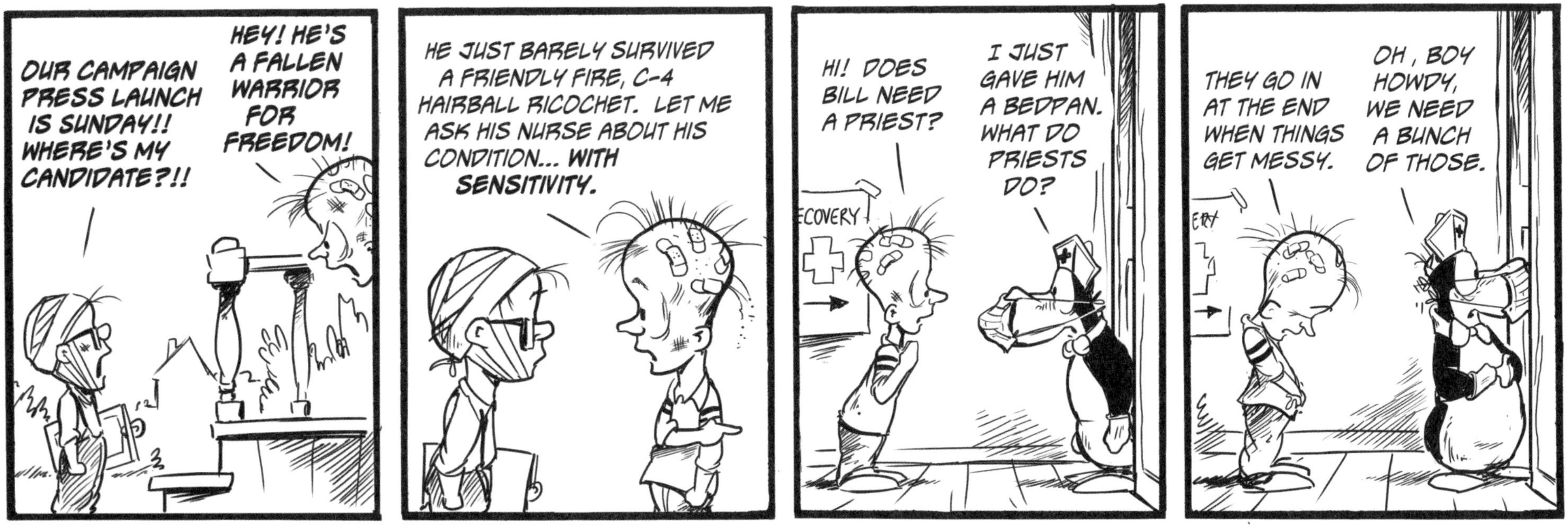
OUR CAMPAIGN PRESS LAUNCH IS SUNDAY!! WHERE'S MY CANDIDATE?!!
HEY! HE'S A FALLEN WARRIOR FOR FREEDOM!
HE JUST BARELY SURVIVED A FRIENDLY FIRE, C-4 HAIRBALL RICOCHET. LET ME ASK HIS NURSE ABOUT HIS CONDITION... WITH SENSITIVITY.
HI! DOES BILL NEED A PRIEST?
I JUST GAVE HIM A BEDPAN. WHAT DO PRIESTS DO?
ECOVERY
THEY GO IN AT THE END WHEN THINGS GET MESSY.
OH, BOY HOWDY, WE NEED A BUNCH OF THOSE.

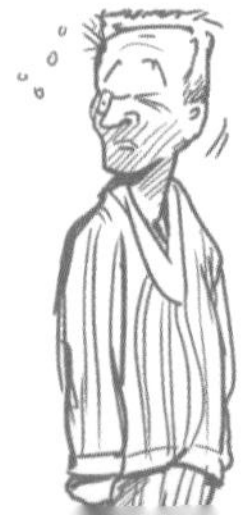

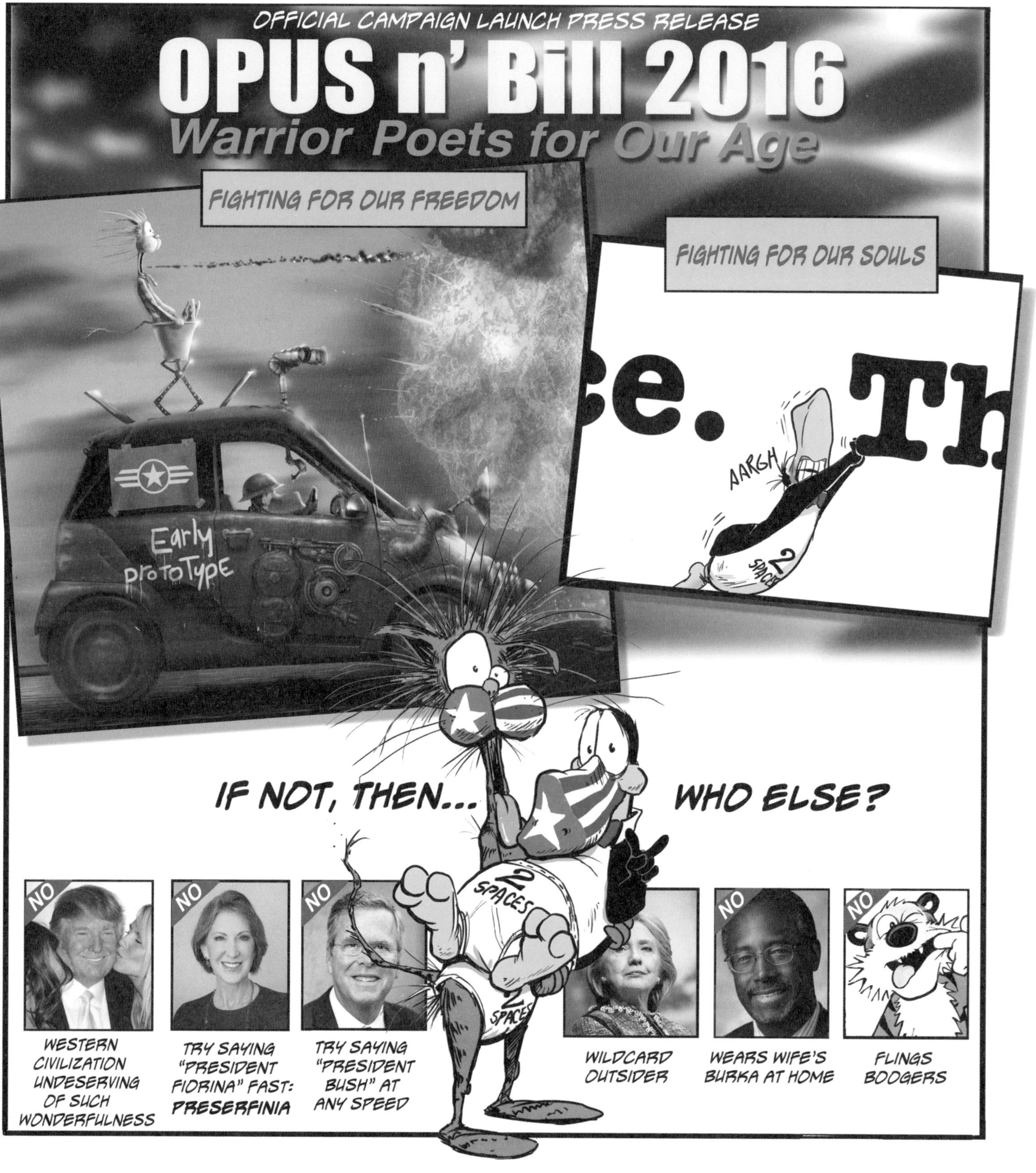
OFFICIAL CAMPAIGN LAUNCH PRESS RELEASE
OPUS n' Bill 2016
Warrior Poets for Our Age
FIGHTING FOR OUR FREEDOM
Early prototype
FIGHTING FOR OUR SOULS
e. Th
AARGH
2 SPACES
IF NOT, THEN... WHO ELSE?
2 SPACES
NO
WESTERN CIVILIZATION UNDESERVING OF SUCH WONDERFULNESS
NO
TRY SAYING "PRESIDENT FIORINA" FAST: PRESERFINIA
NO
TRY SAYING "PRESIDENT BUSH" AT ANY SPEED
WILDCARD OUTSIDER
NO
WEARS WIFE'S BURKA AT HOME
NO
FLINGS BOOGERS

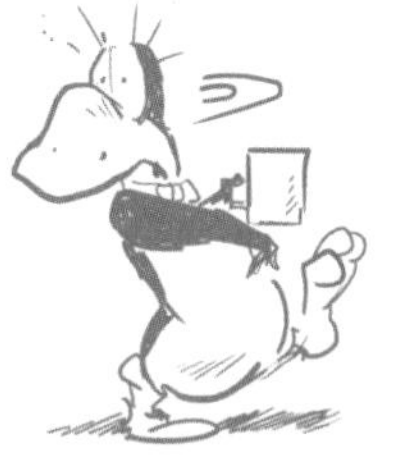

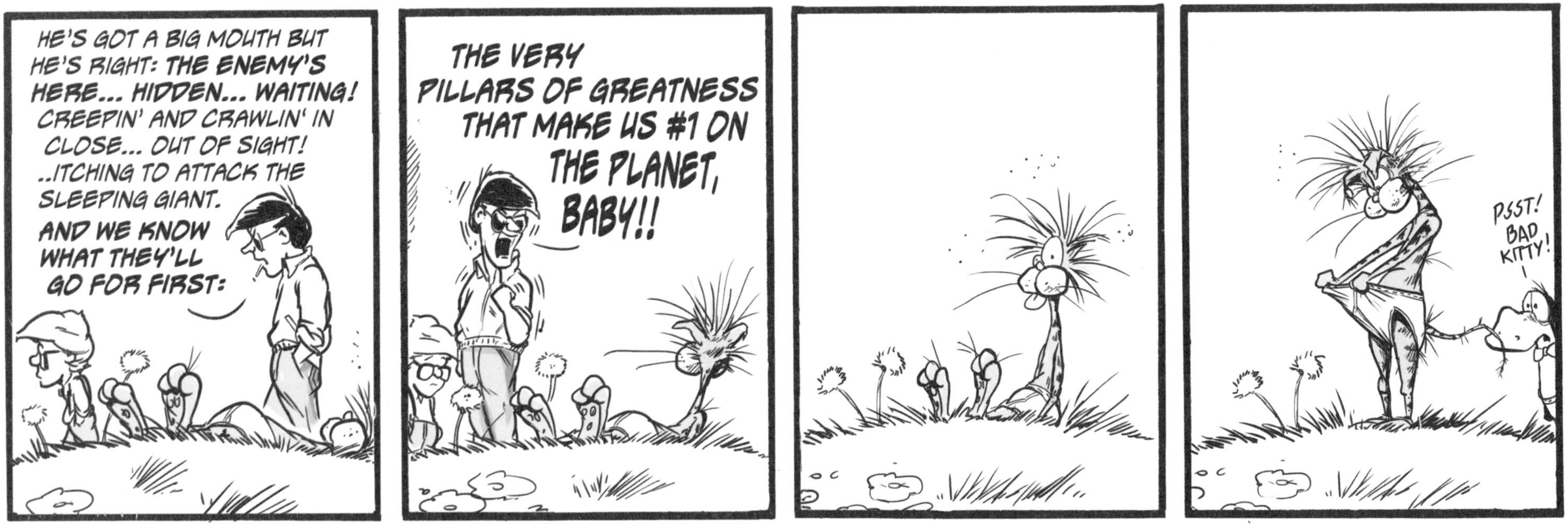
HE'S GOT A BIG MOUTH BUT HE'S RIGHT: THE ENEMY'S HERE... HIDDEN... WAITING! CREEPIN' AND CRAWLIN' IN CLOSE... OUT OF SIGHT! ..ITCHING TO ATTACK THE SLEEPING GIANT.
AND WE KNOW WHAT THEY'LL GO FOR FIRST:
THE VERY PILLARS OF GREATNESS THAT MAKE US #1 ON THE PLANET, BABY!!
PSST! BAD KITTY!

54

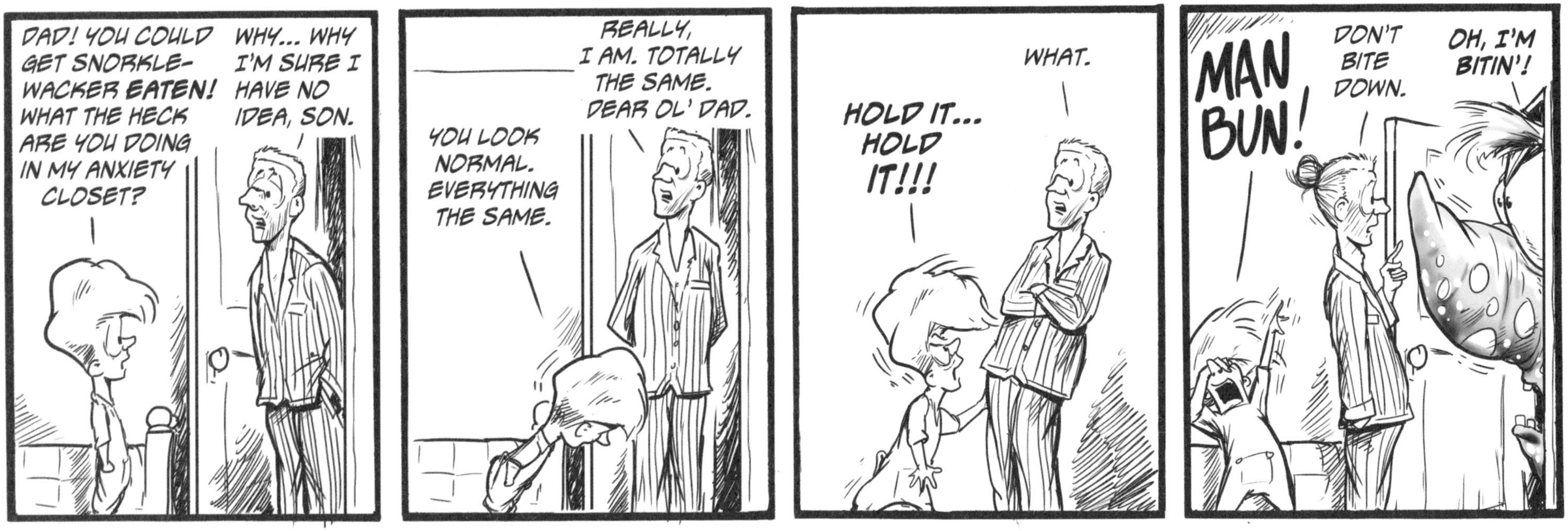
DAD! YOU COULD GET SNORKLE-WACKER EATEN! WHAT THE HECK ARE YOU DOING IN MY ANXIETY CLOSET?
WHY... WHY I'M SURE I HAVE NO IDEA, SON.
YOU LOOK NORMAL. EVERYTHING THE SAME.
REALLY, I AM. TOTALLY THE SAME. DEAR OL' DAD.
HOLD IT... HOLD IT!!!
WHAT.
MAN BUN!
DON'T BITE DOWN.
OH, I'M BITIN'!

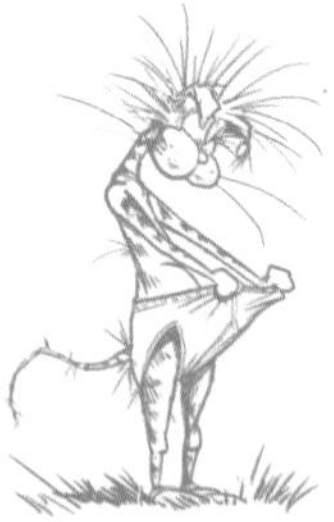

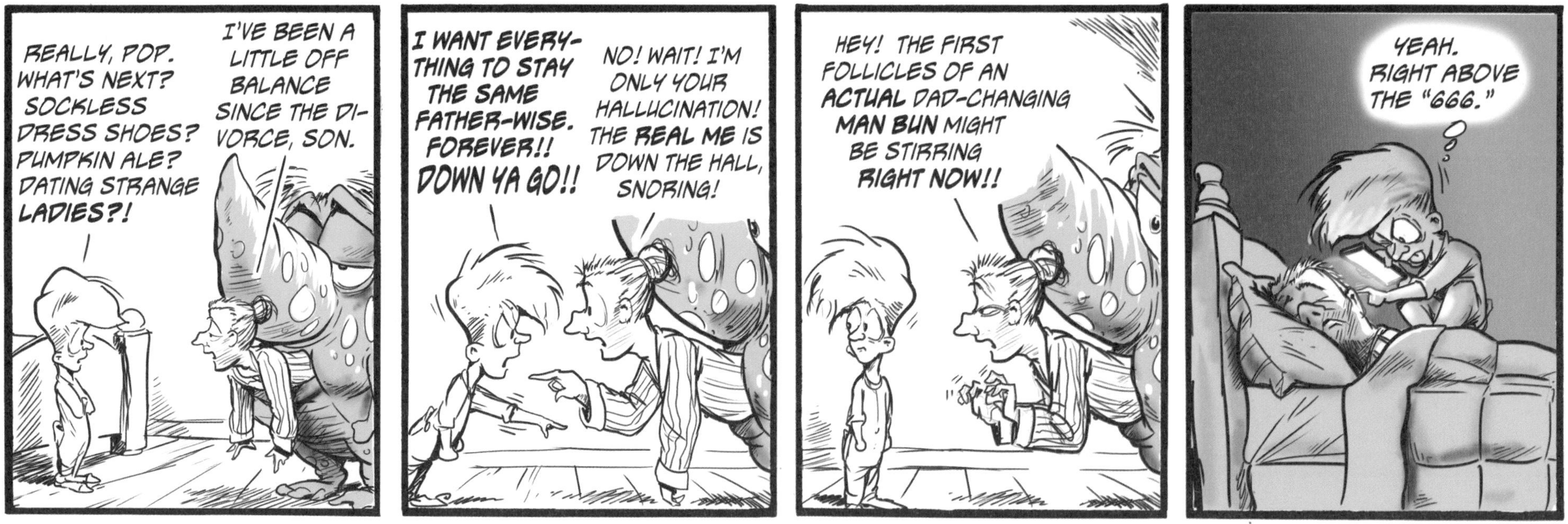
REALLY, POP. WHAT'S NEXT? SOCKLESS DRESS SHOES? PUMPKIN ALE? DATING STRANGE LADIES?!
I'VE BEEN A LITTLE OFF BALANCE SINCE THE DIVORCE, SON.
I WANT EVERYTHING TO STAY THE SAME FATHER-WISE. FOREVER!! DOWN YA GO!!
NO! WAIT! I'M ONLY YOUR HALLUCINATION! THE REAL ME IS DOWN THE HALL, SNORING!
HEY! THE FIRST FOLLICLES OF AN ACTUAL DAD-CHANGING MAN BUN MIGHT BE STIRRING RIGHT NOW!!
YEAH. RIGHT ABOVE THE "666."

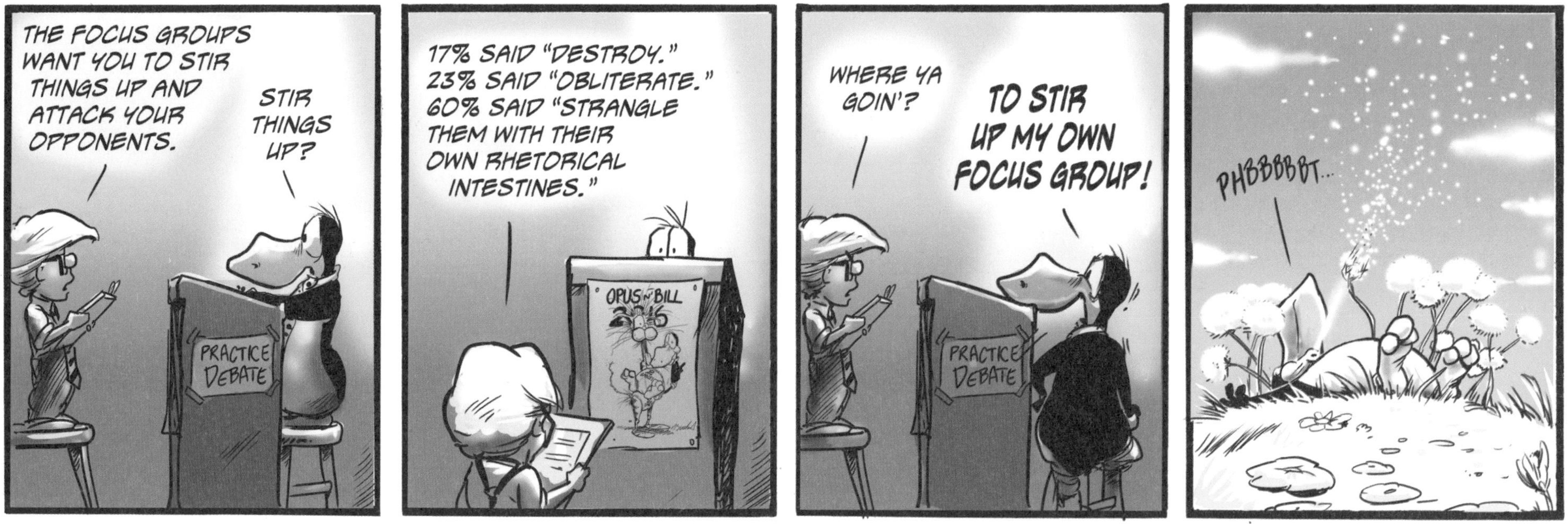
THE FOCUS GROUPS WANT YOU TO STIR THINGS UP AND ATTACK YOUR OPPONENTS.
STIR THINGS UP?
PRACTICE DEBATE
17% SAID "DESTROY." 23% SAID "OBLITERATE." 60% SAID "STRANGLE THEM WITH THEIR OWN RHETORICAL INTESTINES."
OPUS 'N' BILL 2016
WHERE YA GOIN'?
TO STIR UP MY OWN FOCUS GROUP!
PRACTICE DEBATE
PHBBBBBT...

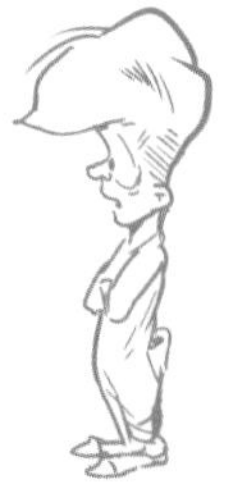

Abby's Inner Workshop

ESSENTIAL POSES TO BALANCE MIND BODY SPIRIT
· Session one ·

With assistance from highly disciplined YOGA Masters

Anjali Mudra
-or-
Prayer Pose

Half Moon Pose

Bended Willow Pose

TOOT

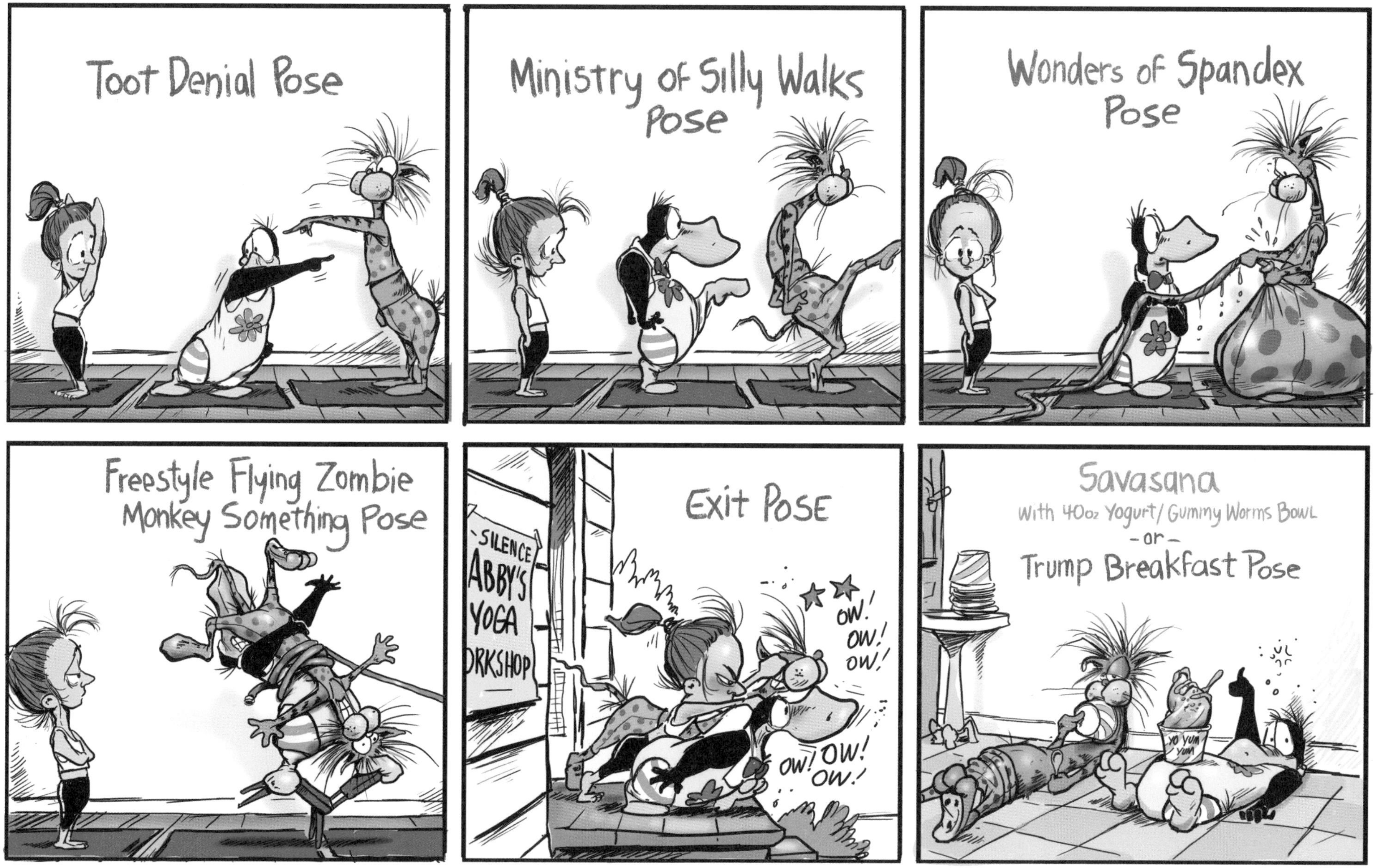
Toot Denial Pose
Ministry of Silly Walks Pose
Wonders of Spandex Pose
Freestyle Flying Zombie Monkey Something Pose
SILENCE
ABBY'S YOGA
RKSHOP
Exit Pose
OW! OW! OW!
OW! OW! OW!
Savasana
With 40oz Yogurt/ Gummy Worms Bowl
-or-
Trump Breakfast Pose
YO YUM YUM

What makes this comic special to me is the myriad of fans who avoid flaming and opt to metaphorically lean over each others' shoulders to revel in *Bloom County's* return. BB has neared or exceeded a Schulz-level of fan appreciation.

—Tyler Barnes

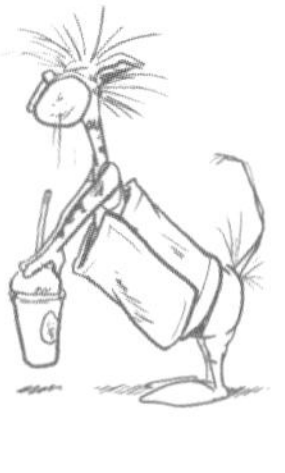

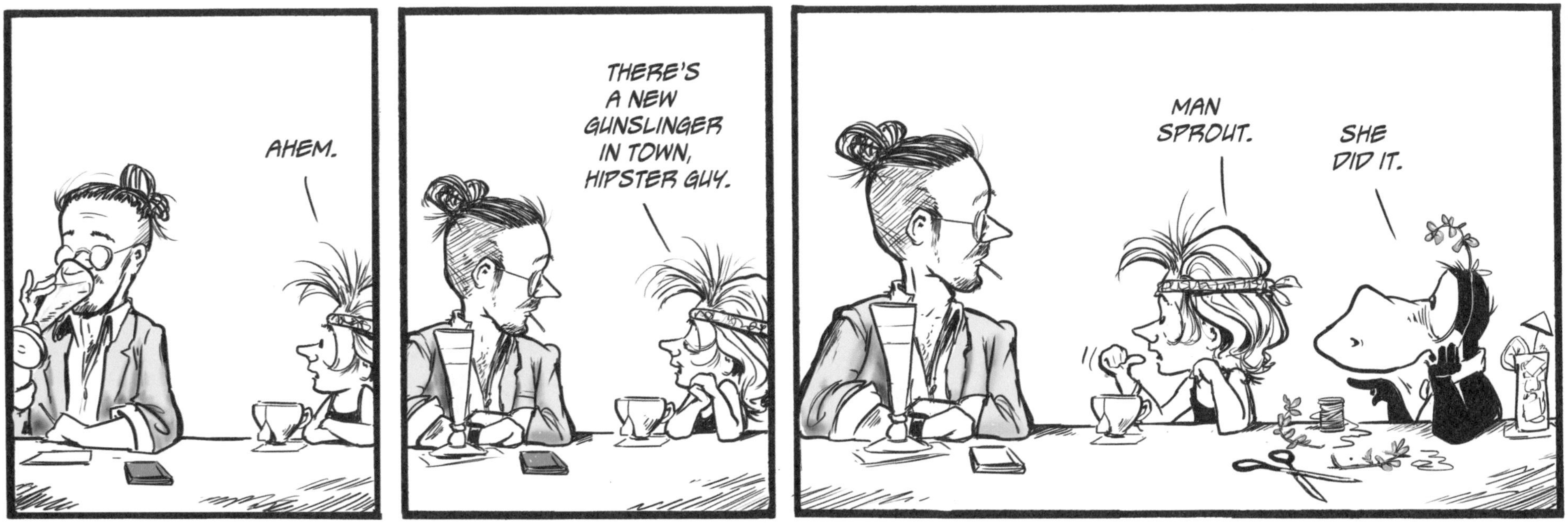
AHEM.
THERE'S A NEW GUNSLINGER IN TOWN, HIPSTER GUY.
MAN SPROUT.
SHE DID IT.

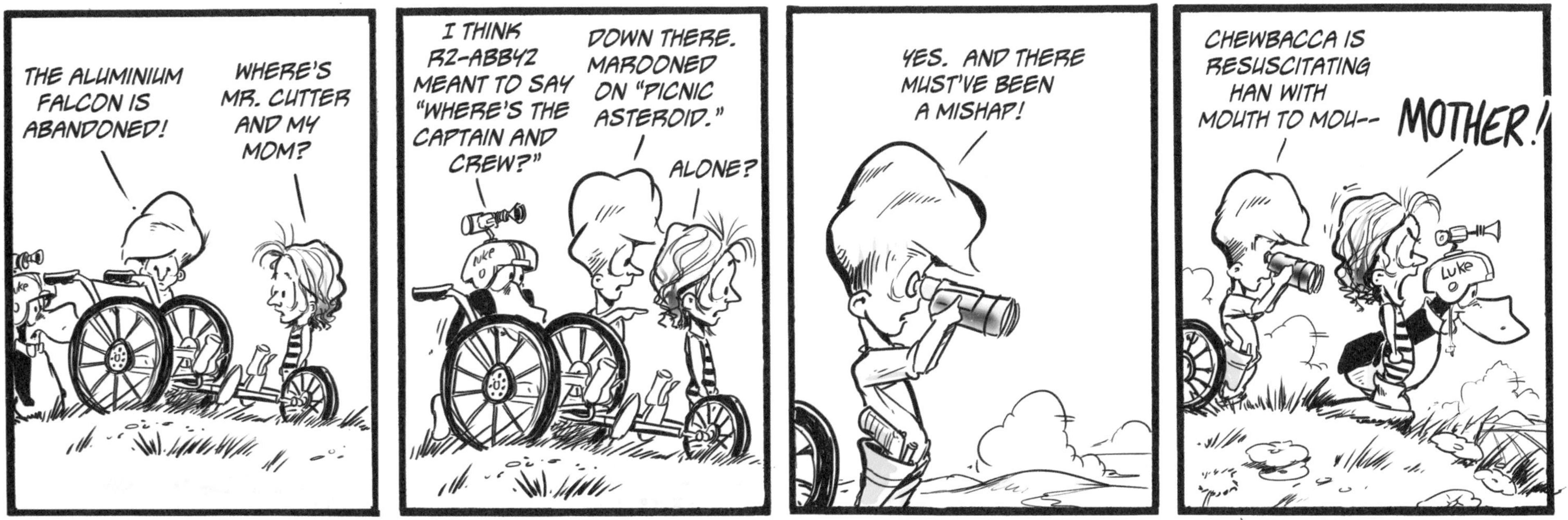
THE ALUMINIUM FALCON IS ABANDONED!
WHERE'S MR. CUTTER AND MY MOM?
I THINK R2-ABBY2 MEANT TO SAY "WHERE'S THE CAPTAIN AND CREW?"
DOWN THERE. MAROONED ON "PICNIC ASTEROID."
ALONE?
YES. AND THERE MUST'VE BEEN A MISHAP!
CHEWBACCA IS RESUSCITATING HAN WITH MOUTH TO MOU--
MOTHER!

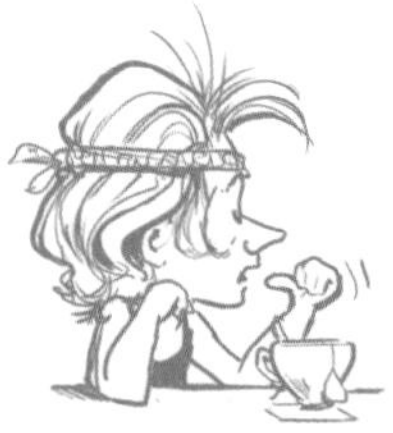

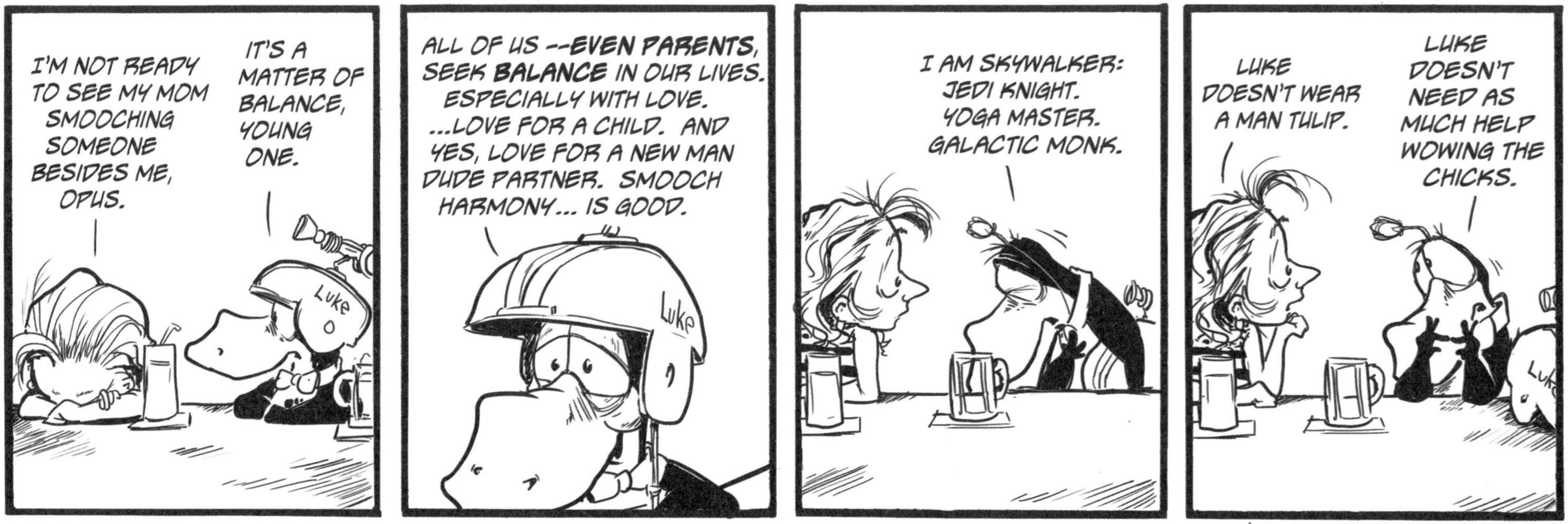
I'M NOT READY TO SEE MY MOM SMOOCHING SOMEONE BESIDES ME, OPUS.
IT'S A MATTER OF BALANCE, YOUNG ONE.
Luke
ALL OF US --EVEN PARENTS, SEEK BALANCE IN OUR LIVES. ESPECIALLY WITH LOVE. ...LOVE FOR A CHILD. AND YES, LOVE FOR A NEW MAN DUDE PARTNER. SMOOCH HARMONY... IS GOOD.
Luke
I AM SKYWALKER: JEDI KNIGHT. YOGA MASTER. GALACTIC MONK.
LUKE DOESN'T WEAR A MAN TULIP.
LUKE DOESN'T NEED AS MUCH HELP WOWING THE CHICKS.

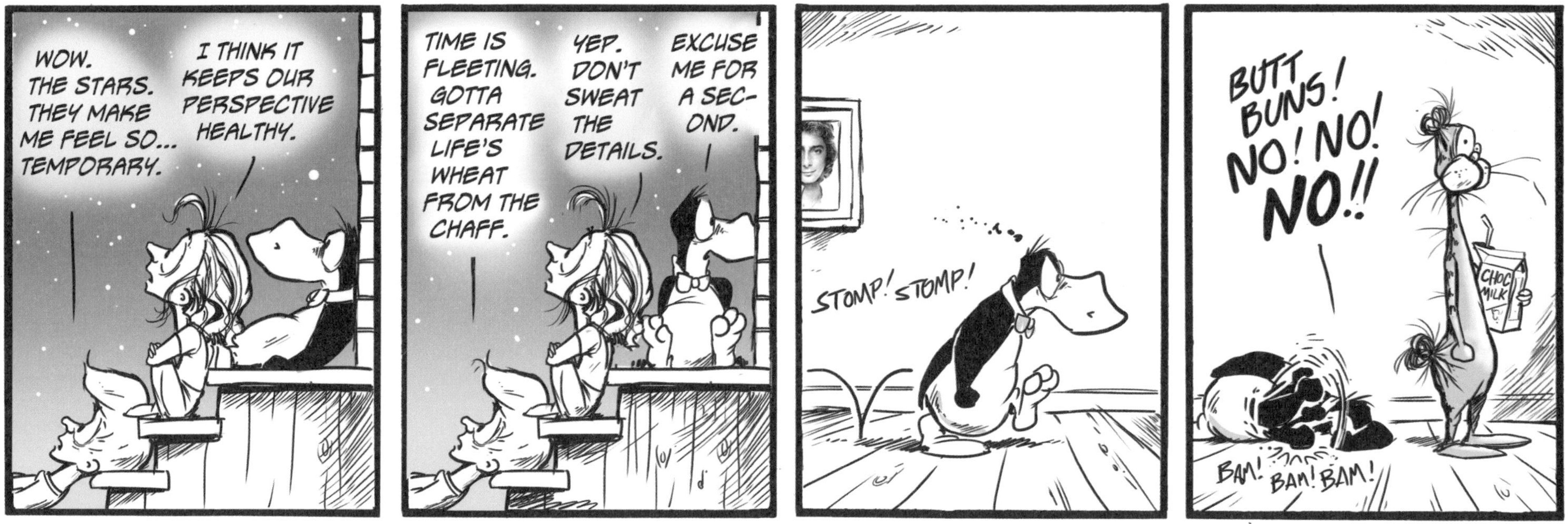
WOW. THE STARS. THEY MAKE ME FEEL SO... TEMPORARY.
I THINK IT KEEPS OUR PERSPECTIVE HEALTHY.
TIME IS FLEETING. GOTTA SEPARATE LIFE'S WHEAT FROM THE CHAFF.
YEP. DON'T SWEAT THE DETAILS.
EXCUSE ME FOR A SEC-OND.
STOMP! STOMP!
BUTT BUNS! NO! NO! NO!!
CHOC MILK
BAM! BAM! BAM!

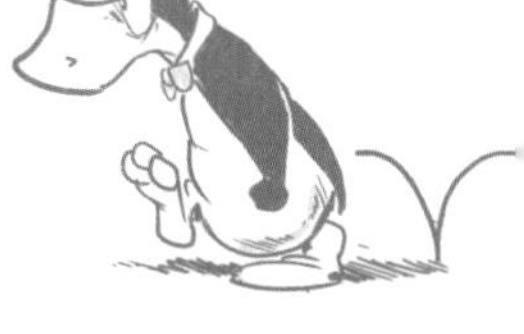

Bloom County 2015
by Berkeley Breathed
LET'S CHECK UPPER MAPLE STREET, BLOOM COUNTY. WE CAN HEAR A SHOWER.
YES! WE HAVE SOMETHING! HERE WE GO, EVERYONE! MULTI-PLATFORM LIVE-STREAMING TO 134 COUNTRIES! !
THERE! YES! WAVING HIS LITTLE SCRUBBER! WAVING! WAVING! WE MIGHT GET LUCKY, LADIES AND GENTLEMEN!

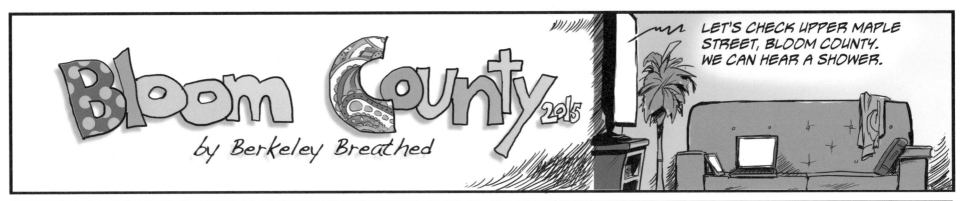

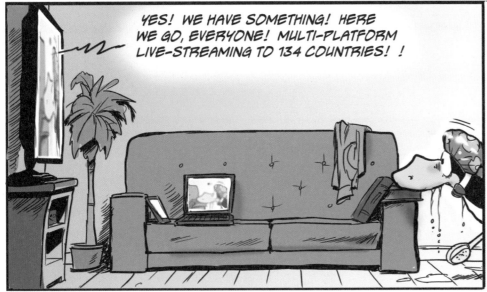

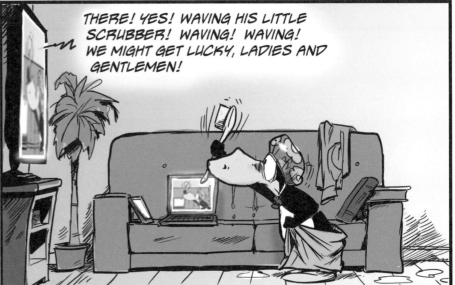

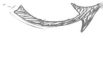

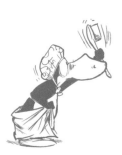

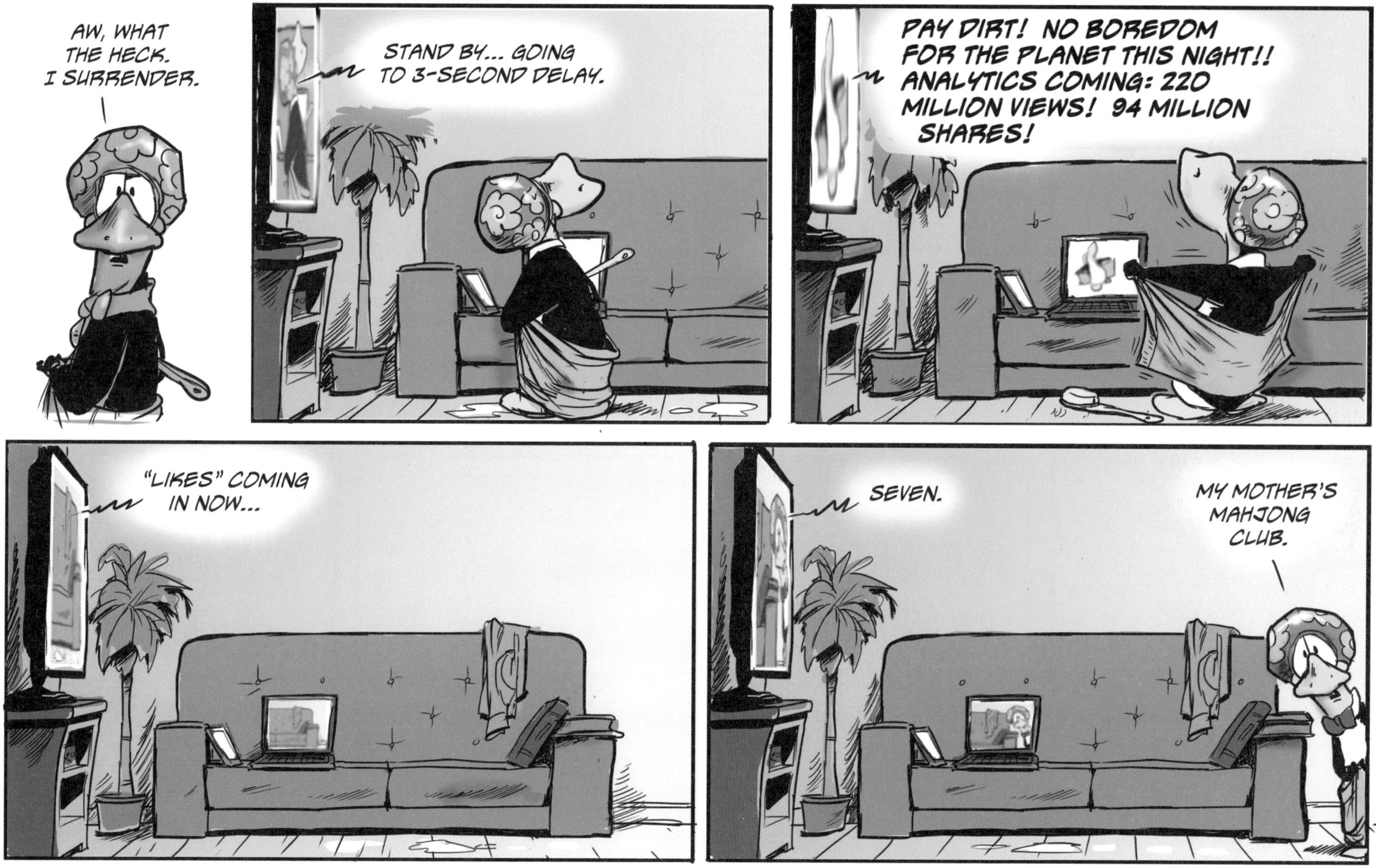
AW, WHAT THE HECK. I SURRENDER.
STAND BY... GOING TO 3-SECOND DELAY.
PAY DIRT! NO BOREDOM FOR THE PLANET THIS NIGHT!! ANALYTICS COMING: 220 MILLION VIEWS! 94 MILLION SHARES!
"LIKES" COMING IN NOW...
SEVEN.
MY MOTHER'S MAHJONG CLUB.

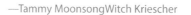

There's just something about that short, stout, flightless waterfowl…

—Tammy MoonsongWitch Kriescher

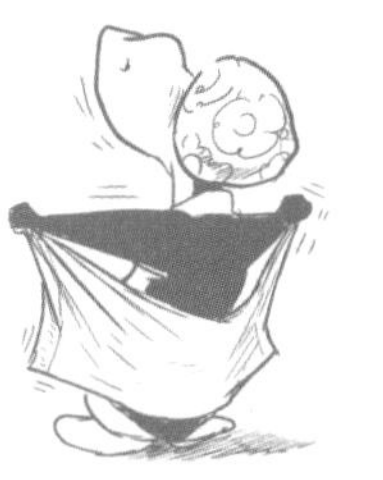

FIRST **STAR WARS** TRAILER ABOUT TO DEBUT. WHERE'S CUTTER JOHN?

NOT HERE. HE SAYS TODAY'S TRAILERS SPOIL EVERY GREAT MOVIE.

THE MAN IS A MONUMENT TO MATURE SELF-DISCIPLINE.

THANK GOD FOR ADULTS IN THIS WORLD.

COZY, I WAS KIDDING. GIVE ME THE KEY. I WASN'T REALLY SERIOUS. I WAS PLAY-- **GIMME THE #⊃✳?! KEY.!!**

THE KEY TO MY HEART? YOU ALREADY HAVE IT, HONEY.

I HAVE A CONTRIBUTION TO YOUR CRUSADE FROM A FREEDOM-LOVING PATRIOT.

THERE'S THE JAR!

OPUS N' BILL 2 SPACES 4 AMERICA

OPUS N' BILL 2 SPACES 4 AMERICA

OPUS! DO YOU KNOW WHAT THIS IS?!!

SURE DO!

~~BRIBE!~~ CAMPAIGN DONOR BONANZA!!

BILL!! NEW LUGGAGE!

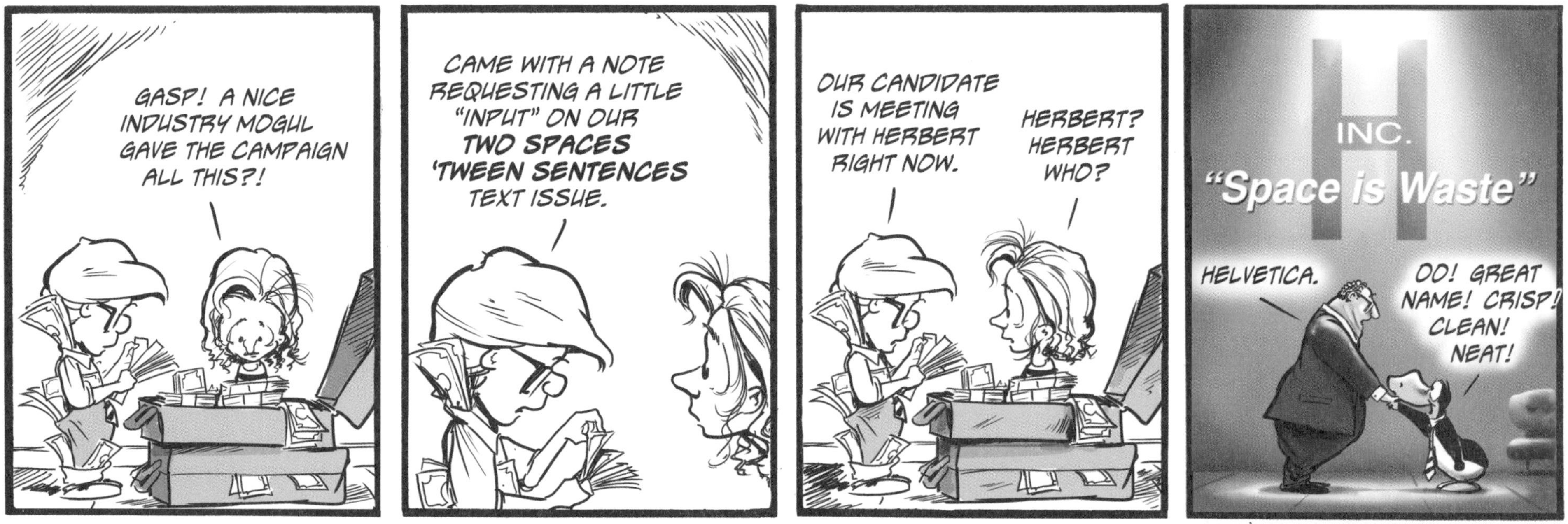
GASP! A NICE INDUSTRY MOGUL GAVE THE CAMPAIGN ALL THIS?!
CAME WITH A NOTE REQUESTING A LITTLE "INPUT" ON OUR **TWO SPACES 'TWEEN SENTENCES** TEXT ISSUE.
OUR CANDIDATE IS MEETING WITH HERBERT RIGHT NOW.
HERBERT? HERBERT WHO?
INC.
"Space is Waste"
HELVETICA.
OO! GREAT NAME! CRISP! CLEAN! NEAT!

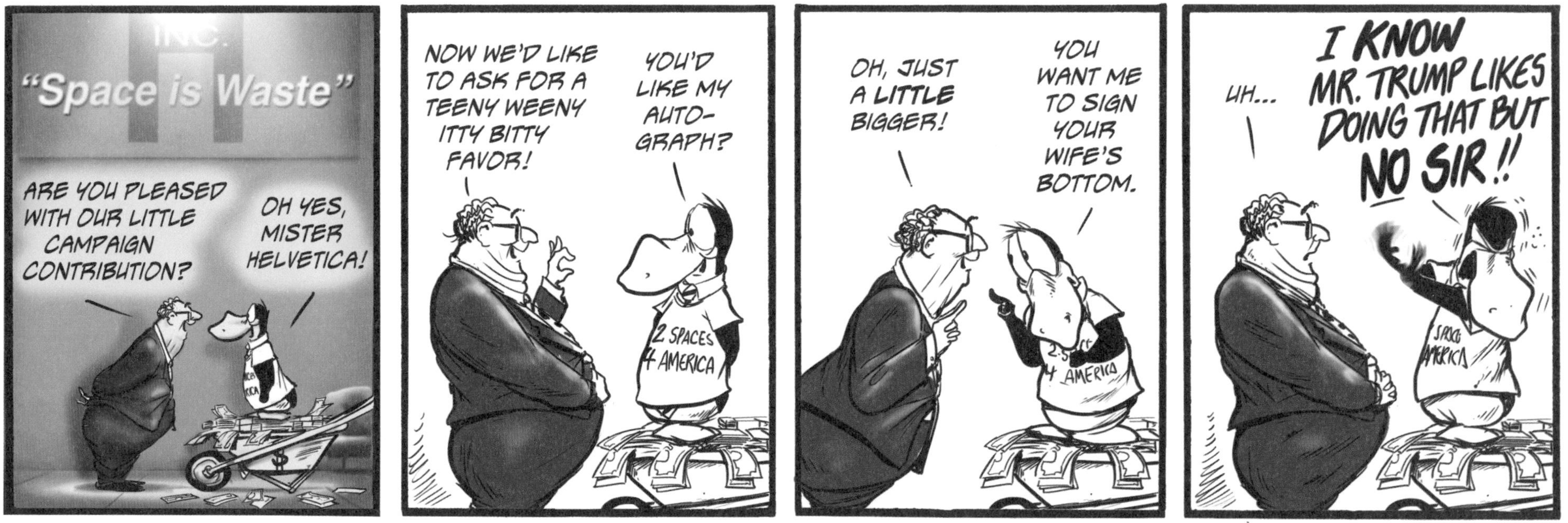
INC.
"Space is Waste"
ARE YOU PLEASED WITH OUR LITTLE CAMPAIGN CONTRIBUTION?
OH YES, MISTER HELVETICA!
NOW WE'D LIKE TO ASK FOR A TEENY WEENY ITTY BITTY FAVOR!
YOU'D LIKE MY AUTO-GRAPH?
2 SPACES 4 AMERICA
OH, JUST A **LITTLE** BIGGER!
YOU WANT ME TO SIGN YOUR WIFE'S BOTTOM.
UH...
I **KNOW** MR. TRUMP LIKES DOING THAT BUT NO SIR!!

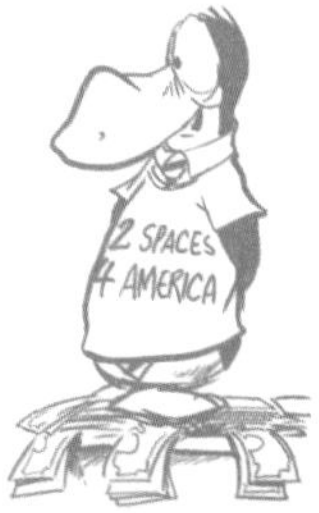
2 SPACES 4 AMERICA

oom County 2015
by Berkeley Breathed
GUYS. I... I'VE STUMBLED ONTO A SHATTERING SECRET...
WOMEN ARE IMPENETRABLE MYSTERIES AND IT'D BE EASIER IF WE WERE ALL GAY?
NO! MR. HELVETICA WHEELED IN TWO TONS OF CASH AND SAID, "NOW MAKE OUR SHARE-HOLDERS HAPPY AND CHANGE YOUR CAMPAIGN SLOGAN!"
2 SPACES 4 AMERICA
TO WHAT?
"SPACES SUCK."
2 SPACES 4 AMERICA
SHORT N' SNAPPY. GOOD!

2 SPACES 4 AMERICA

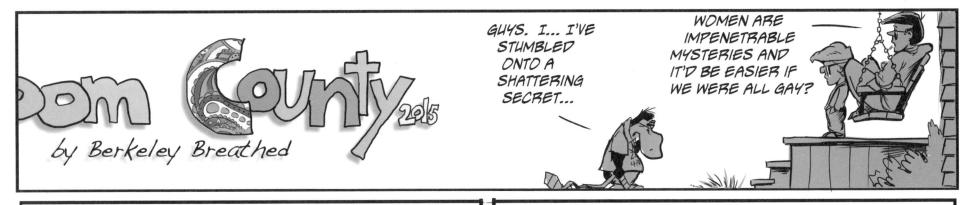

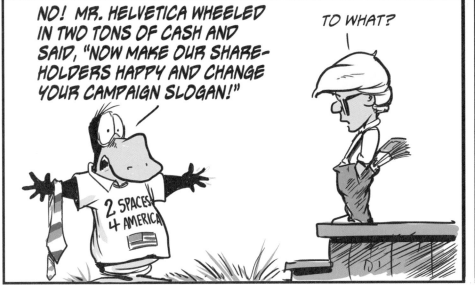

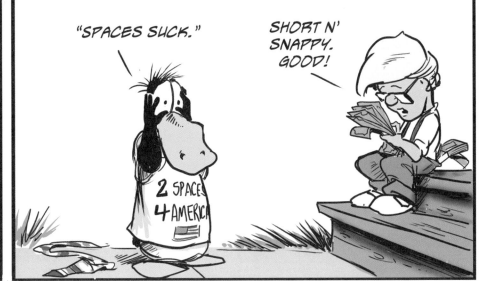

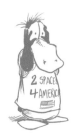

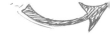

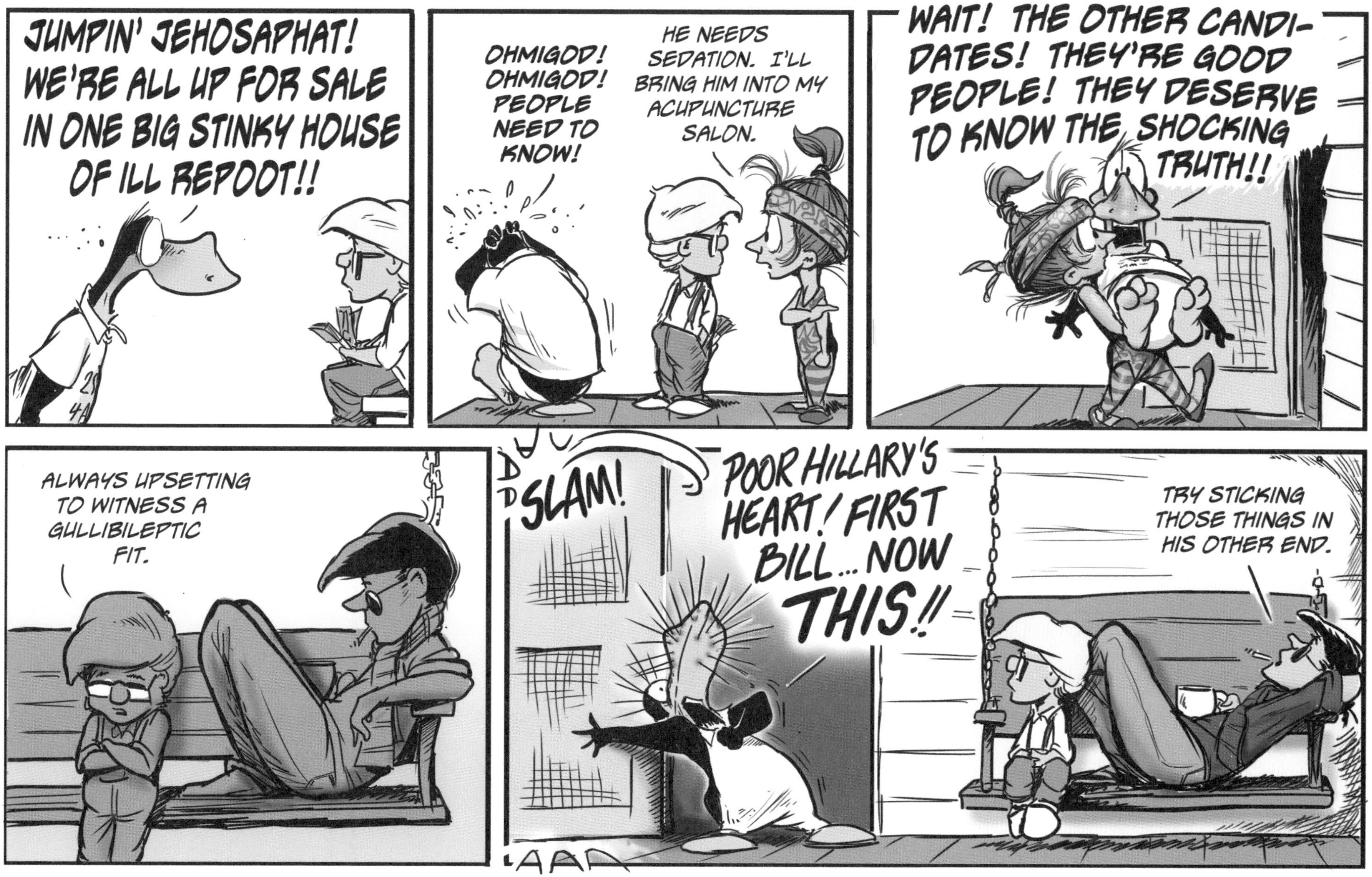
JUMPIN' JEHOSAPHAT! WE'RE ALL UP FOR SALE IN ONE BIG STINKY HOUSE OF ILL REPOOT!!
OHMIGOD! OHMIGOD! PEOPLE NEED TO KNOW!
HE NEEDS SEDATION. I'LL BRING HIM INTO MY ACUPUNCTURE SALON.
WAIT! THE OTHER CANDIDATES! THEY'RE GOOD PEOPLE! THEY DESERVE TO KNOW THE SHOCKING TRUTH!!
ALWAYS UPSETTING TO WITNESS A GULLIBILEPTIC FIT.
SLAM!
POOR HILLARY'S HEART! FIRST BILL... NOW THIS!!
TRY STICKING THOSE THINGS IN HIS OTHER END.

Where can I get the campaign "2 spaces" underwear? Also, is it socially acceptable to wear them on the outside of your pants? Pants optional? I cannot find any information in my trusty etiquette guide.

—Terry Omar

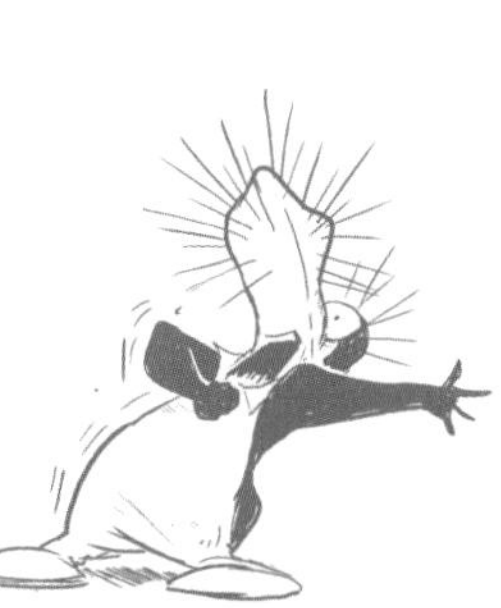

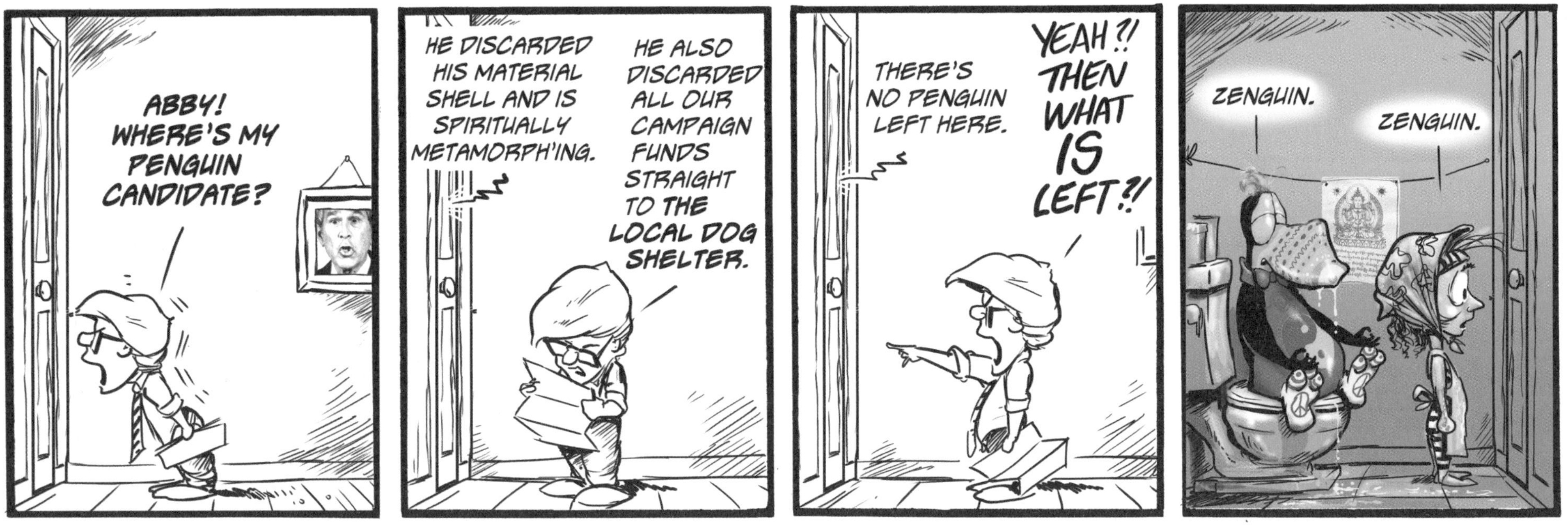
ABBY! WHERE'S MY PENGUIN CANDIDATE?
HE DISCARDED HIS MATERIAL SHELL AND IS SPIRITUALLY METAMORPH'ING.
HE ALSO DISCARDED ALL OUR CAMPAIGN FUNDS STRAIGHT TO THE LOCAL DOG SHELTER.
THERE'S NO PENGUIN LEFT HERE.
YEAH?! THEN WHAT IS LEFT?!
ZENGUIN.
ZENGUIN.

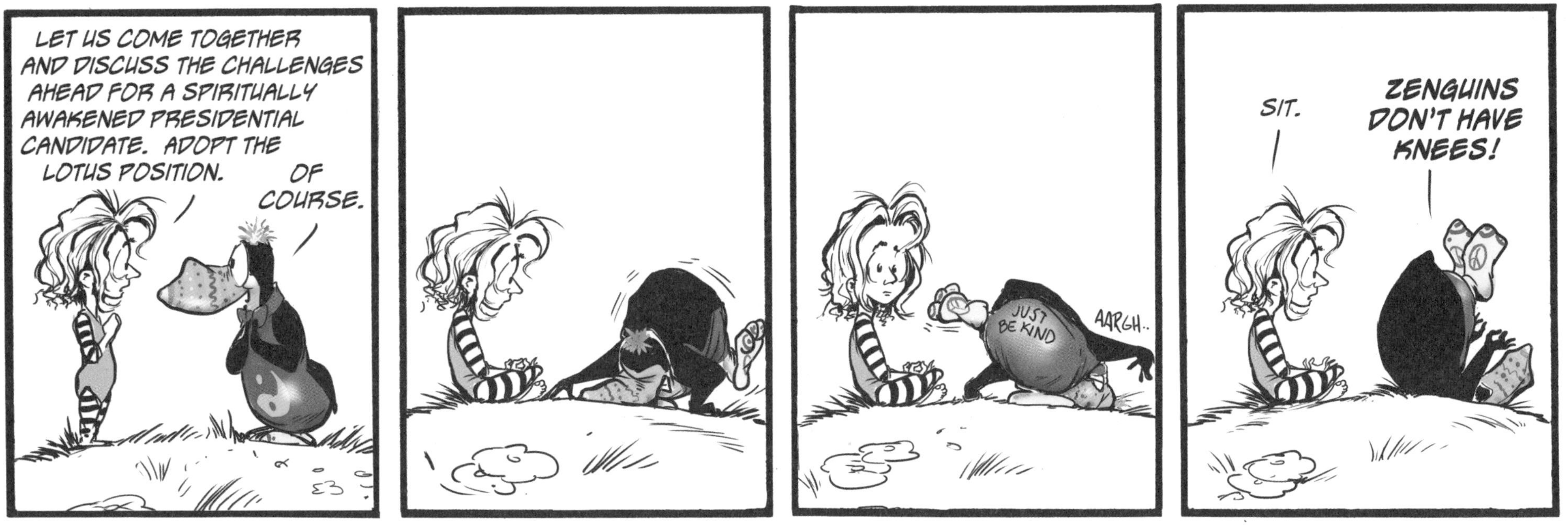
LET US COME TOGETHER AND DISCUSS THE CHALLENGES AHEAD FOR A SPIRITUALLY AWAKENED PRESIDENTIAL CANDIDATE. ADOPT THE LOTUS POSITION.
OF COURSE.
JUST BE KIND
AARGH..
SIT.
ZENGUINS DON'T HAVE KNEES!

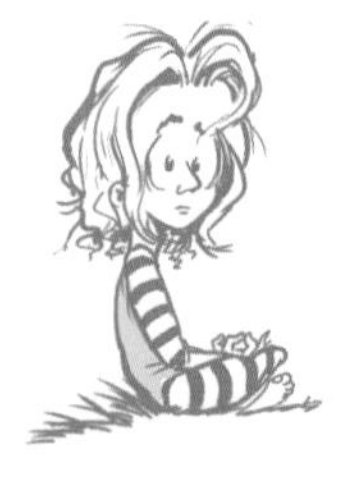

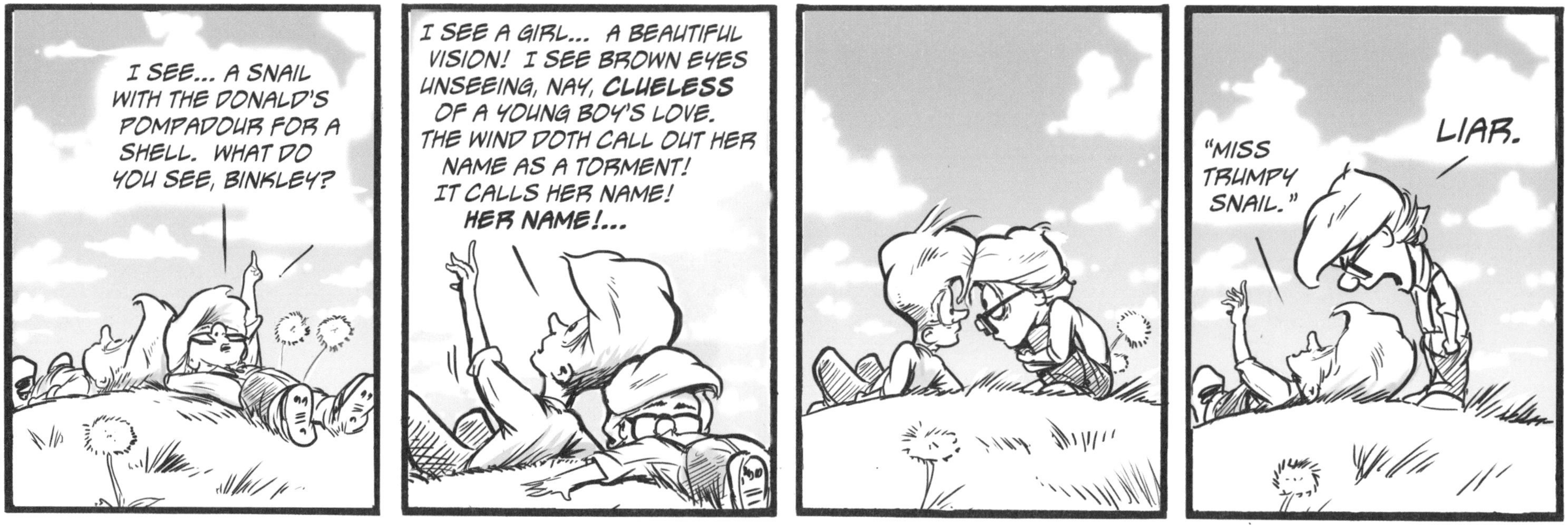
I SEE... A SNAIL WITH THE DONALD'S POMPADOUR FOR A SHELL. WHAT DO YOU SEE, BINKLEY?
I SEE A GIRL... A BEAUTIFUL VISION! I SEE BROWN EYES UNSEEING, NAY, **CLUELESS** OF A YOUNG BOY'S LOVE. THE WIND DOTH CALL OUT HER NAME AS A TORMENT! IT CALLS HER NAME! **HER NAME!...**
"MISS TRUMPY SNAIL."
LIAR.

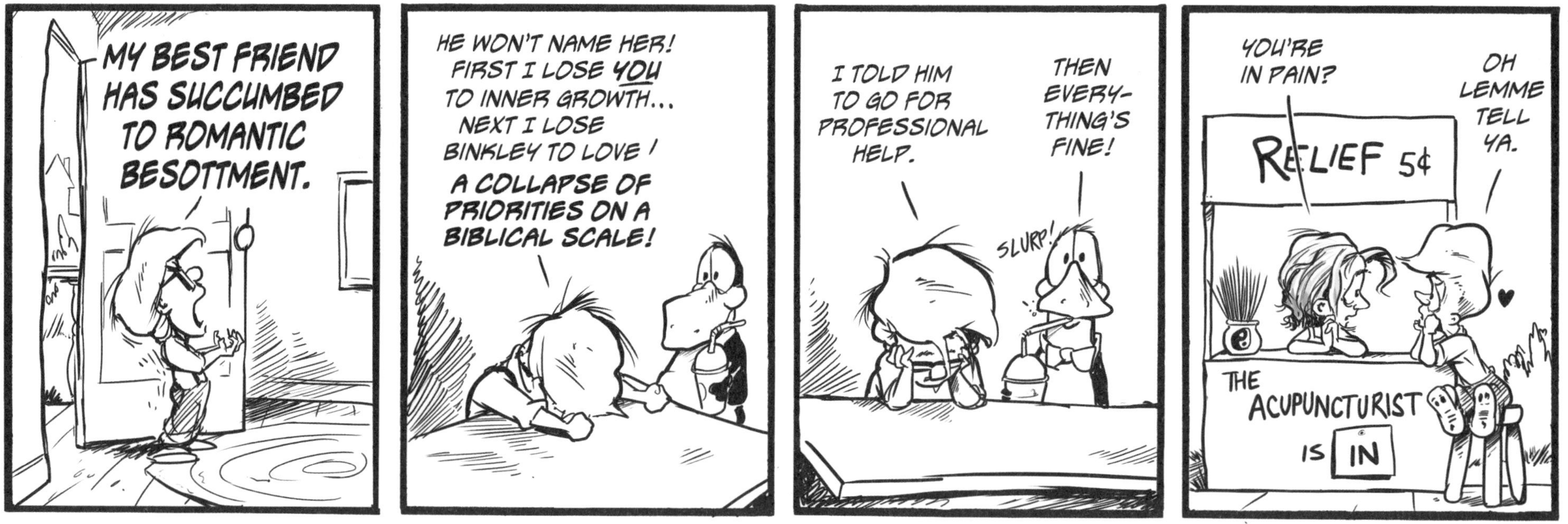
MY BEST FRIEND HAS SUCCUMBED TO ROMANTIC BESOTTMENT.
HE WON'T NAME HER! FIRST I LOSE YOU TO INNER GROWTH... NEXT I LOSE BINKLEY TO LOVE! **A COLLAPSE OF PRIORITIES ON A BIBLICAL SCALE!**
I TOLD HIM TO GO FOR PROFESSIONAL HELP.
THEN EVERY-THING'S FINE!
SLURP!
YOU'RE IN PAIN?
OH LEMME TELL YA.
RELIEF 5¢
THE ACUPUNCTURIST IS IN

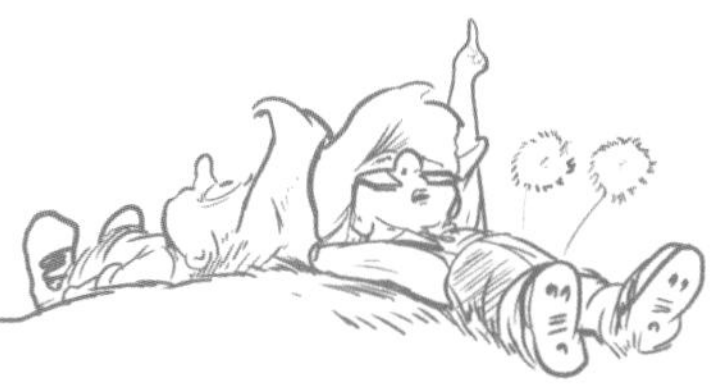

Bloom County 2015

by Berkeley Breathed

OOF.
OH YEAH.

LORDY...

OH GOSH. SORRY. HOPE
I'M NOT DISTURBING YOU
WHILE I DO MY ASS HANA.
ASSINA. ASANA. POSE
THING.

The You Inside

I'VE NOTICED YOU HERE A LOT.
YOU AND YOUR CALM CENTEREDNESS.
IN YOUR CROCHETED HALTER TOP.
I'M SENSING WE'RE
BOTH SEEKERS,
YOU AND I.

The You Inside

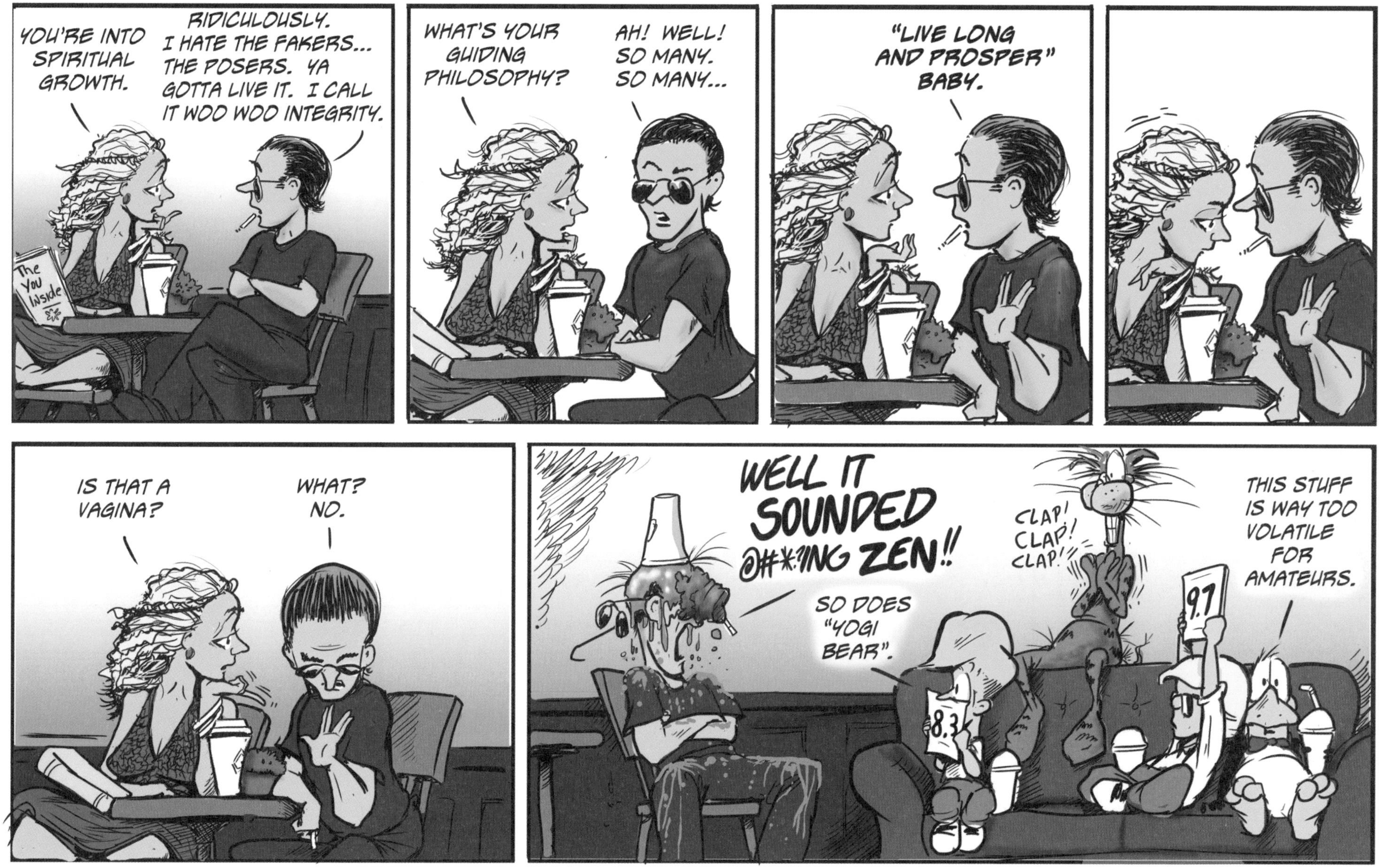
YOU'RE INTO SPIRITUAL GROWTH.
RIDICULOUSLY. I HATE THE FAKERS... THE POSERS. YA GOTTA LIVE IT. I CALL IT WOO WOO INTEGRITY.
The You Inside
WHAT'S YOUR GUIDING PHILOSOPHY?
AH! WELL! SO MANY. SO MANY...
"LIVE LONG AND PROSPER" BABY.
IS THAT A VAGINA?
WHAT? NO.
WELL IT SOUNDED @#*?ING ZEN!!
SO DOES "YOGI BEAR".
CLAP! CLAP! CLAP!
9.7
8.3
THIS STUFF IS WAY TOO VOLATILE FOR AMATEURS.

Sir Breathed, you left *Bloom County* as a brilliant artist and returned as the Buddha. ♥

—Joy Sequoia

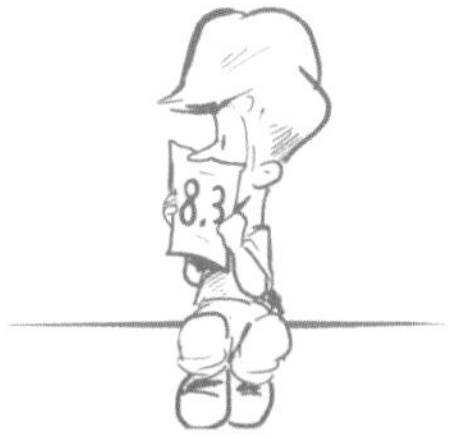
8.3

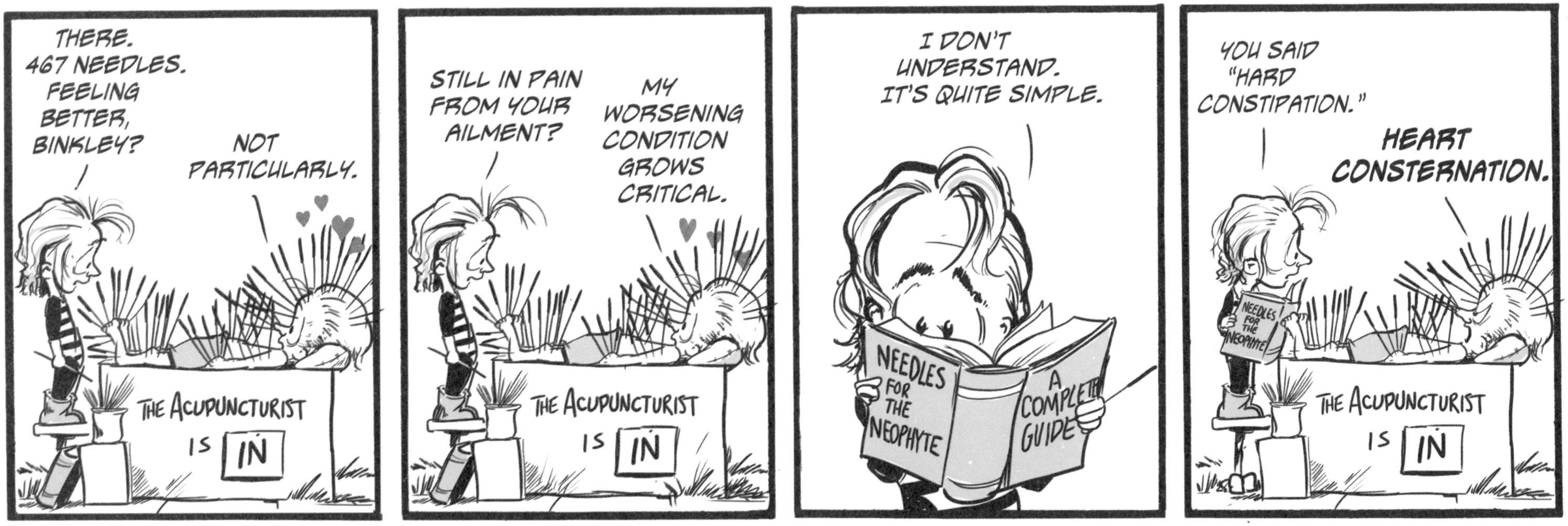
THERE. 467 NEEDLES. FEELING BETTER, BINKLEY?
NOT PARTICULARLY.
THE ACUPUNCTURIST IS IN
STILL IN PAIN FROM YOUR AILMENT?
MY WORSENING CONDITION GROWS CRITICAL.
THE ACUPUNCTURIST IS IN
I DON'T UNDERSTAND. IT'S QUITE SIMPLE.
NEEDLES FOR THE NEOPHYTE
A COMPLETE GUIDE
YOU SAID "HARD CONSTIPATION."
HEART CONSTERNATION.
NEEDLES FOR THE NEOPHYTE
THE ACUPUNCTURIST IS IN

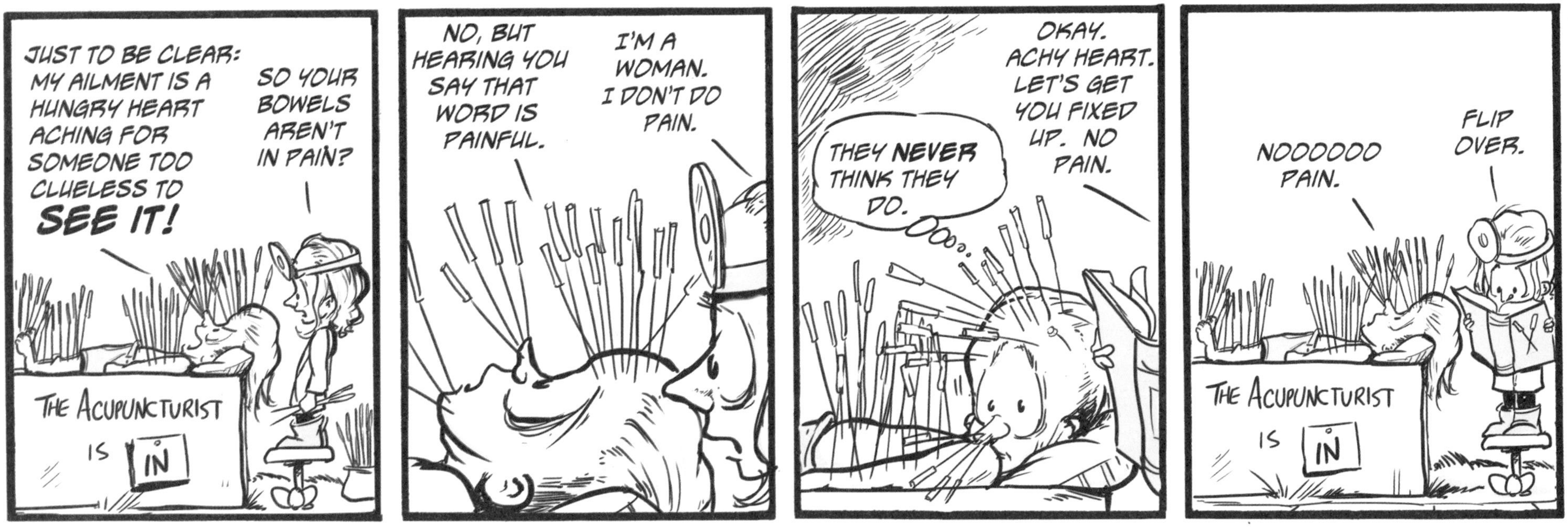
JUST TO BE CLEAR: MY AILMENT IS A HUNGRY HEART ACHING FOR SOMEONE TOO CLUELESS TO **SEE IT!**
SO YOUR BOWELS AREN'T IN PAIN?
THE ACUPUNCTURIST IS IN
NO, BUT HEARING YOU SAY THAT WORD IS PAINFUL.
I'M A WOMAN. I DON'T DO PAIN.
THEY **NEVER** THINK THEY DO.
OKAY. ACHY HEART. LET'S GET YOU FIXED UP. NO PAIN.
NOOOOOO PAIN.
FLIP OVER.
THE ACUPUNCTURIST IS IN

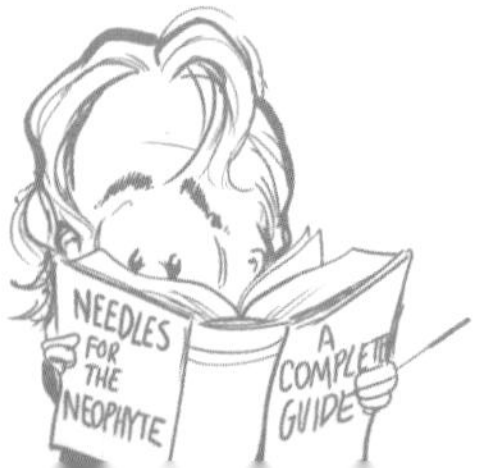
NEEDLES FOR THE NEOPHYTE
A COMPLETE GUIDE

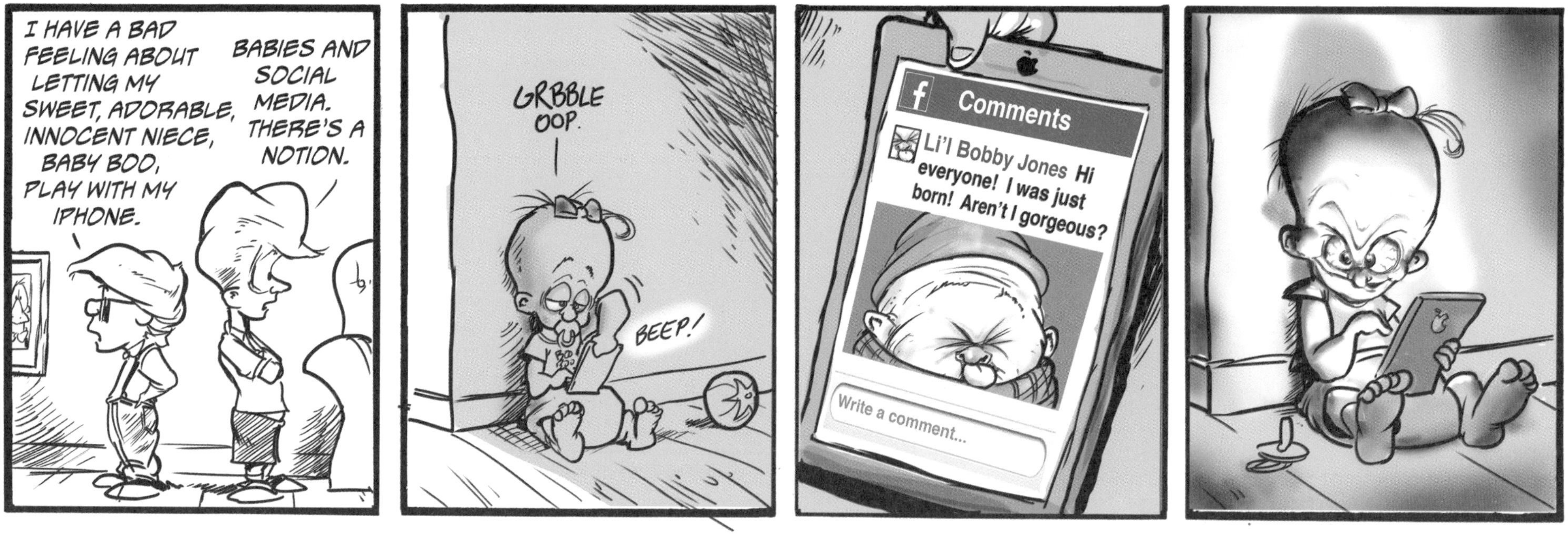
I HAVE A BAD FEELING ABOUT LETTING MY SWEET, ADORABLE, INNOCENT NIECE, BABY BOO, PLAY WITH MY IPHONE.
BABIES AND SOCIAL MEDIA. THERE'S A NOTION.
GRBBLE OOP.
BEEP!
Comments
Li'l Bobby Jones Hi everyone! I was just born! Aren't I gorgeous?
Write a comment...

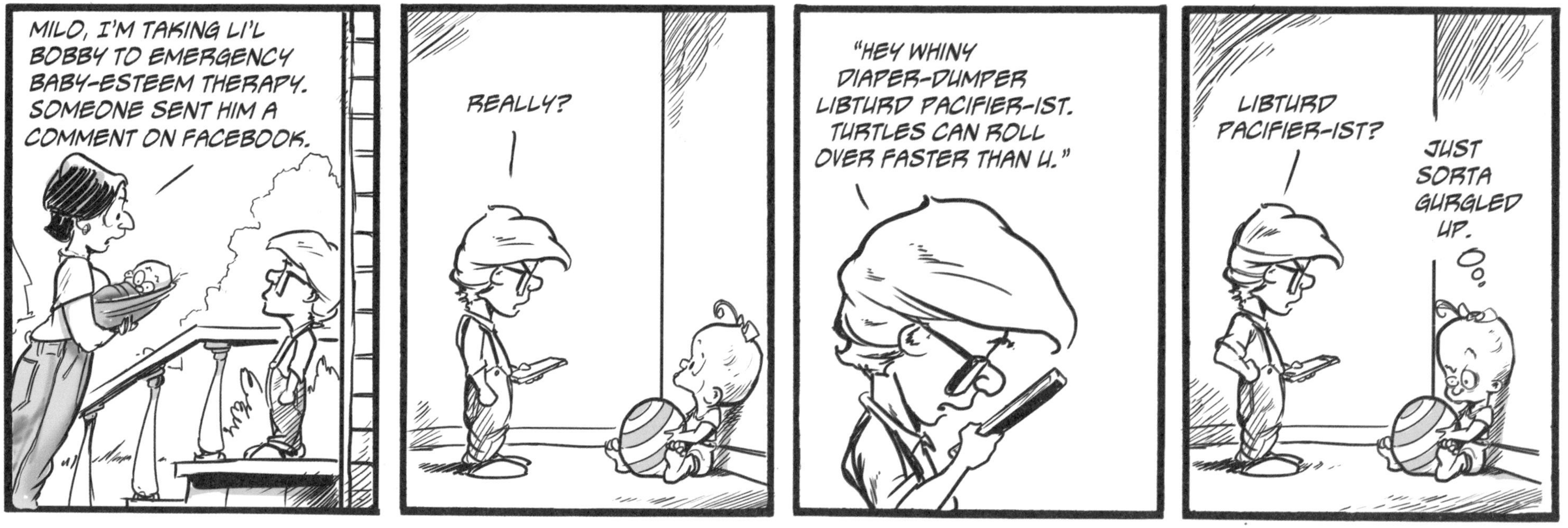
MILO, I'M TAKING LI'L BOBBY TO EMERGENCY BABY-ESTEEM THERAPY. SOMEONE SENT HIM A COMMENT ON FACEBOOK.
REALLY?
"HEY WHINY DIAPER-DUMPER LIBTURD PACIFIER-IST. TURTLES CAN ROLL OVER FASTER THAN U."
LIBTURD PACIFIER-IST?
JUST SORTA GURGLED UP.

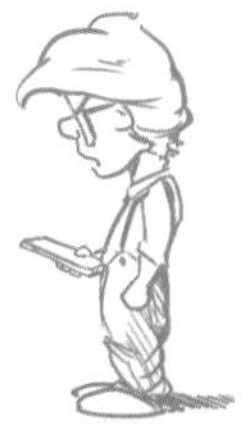

Bloom County 2015
by Berkeley Breathed
WHEN BABIES HAVE PHONES.
Comments
Like
Buzztot15 Hi. That soft spot on top of ur head iz wher they filled it with banana pudding
KANYE Brand MoFlo Breast Pumps
Buzztot15 U guYz SUK SUK SUK SUK SUK HAHAHAHAHA
WELCOME

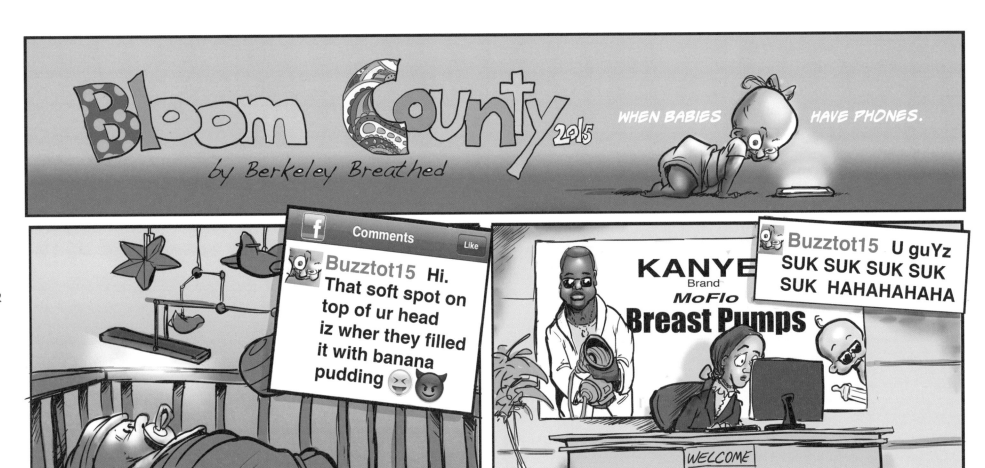

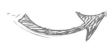

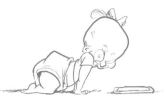

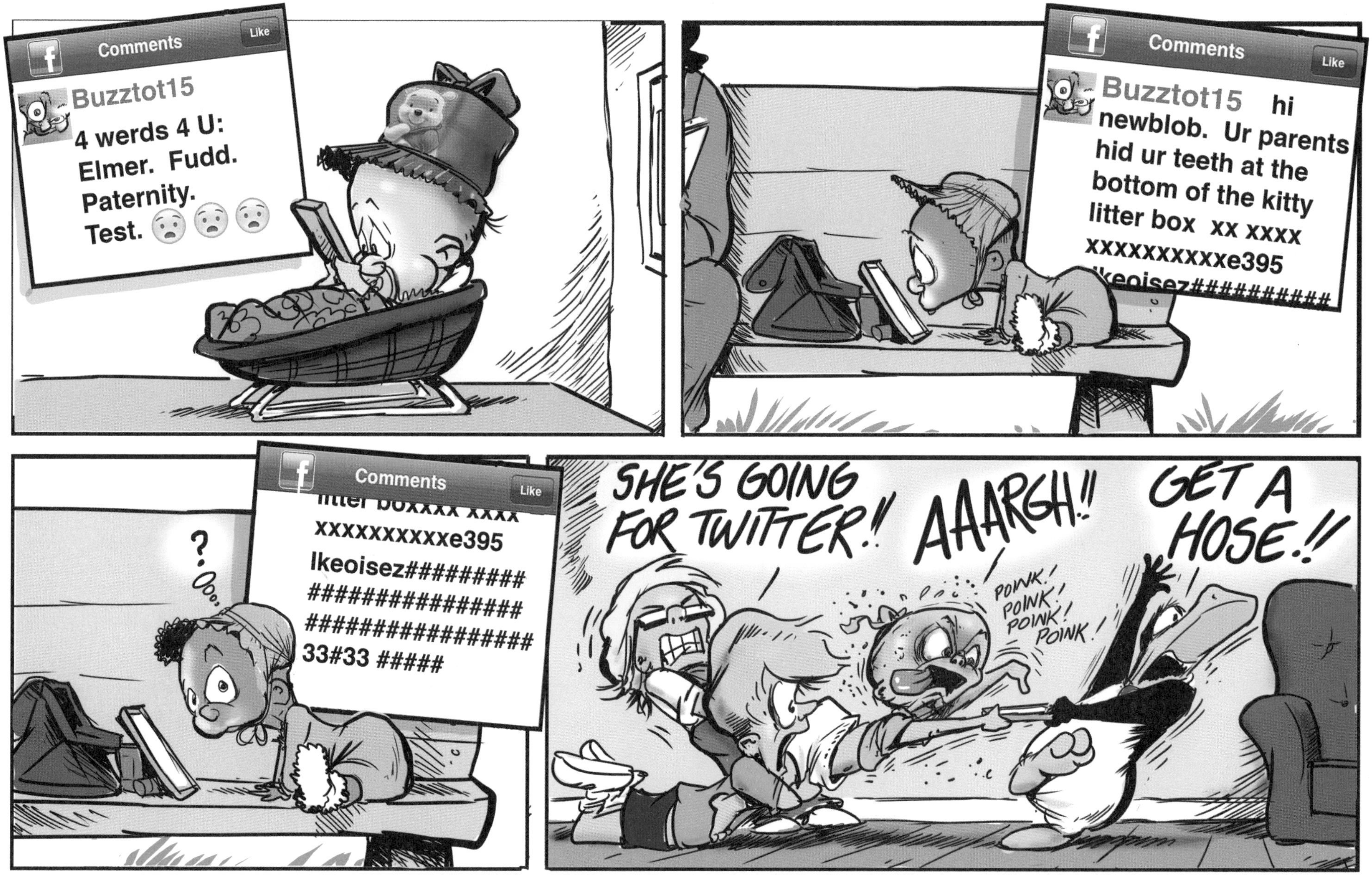
Comments
Like
Buzztot15
4 werds 4 U:
Elmer. Fudd.
Paternity.
Test.
Comments
Like
Buzztot15 hi
newblob. Ur parents
hid ur teeth at the
bottom of the kitty
litter box xx xxxx
xxxxxxxxxxe395
?
Comments
Like
xxxxxxxxxxe395
lkeoisez#########
################
#################
33#33 #####
SHE'S GOING FOR TWITTER!!
AAARGH!!
POINK! POINK! POINK! POINK!
GET A HOSE!!

Is there anything—ANYTHING??—in life better than signing into Facebook and having *Bloom County* at the very top of your timeline? I think not. It's 8:00 A.M. and my day is complete.

—Kathy Fiebig

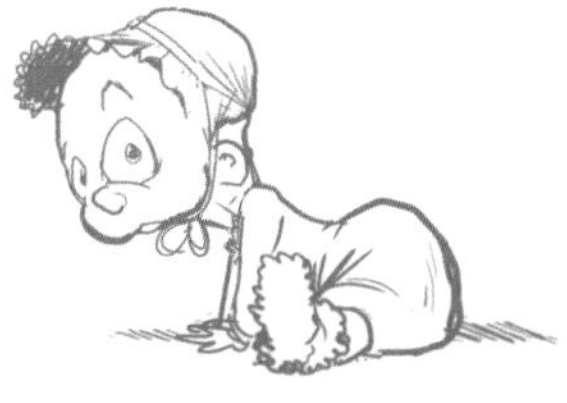

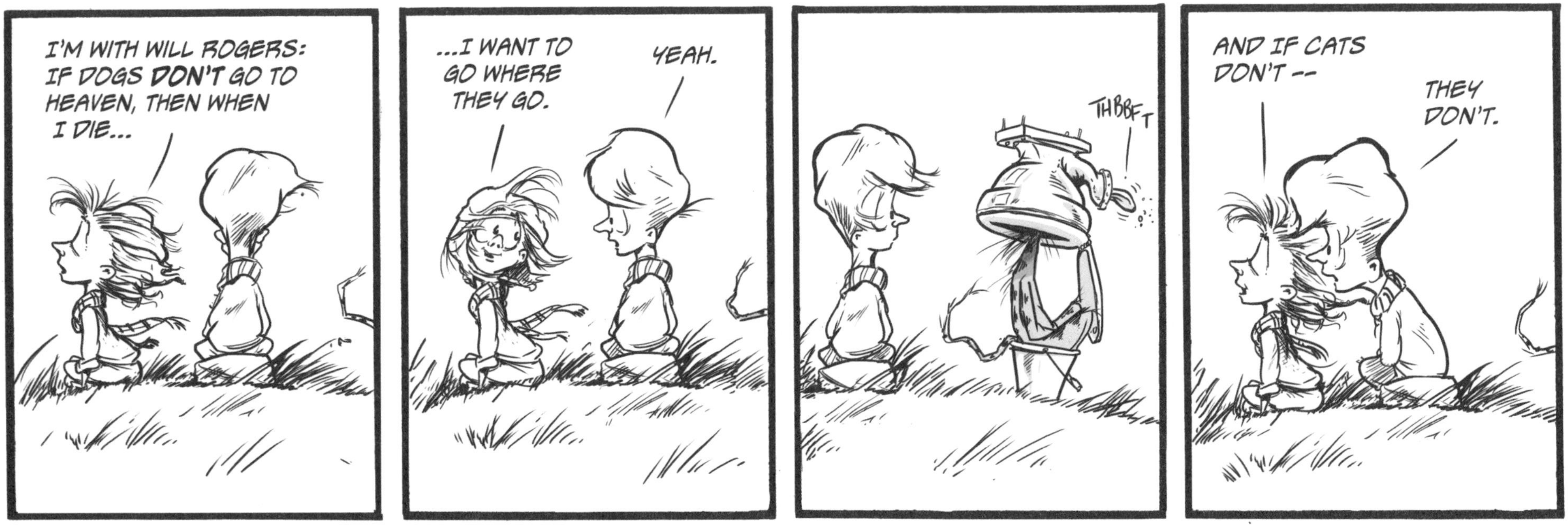
I'M WITH WILL ROGERS: IF DOGS **DON'T** GO TO HEAVEN, THEN WHEN I DIE...
...I WANT TO GO WHERE THEY GO.
YEAH.
THBBFT
AND IF CATS DON'T --
THEY DON'T.

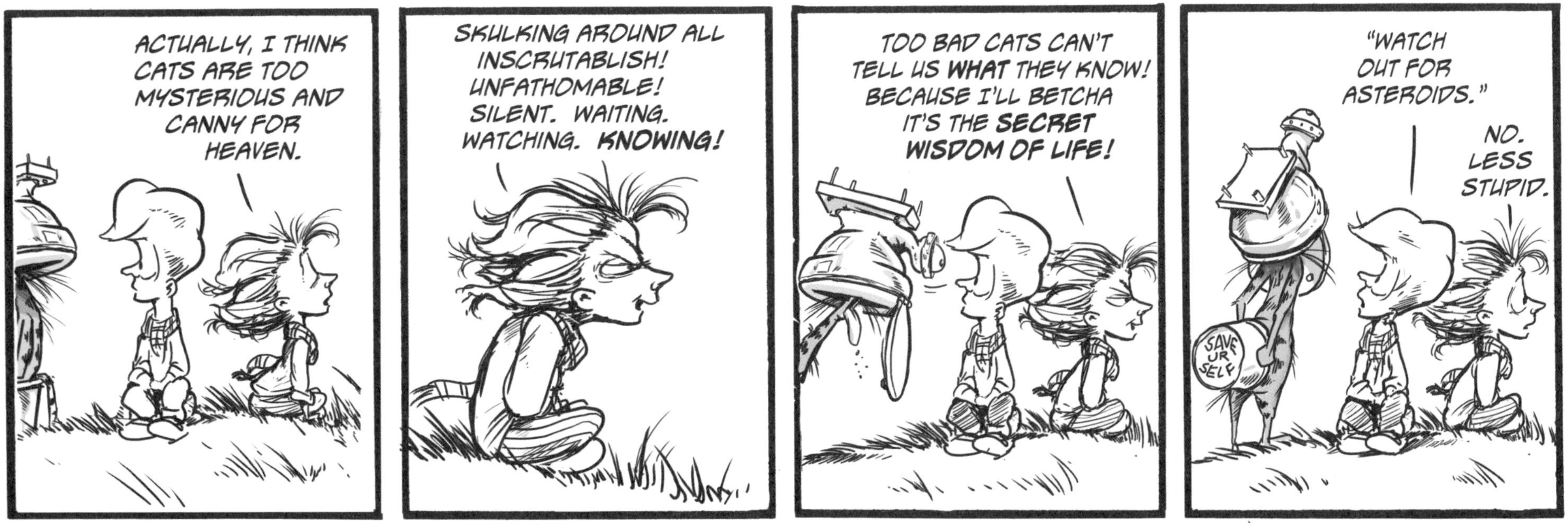
ACTUALLY, I THINK CATS ARE TOO MYSTERIOUS AND CANNY FOR HEAVEN.
SKULKING AROUND ALL INSCRUTABLISH! UNFATHOMABLE! SILENT. WAITING. WATCHING. **KNOWING!**
TOO BAD CATS CAN'T TELL US **WHAT** THEY KNOW! BECAUSE I'LL BETCHA IT'S THE **SECRET WISDOM OF LIFE!**
SAVE UR SELF
"WATCH OUT FOR ASTEROIDS."
NO. LESS STUPID.

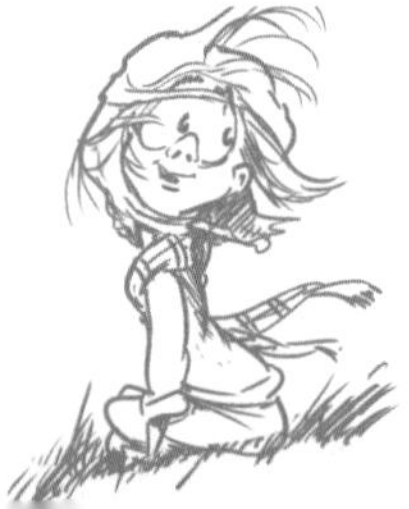

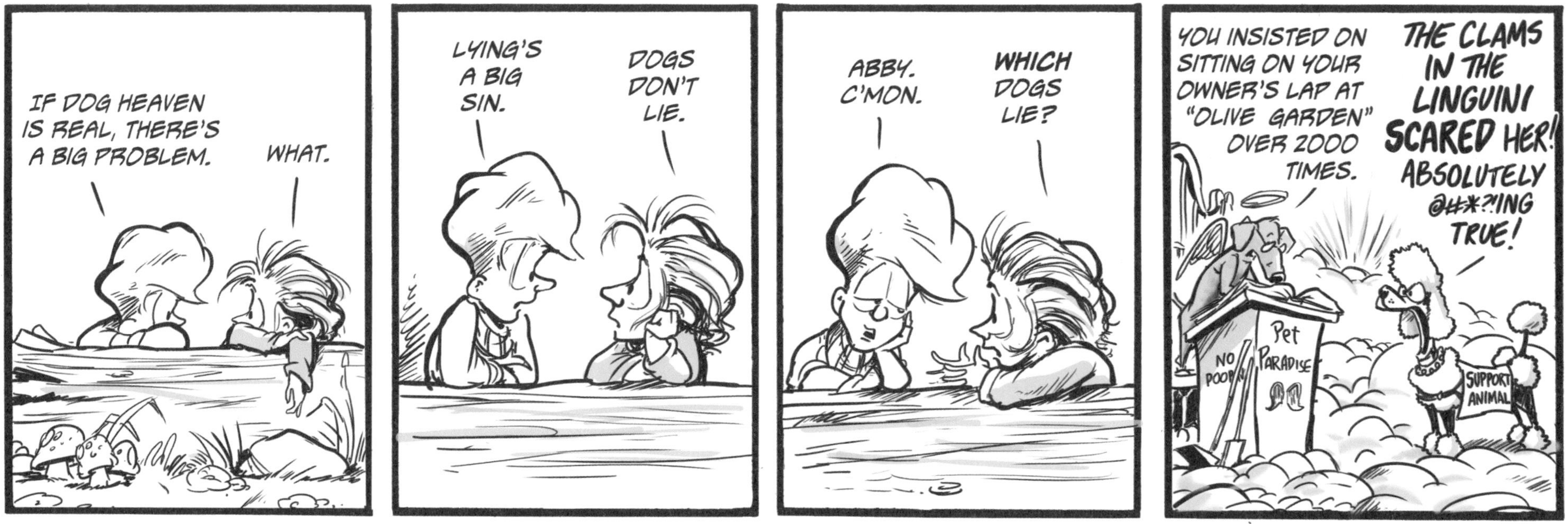
IF DOG HEAVEN IS REAL, THERE'S A BIG PROBLEM.
WHAT.
LYING'S A BIG SIN.
DOGS DON'T LIE.
ABBY. C'MON.
WHICH DOGS LIE?
YOU INSISTED ON SITTING ON YOUR OWNER'S LAP AT "OLIVE GARDEN" OVER 2000 TIMES.
THE CLAMS IN THE LINGUINI SCARED HER! ABSOLUTELY @#*?!ING TRUE!
NO POOPING
Pet PARADISE
SUPPORT ANIMAL

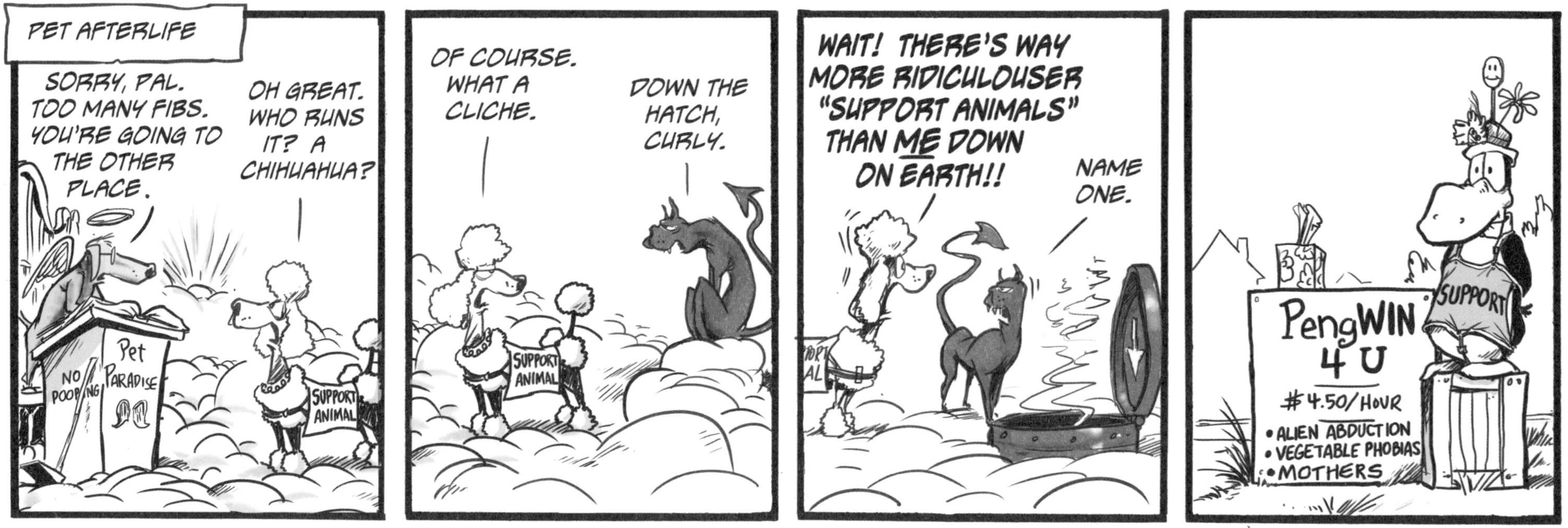
PET AFTERLIFE
SORRY, PAL. TOO MANY FIBS. YOU'RE GOING TO THE OTHER PLACE.
OH GREAT. WHO RUNS IT? A CHIHUAHUA?
NO POOPING
Pet PARADISE
SUPPORT ANIMAL
OF COURSE. WHAT A CLICHE.
DOWN THE HATCH, CURLY.
SUPPORT ANIMAL
WAIT! THERE'S WAY MORE RIDICULOUSER "SUPPORT ANIMALS" THAN ME DOWN ON EARTH!!
NAME ONE.
SUPPORT
PengWIN 4 U
$4.50/HOUR
• ALIEN ABDUCTION
• VEGETABLE PHOBIAS
• MOTHERS

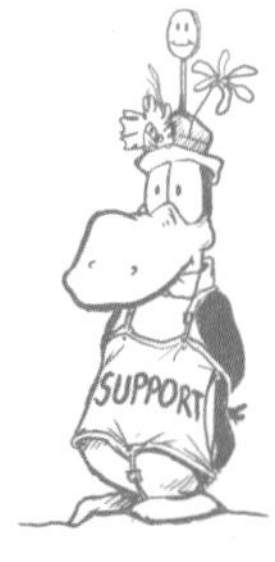
SUPPORT

Bloom County 2015
by Berkeley Breathed
OFF TO WORK!
FOX NEWS channel
PHILBERT... I... UH... YOU SHOULD KNOW... UH..
I'M GONNA TALK TO MY SUPPORT PENGUIN.

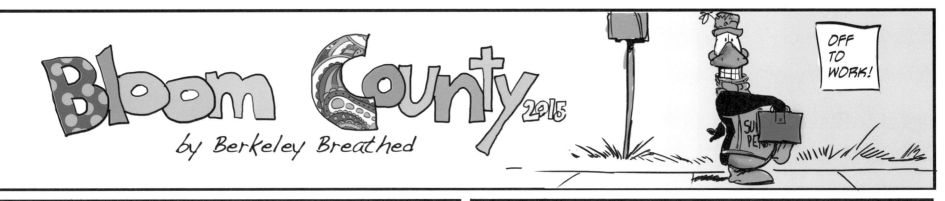

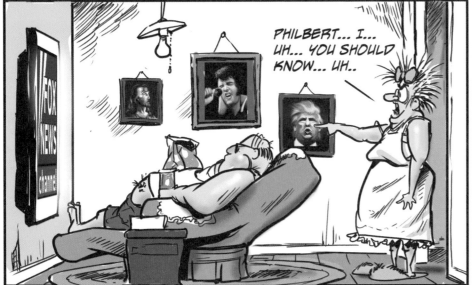

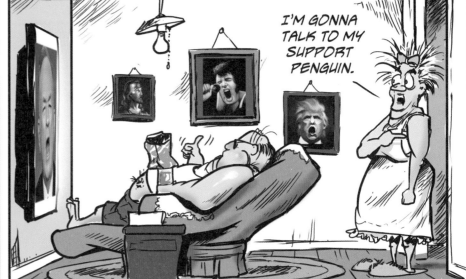

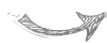

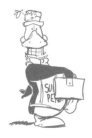

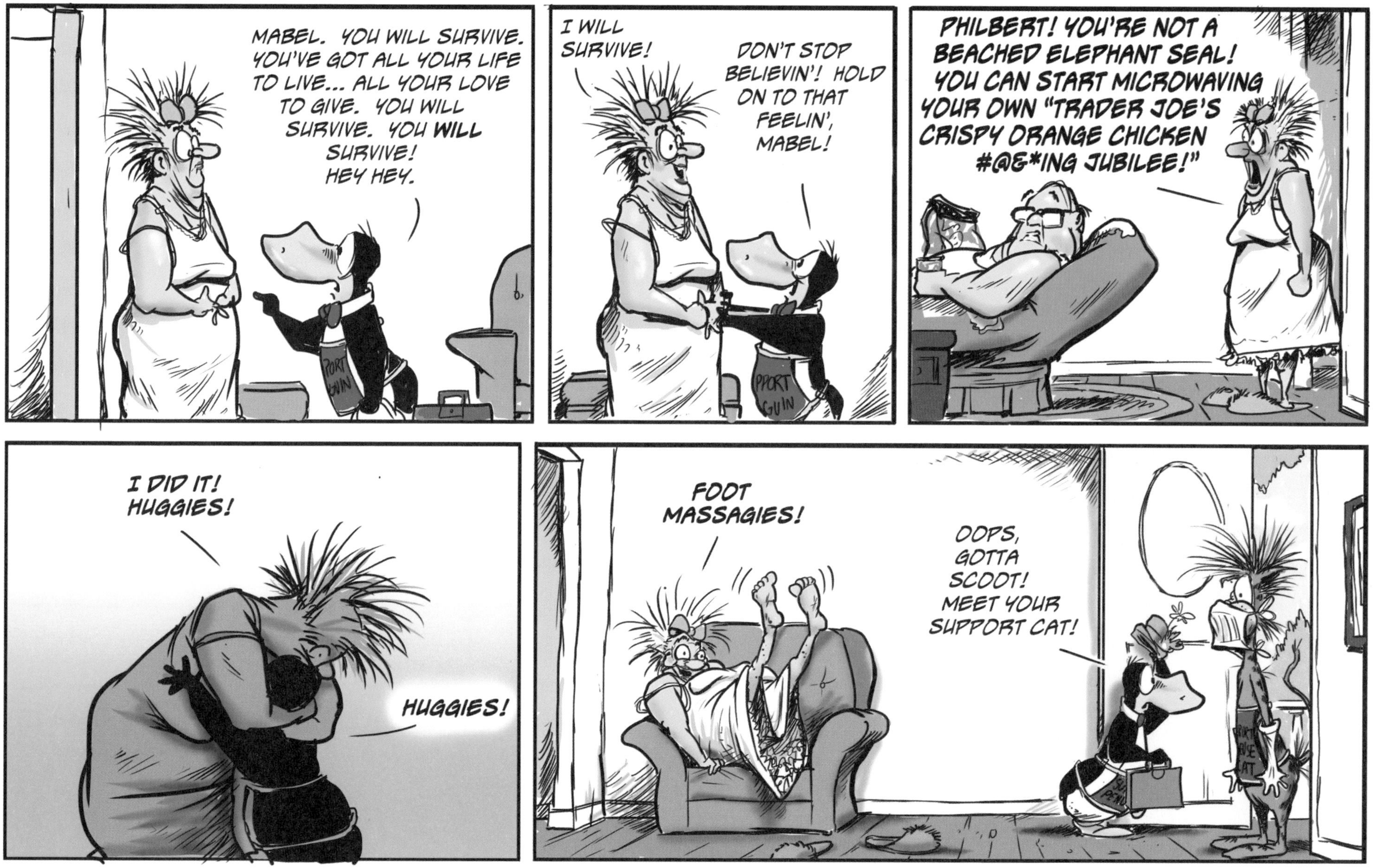
MABEL. YOU WILL SURVIVE. YOU'VE GOT ALL YOUR LIFE TO LIVE... ALL YOUR LOVE TO GIVE. YOU WILL SURVIVE. YOU WILL SURVIVE! HEY HEY.
I WILL SURVIVE!
DON'T STOP BELIEVIN'! HOLD ON TO THAT FEELIN', MABEL!
PHILBERT! YOU'RE NOT A BEACHED ELEPHANT SEAL! YOU CAN START MICROWAVING YOUR OWN "TRADER JOE'S CRISPY ORANGE CHICKEN #@&*ING JUBILEE!"
I DID IT! HUGGIES!
HUGGIES!
FOOT MASSAGIES!
OOPS, GOTTA SCOOT! MEET YOUR SUPPORT CAT!

That's enough empathy indoctrination for one day, sir. Just how much love and compassion do you think we can take, fer cryin' out loud?!? Thank you, I feel more human now, thanks in part to a cartoon penguin—is that weird?

—Lars Blackmore

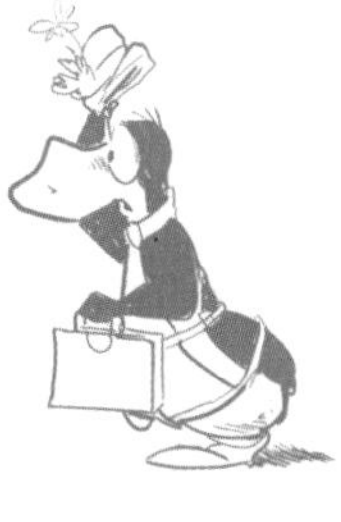

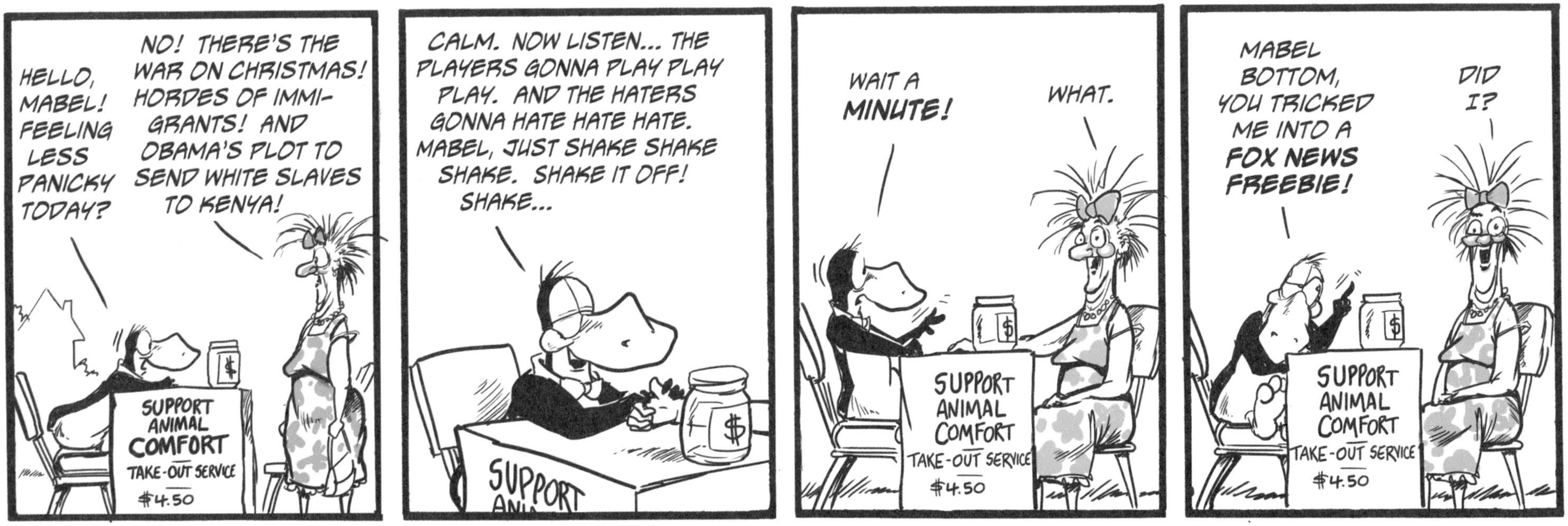
HELLO, MABEL! FEELING LESS PANICKY TODAY?
NO! THERE'S THE WAR ON CHRISTMAS! HORDES OF IMMI-GRANTS! AND OBAMA'S PLOT TO SEND WHITE SLAVES TO KENYA!
SUPPORT ANIMAL COMFORT
TAKE-OUT SERVICE
$4.50
CALM. NOW LISTEN... THE PLAYERS GONNA PLAY PLAY PLAY. AND THE HATERS GONNA HATE HATE HATE. MABEL, JUST SHAKE SHAKE SHAKE. SHAKE IT OFF! SHAKE...
WAIT A **MINUTE!**
WHAT.
SUPPORT ANIMAL COMFORT
TAKE-OUT SERVICE
$4.50
MABEL BOTTOM, YOU TRICKED ME INTO A **FOX NEWS FREEBIE!**
DID I?
SUPPORT ANIMAL COMFORT
TAKE-OUT SERVICE
$4.50

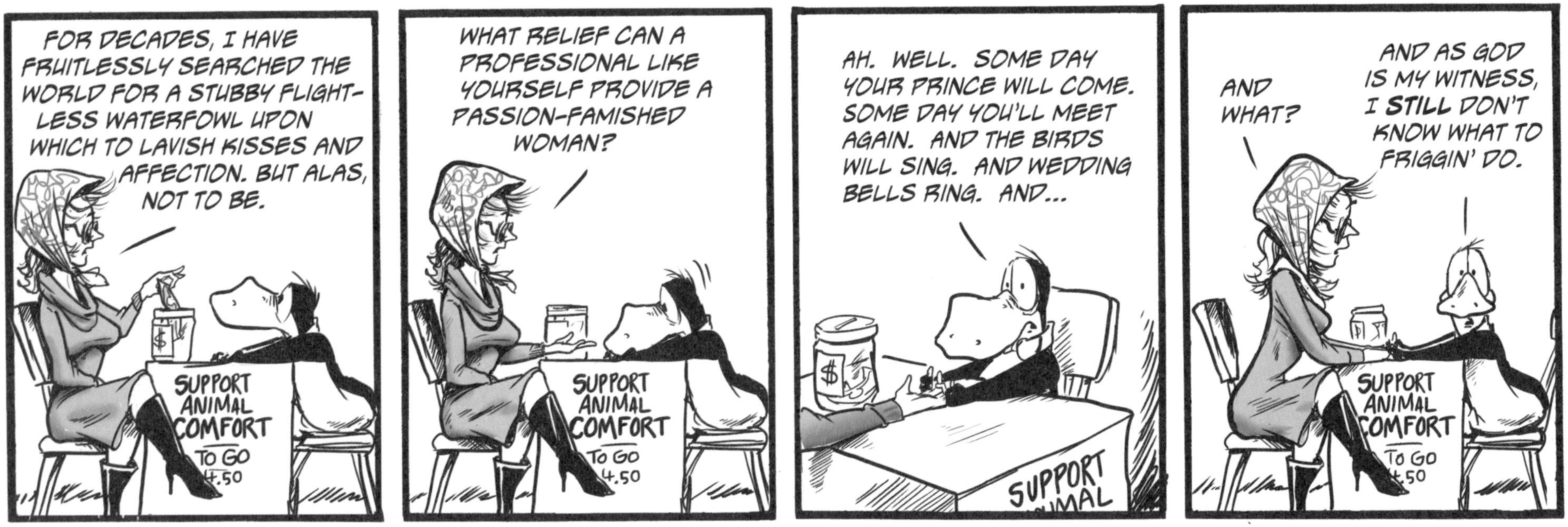
FOR DECADES, I HAVE FRUITLESSLY SEARCHED THE WORLD FOR A STUBBY FLIGHT-LESS WATERFOWL UPON WHICH TO LAVISH KISSES AND AFFECTION. BUT ALAS, NOT TO BE.
SUPPORT ANIMAL COMFORT
TO GO
WHAT RELIEF CAN A PROFESSIONAL LIKE YOURSELF PROVIDE A PASSION-FAMISHED WOMAN?
AH. WELL. SOME DAY YOUR PRINCE WILL COME. SOME DAY YOU'LL MEET AGAIN. AND THE BIRDS WILL SING. AND WEDDING BELLS RING. AND...
AND WHAT?
AND AS GOD IS MY WITNESS, I **STILL** DON'T KNOW WHAT TO FRIGGIN' DO.
SUPPORT ANIMAL COMFORT
TO GO

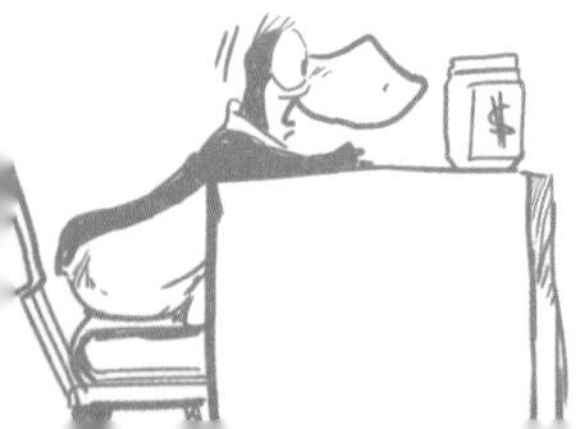

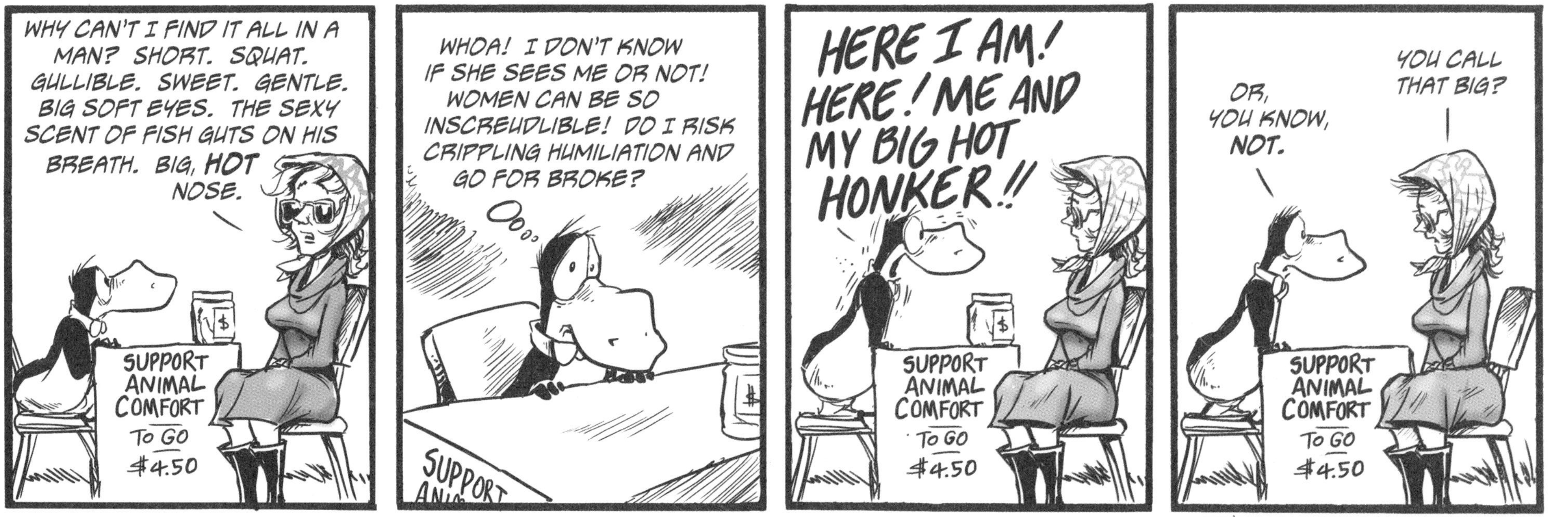
WHY CAN'T I FIND IT ALL IN A MAN? SHORT. SQUAT. GULLIBLE. SWEET. GENTLE. BIG SOFT EYES. THE SEXY SCENT OF FISH GUTS ON HIS BREATH. BIG, HOT NOSE.
SUPPORT ANIMAL COMFORT
TO GO
$4.50
WHOA! I DON'T KNOW IF SHE SEES ME OR NOT! WOMEN CAN BE SO INSCREUDLIBLE! DO I RISK CRIPPLING HUMILIATION AND GO FOR BROKE?
HERE I AM! HERE! ME AND MY BIG HOT HONKER!!
SUPPORT ANIMAL COMFORT
TO GO
$4.50
OR, YOU KNOW, NOT.
YOU CALL THAT BIG?
SUPPORT ANIMAL COMFORT
TO GO
$4.50

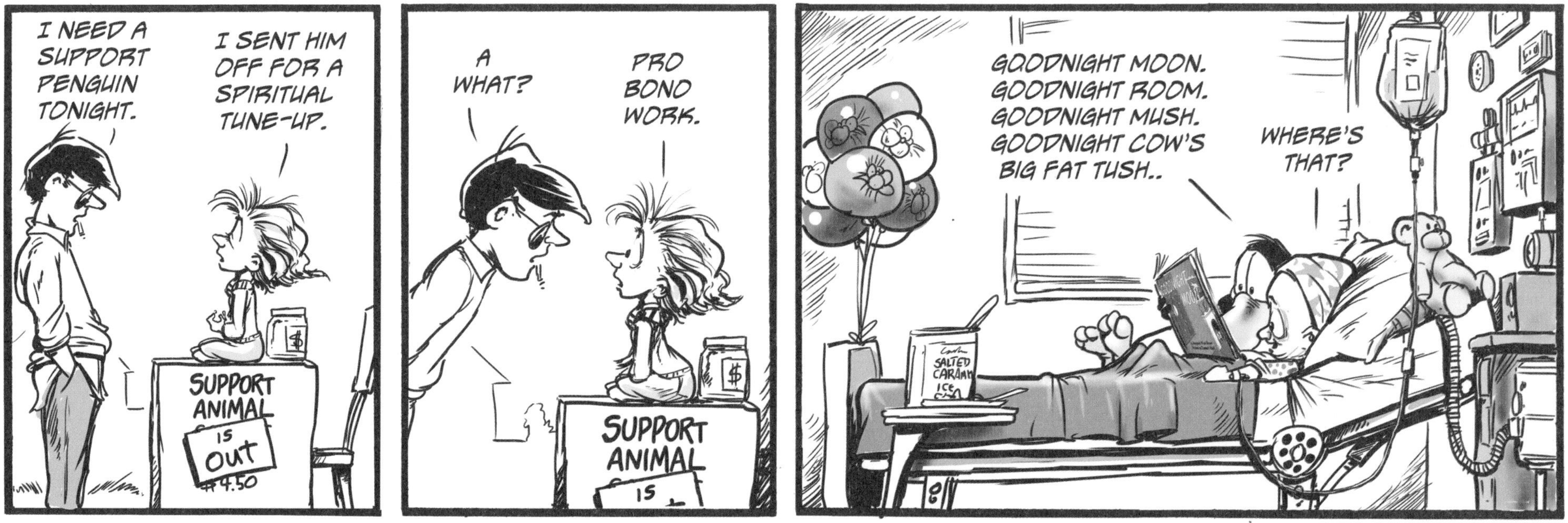
I NEED A SUPPORT PENGUIN TONIGHT.
I SENT HIM OFF FOR A SPIRITUAL TUNE-UP.
SUPPORT ANIMAL
IS OUT
A WHAT?
PRO BONO WORK.
SUPPORT ANIMAL
IS
GOODNIGHT MOON. GOODNIGHT ROOM. GOODNIGHT MUSH. GOODNIGHT COW'S BIG FAT TUSH..
WHERE'S THAT?
SALTED

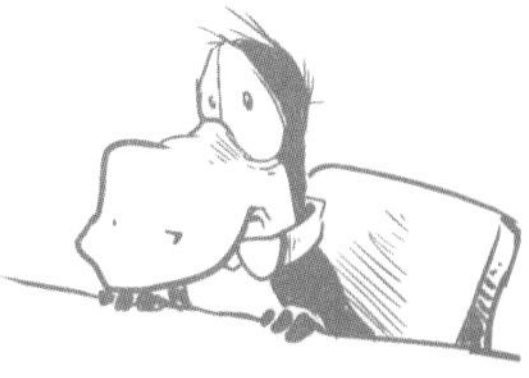

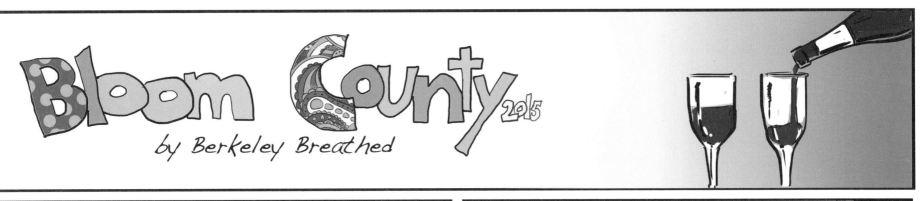

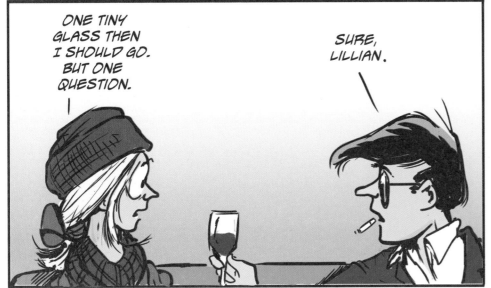

Bloom County 2015
by Berkeley Breathed
ONE TINY GLASS THEN I SHOULD GO. BUT ONE QUESTION.
SURE, LILLIAN.
IT'S "VIVIAN." WHO'S THE LITTLE GUY THAT SMELLS LIKE OLD SOCKS AND FISH STICKS?
MY HOSPITALITY SUPPORT ANIMAL.

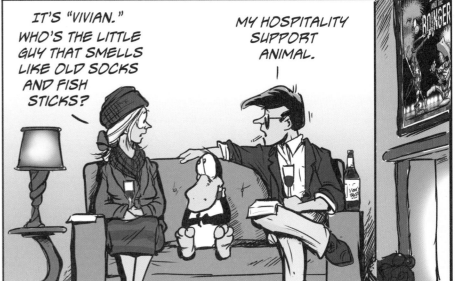

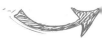

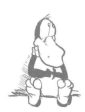

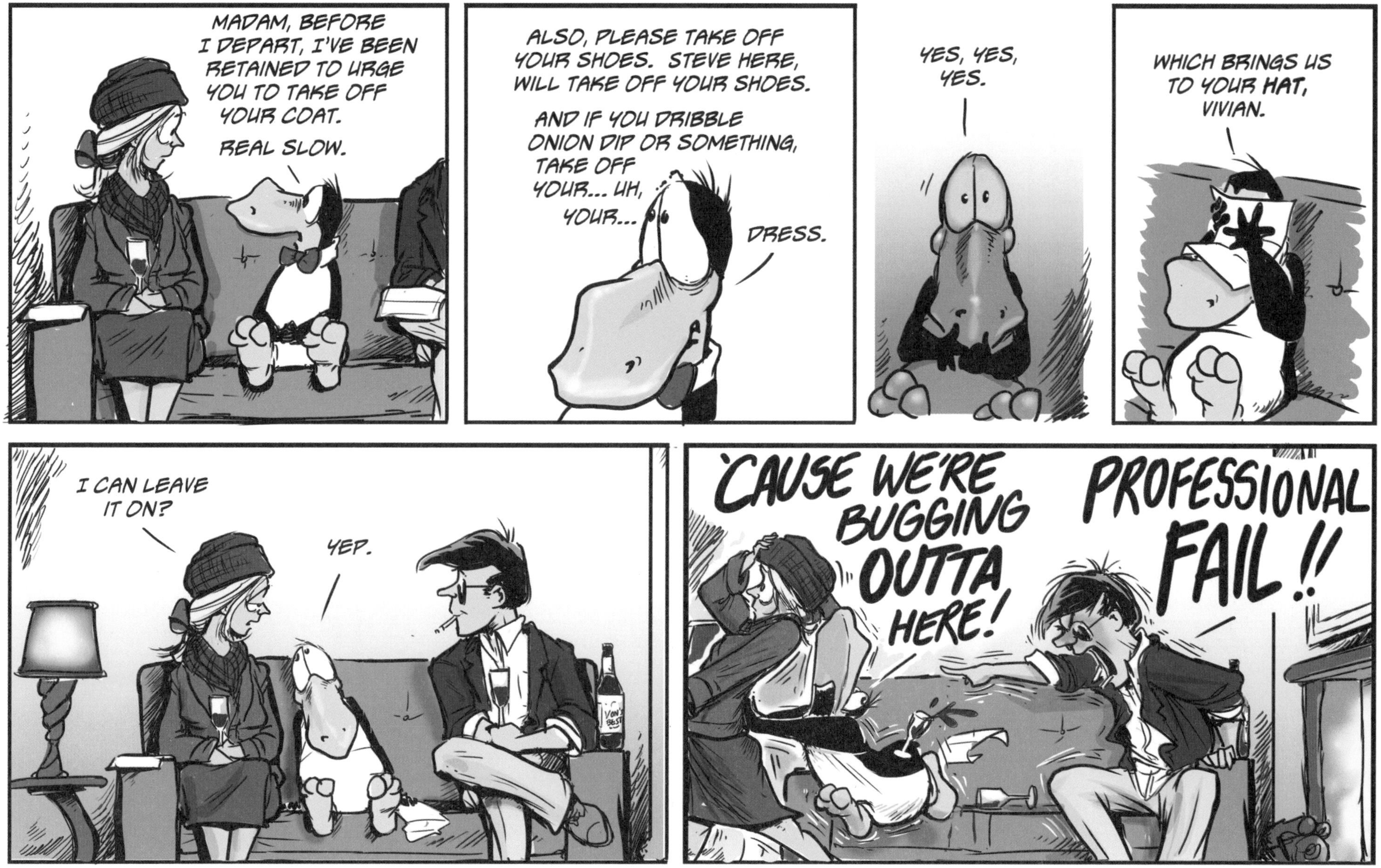
MADAM, BEFORE I DEPART, I'VE BEEN RETAINED TO URGE YOU TO TAKE OFF YOUR COAT.
REAL SLOW.
ALSO, PLEASE TAKE OFF YOUR SHOES. STEVE HERE, WILL TAKE OFF YOUR SHOES.
AND IF YOU DRIBBLE ONION DIP OR SOMETHING, TAKE OFF YOUR... UH, YOUR...
DRESS.
YES, YES, YES.
WHICH BRINGS US TO YOUR HAT, VIVIAN.
I CAN LEAVE IT ON?
YEP.
'CAUSE WE'RE BUGGING OUTTA HERE!
PROFESSIONAL FAIL!!

Opus has literally been my support penguin since 1986. He's tattooed on my arm, he has been allowed into every surgery with me since that year, he always goes with me to the dentist, he sleeps with me when life becomes overwhelming. Do I get funny looks? Do I care? Mr. Breathed—have you been following me, because this is not a new concept. 😉

—Merla Miller

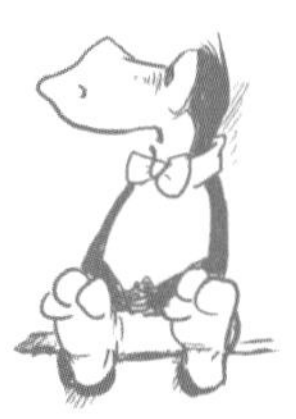

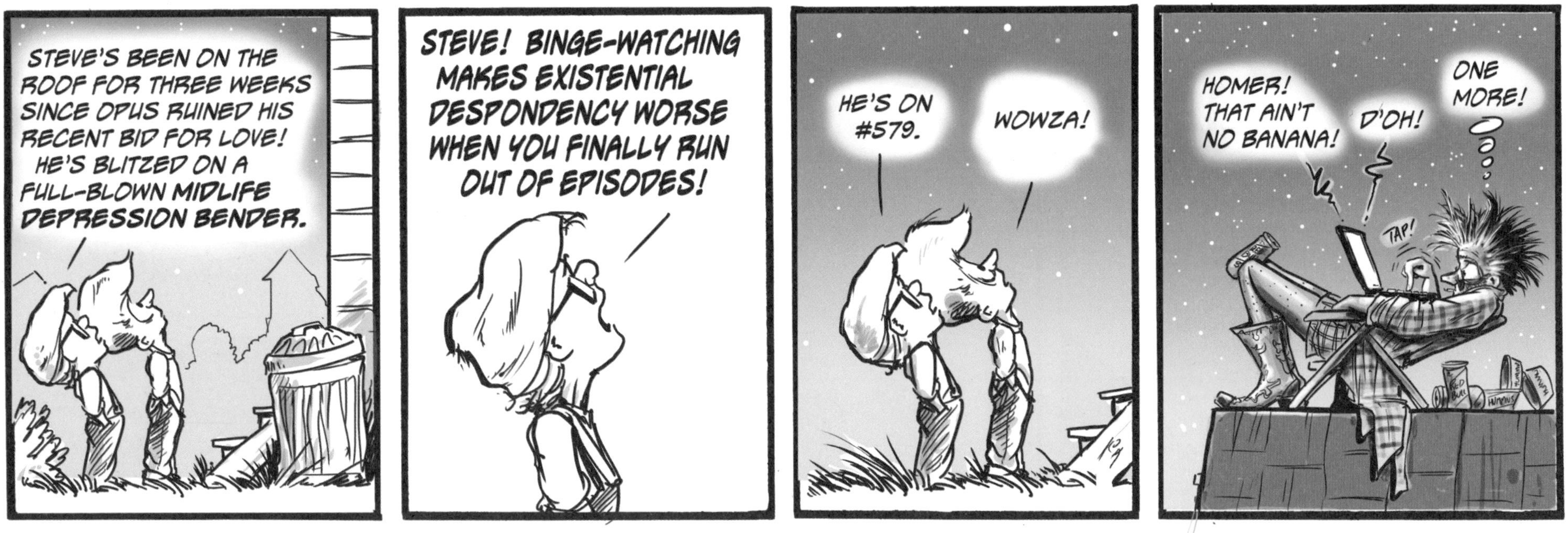
STEVE'S BEEN ON THE ROOF FOR THREE WEEKS SINCE OPUS RUINED HIS RECENT BID FOR LOVE! HE'S BLITZED ON A FULL-BLOWN MIDLIFE DEPRESSION BENDER.
STEVE! BINGE-WATCHING MAKES EXISTENTIAL DESPONDENCY WORSE WHEN YOU FINALLY RUN OUT OF EPISODES!
HE'S ON #579.
WOWZA!
HOMER! THAT AIN'T NO BANANA!
D'OH!
ONE MORE!
TAP!

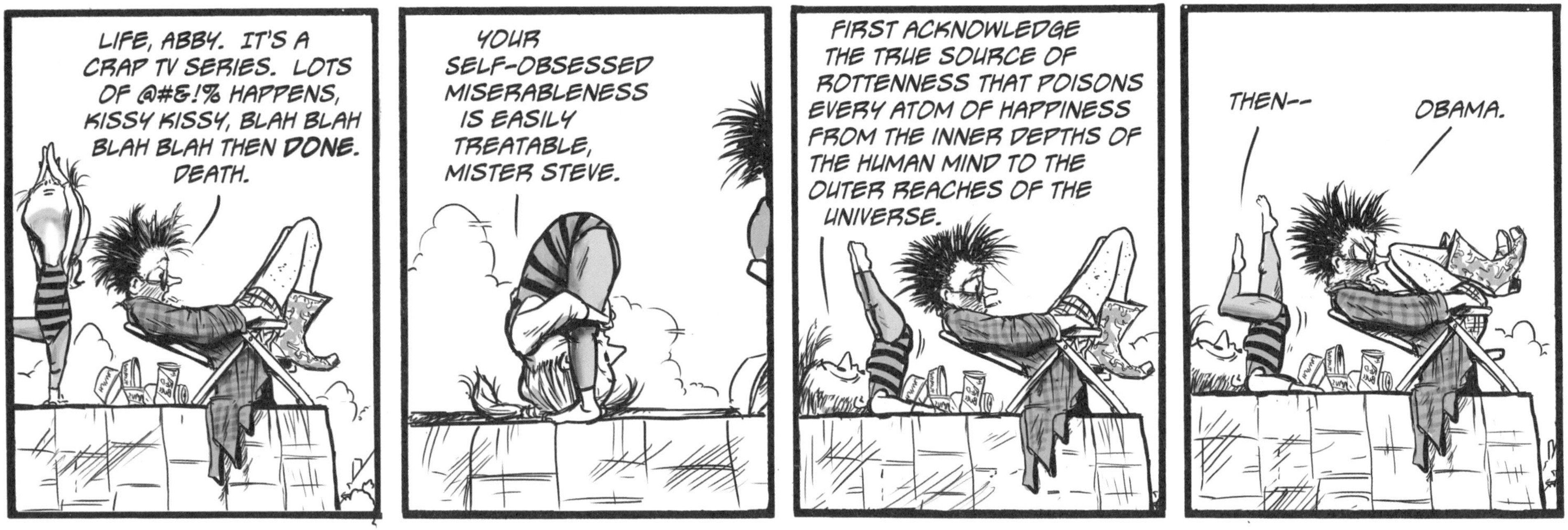
LIFE, ABBY. IT'S A CRAP TV SERIES. LOTS OF @#&!% HAPPENS, KISSY KISSY, BLAH BLAH BLAH BLAH THEN DONE. DEATH.
YOUR SELF-OBSESSED MISERABLENESS IS EASILY TREATABLE, MISTER STEVE.
FIRST ACKNOWLEDGE THE TRUE SOURCE OF ROTTENNESS THAT POISONS EVERY ATOM OF HAPPINESS FROM THE INNER DEPTHS OF THE HUMAN MIND TO THE OUTER REACHES OF THE UNIVERSE.
THEN--
OBAMA.

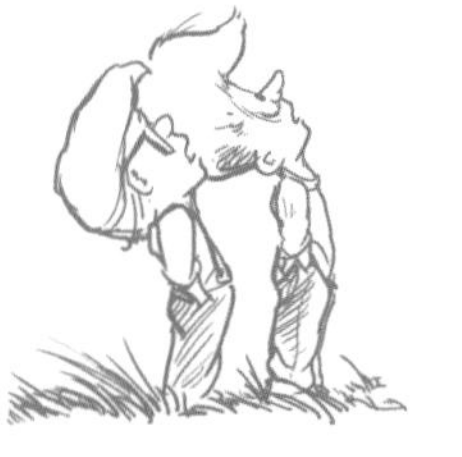

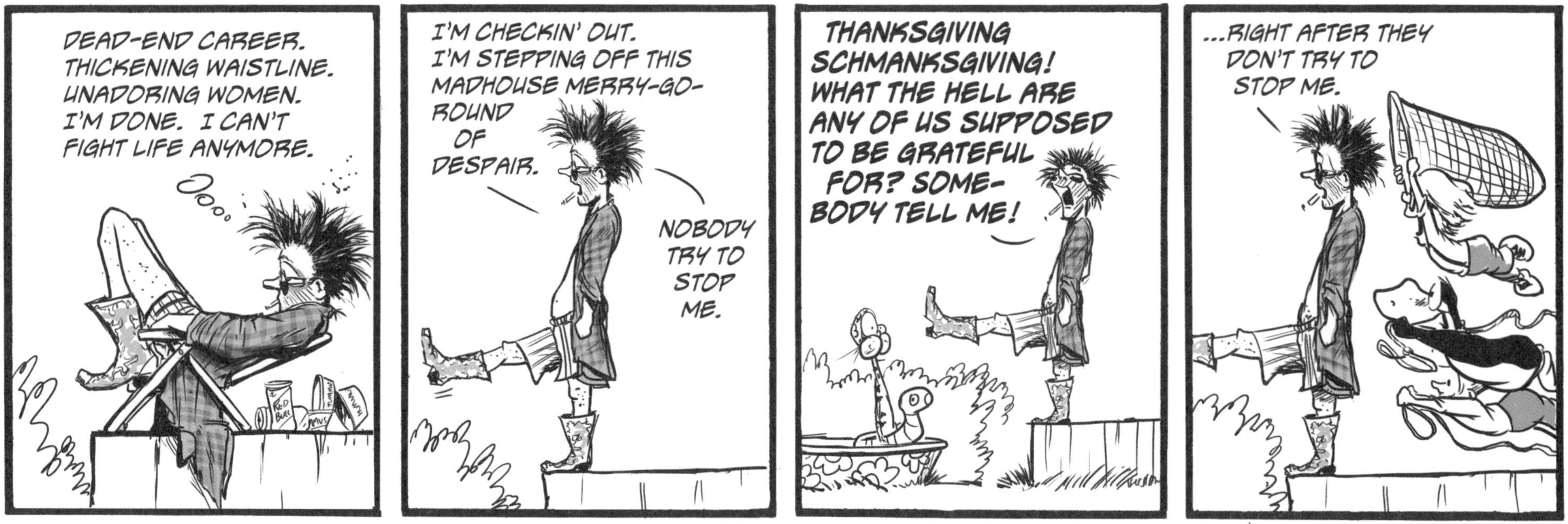
DEAD-END CAREER. THICKENING WAISTLINE. UNADORING WOMEN. I'M DONE. I CAN'T FIGHT LIFE ANYMORE.
I'M CHECKIN' OUT. I'M STEPPING OFF THIS MADHOUSE MERRY-GO-ROUND OF DESPAIR.
NOBODY TRY TO STOP ME.
THANKSGIVING SCHMANKSGIVING! WHAT THE HELL ARE ANY OF US SUPPOSED TO BE GRATEFUL FOR? SOME-BODY TELL ME!
...RIGHT AFTER THEY DON'T TRY TO STOP ME.

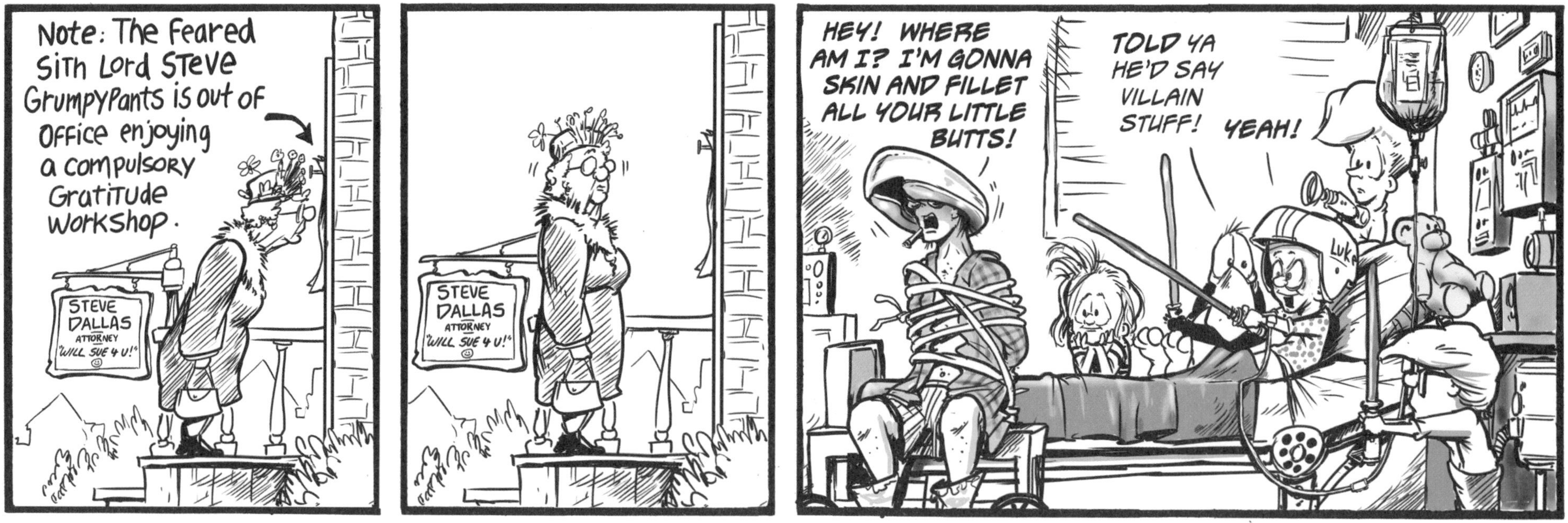
Note: The Feared Sith Lord Steve GrumpyPants is out of Office enjoying a compulsory Gratitude Workshop.
STEVE DALLAS ATTORNEY "WILL SUE 4 U!"
STEVE DALLAS ATTORNEY "WILL SUE 4 U!"
HEY! WHERE AM I? I'M GONNA SKIN AND FILLET ALL YOUR LITTLE BUTTS!
TOLD YA HE'D SAY VILLAIN STUFF!
YEAH!
LUKE

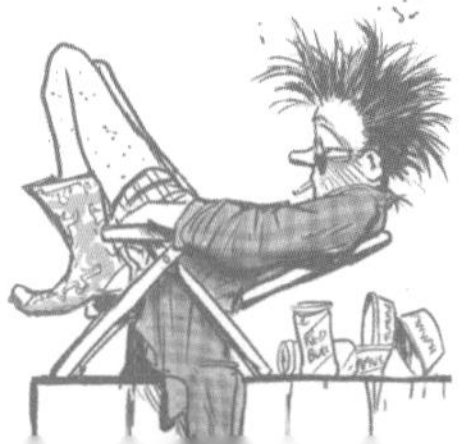

Bloom County 2015
by Berkeley Breathed
ONE OF YOU LITTLE CRIMINAL TYKES UNTIE ME! AND GET THIS THING OFF MY HEAD!
I WAS BUSY AND HAPPY WALLOWING IN SELF-PITY. WHY WAS THAT INTERRUPTED?
AND WHO IS THAT?
SAM THE LION. A JEDI BATTLING IMPERIAL WHITE BLOOD CELL DRONES. HE'S TRYING TO GET BACK TO THE BEDROOM PLANET "HOME" IN THE ELM STREET SYSTEM.

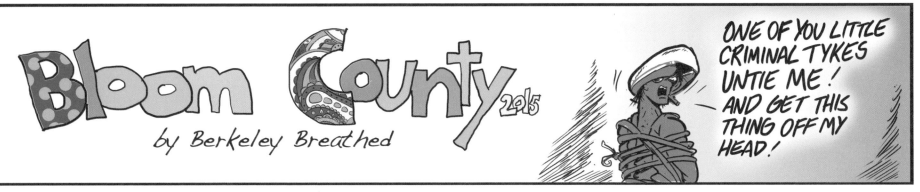

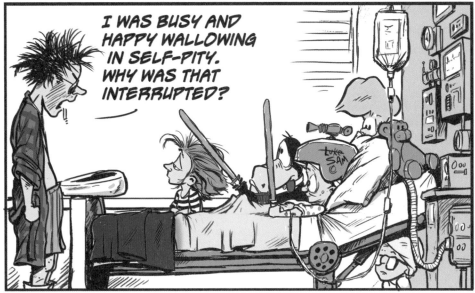

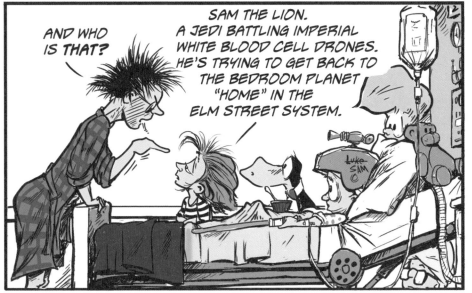

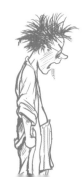

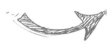

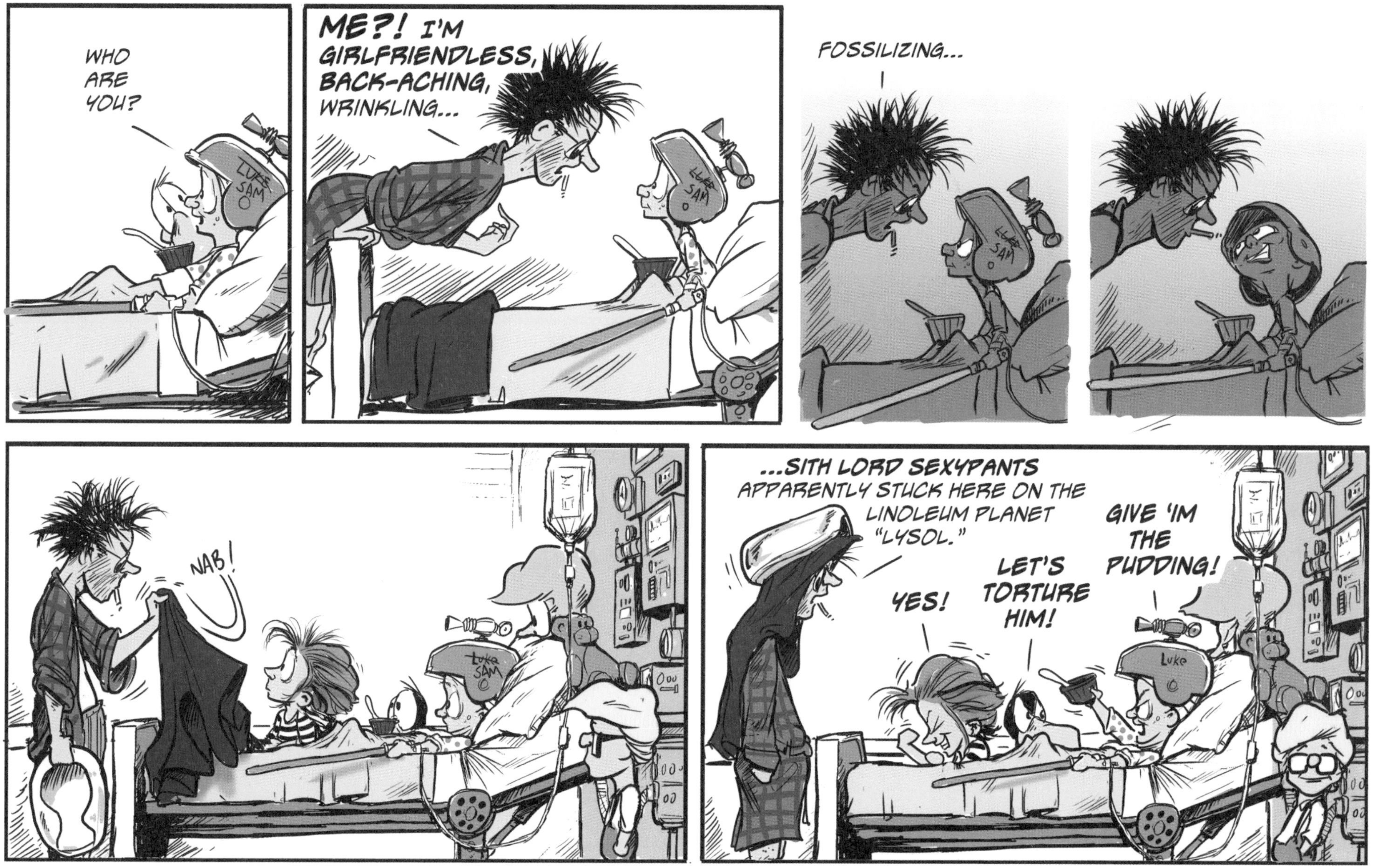
WHO ARE YOU?
ME?! I'M GIRLFRIENDLESS, BACK-ACHING, WRINKLING...
FOSSILIZING...
NAB!
...SITH LORD SEXYPANTS APPARENTLY STUCK HERE ON THE LINOLEUM PLANET "LYSOL."
YES!
LET'S TORTURE HIM!
GIVE 'IM THE PUDDING!

Mr. Breathed, on behalf of cancer patients, you have outdone yourself by not only creating laughter, which is the best medicine, but also introducing a new character in addition by having Steve Dallas transform into the Sith Lord of Sexypants. Good job!

—Alan Mortensen

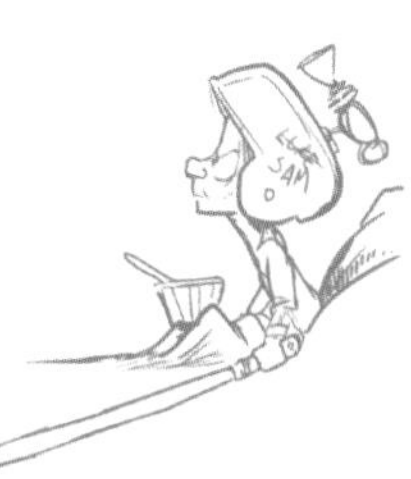

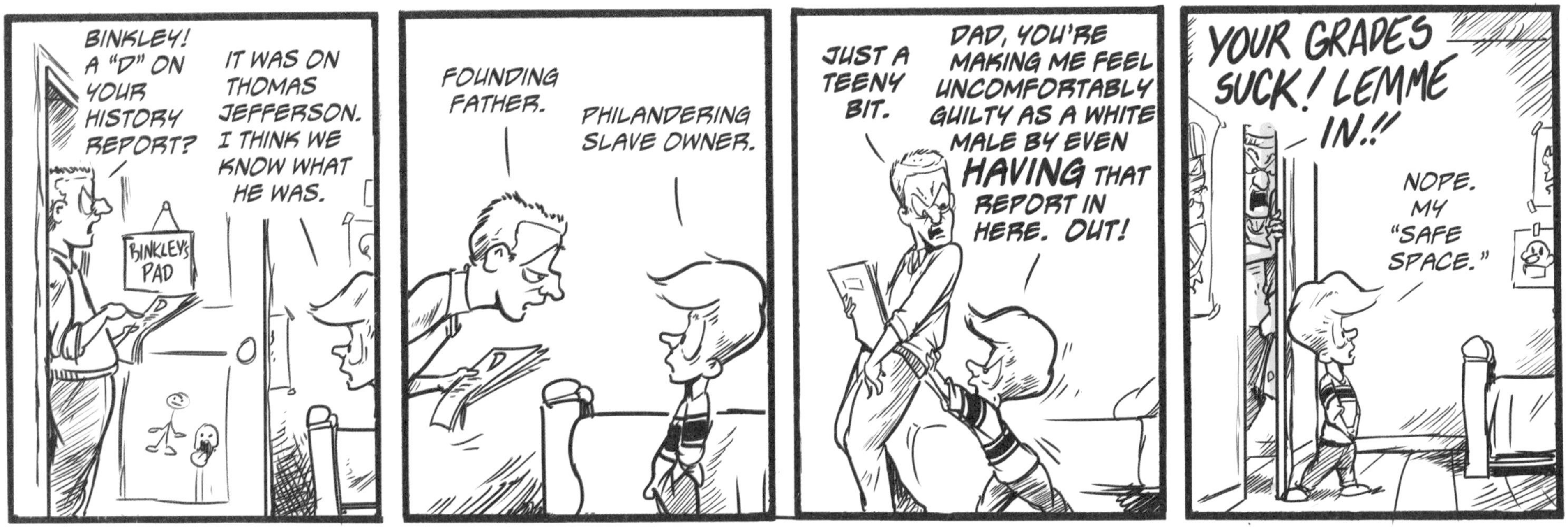
BINKLEY! A "D" ON YOUR HISTORY REPORT?
IT WAS ON THOMAS JEFFERSON. I THINK WE KNOW WHAT HE WAS.
BINKLEY'S PAD
FOUNDING FATHER.
PHILANDERING SLAVE OWNER.
JUST A TEENY BIT.
DAD, YOU'RE MAKING ME FEEL UNCOMFORTABLY GUILTY AS A WHITE MALE BY EVEN HAVING THAT REPORT IN HERE. OUT!
YOUR GRADES SUCK! LEMME IN.!!
NOPE. MY "SAFE SPACE."

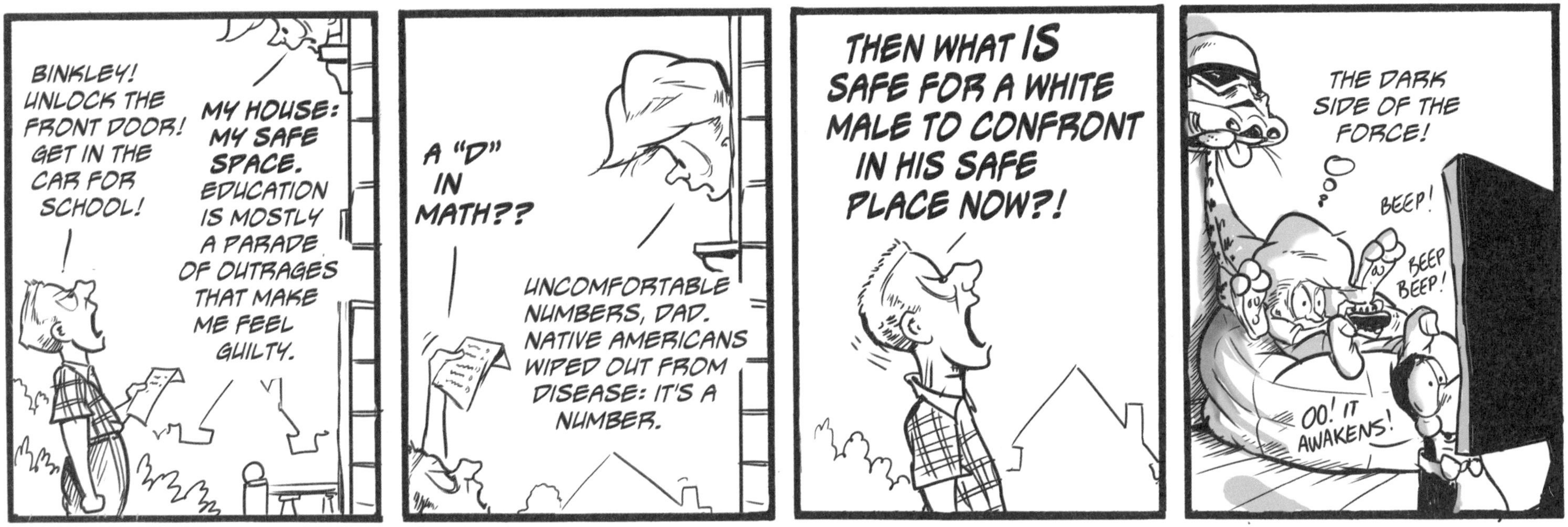
BINKLEY! UNLOCK THE FRONT DOOR! GET IN THE CAR FOR SCHOOL!
MY HOUSE: MY SAFE SPACE. EDUCATION IS MOSTLY A PARADE OF OUTRAGES THAT MAKE ME FEEL GUILTY.
A "D" IN MATH??
UNCOMFORTABLE NUMBERS, DAD. NATIVE AMERICANS WIPED OUT FROM DISEASE: IT'S A NUMBER.
THEN WHAT IS SAFE FOR A WHITE MALE TO CONFRONT IN HIS SAFE PLACE NOW?!
THE DARK SIDE OF THE FORCE!
BEEP!
BEEP BEEP!
OO! IT AWAKENS!

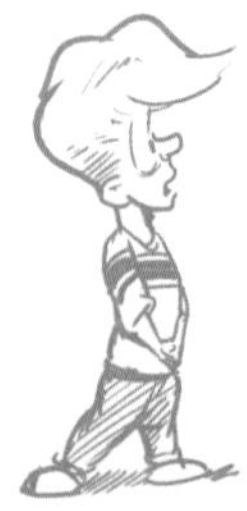

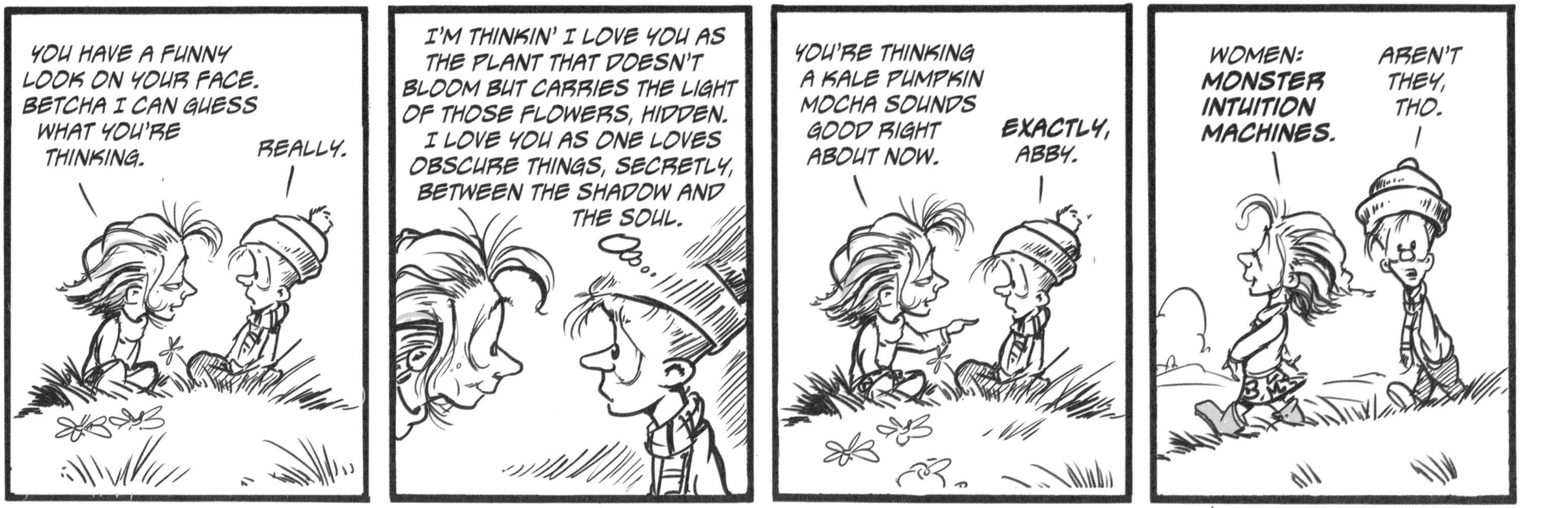
YOU HAVE A FUNNY LOOK ON YOUR FACE. BETCHA I CAN GUESS WHAT YOU'RE THINKING.
REALLY.
I'M THINKIN' I LOVE YOU AS THE PLANT THAT DOESN'T BLOOM BUT CARRIES THE LIGHT OF THOSE FLOWERS, HIDDEN. I LOVE YOU AS ONE LOVES OBSCURE THINGS, SECRETLY, BETWEEN THE SHADOW AND THE SOUL.
YOU'RE THINKING A KALE PUMPKIN MOCHA SOUNDS GOOD RIGHT ABOUT NOW.
EXACTLY, ABBY.
WOMEN: MONSTER INTUITION MACHINES.
AREN'T THEY, THO.

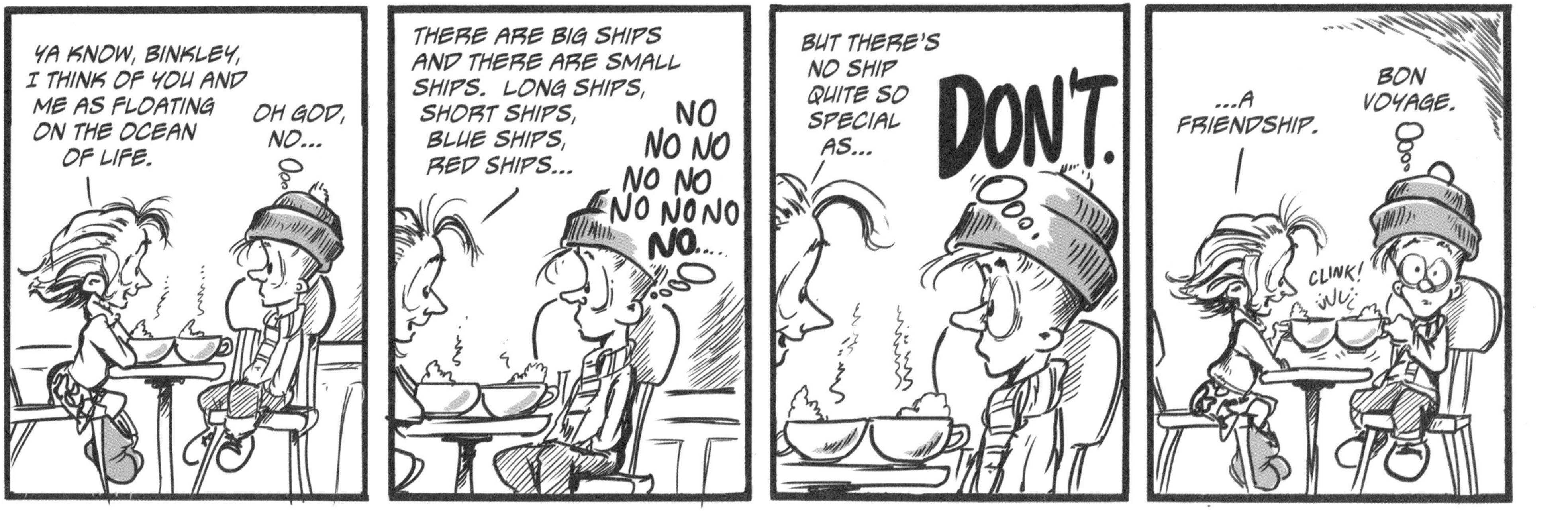
YA KNOW, BINKLEY, I THINK OF YOU AND ME AS FLOATING ON THE OCEAN OF LIFE.
OH GOD, NO...
THERE ARE BIG SHIPS AND THERE ARE SMALL SHIPS. LONG SHIPS, SHORT SHIPS, BLUE SHIPS, RED SHIPS...
NO NO NO NO NO NO NO NO NO...
BUT THERE'S NO SHIP QUITE SO SPECIAL AS...
DON'T.
...A FRIENDSHIP.
BON VOYAGE.
CLINK!

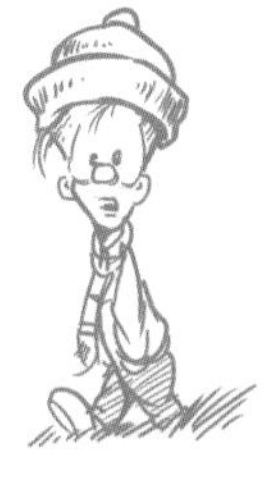

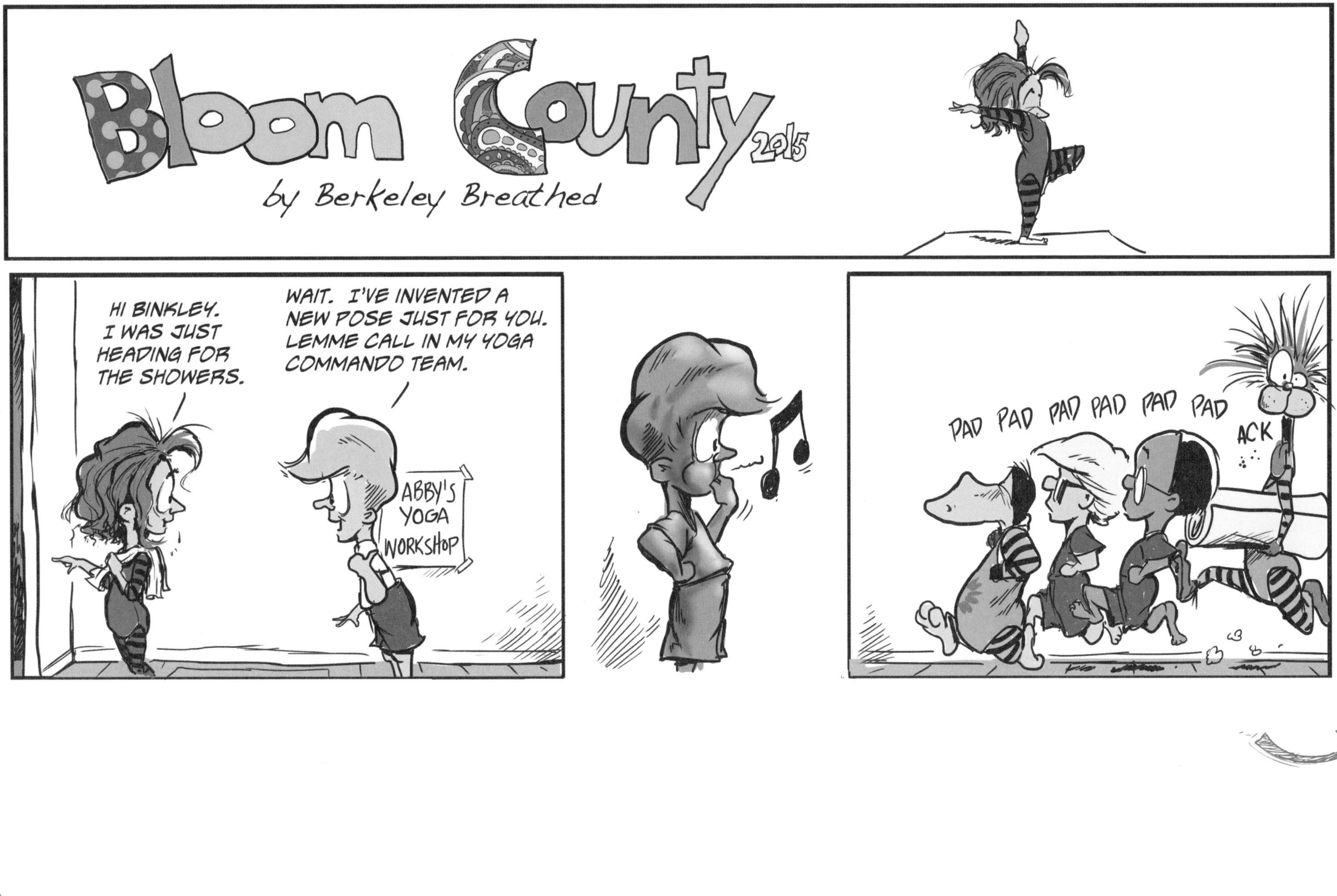
Bloom County 2015
by Berkeley Breathed
HI BINKLEY. I WAS JUST HEADING FOR THE SHOWERS.
WAIT. I'VE INVENTED A NEW POSE JUST FOR YOU. LEMME CALL IN MY YOGA COMMANDO TEAM.
ABBY'S YOGA WORKSHOP
PAD PAD PAD PAD PAD PAD
ACK

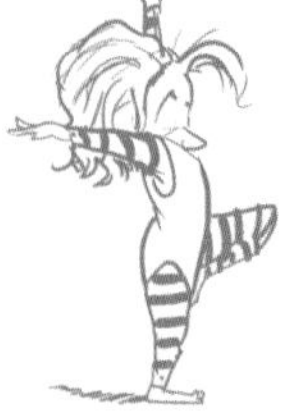

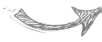

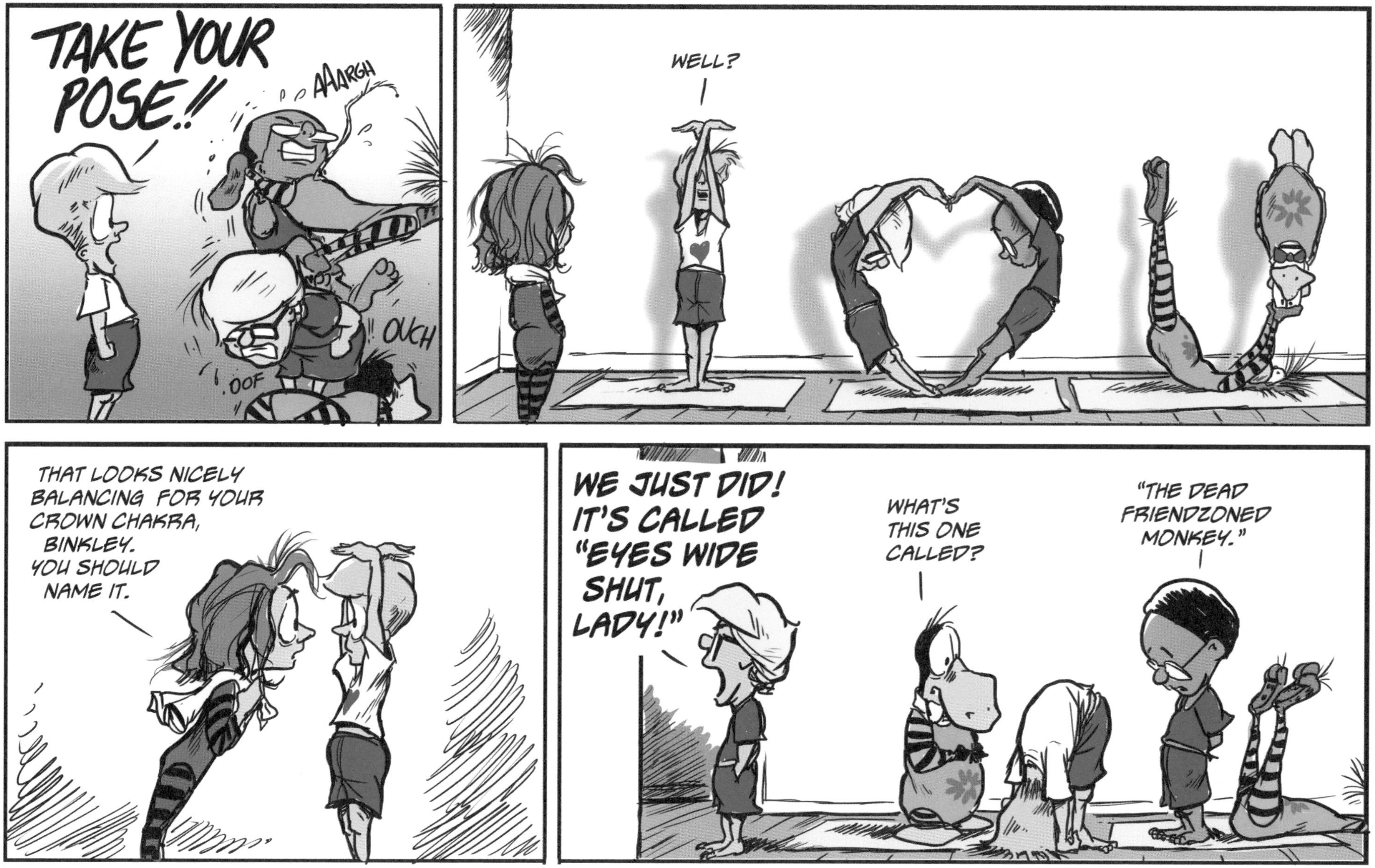
TAKE YOUR POSE.!!
AAARGH
OUCH
OOF
WELL?
THAT LOOKS NICELY BALANCING FOR YOUR CROWN CHAKRA, BINKLEY. YOU SHOULD NAME IT.
WE JUST DID! IT'S CALLED "EYES WIDE SHUT, LADY!"
WHAT'S THIS ONE CALLED?
"THE DEAD FRIENDZONED MONKEY."

Spent yesterday in outrage and shame, and now, Mr. Breathed and Opus and Abby have given me tears of relief. Yes, amen, thank you for returning a moon to say goodnight to, in the darkness of 2015.

—Donna Keller

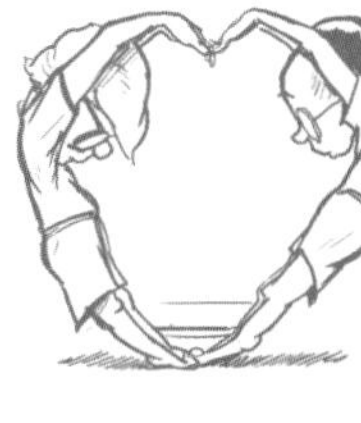

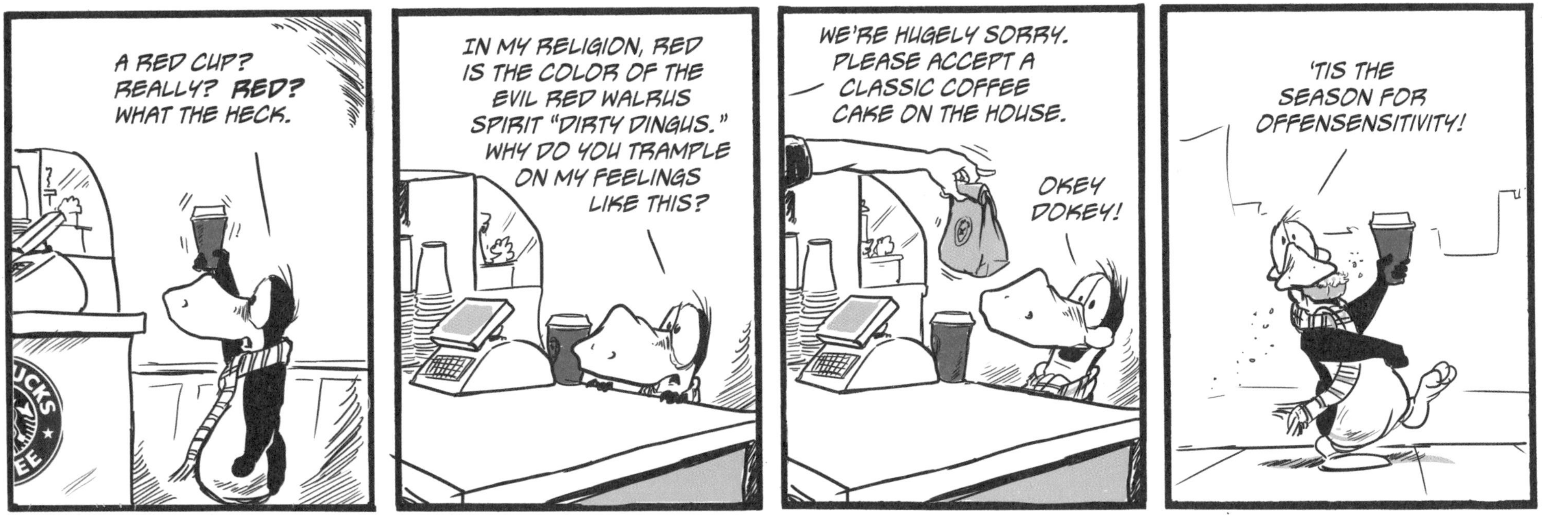
A RED CUP? REALLY? RED? WHAT THE HECK.
IN MY RELIGION, RED IS THE COLOR OF THE EVIL RED WALRUS SPIRIT "DIRTY DINGUS." WHY DO YOU TRAMPLE ON MY FEELINGS LIKE THIS?
WE'RE HUGELY SORRY. PLEASE ACCEPT A CLASSIC COFFEE CAKE ON THE HOUSE.
OKEY DOKEY!
'TIS THE SEASON FOR OFFENSENSITIVITY!

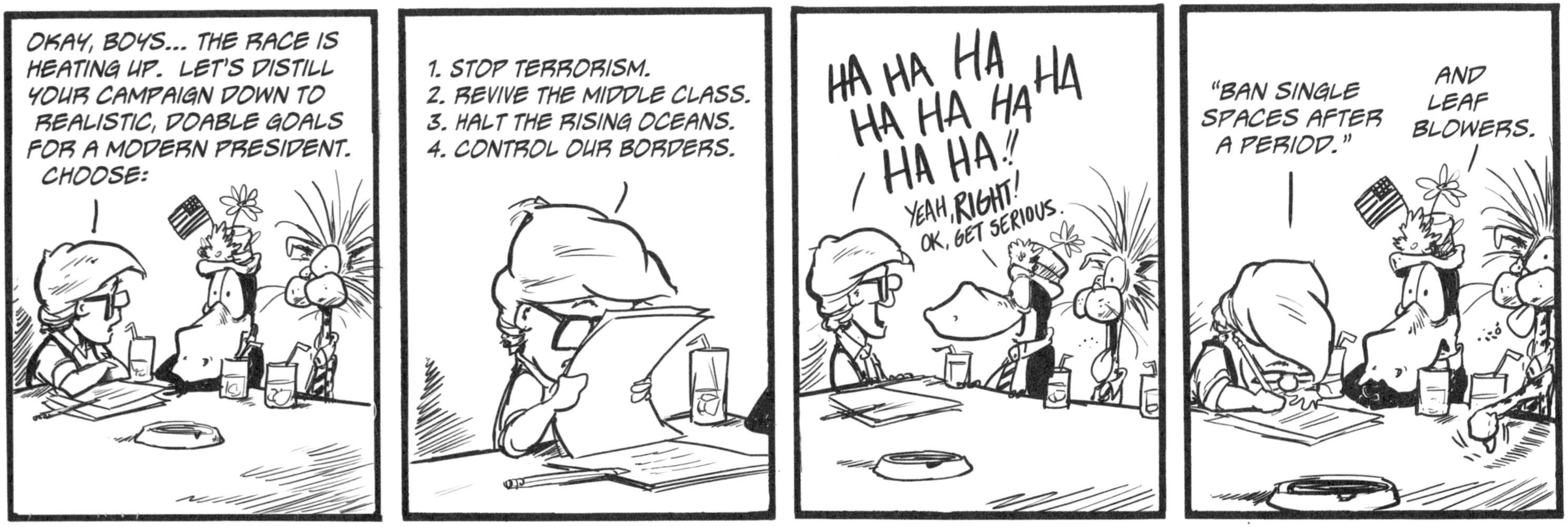
OKAY, BOYS... THE RACE IS HEATING UP. LET'S DISTILL YOUR CAMPAIGN DOWN TO REALISTIC, DOABLE GOALS FOR A MODERN PRESIDENT. CHOOSE:
1. STOP TERRORISM.
2. REVIVE THE MIDDLE CLASS.
3. HALT THE RISING OCEANS.
4. CONTROL OUR BORDERS.
HA HA HA HA HA HA HA HA HA HA!!
YEAH, RIGHT! OK, GET SERIOUS.
"BAN SINGLE SPACES AFTER A PERIOD."
AND LEAF BLOWERS.

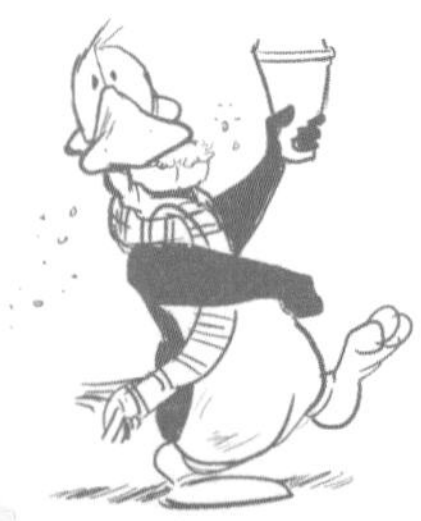

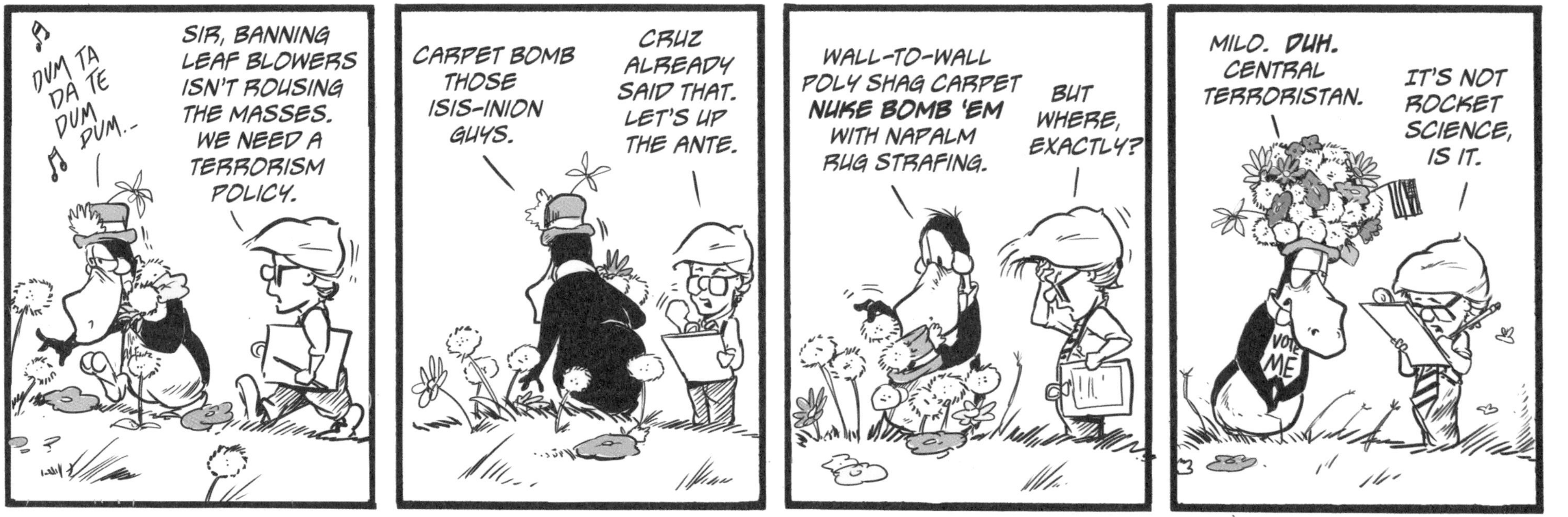
DUM TA DA TE DUM DUM..
SIR, BANNING LEAF BLOWERS ISN'T ROUSING THE MASSES. WE NEED A TERRORISM POLICY.
CARPET BOMB THOSE ISIS-INION GUYS.
CRUZ ALREADY SAID THAT. LET'S UP THE ANTE.
WALL-TO-WALL POLY SHAG CARPET NUKE BOMB 'EM WITH NAPALM RUG STRAFING.
BUT WHERE, EXACTLY?
MILO. DUH. CENTRAL TERRORISTAN.
IT'S NOT ROCKET SCIENCE, IS IT.
VOTE ME

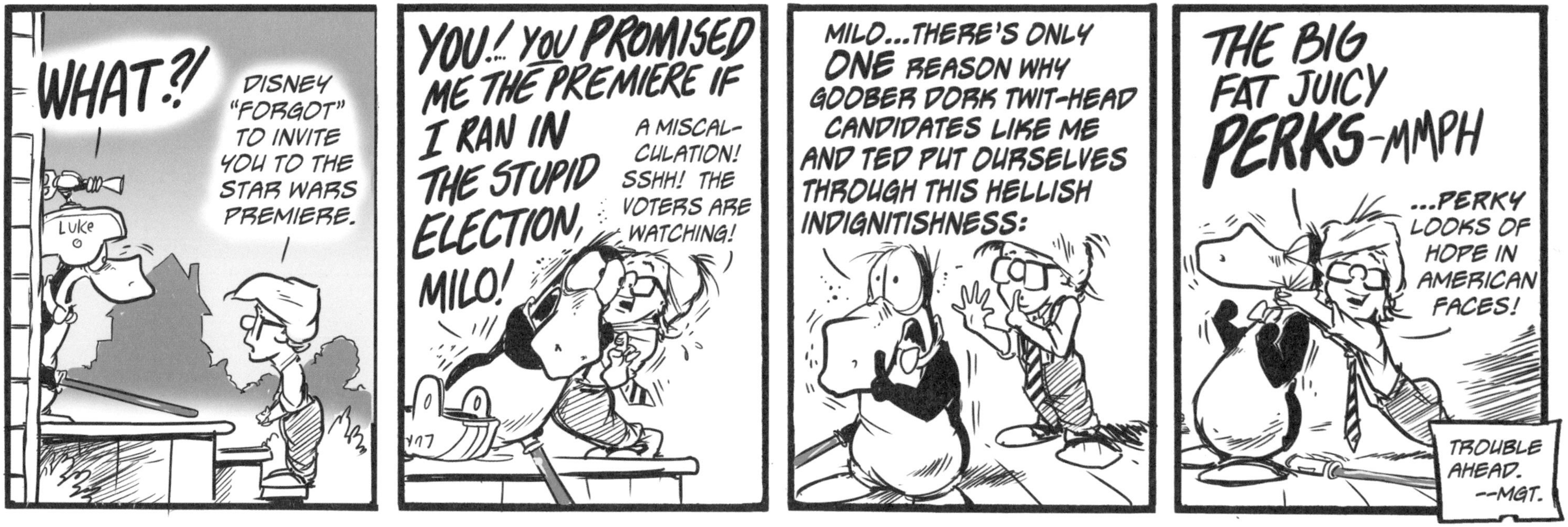
WHAT?!
DISNEY "FORGOT" TO INVITE YOU TO THE STAR WARS PREMIERE.
LUKE
YOU!.. YOU PROMISED ME THE PREMIERE IF I RAN IN THE STUPID ELECTION, MILO!
A MISCAL-CULATION! SSHH! THE VOTERS ARE WATCHING!
MILO... THERE'S ONLY ONE REASON WHY GOOBER DORK TWIT-HEAD CANDIDATES LIKE ME AND TED PUT OURSELVES THROUGH THIS HELLISH INDIGNITISHNESS:
THE BIG FAT JUICY PERKS-MMPH
...PERKY LOOKS OF HOPE IN AMERICAN FACES!
TROUBLE AHEAD. --MGT.

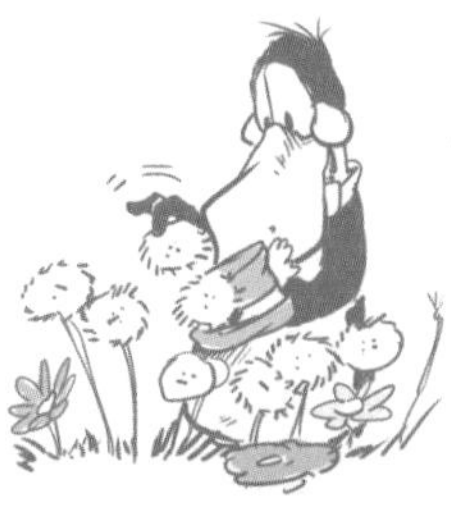

92

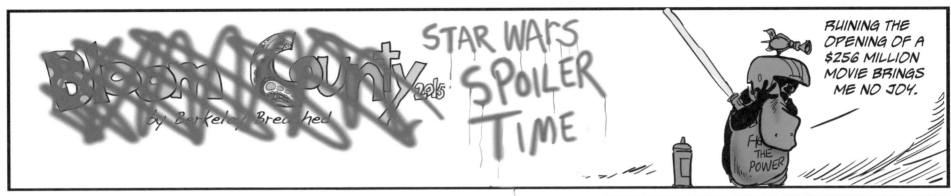

Bloom County 2015
by Berkeley Breathed
STAR WARS SPOILER TIME
RUINING THE OPENING OF A $256 MILLION MOVIE BRINGS ME NO JOY.
FIGHT THE POWER
IT'S DISNEY, THE GALACTIC CORPORATE EMPIRE. THEY'LL STOP YOU, OPUS.
INCONCEIBABLE!! LET 'EM TRY!! WE'RE ON SOCIAL MEDIA, BABY! THE UNTOUCHABLE REBEL ALLIANCE OF FREEDOM AND AUTOMINY!!
I GOT THE EXPLOSIVE, BOOTLEGGED, HI-RES PLOT SPOILER IMAGES RIGHT HERE!
THBBFT!
HERE YOU CAN CLEARLY SEE LUKE'S STINKY SMELLY SEVERED HAND ATTACHED TO [redacted]'S FOREHEAD, HOLDING [redacted]'S LITTLE SCRUBBY BRUSH.
FIGHT THE POWER

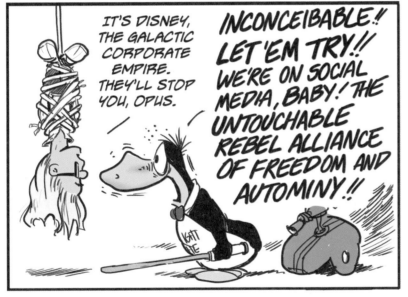

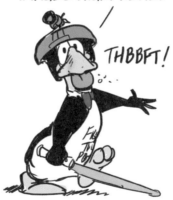

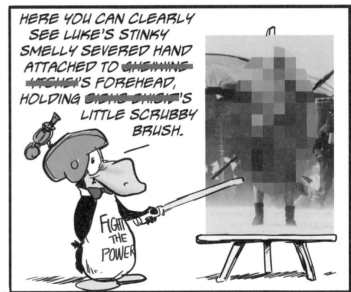

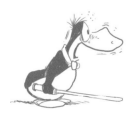

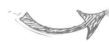

NEXT, LOOK CAREFULLY AND YOU CAN SEE THAT KYLO REN IS ACTUALLY ~~THEIR CHENEY'S~~ 'S FRATERNAL TWIN, THE LOVE CHILD OF ~~PELOSI~~.

FIGHT THE POWER

AND OOPS! HIDE THE NEXT PIC FROM GRANDMA! I HAVE ONLY THREE WORDS:

C-3POH LORDY MOSES!

FIGHT THE POWER

FACEBOOK SPOILER-BOMBING COMPLETE, MILO!! WELL, I THINK WE'VE LEARNED SOMETHING PRET-TY IMPORTANT TODAY!

GHT-HE WER

ZUCKERBERG'S ~~ASS~~ CAN BE BOUGHT.

INCONCEIBABLE.

POWER

Berkeley Breathed's *Bloom County*, you are the cream in my coffee, the milky in my way, the light in my saber…

—Darlene Click

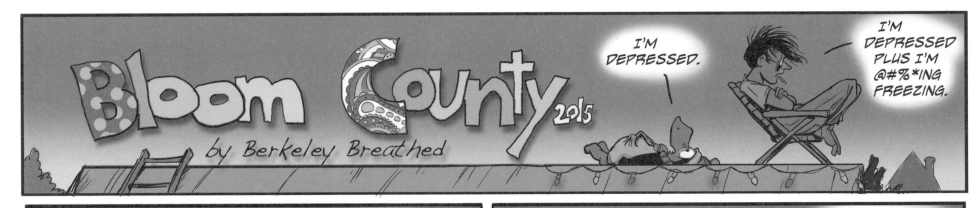

Bloom County 2015
by Berkeley Breathed

I'M DEPRESSED.

I'M DEPRESSED PLUS I'M @#%*ING FREEZING.

94

STAR WARS DIDN'T BRING AS MUCH MEANING TO MY LIFE AS I'D HOPED. I'M REALLY DEPRESSED.

I'M PAST DEPRESSION AND WELL INTO CHRISTMAS DESPONDENCY.

IT'S LIKE WE'RE LOCKED INTO SOME HORRIBLE BLEAKNESS COMPETITION.

WELL, IF YOU FIGURE OUT THE SECRET, MAGIC, COSMIC TRICK FOR HOW TO LOSE A GLOOM SWEEPSTAKES, LEMME KNOW!

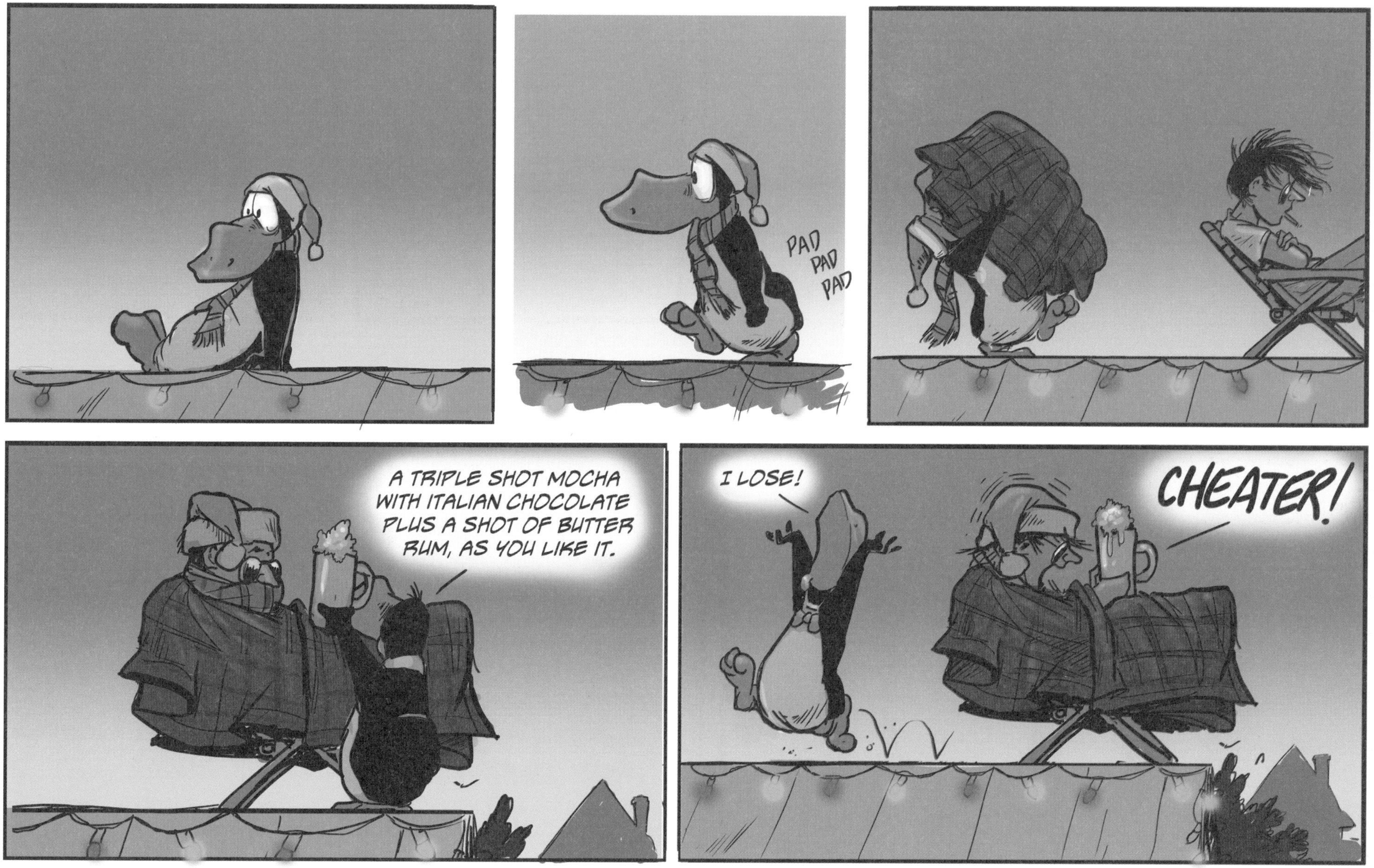
PAD
PAD
PAD
A TRIPLE SHOT MOCHA WITH ITALIAN CHOCOLATE PLUS A SHOT OF BUTTER RUM, AS YOU LIKE IT.
I LOSE!
CHEATER!

I am not only humbled by today's heartfelt strip, but by all the wonderful comments. As many have said, this is a wonderfully tender reminder of what humanity is, and from a lovely penguin. I love that the readers of the strip "get it." Good night, Opus, you sweet, sweet penguin.

—Didi McPhillips

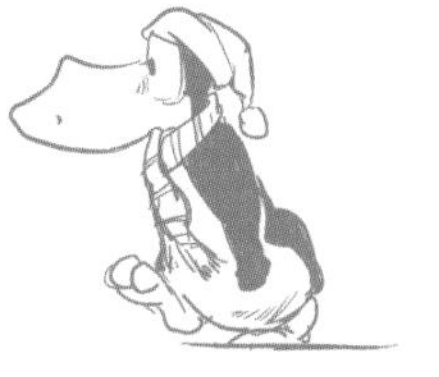

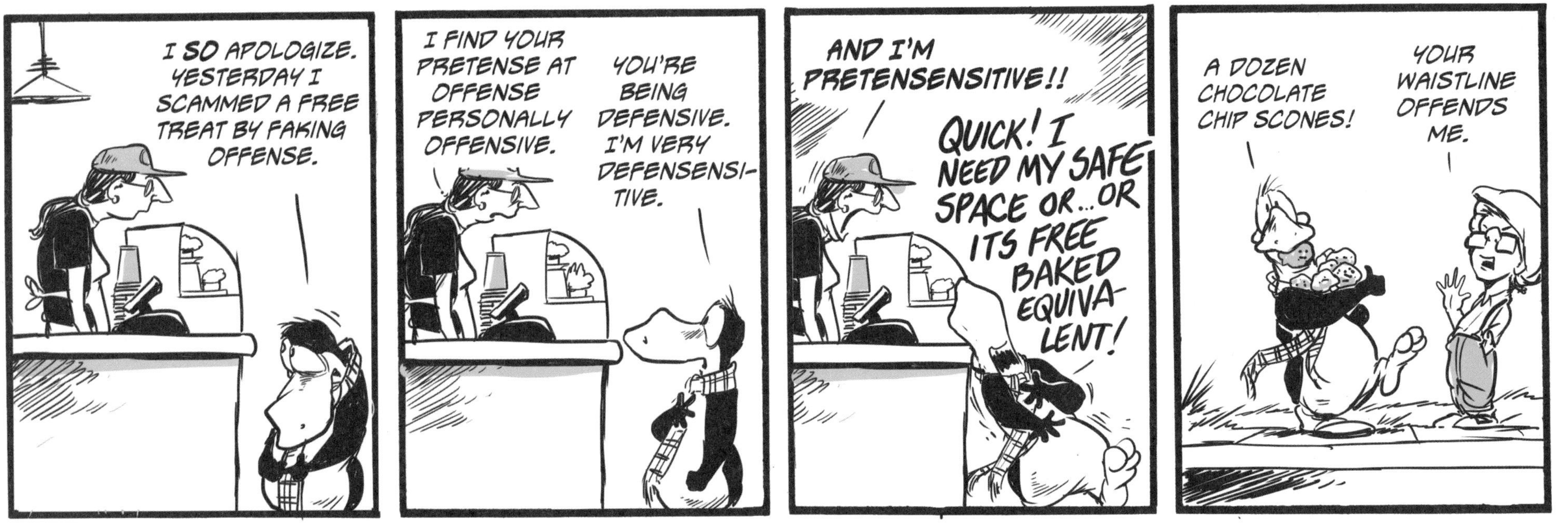
I SO APOLOGIZE. YESTERDAY I SCAMMED A FREE TREAT BY FAKING OFFENSE.
I FIND YOUR PRETENSE AT OFFENSE PERSONALLY OFFENSIVE.
YOU'RE BEING DEFENSIVE. I'M VERY DEFENSENSI-TIVE.
AND I'M PRETENSENSITIVE!!
QUICK! I NEED MY SAFE SPACE OR...OR ITS FREE BAKED EQUIVA-LENT!
A DOZEN CHOCOLATE CHIP SCONES!
YOUR WAISTLINE OFFENDS ME.

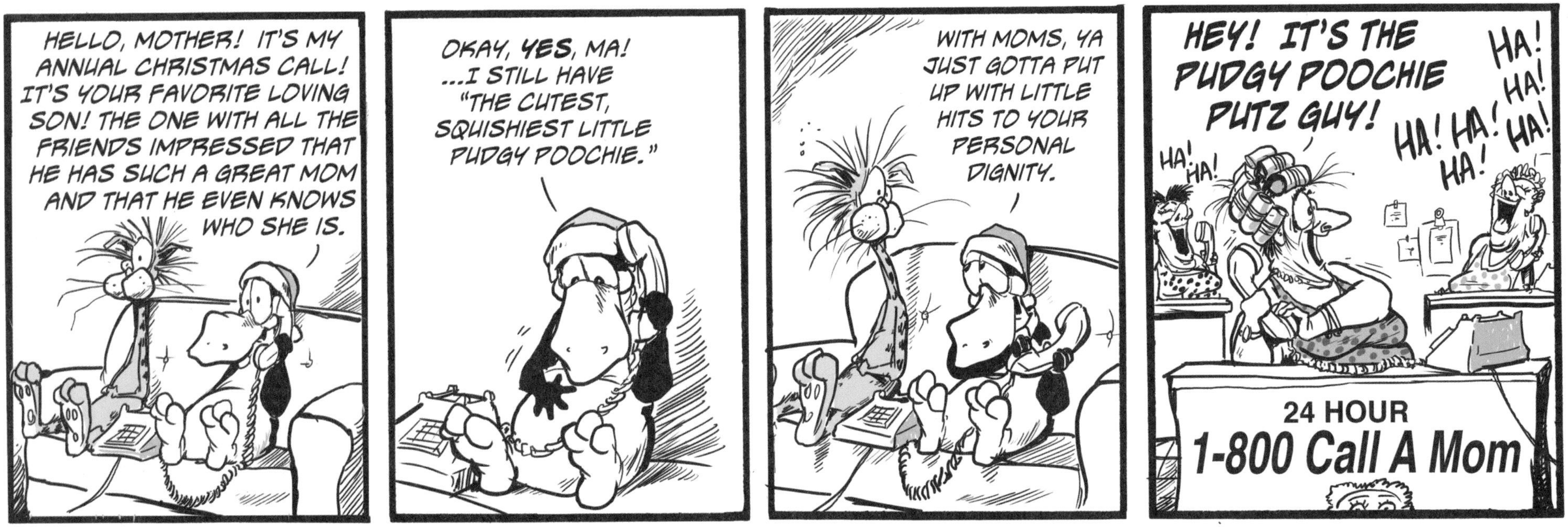
HELLO, MOTHER! IT'S MY ANNUAL CHRISTMAS CALL! IT'S YOUR FAVORITE LOVING SON! THE ONE WITH ALL THE FRIENDS IMPRESSED THAT HE HAS SUCH A GREAT MOM AND THAT HE EVEN KNOWS WHO SHE IS.
OKAY, YES, MA! ...I STILL HAVE "THE CUTEST, SQUISHIEST LITTLE PUDGY POOCHIE."
WITH MOMS, YA JUST GOTTA PUT UP WITH LITTLE HITS TO YOUR PERSONAL DIGNITY.
HEY! IT'S THE PUDGY POOCHIE PUTZ GUY!
HA! HA!
HA! HA! HA!
HA! HA! HA!
24 HOUR
1-800 Call A Mom

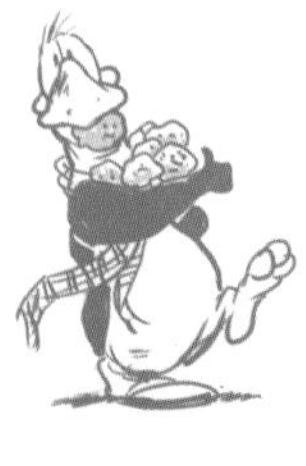

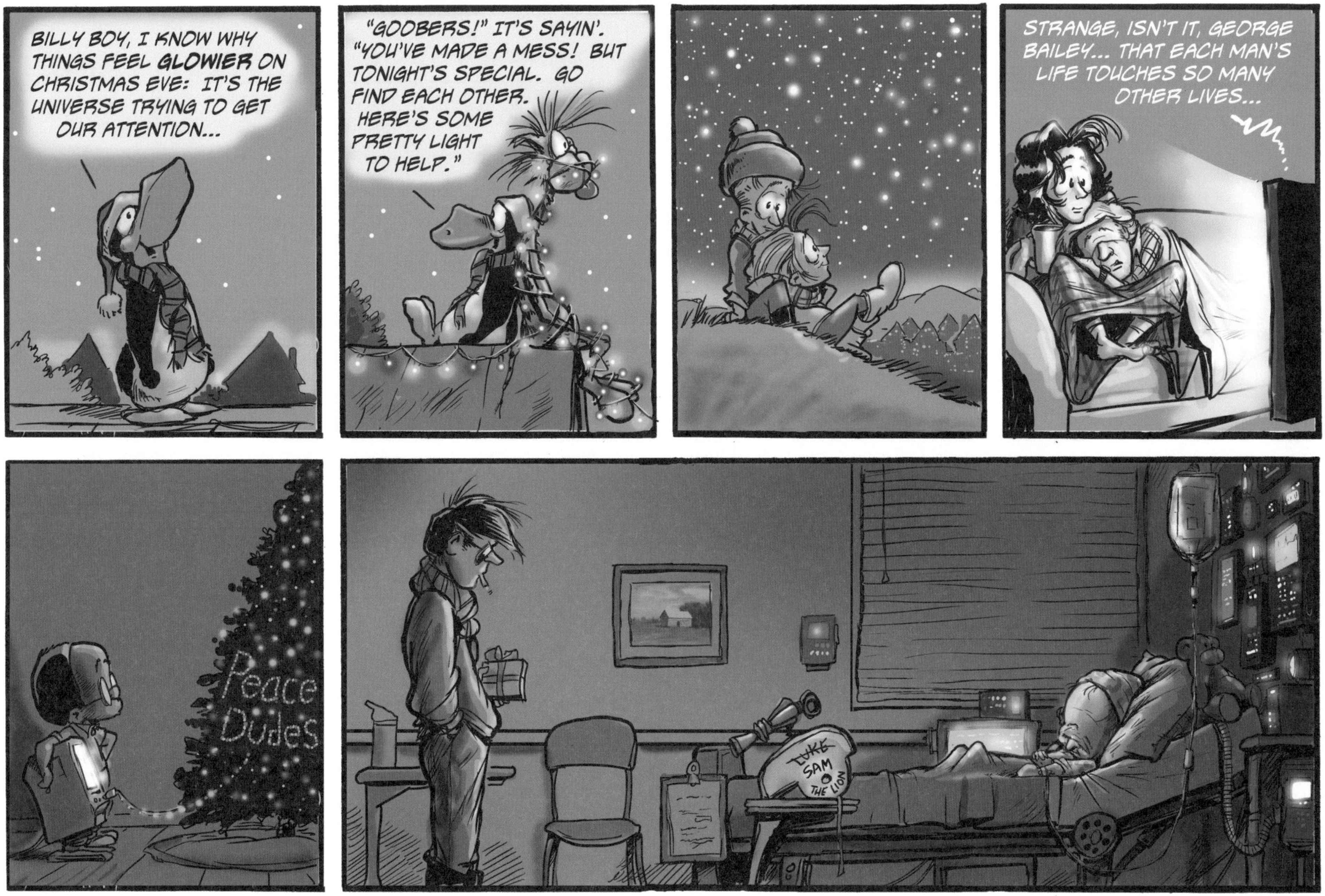
BILLY BOY, I KNOW WHY THINGS FEEL **GLOWIER** ON CHRISTMAS EVE: IT'S THE UNIVERSE TRYING TO GET OUR ATTENTION...
"GOOBERS!" IT'S SAYIN'. "YOU'VE MADE A MESS! BUT TONIGHT'S SPECIAL. GO FIND EACH OTHER. HERE'S SOME PRETTY LIGHT TO HELP."
STRANGE, ISN'T IT, GEORGE BAILEY... THAT EACH MAN'S LIFE TOUCHES SO MANY OTHER LIVES...
Peace Dudes
~~LUKE~~
SAM
THE LION

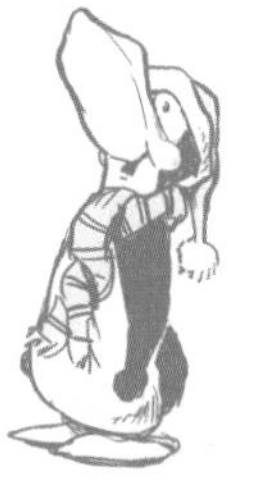

Bloom County 2015
by Berkeley Breathed
HELLO!? 9-1-1? I'VE BEEN BURGLED!!
Sam the LION
STAY OUT WOOKIES OK
MY SON'S ROOM HAS BEEN CLEANED OUT!! POSTERS! TOYS! MODELS! THE ROCKET BED I MADE HIM! GONE!!
Sam the LION
HE'S BEEN AT BLOOM COUNTY MEMORIAL FOR FIVE WEEKS AND HAD A MISERABLE PROCEDURE YESTERDAY. I CAME BACK FOR SOME SLEEP AND I GET UP TO FIND THIS!!

98

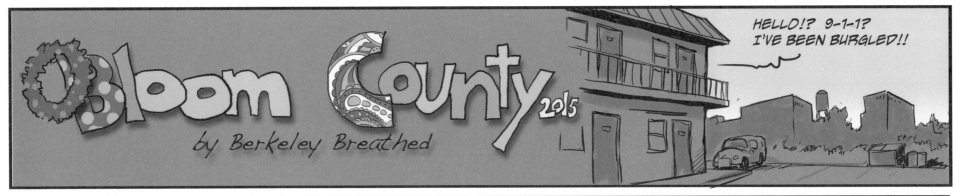

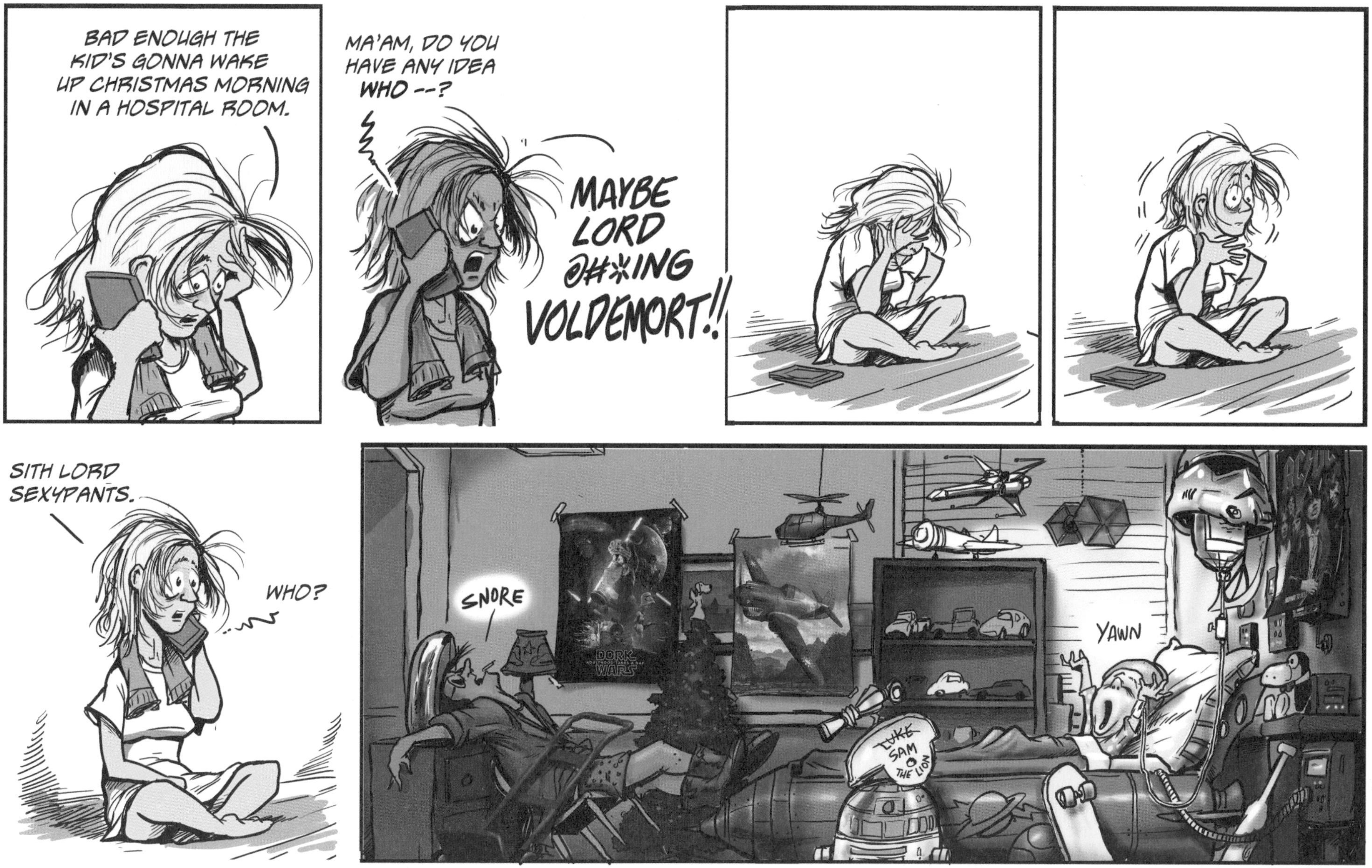
BAD ENOUGH THE KID'S GONNA WAKE UP CHRISTMAS MORNING IN A HOSPITAL ROOM.
MA'AM, DO YOU HAVE ANY IDEA WHO --?
MAYBE LORD @#*ING VOLDEMORT!!
SITH LORD SEXYPANTS.
WHO?
SNORE
DORK WARS
LUKE SAM THE LION
YAWN

Bloom County is more than a simple comic strip to me. It evokes emotion and it ignites thought processes that force me to think outside of my own little box. It has been a part of me for over 30 years and I believe I am a better person because of your influence, Mr. Breathed. Thank you & Merry Christmas.

Crap, someone's cutting onions in here again…

—Dion Vansevenant

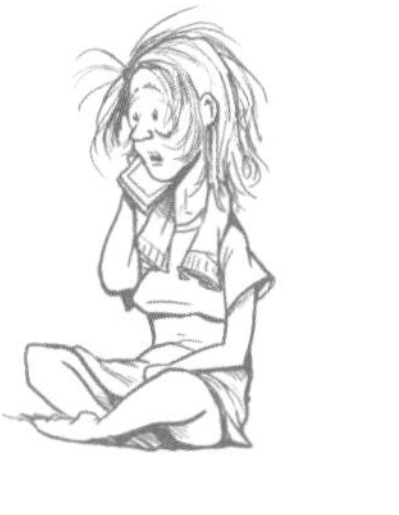

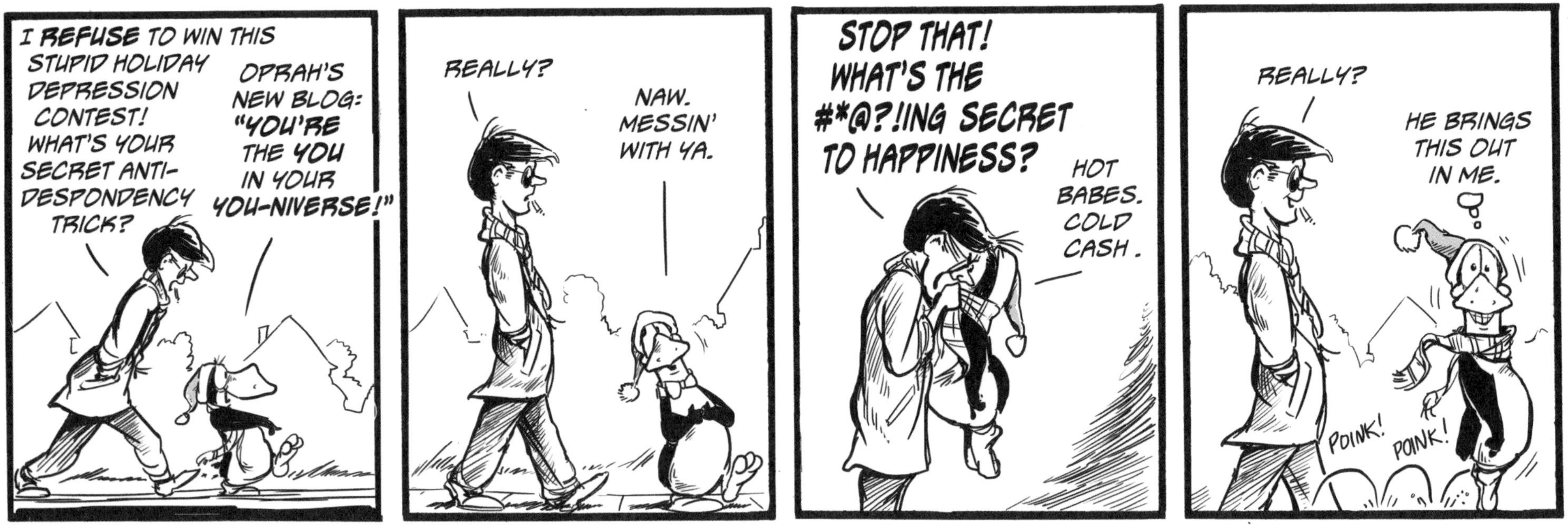
I **REFUSE** TO WIN THIS STUPID HOLIDAY DEPRESSION CONTEST! WHAT'S YOUR SECRET ANTI-DESPONDENCY TRICK?
OPRAH'S NEW BLOG: "**YOU'RE** THE **YOU** IN YOUR **YOU-NIVERSE!**"
REALLY?
NAW. MESSIN' WITH YA.
STOP THAT! WHAT'S THE #*@?!ING SECRET TO HAPPINESS?
HOT BABES. COLD CASH.
REALLY?
HE BRINGS THIS OUT IN ME.
POINK!
POINK!

100

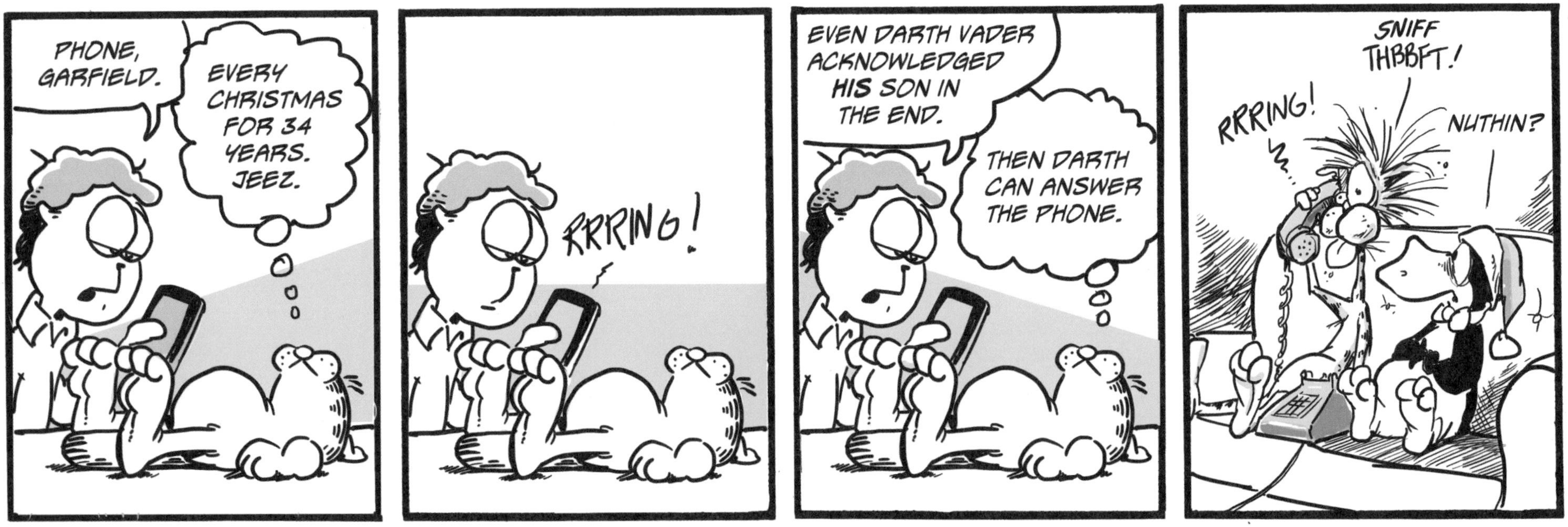
PHONE, GARFIELD.
EVERY CHRISTMAS FOR 34 YEARS. JEEZ.
RRRING!
EVEN DARTH VADER ACKNOWLEDGED **HIS** SON IN THE END.
THEN DARTH CAN ANSWER THE PHONE.
RRRING!
SNIFF THBBFT!
NUTHIN?

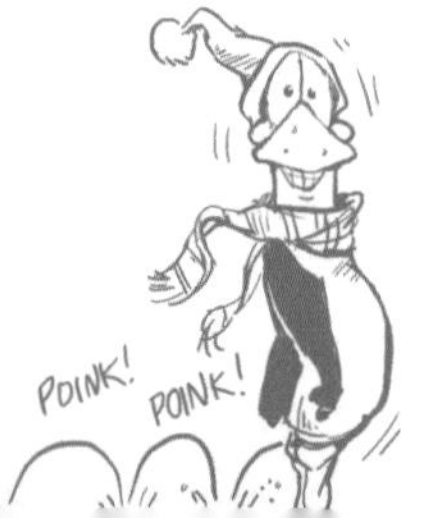
POINK!
POINK!

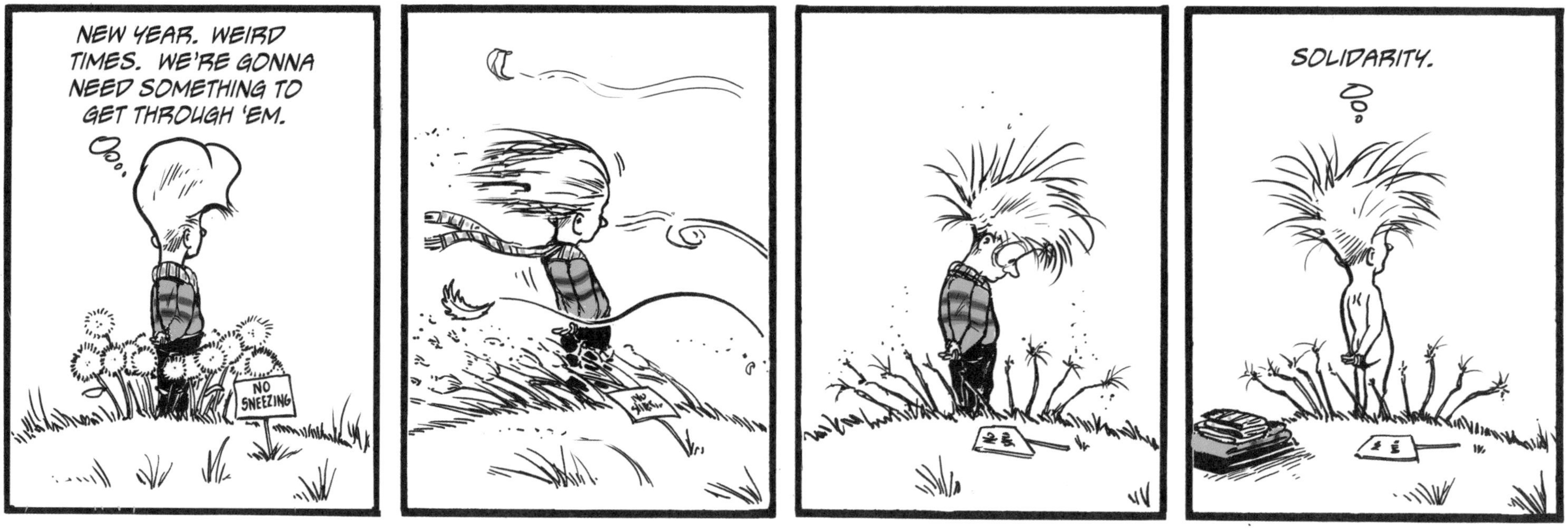
NEW YEAR. WEIRD TIMES. WE'RE GONNA NEED SOMETHING TO GET THROUGH 'EM.
NO SNEEZING
SOLIDARITY.

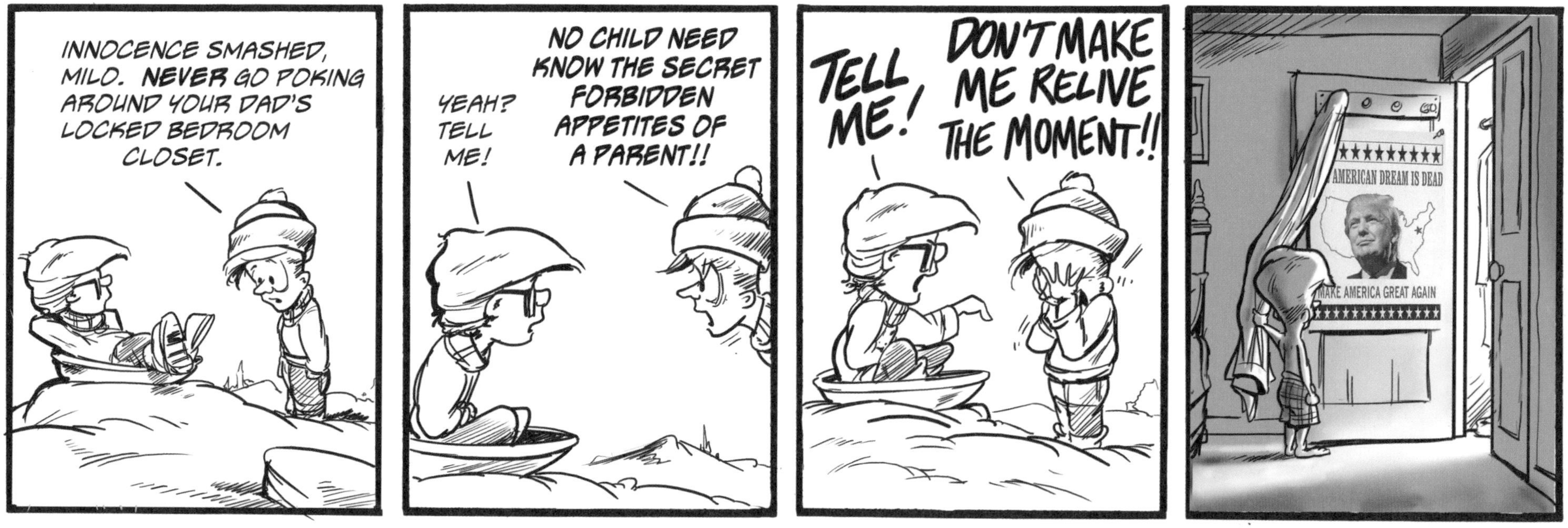
INNOCENCE SMASHED, MILO. **NEVER** GO POKING AROUND YOUR DAD'S LOCKED BEDROOM CLOSET.
YEAH? TELL ME!
NO CHILD NEED KNOW THE SECRET FORBIDDEN APPETITES OF A PARENT!!
TELL ME!
DON'T MAKE ME RELIVE THE MOMENT!!
AMERICAN DREAM IS DEAD
MAKE AMERICA GREAT AGAIN

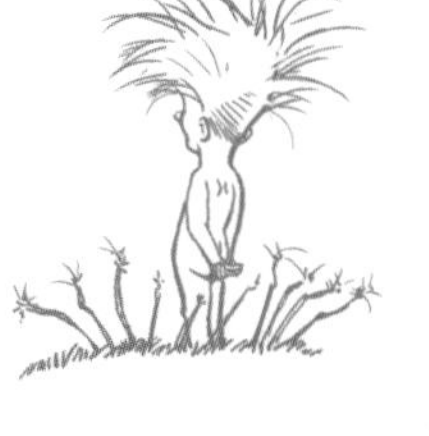

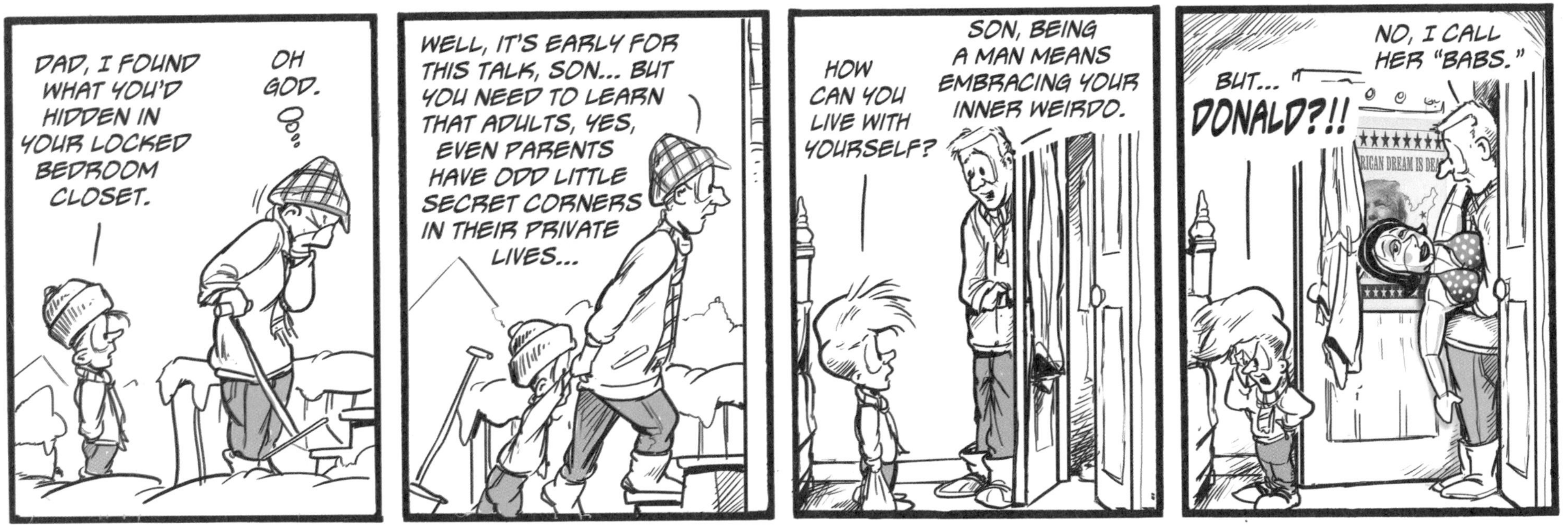
DAD, I FOUND WHAT YOU'D HIDDEN IN YOUR LOCKED BEDROOM CLOSET.
OH GOD.
WELL, IT'S EARLY FOR THIS TALK, SON... BUT YOU NEED TO LEARN THAT ADULTS, YES, EVEN PARENTS HAVE ODD LITTLE SECRET CORNERS IN THEIR PRIVATE LIVES...
HOW CAN YOU LIVE WITH YOURSELF?
SON, BEING A MAN MEANS EMBRACING YOUR INNER WEIRDO.
BUT... DONALD?!!
NO, I CALL HER "BABS."

102

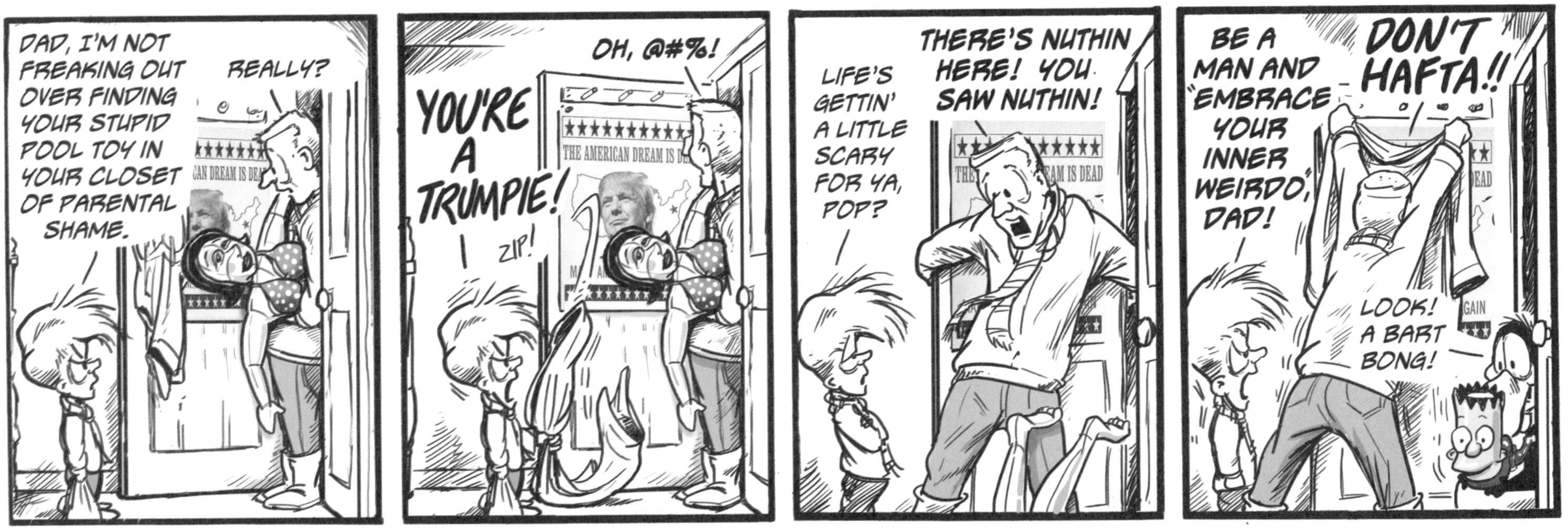
DAD, I'M NOT FREAKING OUT OVER FINDING YOUR STUPID POOL TOY IN YOUR CLOSET OF PARENTAL SHAME.
REALLY?
YOU'RE A TRUMPIE!
OH, @#%!
ZIP!
LIFE'S GETTIN' A LITTLE SCARY FOR YA, POP?
THERE'S NUTHIN HERE! YOU SAW NUTHIN!
BE A MAN AND "EMBRACE YOUR INNER WEIRDO," DAD!
DON'T HAFTA!!
LOOK! A BART BONG!

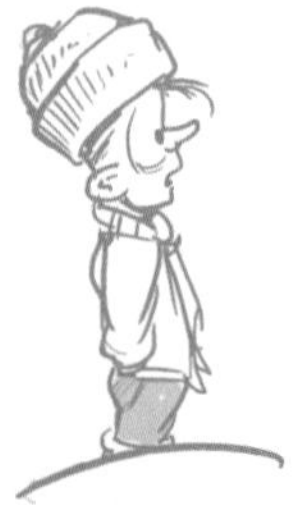

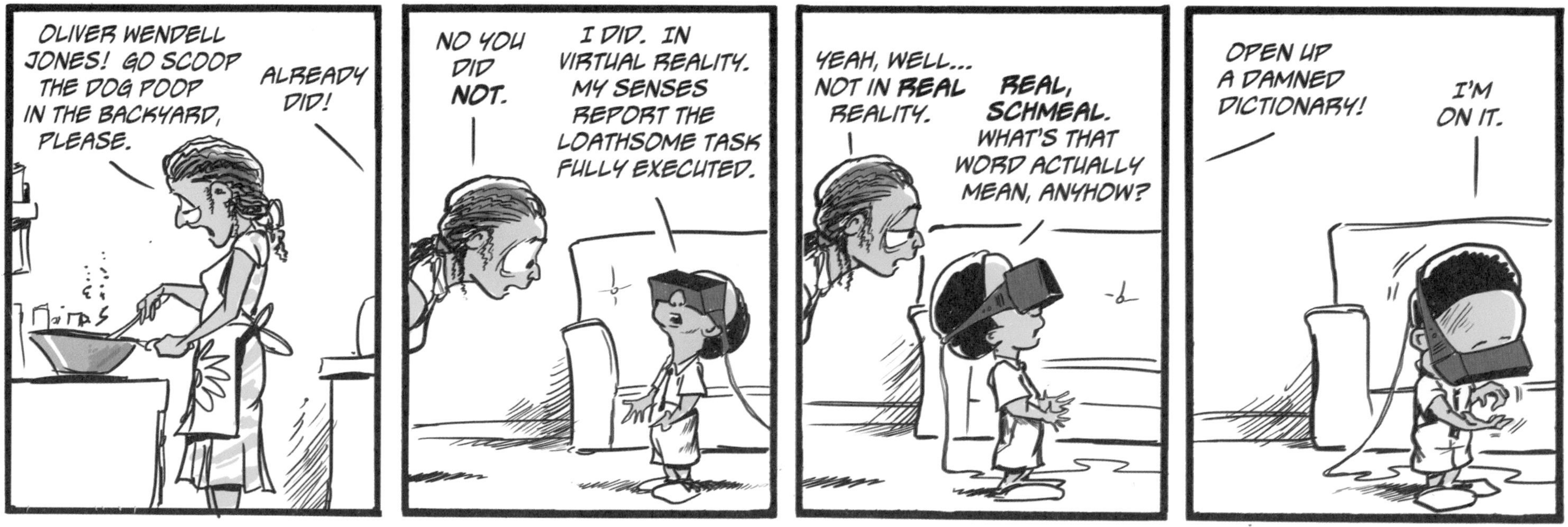
OLIVER WENDELL JONES! GO SCOOP THE DOG POOP IN THE BACKYARD, PLEASE.
ALREADY DID!
NO YOU DID **NOT**.
I DID. IN VIRTUAL REALITY. MY SENSES REPORT THE LOATHSOME TASK FULLY EXECUTED.
YEAH, WELL... NOT IN **REAL** REALITY.
REAL, SCHMEAL. WHAT'S THAT WORD ACTUALLY MEAN, ANYHOW?
OPEN UP A DAMNED DICTIONARY!
I'M ON IT.

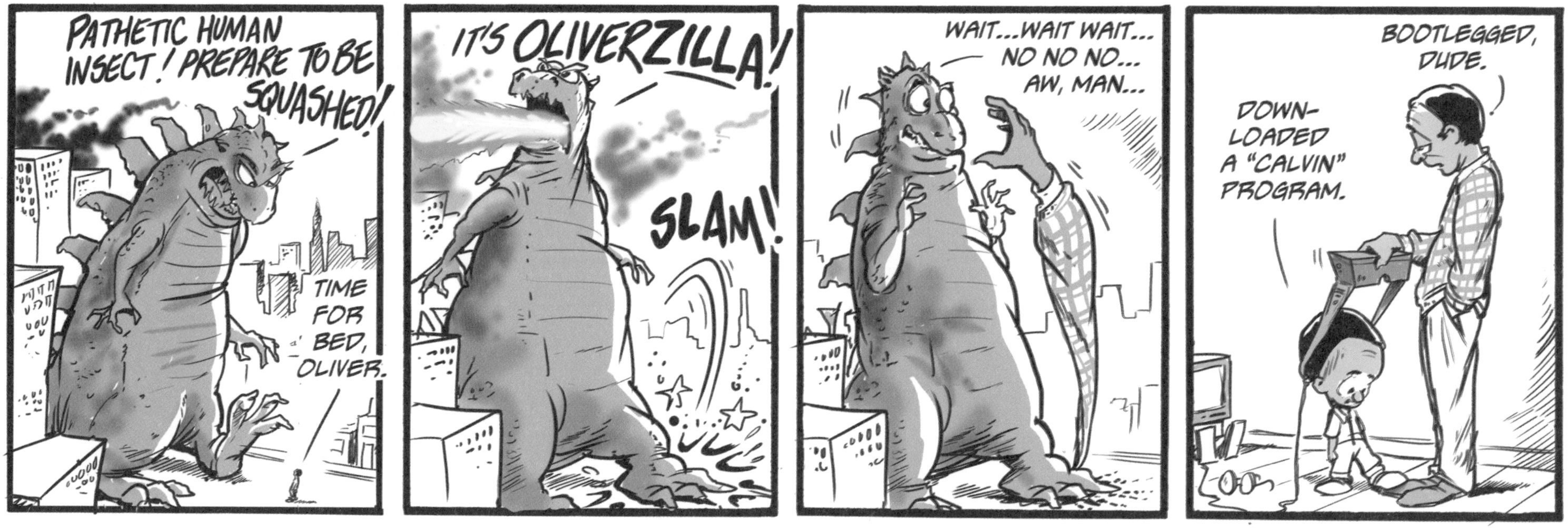
PATHETIC HUMAN INSECT! PREPARE TO BE SQUASHED!
TIME FOR BED, OLIVER.
IT'S OLIVERZILLA!
SLAM!
WAIT...WAIT WAIT... NO NO NO... AW, MAN...
BOOTLEGGED, DUDE.
DOWN-LOADED A "CALVIN" PROGRAM.

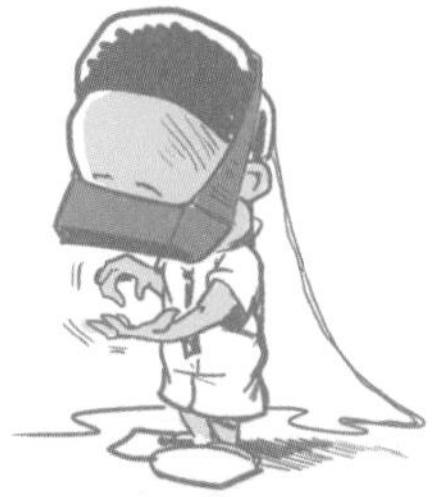

Bloom County
by Berkeley Breathed

OLIVER! GO SHOVEL THE BACK PORCH!

CAN'T, O' FOSSILIZED FATHER DUDE STUCK IN THE ANCIENT BORING "REAL" WORLD OF BORING LIMITATIONS... I'M BUSY BUILDING A FULL-SCALE MODEL OF THE TAJ MAHAL IN VIRTUAL LEGOS.

NOW I HAVE FINISHED RUNNING MY VIRTUAL 12-MINUTE MARATHON AND AM RELAXING ON MY RAFT. OH, LOOK! JENNIFER LAWRENCE IS COMING OVER FOR A FLOAT AND A CANOODLE!

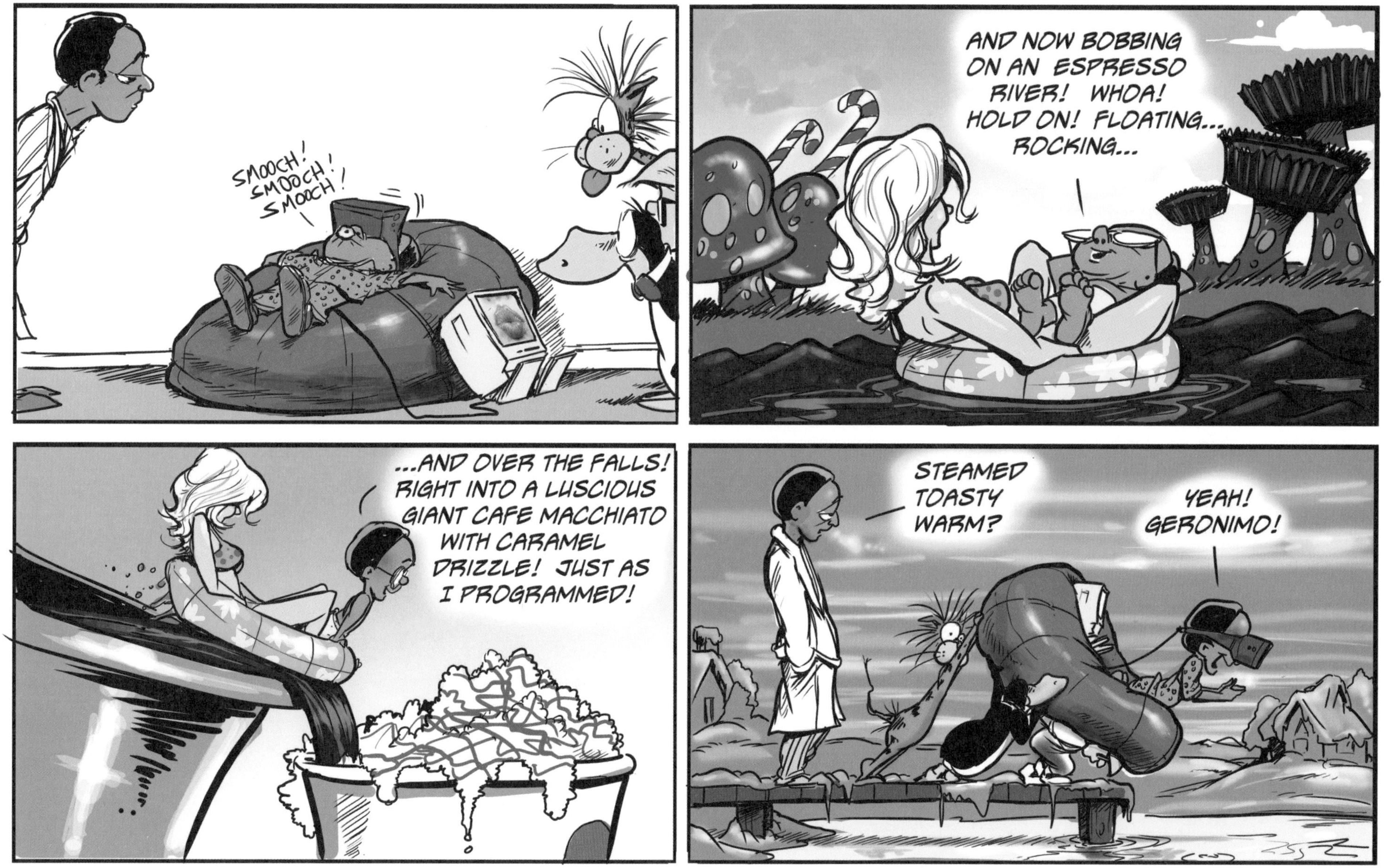
SMOOCH! SMOOCH! SMOOCH!
AND NOW BOBBING ON AN ESPRESSO RIVER! WHOA! HOLD ON! FLOATING... ROCKING...
...AND OVER THE FALLS! RIGHT INTO A LUSCIOUS GIANT CAFE MACCHIATO WITH CARAMEL DRIZZLE! JUST AS I PROGRAMMED!
STEAMED TOASTY WARM?
YEAH! GERONIMO!

Dear Mr. Breathed, I recently lost my father to his second battle with cancer. I'm now in the process of cleaning up his affairs and getting his belongings in order. As I do so I keep finding *Bloom County* comic strips he saved from the newspapers and the graphic-novel books everywhere in his stuff. It was always his favorite comic. I even remember Dad teaching me to read with them. I just wanted to take a minute to thank you for your years of entertainment. And for bringing joy into his life, along with countless others. Keep up the great work.

—Kerrigan Mullis

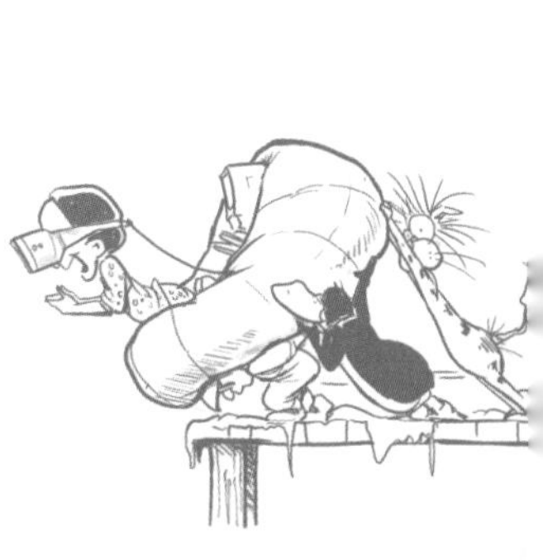

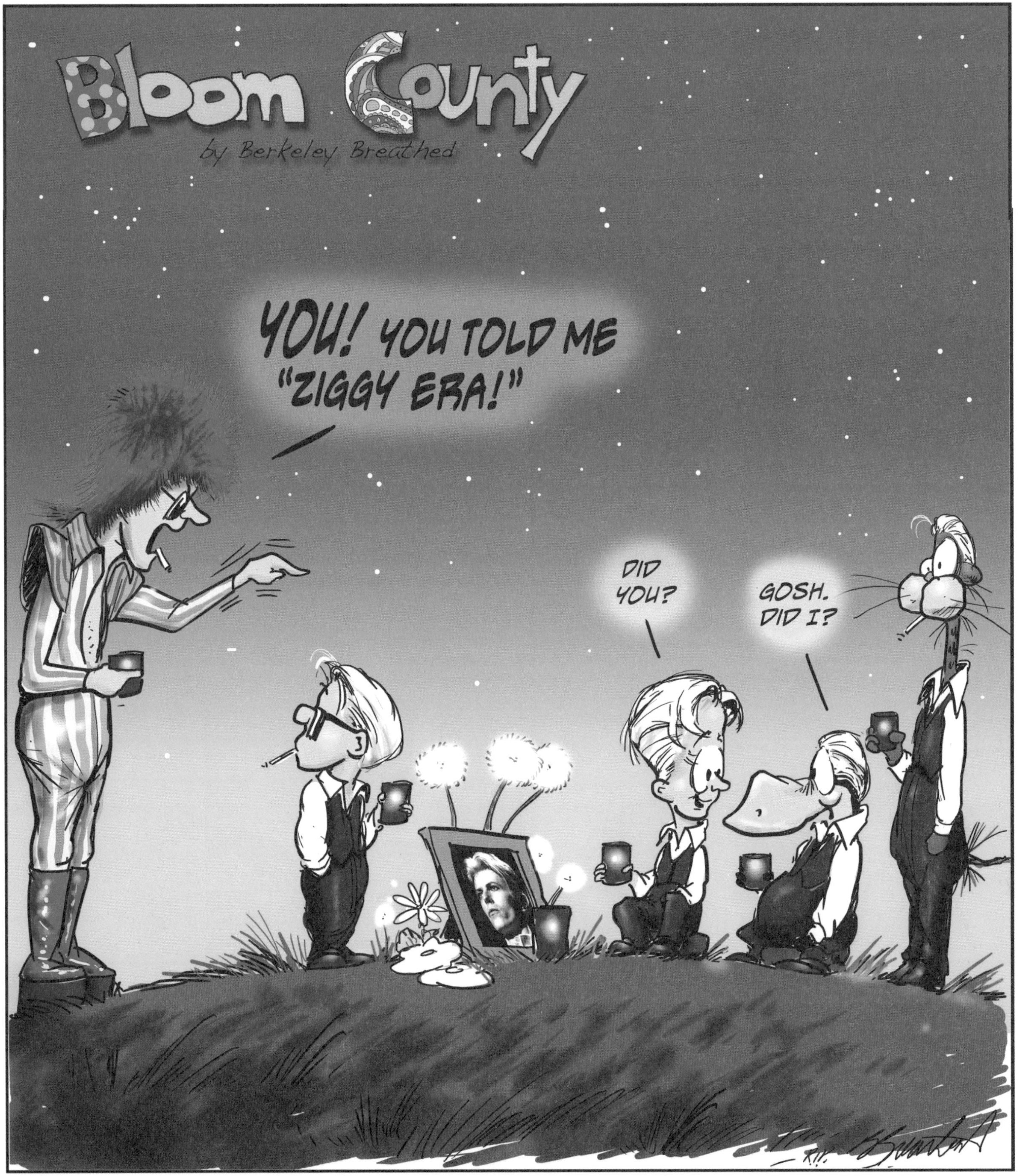
Bloom County
by Berkeley Breathed
YOU! YOU TOLD ME "ZIGGY ERA!"
DID YOU?
GOSH. DID I?

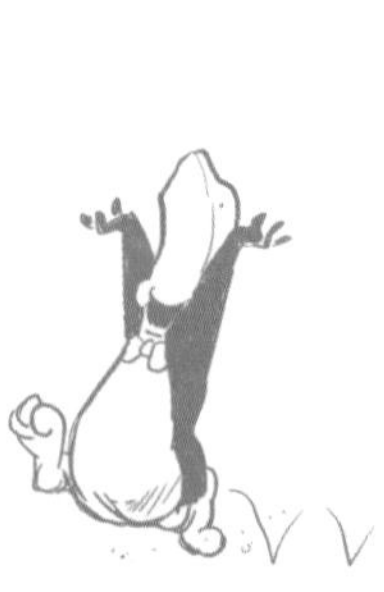

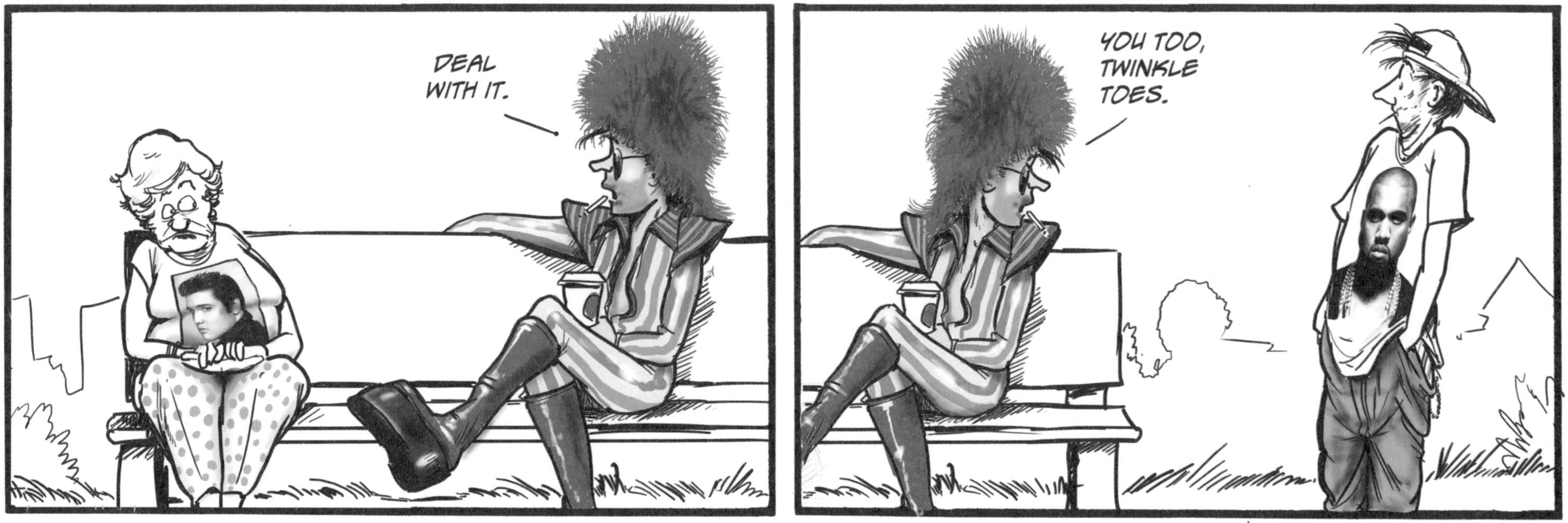
DEAL WITH IT.
YOU TOO, TWINKLE TOES.

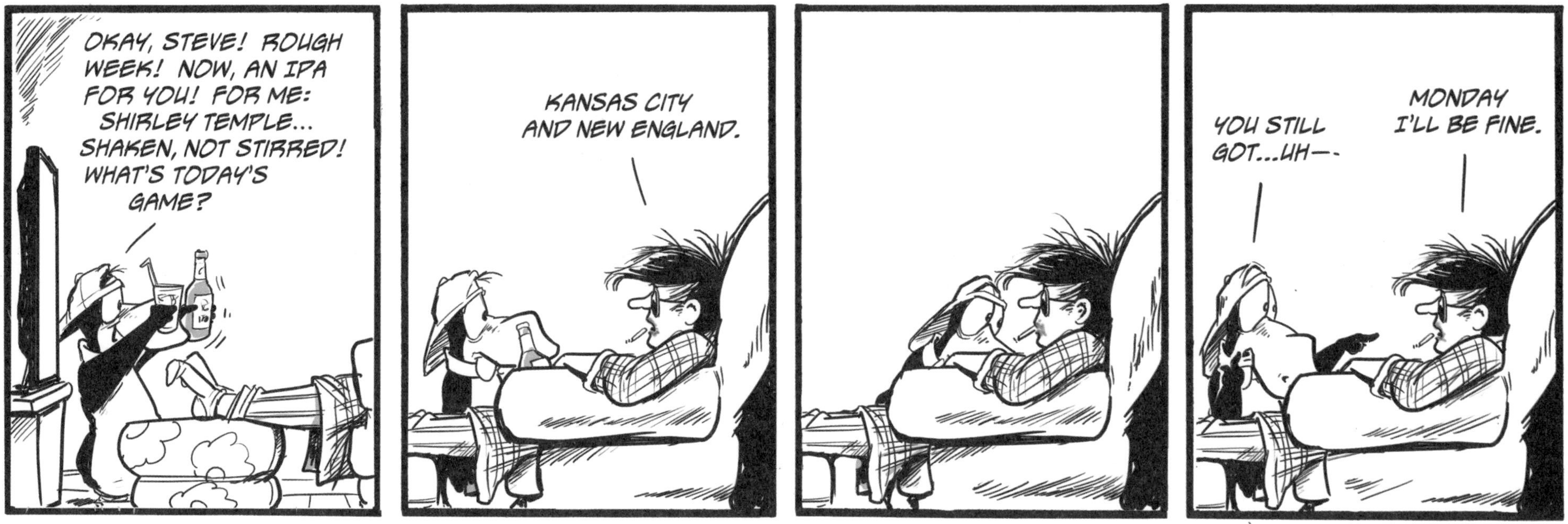
OKAY, STEVE! ROUGH WEEK! NOW, AN IPA FOR YOU! FOR ME: SHIRLEY TEMPLE... SHAKEN, NOT STIRRED! WHAT'S TODAY'S GAME?
KANSAS CITY AND NEW ENGLAND.
YOU STILL GOT...UH—
MONDAY I'LL BE FINE.

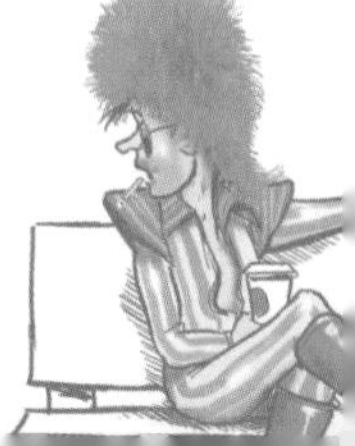

Bloom County
2006 2016
by Berkeley Breathed
STEVE! MY LAWYER! THANK GOODNESS!
THEY SAID YOU ATTACKED A WOMAN.
JAIL
SHE'S PRESSING CHARGES. WHAT THE @#% HAPPENED?
WHOLESALE FIBNICITY! I DID MY CIVIC DUTY!!
SO... I'M AT THE "HUNGRY HOOFBRAU" EATING HERRINGSCHNITZEL WHEN I HEAR A LADY CHOKING ON A SAUSAGE...
THEN WHAT?

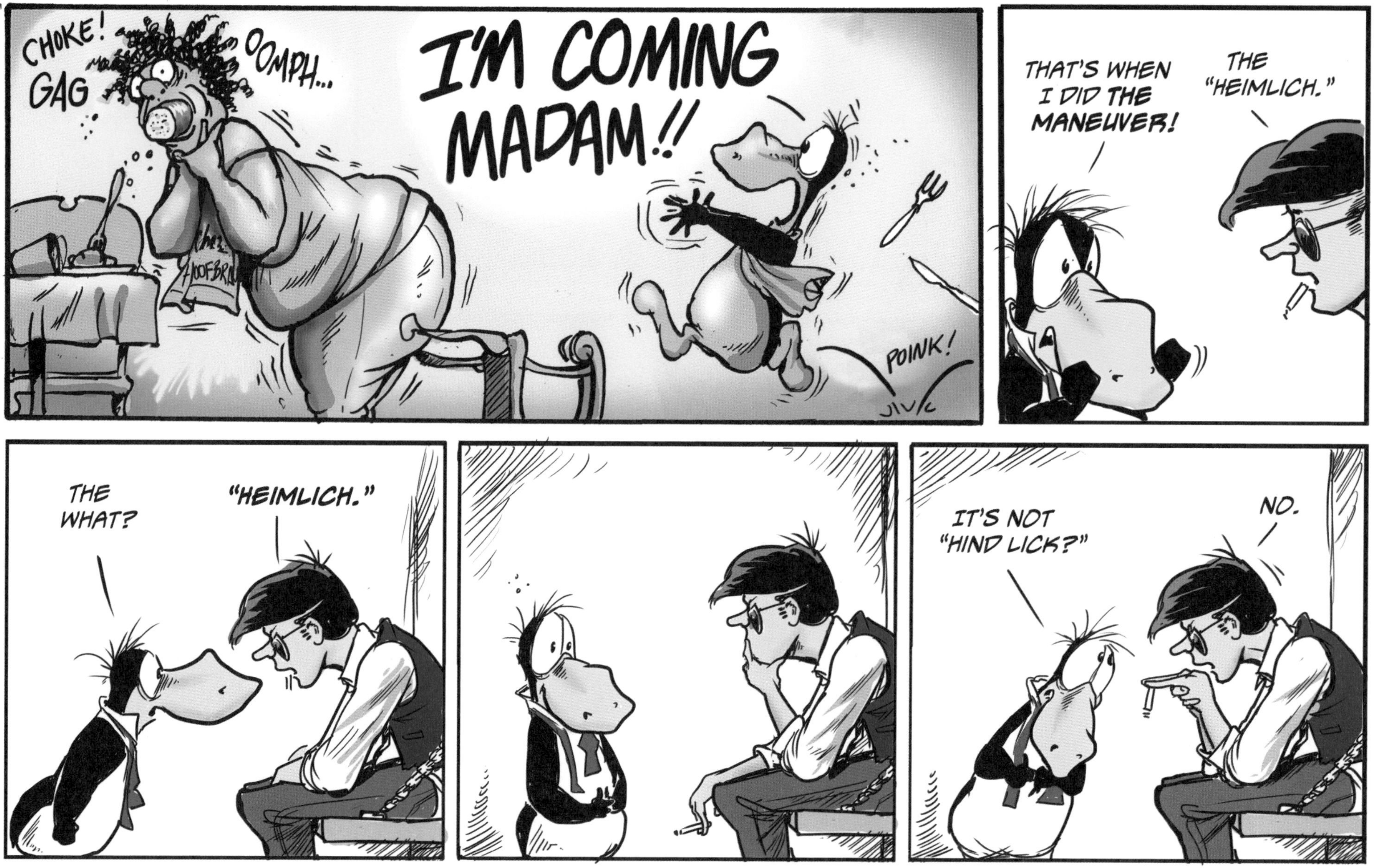
CHOKE!
GAG
OOMPH...
I'M COMING MADAM!!
POINK!
THAT'S WHEN I DID THE MANEUVER!
THE "HEIMLICH."
THE WHAT?
"HEIMLICH."
IT'S NOT "HIND LICK?"
NO.

A VERY RARE example of something being just as good the second time around. *Bloom County* restores faith in beauty.

—Rubin Drew

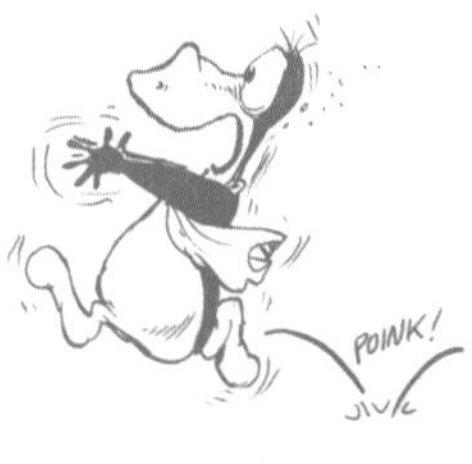
POINK!

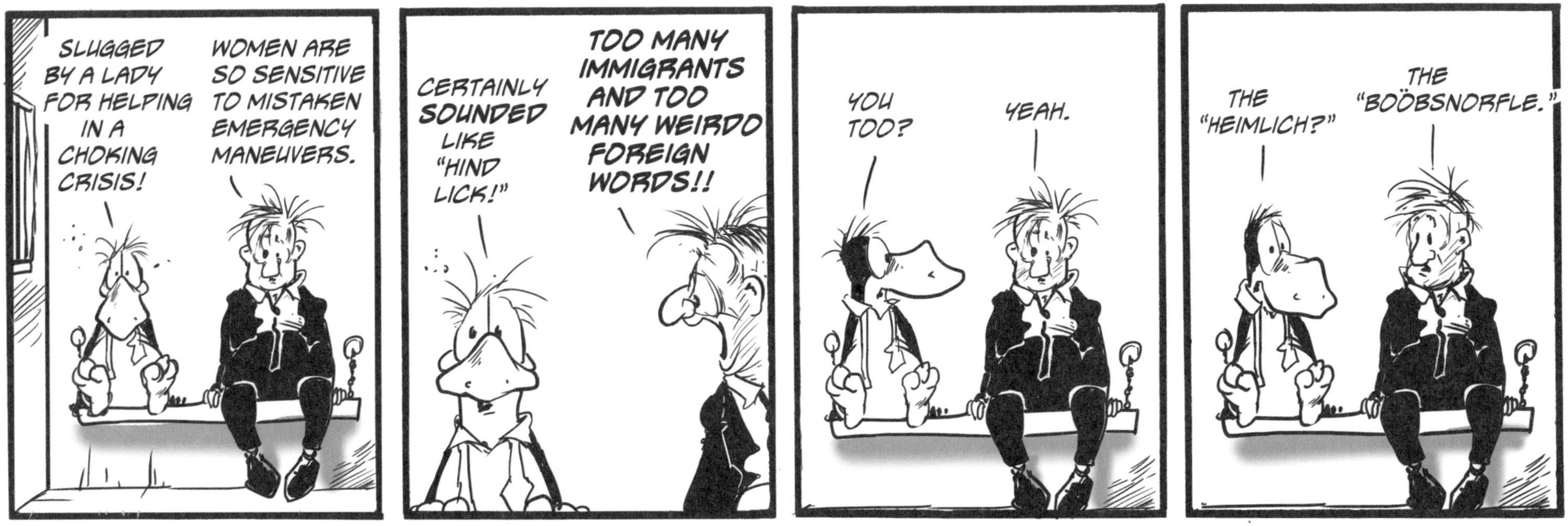
SLUGGED BY A LADY FOR HELPING IN A CHOKING CRISIS!
WOMEN ARE SO SENSITIVE TO MISTAKEN EMERGENCY MANEUVERS.
CERTAINLY SOUNDED LIKE "HIND LICK!"
TOO MANY IMMIGRANTS AND TOO MANY WEIRDO FOREIGN WORDS!!
YOU TOO?
YEAH.
THE "HEIMLICH?"
THE "BOÖBSNORFLE."

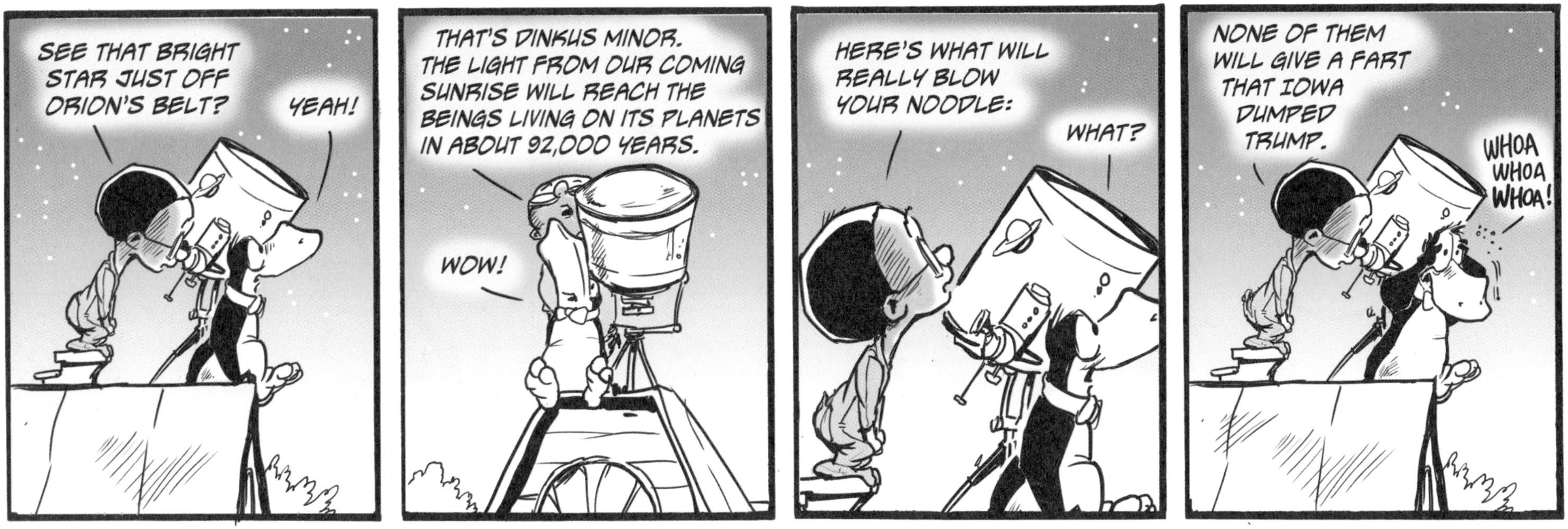
SEE THAT BRIGHT STAR JUST OFF ORION'S BELT?
YEAH!
THAT'S DINKUS MINOR. THE LIGHT FROM OUR COMING SUNRISE WILL REACH THE BEINGS LIVING ON ITS PLANETS IN ABOUT 92,000 YEARS.
WOW!
HERE'S WHAT WILL REALLY BLOW YOUR NOODLE:
WHAT?
NONE OF THEM WILL GIVE A FART THAT IOWA DUMPED TRUMP.
WHOA WHOA WHOA!

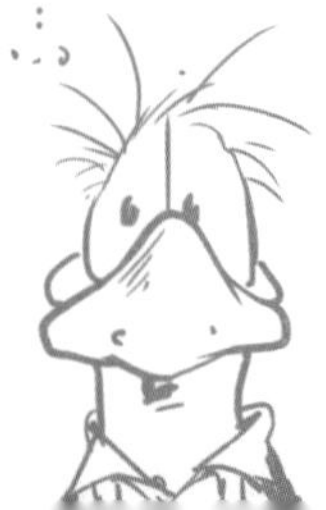

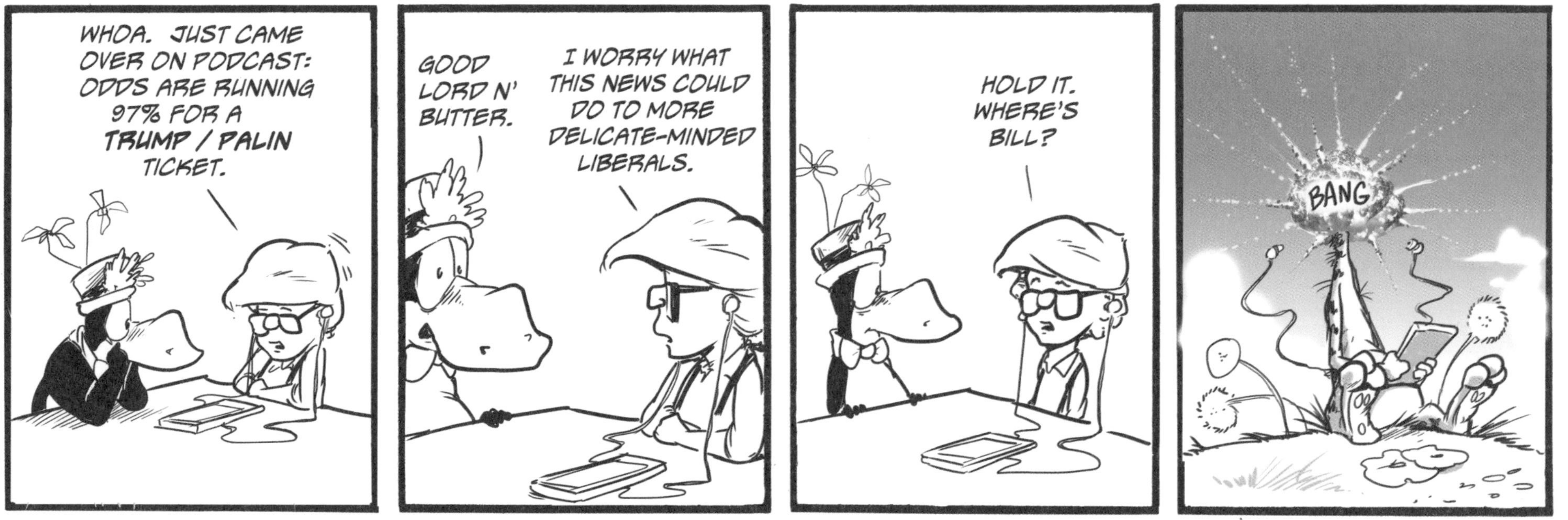
WHOA. JUST CAME OVER ON PODCAST: ODDS ARE RUNNING 97% FOR A TRUMP / PALIN TICKET.
GOOD LORD N' BUTTER.
I WORRY WHAT THIS NEWS COULD DO TO MORE DELICATE-MINDED LIBERALS.
HOLD IT. WHERE'S BILL?
BANG

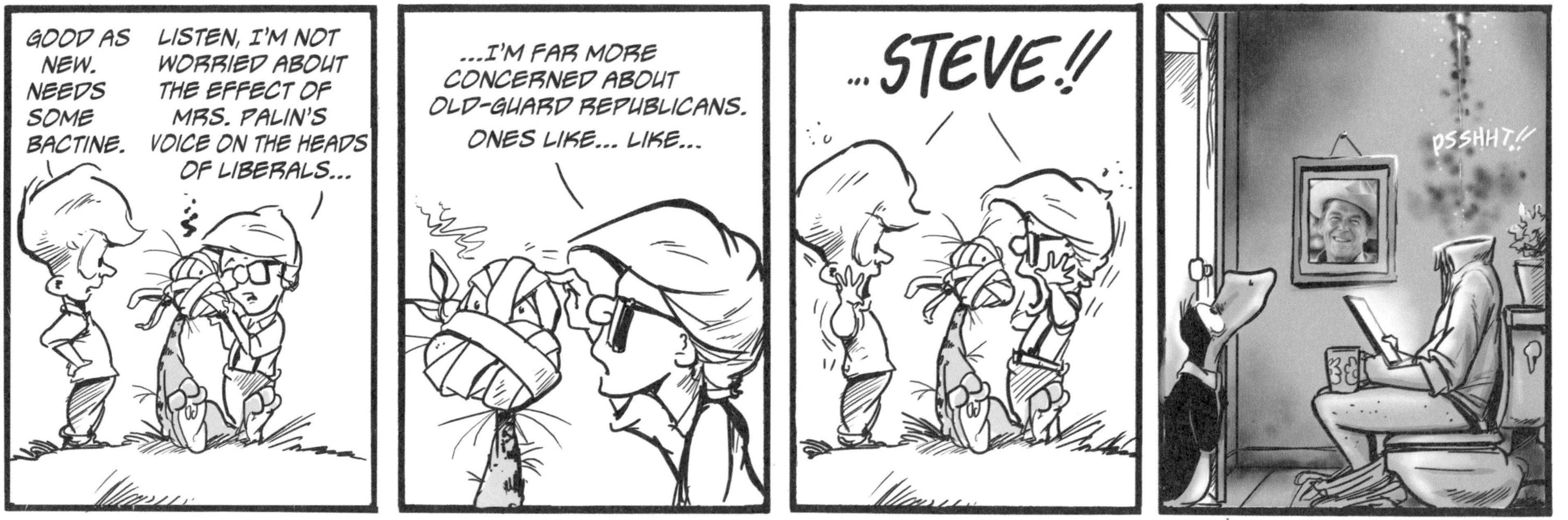
GOOD AS NEW. NEEDS SOME BACTINE.
LISTEN, I'M NOT WORRIED ABOUT THE EFFECT OF MRS. PALIN'S VOICE ON THE HEADS OF LIBERALS...
...I'M FAR MORE CONCERNED ABOUT OLD-GUARD REPUBLICANS.
ONES LIKE... LIKE...
...STEVE!!
PSSHHT!!

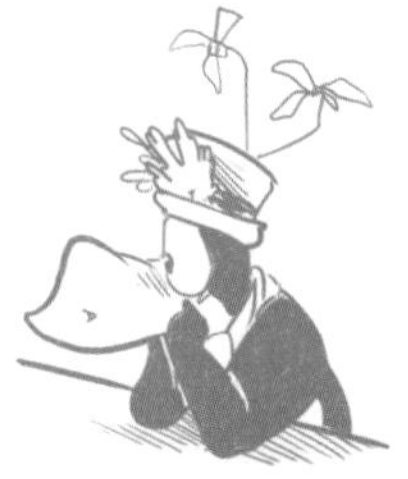

Bloom County
by Berkeley Breathed
YOUR KINGDOM IS FINISHED! PREPARE TO TASTE THE STEELY KISS OF MY BLADE!
CLOSE THE GATES!!
STORM THE WALLS!!
GODLESS BARBARIAN USURPER!! HIDE THE WOMEN!!
SEIZE THE THRONE! GUT 'EM LIKE TROUT!!
FOUL, SMELLY APOSTATE!!
WOOSH! WOOSH!

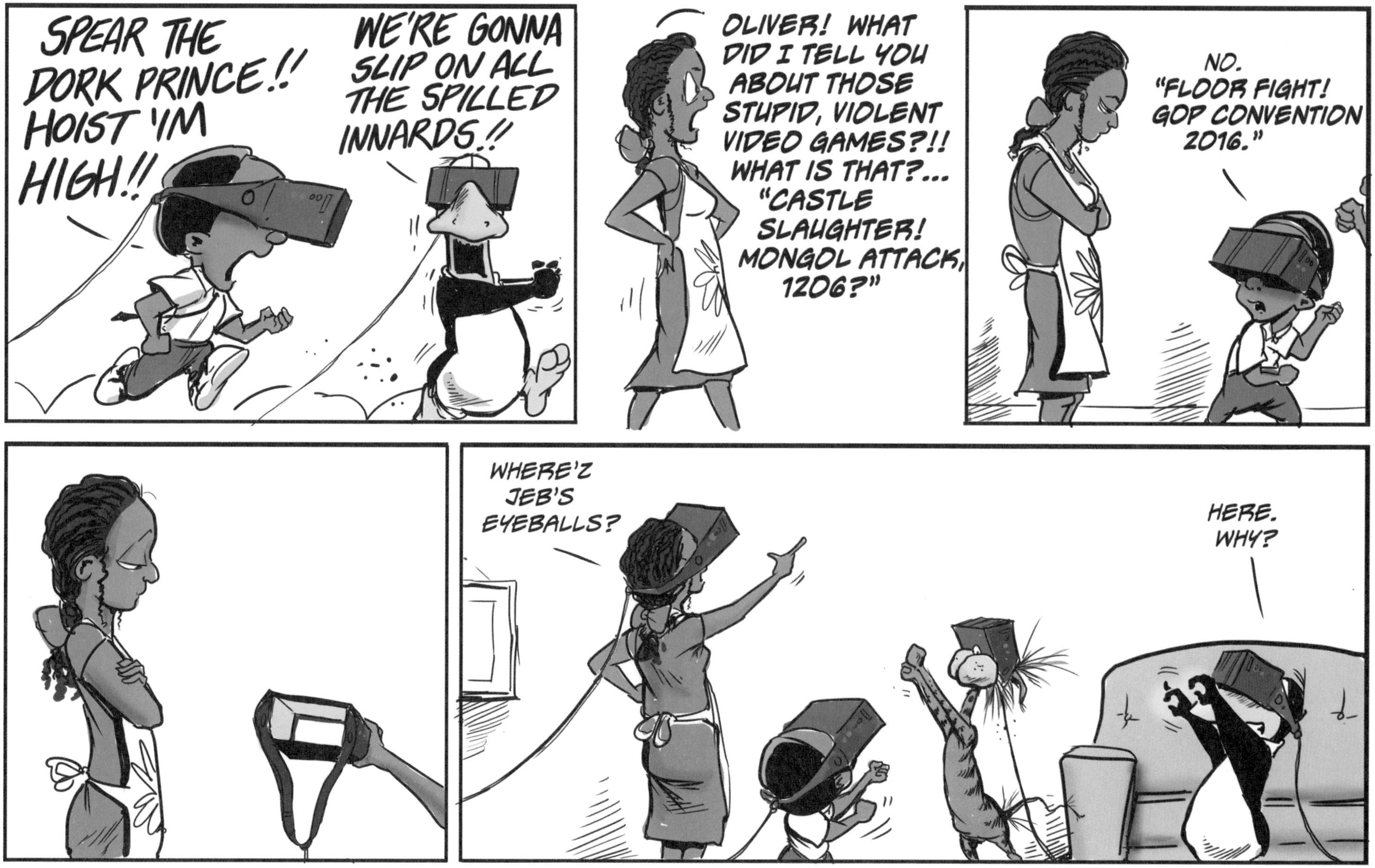
SPEAR THE DORK PRINCE!! HOIST 'IM HIGH!!
WE'RE GONNA SLIP ON ALL THE SPILLED INNARDS!!
OLIVER! WHAT DID I TELL YOU ABOUT THOSE STUPID, VIOLENT VIDEO GAMES?!! WHAT IS THAT?... "CASTLE SLAUGHTER! MONGOL ATTACK, 1206?"
NO. "FLOOR FIGHT! GOP CONVENTION 2016."
WHERE'Z JEB'S EYEBALLS?
HERE. WHY?

My son was born in 1994 and as soon as he could, he started reading all the *Bloom County* books. He loved them. Not only did he still get the humor, but he still uses them to this day as references when discussing U.S. politics with anyone.

You have two diehard fans here in Canada, and in this case, two generations' worth.

—Amy Hughes-Littlejohn

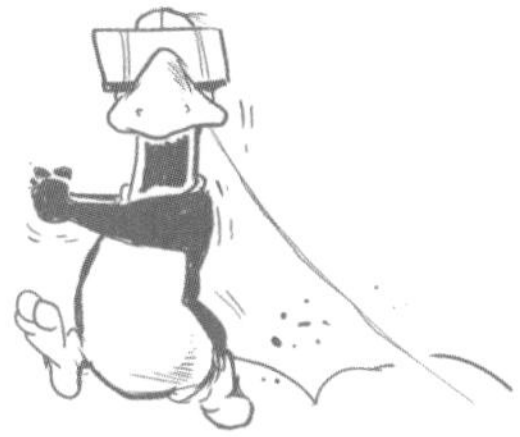

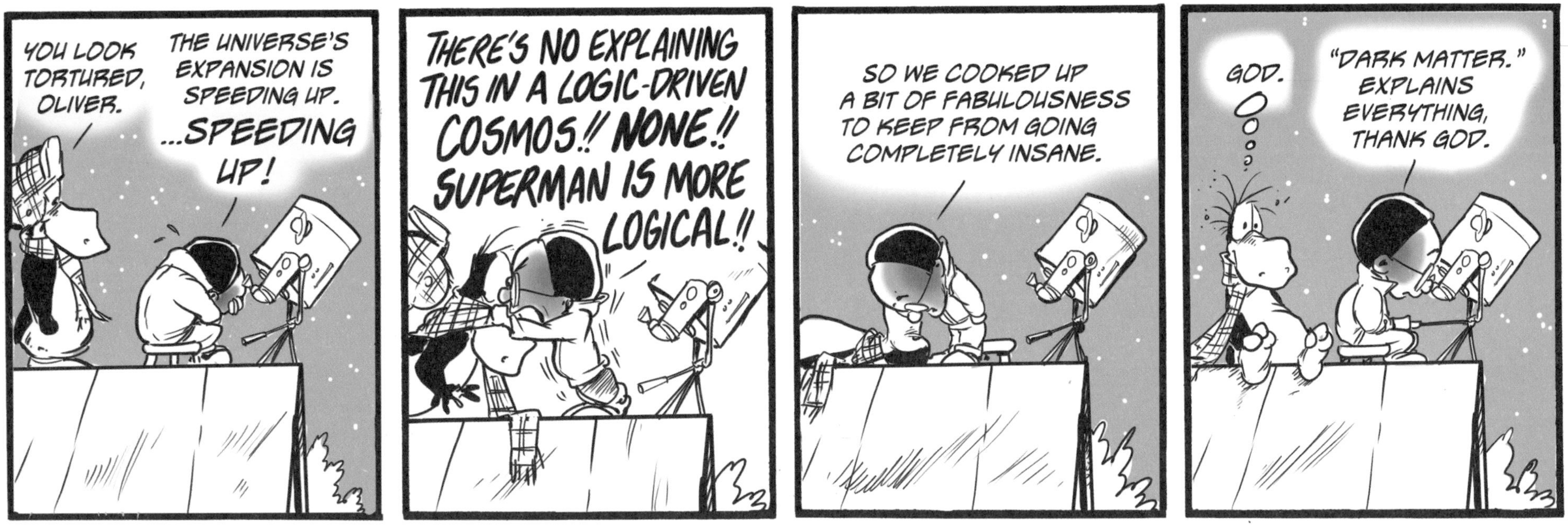
YOU LOOK TORTURED, OLIVER.
THE UNIVERSE'S EXPANSION IS SPEEDING UP. ...SPEEDING UP!
THERE'S NO EXPLAINING THIS IN A LOGIC-DRIVEN COSMOS!! NONE!! SUPERMAN IS MORE LOGICAL!!
SO WE COOKED UP A BIT OF FABULOUSNESS TO KEEP FROM GOING COMPLETELY INSANE.
GOD.
"DARK MATTER." EXPLAINS EVERYTHING, THANK GOD.

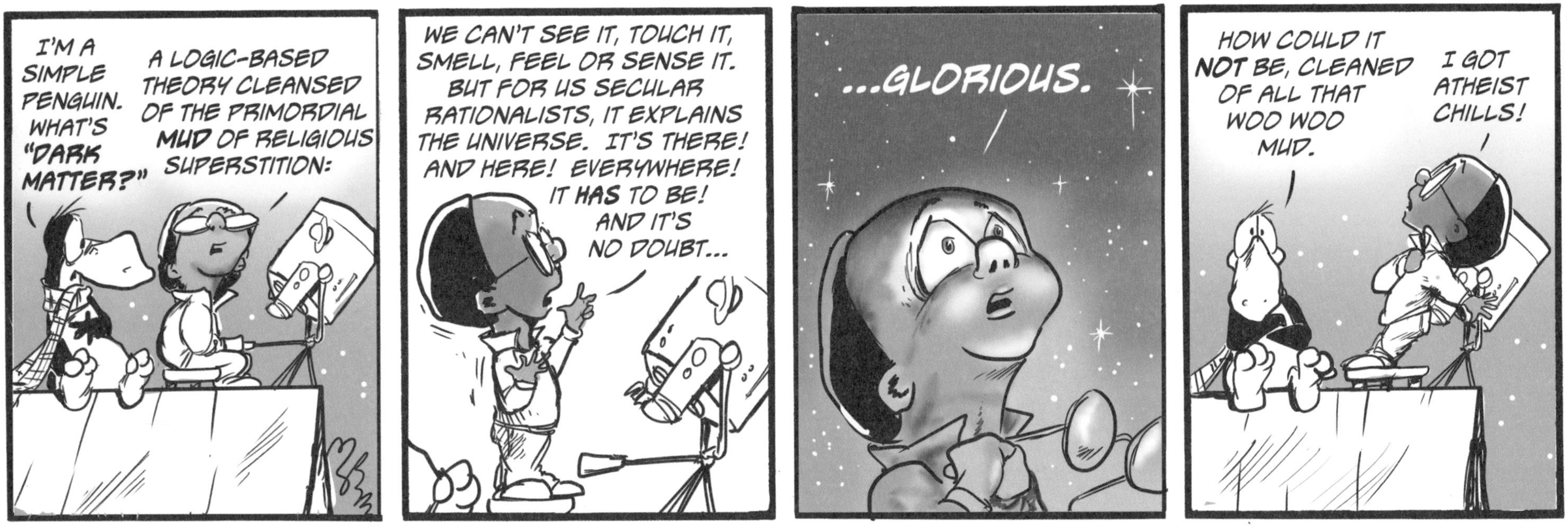
I'M A SIMPLE PENGUIN. WHAT'S "DARK MATTER?"
A LOGIC-BASED THEORY CLEANSED OF THE PRIMORDIAL MUD OF RELIGIOUS SUPERSTITION:
WE CAN'T SEE IT, TOUCH IT, SMELL, FEEL OR SENSE IT. BUT FOR US SECULAR RATIONALISTS, IT EXPLAINS THE UNIVERSE. IT'S THERE! AND HERE! EVERYWHERE! IT HAS TO BE! AND IT'S NO DOUBT...
...GLORIOUS.
HOW COULD IT NOT BE, CLEANED OF ALL THAT WOO WOO MUD.
I GOT ATHEIST CHILLS!

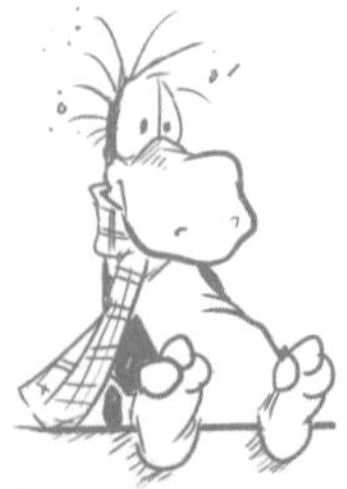

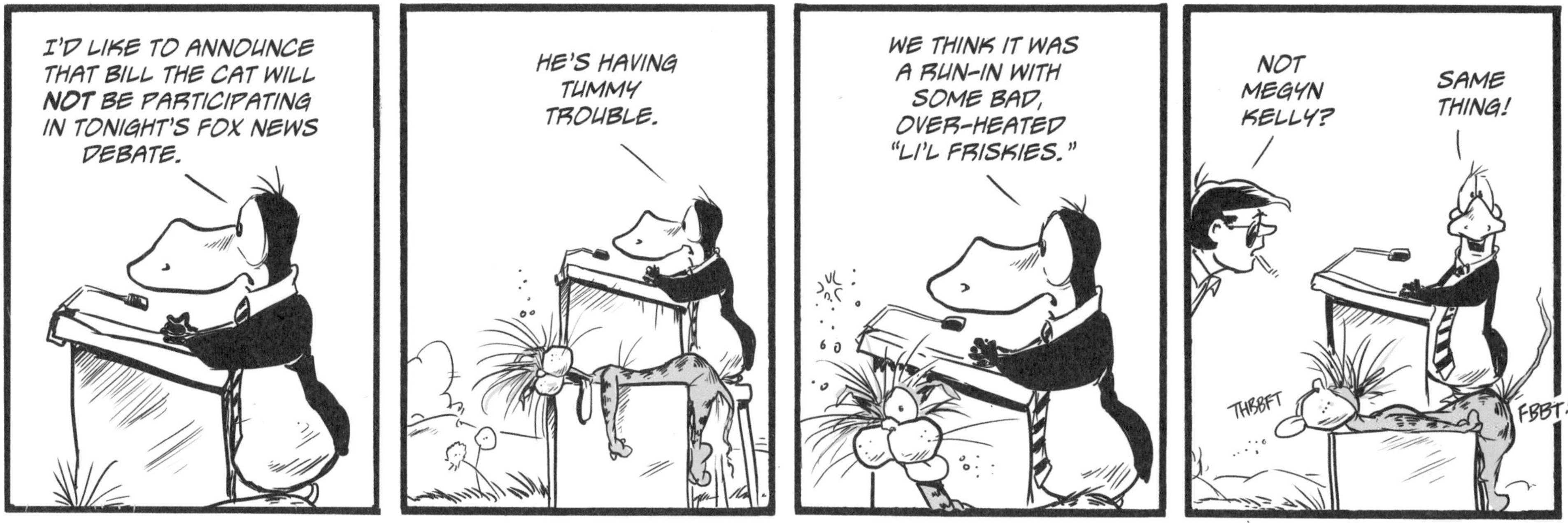

I'D LIKE TO ANNOUNCE THAT BILL THE CAT WILL **NOT** BE PARTICIPATING IN TONIGHT'S FOX NEWS DEBATE.
HE'S HAVING TUMMY TROUBLE.
WE THINK IT WAS A RUN-IN WITH SOME BAD, OVER-HEATED "LI'L FRISKIES."
NOT MEGYN KELLY?
SAME THING!
THBBFT
FBBT!

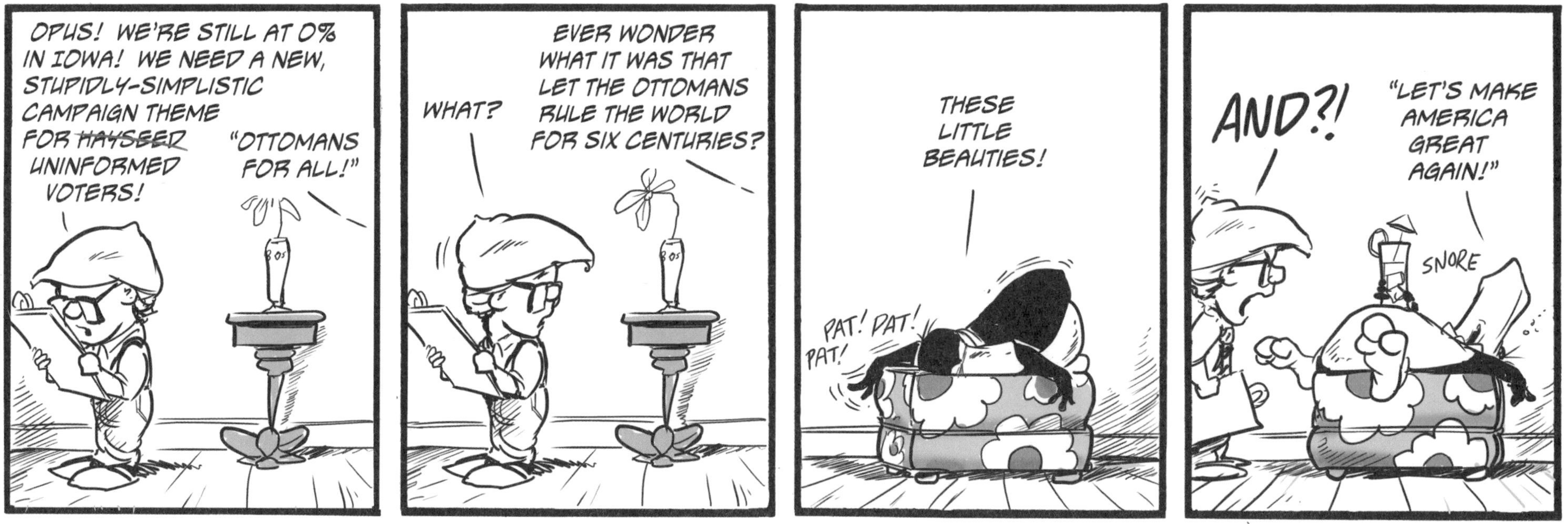

OPUS! WE'RE STILL AT 0% IN IOWA! WE NEED A NEW, STUPIDLY-SIMPLISTIC CAMPAIGN THEME FOR ~~HAYSEED~~ UNINFORMED VOTERS!
"OTTOMANS FOR ALL!"
WHAT?
EVER WONDER WHAT IT WAS THAT LET THE OTTOMANS RULE THE WORLD FOR SIX CENTURIES?
THESE LITTLE BEAUTIES!
PAT! PAT! PAT!
AND?!
"LET'S MAKE AMERICA GREAT AGAIN!"
SNORE

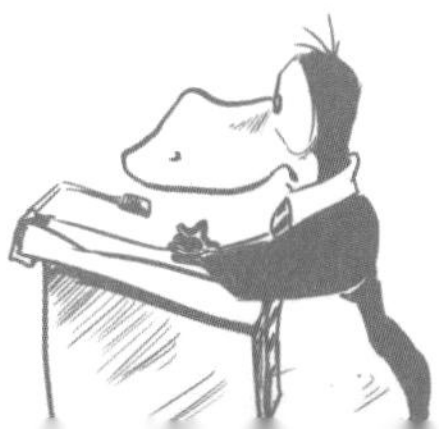

Bloom County
by Berkeley Breathed
THERE SHE IS! LIKE A PORT IN A STORM!
OPUS! BOUNCY, UPHOLSTERED FOOTSTOOLS WON'T MAKE AMERICA GREAT AGAIN!
THBBF
OH YEAH? WHAT'S THAT BERNIE DUDE'S PLAN FOR NATIONAL RE-GLORY?
TURN BANKS INTO FREE-RANGE CHICKEN COOPS.
DONALD'S PLAN?

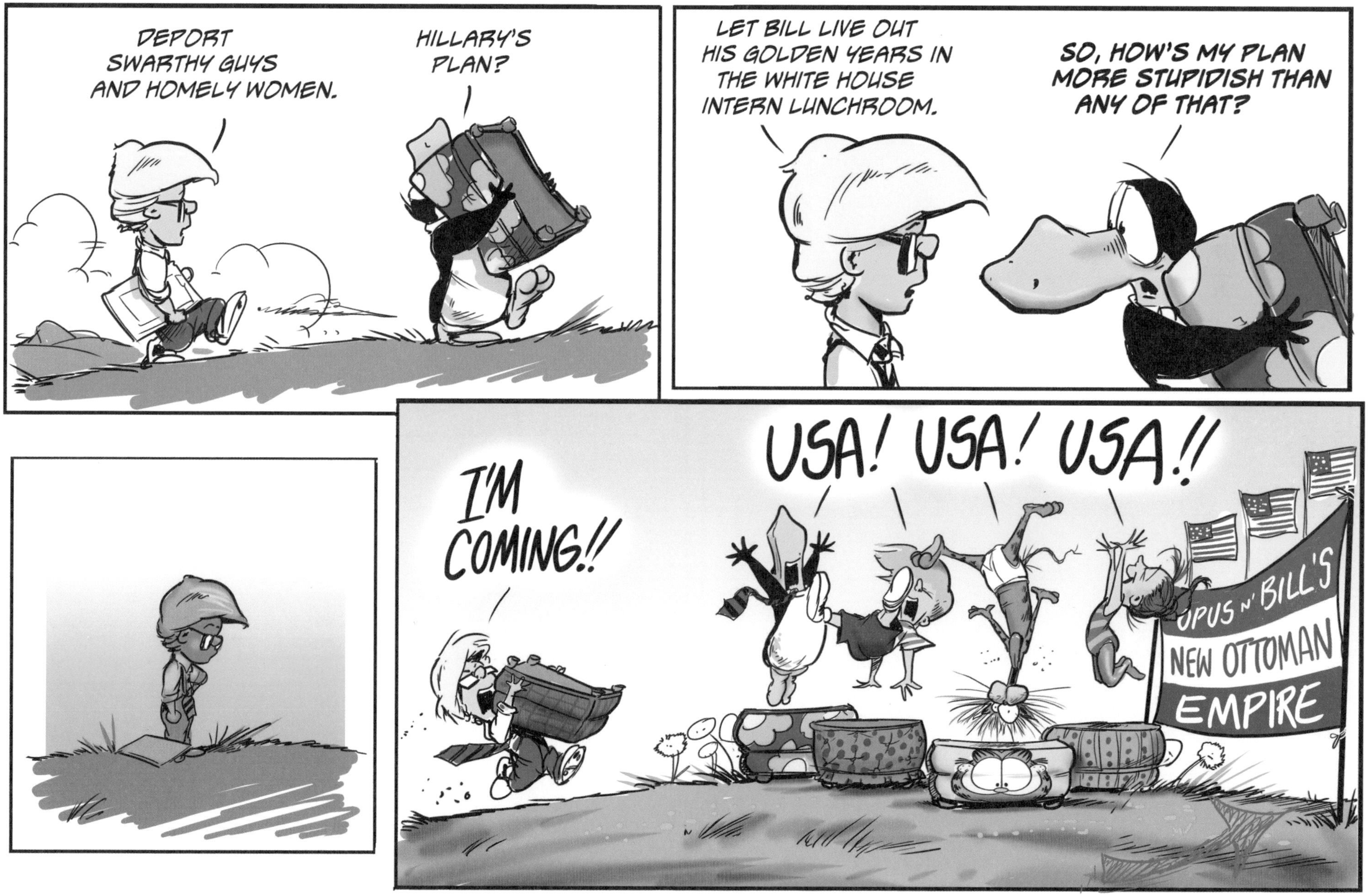
DEPORT SWARTHY GUYS AND HOMELY WOMEN.
HILLARY'S PLAN?
LET BILL LIVE OUT HIS GOLDEN YEARS IN THE WHITE HOUSE INTERN LUNCHROOM.
SO, HOW'S MY PLAN MORE STUPIDISH THAN ANY OF THAT?
I'M COMING!!
USA! USA! USA!!
OPUS N' BILL'S NEW OTTOMAN EMPIRE

Thank you for doing all this again. As a conservative, I am so tired of all the fear and anger from my side of the aisle. You reinforce the idea that we can have a discussion with each other, care about each other, laugh with and at each other and still be friends…

—Richard Berkstresser

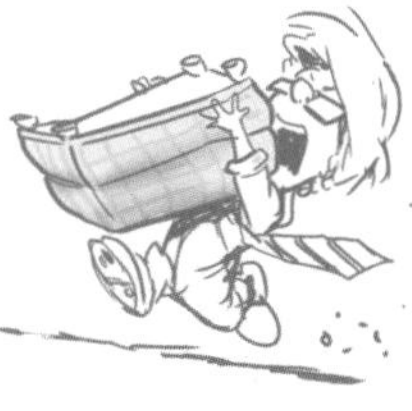

Bloom County
by Berkeley Breathed

CULTURAL ABBOBRITION... APOBOBOIATION... APPROBUBBLE--

WHAT'S "CULTURAL APPROPRIATION," MILO?

IT'S WHAT HAS EXTREMIST CHAR TREUSE'S KNICKERS IN A TWIST AT THE RADICAL MIDWEST IMAGE, INTELLECT & LUTEFISK FRONT*:

THE COFFEE CAT

* M.I.I.L.F.

IT'S WHEN A VASTLY ADVANCED CULTURE LIKE OURS PLAYFULLY "APPROPRIATES" THE WHIMSICAL ASPECTS OF ANOTHER CULTURE FOR REASONS OF AMUSEMENT.

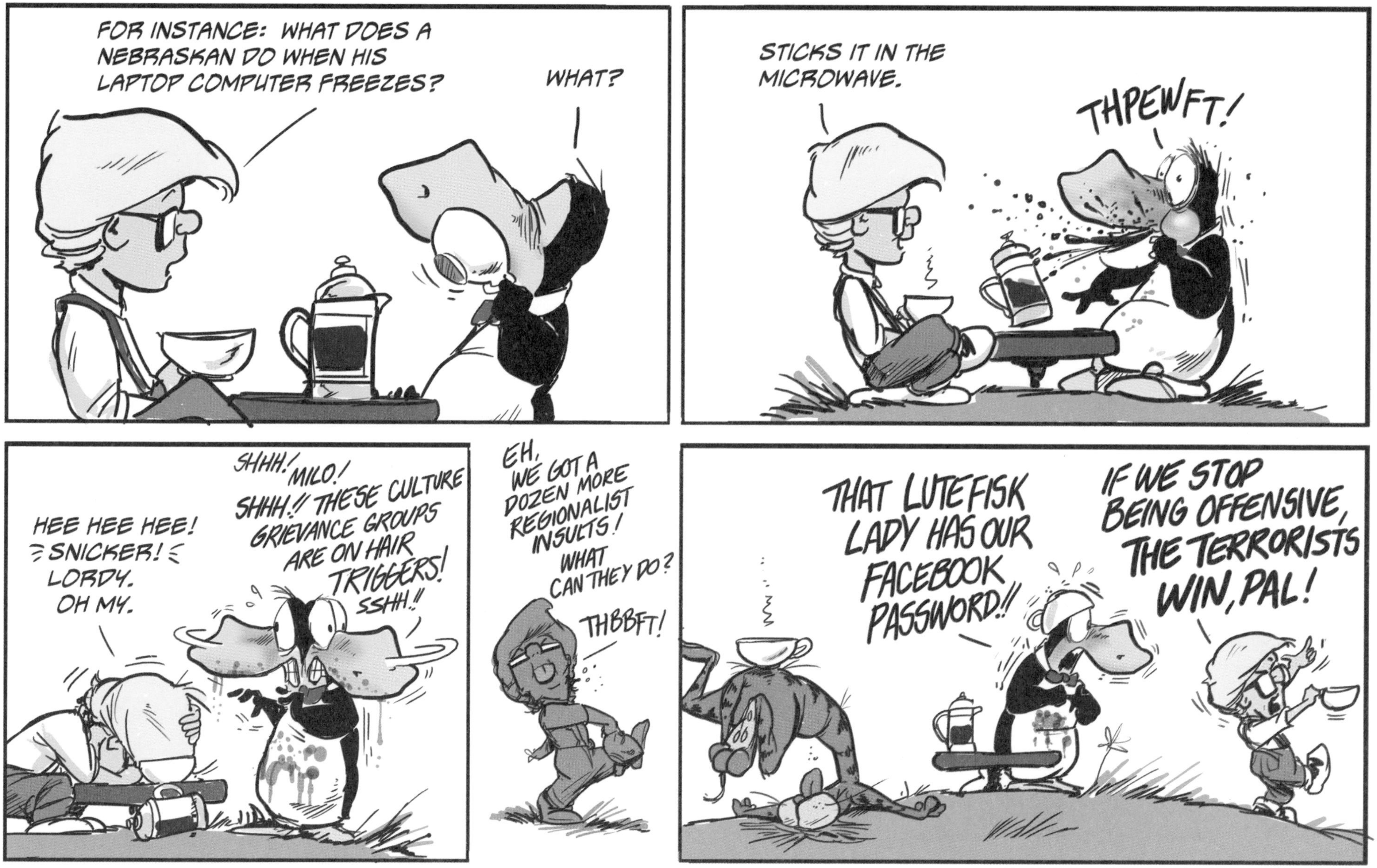
FOR INSTANCE: WHAT DOES A NEBRASKAN DO WHEN HIS LAPTOP COMPUTER FREEZES?
WHAT?
STICKS IT IN THE MICROWAVE.
THPEWFT!
HEE HEE HEE! SNICKER! LORDY. OH MY.
SHHH! MILO! SHHH!! THESE CULTURE GRIEVANCE GROUPS ARE ON HAIR TRIGGERS! SSHH!!
EH, WE GOT A DOZEN MORE REGIONALIST INSULTS! WHAT CAN THEY DO?
THBBFT!
THAT LUTEFISK LADY HAS OUR FACEBOOK PASSWORD!!
IF WE STOP BEING OFFENSIVE, THE TERRORISTS WIN, PAL!

I'm sure you've heard this over and over, but thank you, thank you so much. I didn't realize how much I missed these people until you brought them back. It's almost like no time has passed. Finally my kids understand that weird creepy orange stuffed animal.

—Heather Anderson

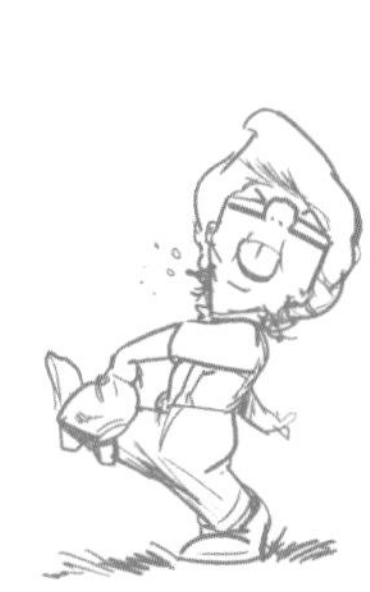

120

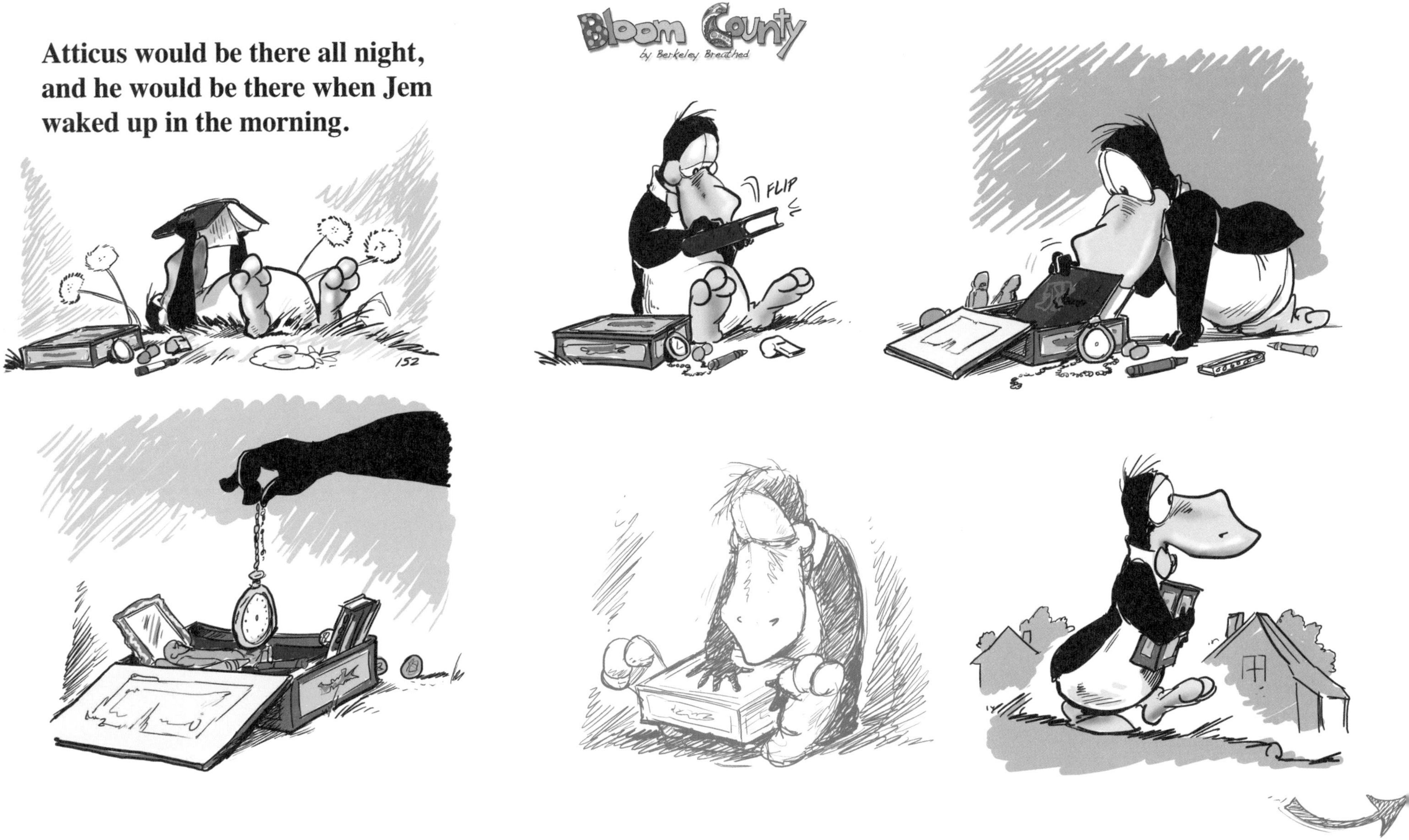
Atticus would be there all night, and he would be there when Jem waked up in the morning.
Bloom County
by Berkeley Breathed
152
FLIP

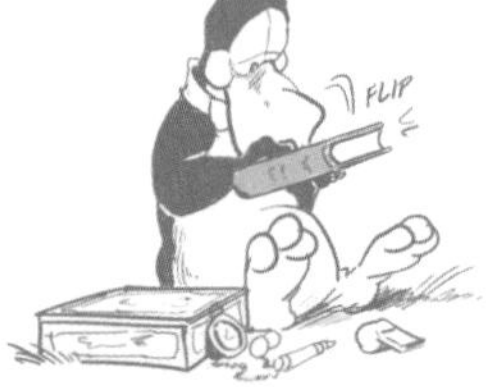
FLIP

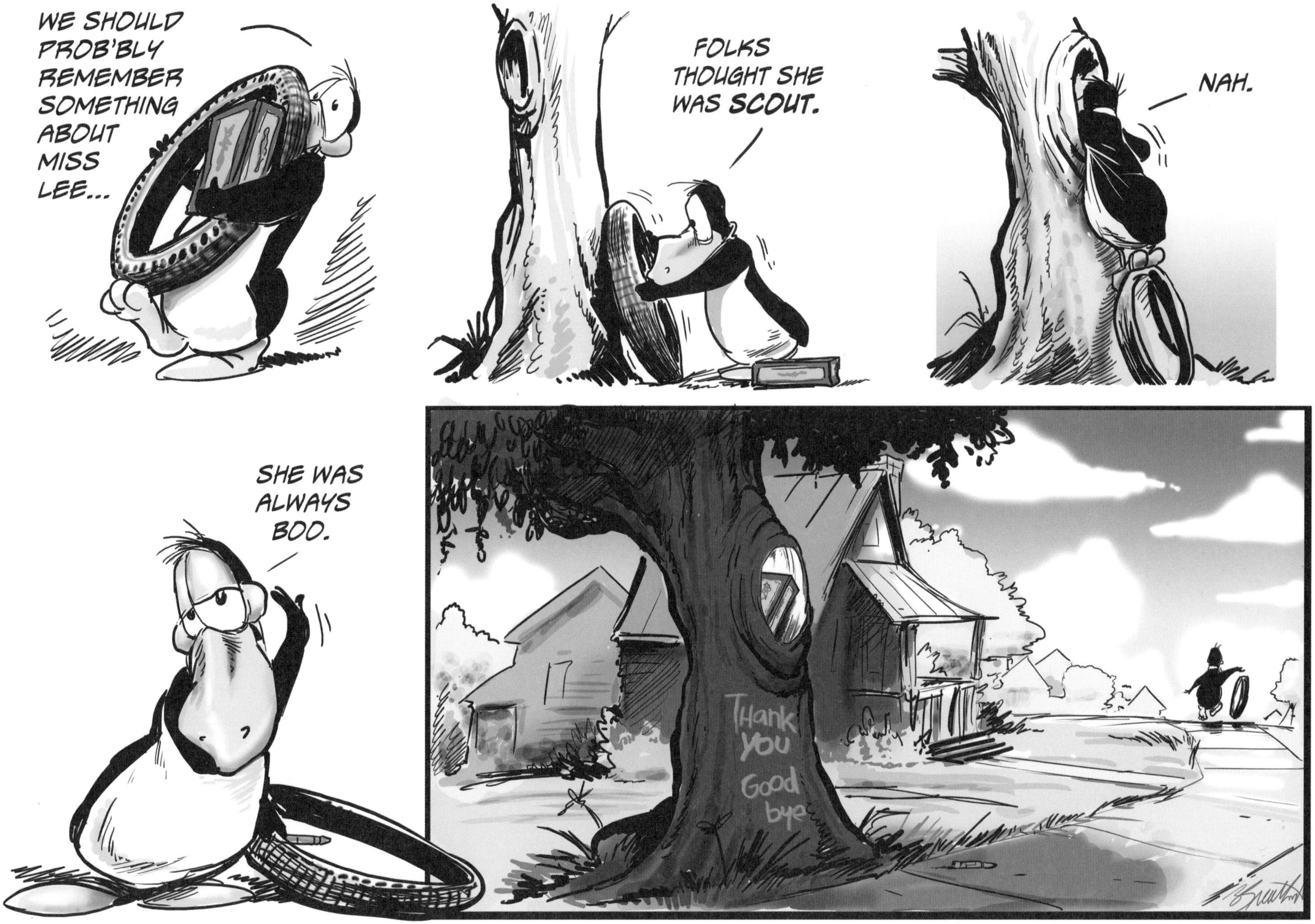
WE SHOULD PROB'BLY REMEMBER SOMETHING ABOUT MISS LEE...
FOLKS THOUGHT SHE WAS SCOUT.
NAH.
SHE WAS ALWAYS BOO.
Thank you Good bye

How wonderful to learn that two of my favorite creative geniuses—Berkeley Breathed and Harper Lee—admired one another, too. It makes me feel like part of an extended, yet intimate, family.

—Erin Naillon

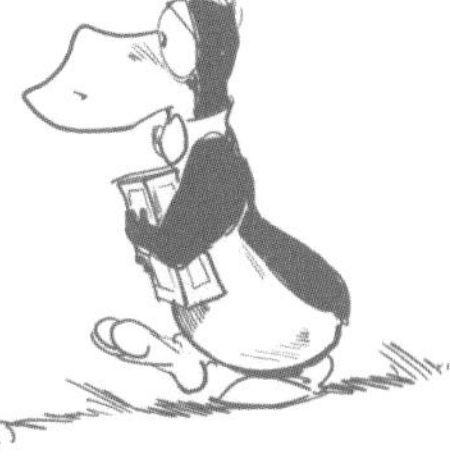

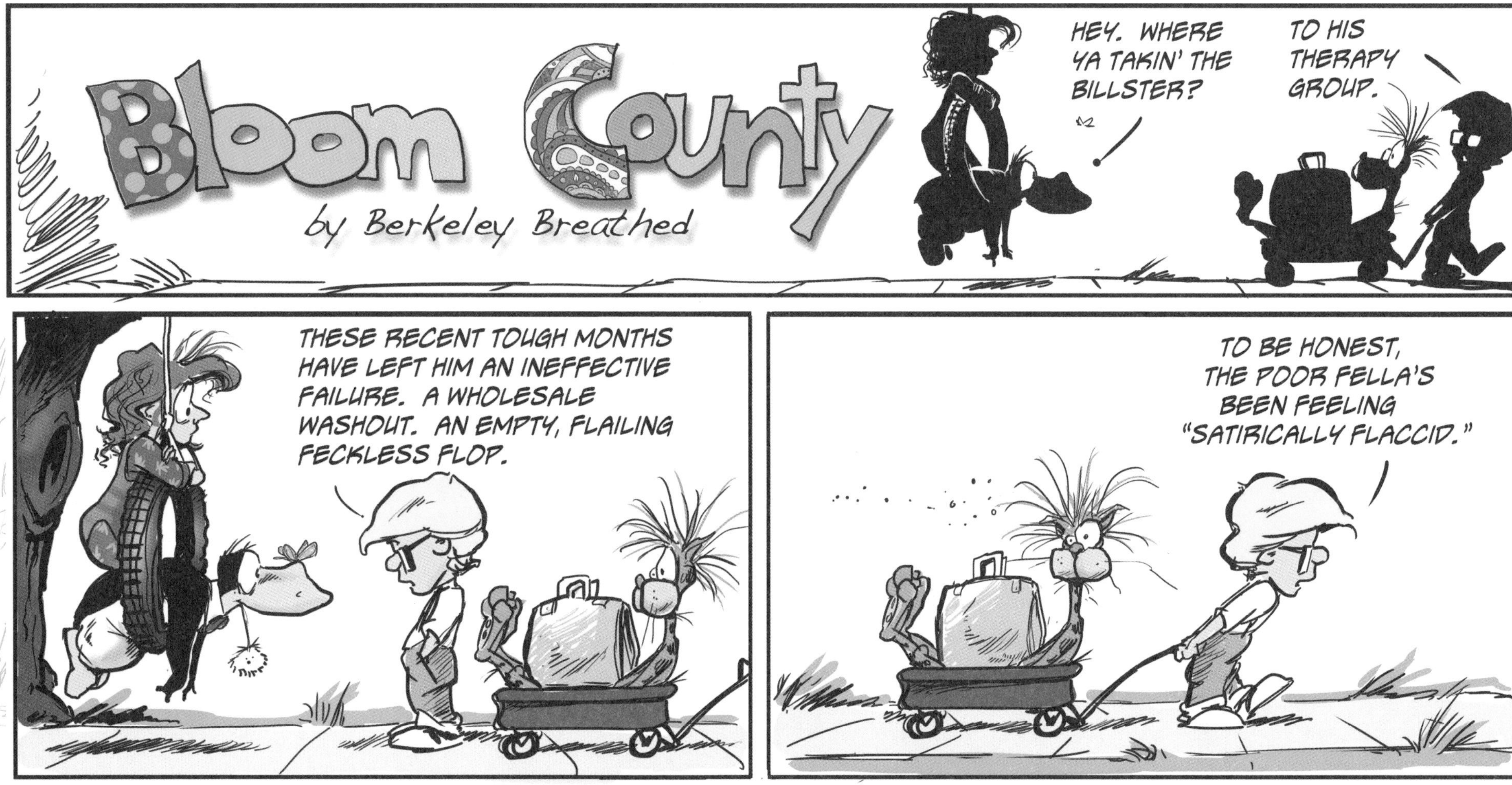
Bloom County
by Berkeley Breathed
HEY. WHERE YA TAKIN' THE BILLSTER?
TO HIS THERAPY GROUP.
THESE RECENT TOUGH MONTHS HAVE LEFT HIM AN INEFFECTIVE FAILURE. A WHOLESALE WASHOUT. AN EMPTY, FLAILING FECKLESS FLOP.
TO BE HONEST, THE POOR FELLA'S BEEN FEELING "SATIRICALLY FLACCID."

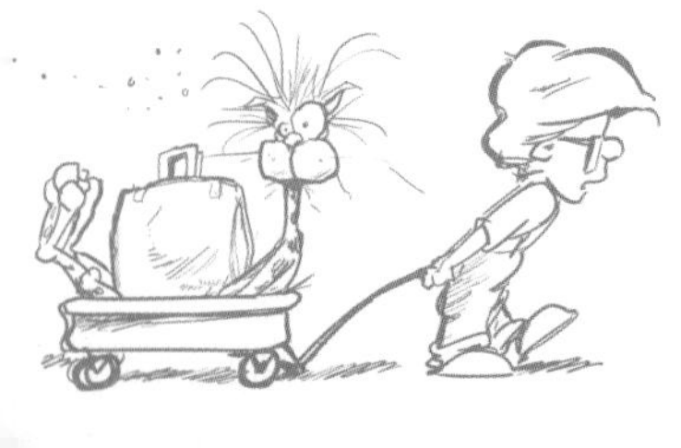

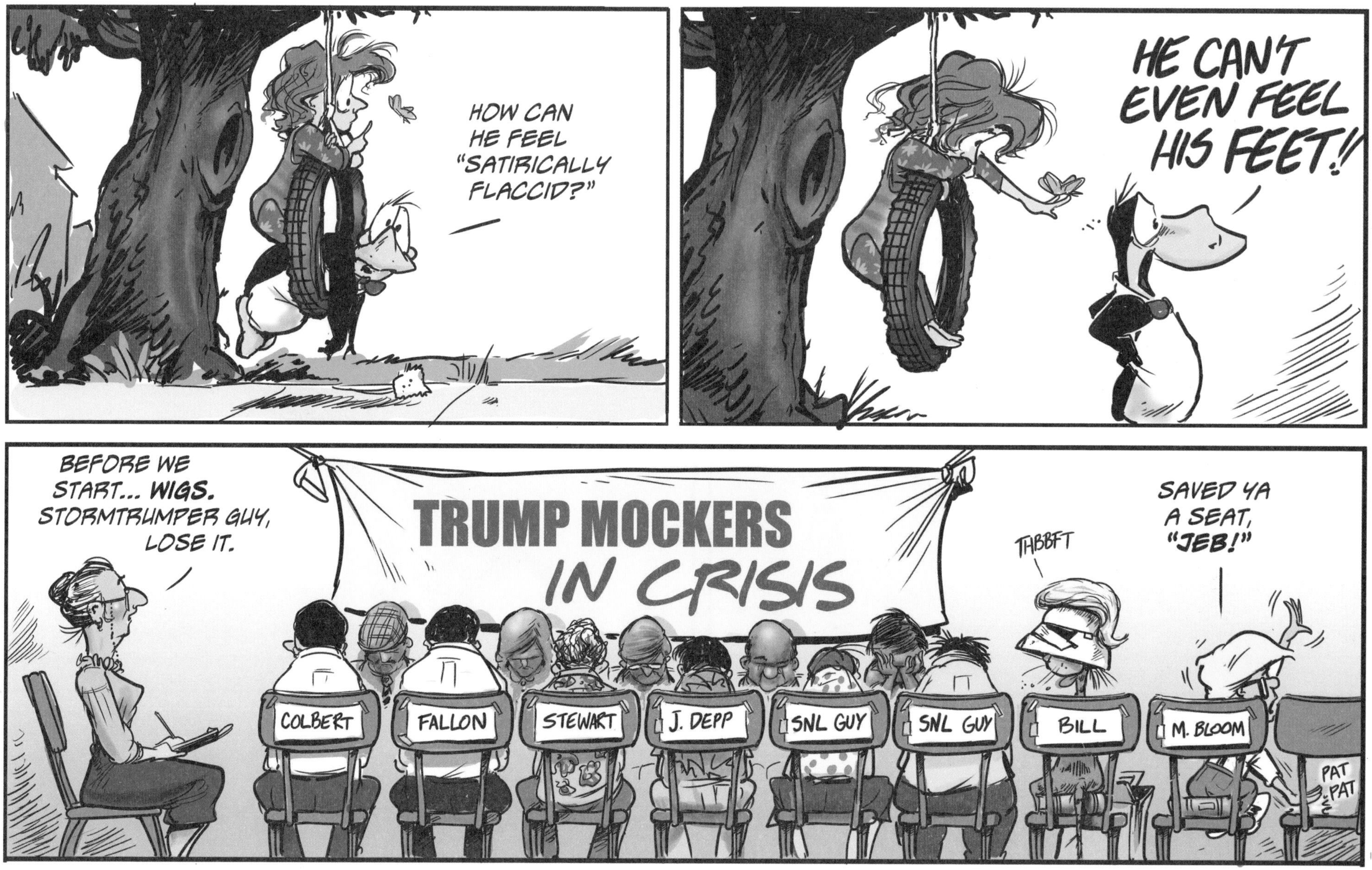
HOW CAN HE FEEL "SATIRICALLY FLACCID?"
HE CAN'T EVEN FEEL HIS FEET!!
BEFORE WE START... **WIGS.** STORMTRUMPER GUY, LOSE IT.
TRUMP MOCKERS
IN CRISIS
THBBFT
SAVED YA A SEAT, **"JEB!"**
COLBERT
FALLON
STEWART
J. DEPP
SNL GUY
SNL GUY
BILL
M. BLOOM
PAT PAT

Oh, Facebook, I have such a love/hate relationship with you. I love seeing what my far-flung friends are doing and delight in their posts, the creative and artistic sharing, the uplifting and inspirational material, and, yes, the cat (and other animal) videos. However, I hate the trolls, political and religious fights, the insensitivity that anonymity can bring and the sometimes vapid narcissism.

But you have brought *Bloom County* back into my life and, for that, all is forgiven.

—Marilyn Hoffman

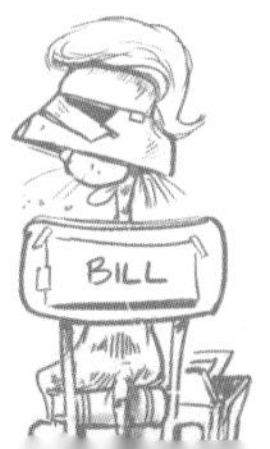
BILL

A CAT? YOU WANT GOOD 'OL BILL TO DO A PAINTING?
Bloom County
by Berkeley Breathed
I'VE SEEN THEM GIVE ELEPHANTS A BRUSH AND LET 'EM GO AT IT WITH A CANVAS.
IT'S MYSTERIOUS AND ASTONISHING. THEY CREATE SUBLIMELY PRIMAL EXPRESSIONS OF UNIVERSAL, NATURAL TRUTH. EVEN BEAUTY.
HERE YA GO, BIG FELLA. JUST... YOU KNOW, LET IT FLOW. MAYBE WE CAN SELL THESE BABIES.

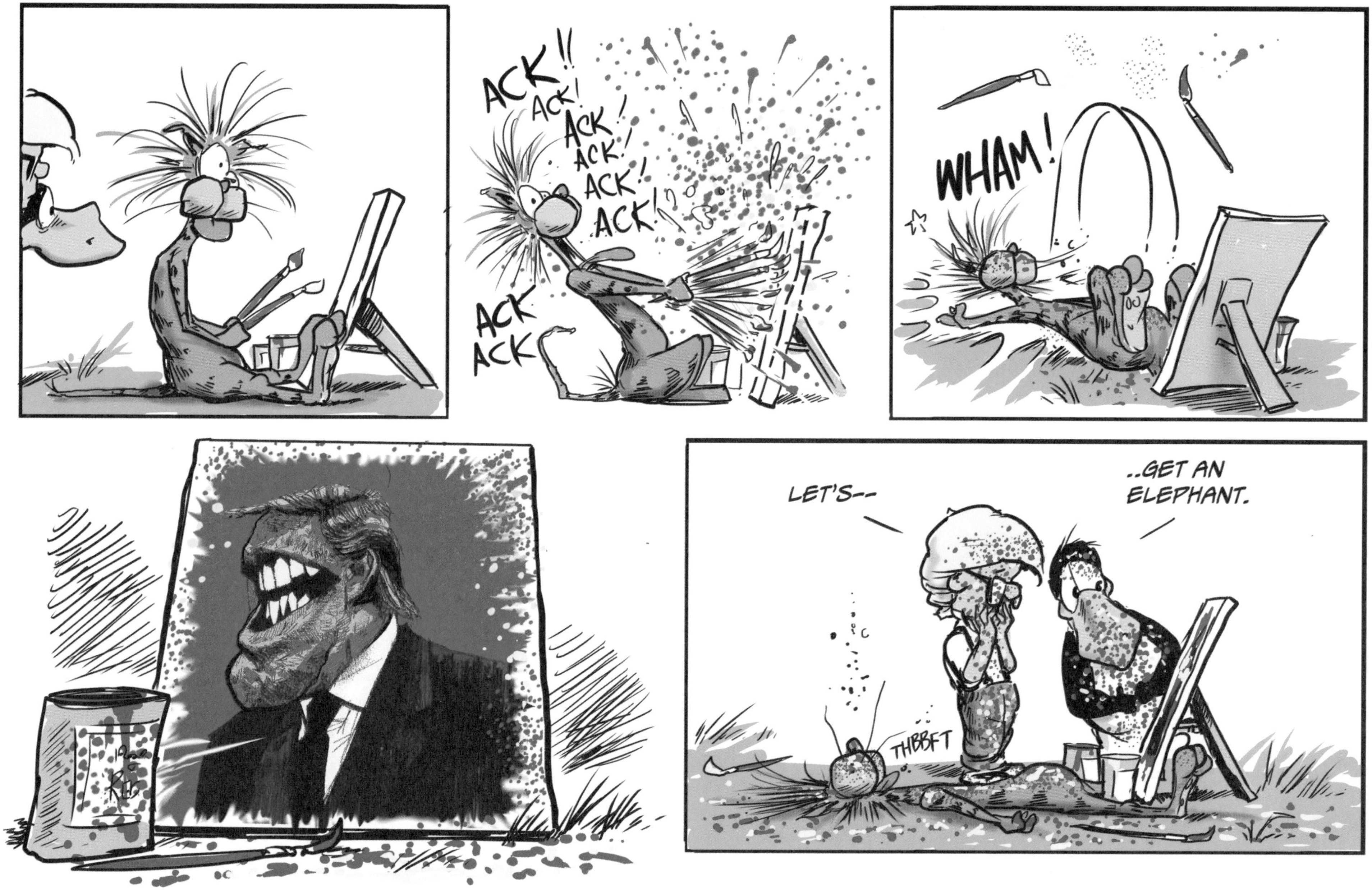

ACK!!
ACK!
ACK!
ACK!
ACK!
ACK!
ACK
ACK
WHAM!
LET'S--
..GET AN ELEPHANT.
THBBFT

When I was seven years old I was dumpster-diving in Long Island New York. I found a collection of porn, a cracked jet pilot's helmet, and one of the most important discoveries of my life: *Bloom County Penguin Dreams* and *Stranger Things*. It changed my life. From that point on I wanted to be a cartoonist. I even tried to get published by the local newspaper when I was 11. Right now I'm a 24-year-old self-employed artist. I kinda said screw retail…I'll go starve. But I'm happy and I wanted to say thanks.

—Joshua Van Fonda

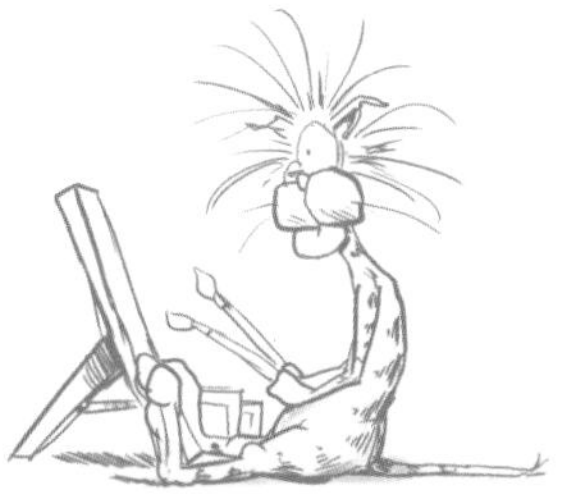

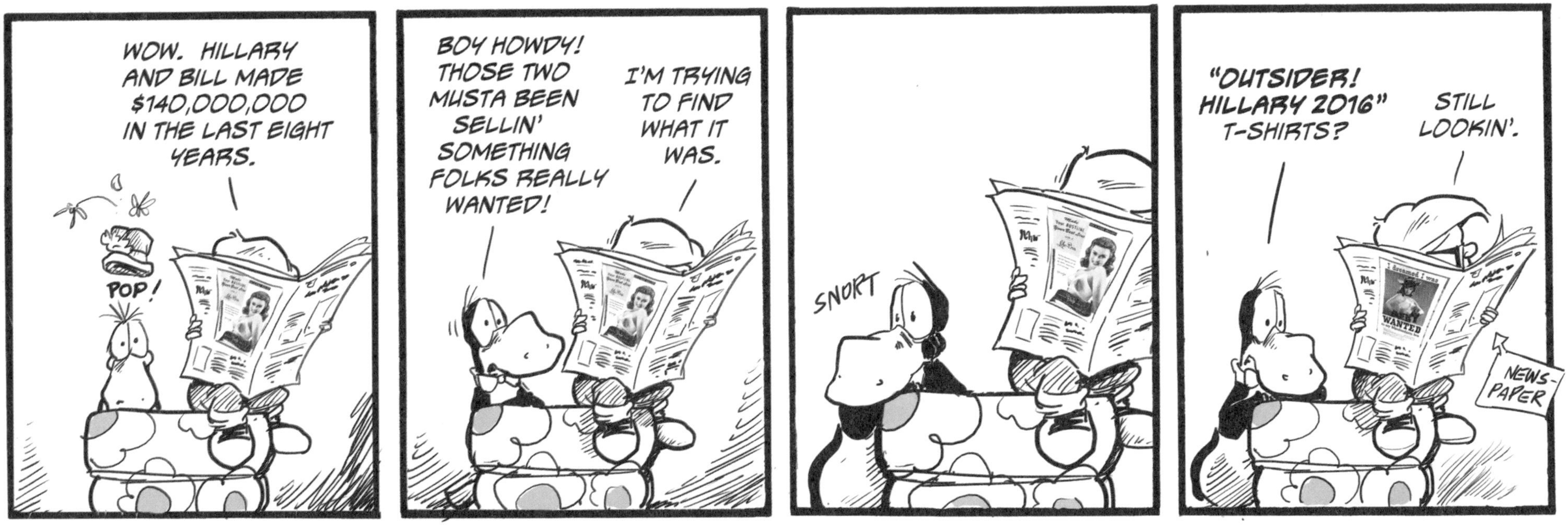
WOW. HILLARY AND BILL MADE $140,000,000 IN THE LAST EIGHT YEARS.
POP!
BOY HOWDY! THOSE TWO MUSTA BEEN SELLIN' SOMETHING FOLKS REALLY WANTED!
I'M TRYING TO FIND WHAT IT WAS.
SNORT
"OUTSIDER! HILLARY 2016" T-SHIRTS?
STILL LOOKIN'.
NEWS-PAPER
WANTED

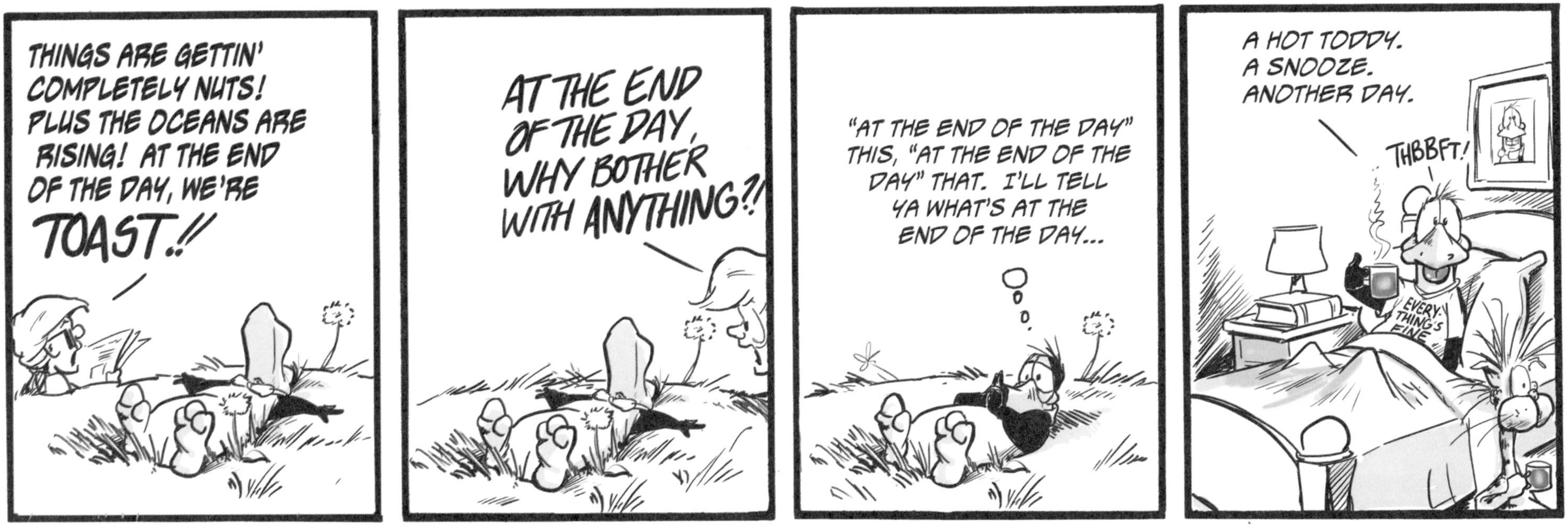
THINGS ARE GETTIN' COMPLETELY NUTS! PLUS THE OCEANS ARE RISING! AT THE END OF THE DAY, WE'RE TOAST.!!
AT THE END OF THE DAY, WHY BOTHER WITH ANYTHING?!
"AT THE END OF THE DAY" THIS, "AT THE END OF THE DAY" THAT. I'LL TELL YA WHAT'S AT THE END OF THE DAY...
A HOT TODDY. A SNOOZE. ANOTHER DAY.
THBBFT!
EVERY-THING'S FINE

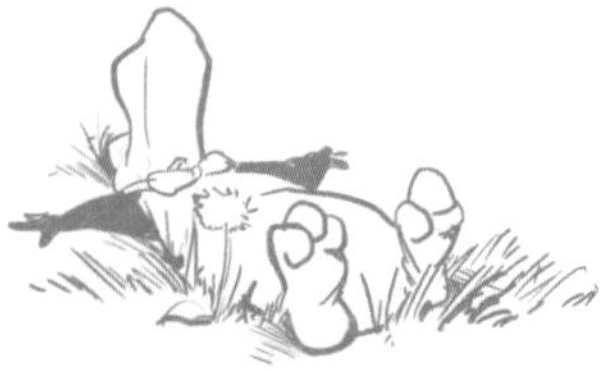

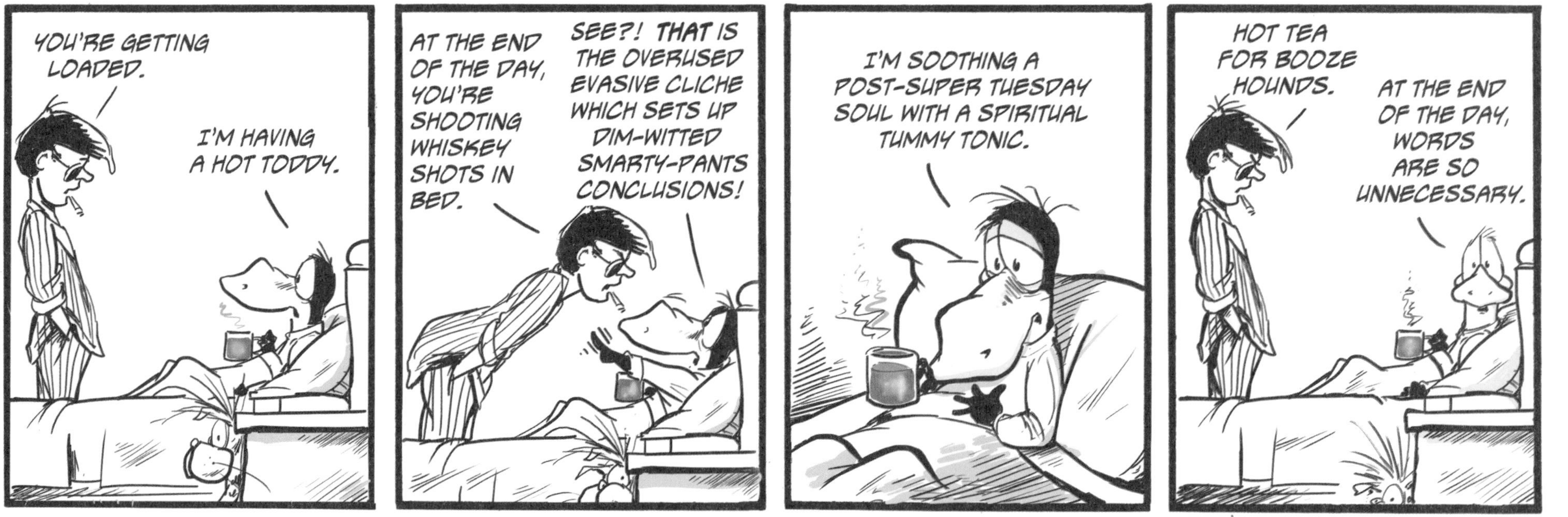
YOU'RE GETTING LOADED.
I'M HAVING A HOT TODDY.
AT THE END OF THE DAY, YOU'RE SHOOTING WHISKEY SHOTS IN BED.
SEE?! THAT IS THE OVERUSED EVASIVE CLICHE WHICH SETS UP DIM-WITTED SMARTY-PANTS CONCLUSIONS!
I'M SOOTHING A POST-SUPER TUESDAY SOUL WITH A SPIRITUAL TUMMY TONIC.
HOT TEA FOR BOOZE HOUNDS.
AT THE END OF THE DAY, WORDS ARE SO UNNECESSARY.

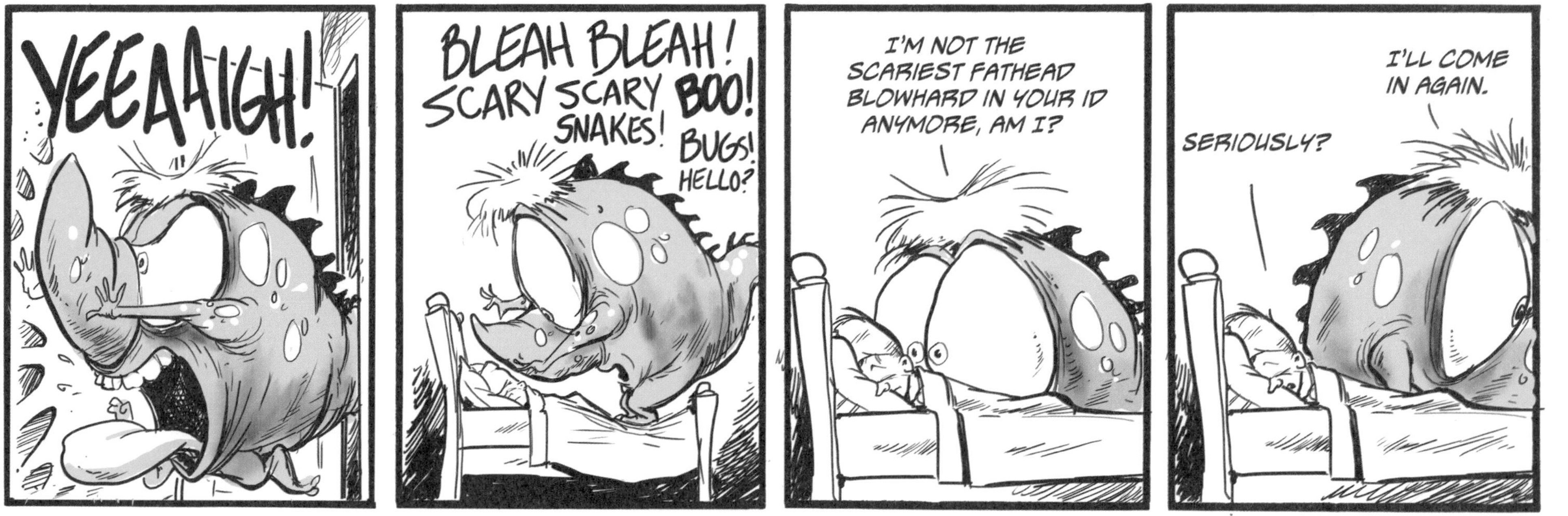
YEEAAIGH!
BLEAH BLEAH! SCARY SCARY SNAKES! BOO! BUGS! HELLO?
I'M NOT THE SCARIEST FATHEAD BLOWHARD IN YOUR ID ANYMORE, AM I?
SERIOUSLY?
I'LL COME IN AGAIN.

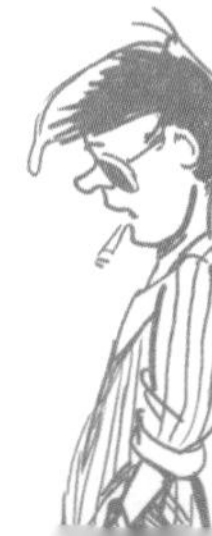

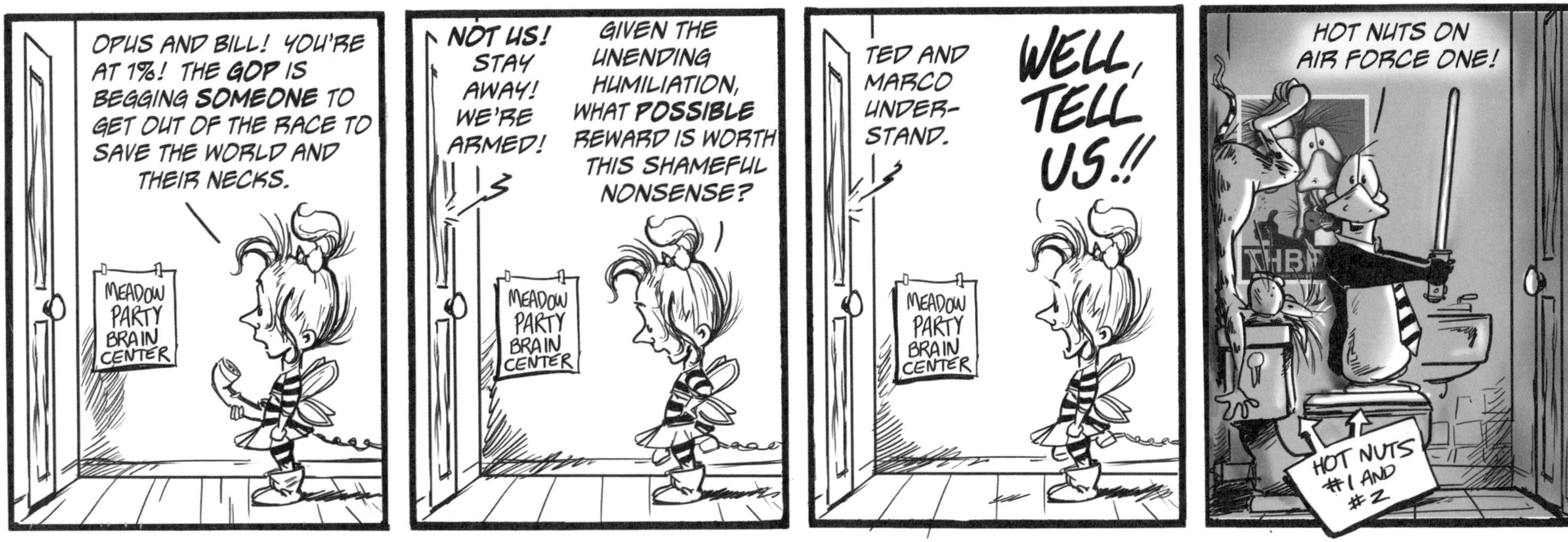
OPUS AND BILL! YOU'RE AT 1%! THE GOP IS BEGGING SOMEONE TO GET OUT OF THE RACE TO SAVE THE WORLD AND THEIR NECKS.
MEADOW PARTY BRAIN CENTER
NOT US! STAY AWAY! WE'RE ARMED!
GIVEN THE UNENDING HUMILIATION, WHAT POSSIBLE REWARD IS WORTH THIS SHAMEFUL NONSENSE?
MEADOW PARTY BRAIN CENTER
TED AND MARCO UNDER-STAND.
WELL, TELL US!!
MEADOW PARTY BRAIN CENTER
HOT NUTS ON AIR FORCE ONE!
HOT NUTS #1 AND #2

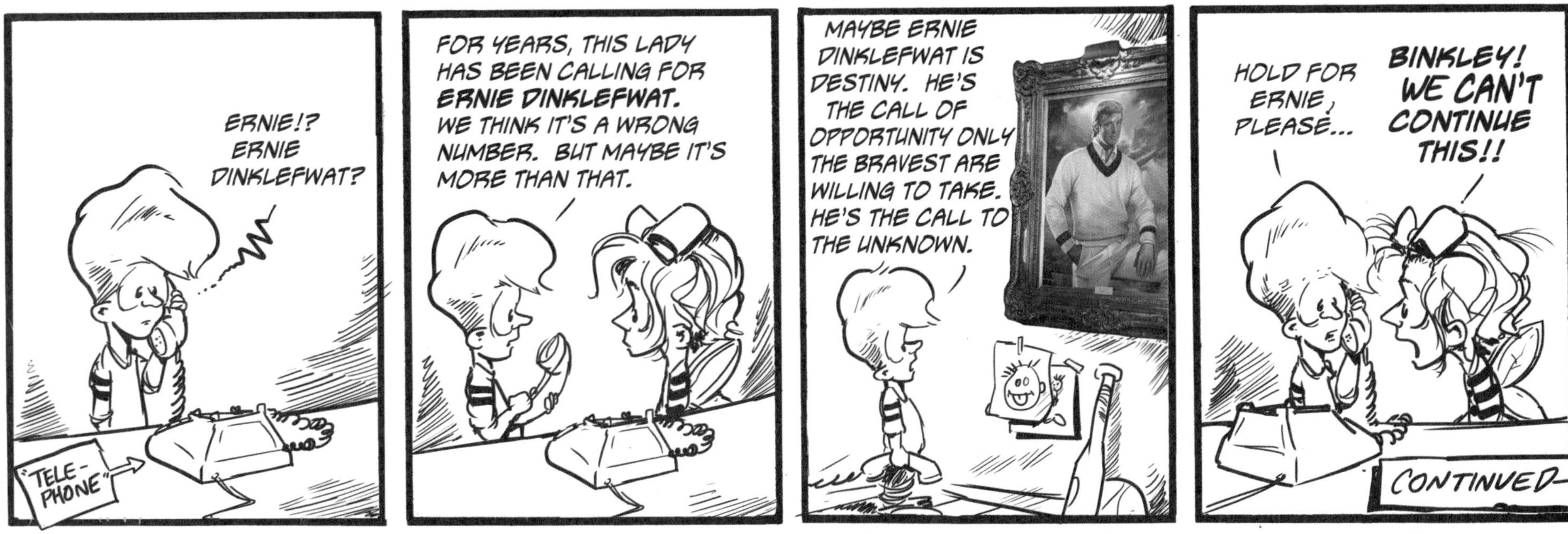
ERNIE!? ERNIE DINKLEFWAT?
"TELE-PHONE"
FOR YEARS, THIS LADY HAS BEEN CALLING FOR ERNIE DINKLEFWAT. WE THINK IT'S A WRONG NUMBER. BUT MAYBE IT'S MORE THAN THAT.
MAYBE ERNIE DINKLEFWAT IS DESTINY. HE'S THE CALL OF OPPORTUNITY ONLY THE BRAVEST ARE WILLING TO TAKE. HE'S THE CALL TO THE UNKNOWN.
HOLD FOR ERNIE, PLEASE...
BINKLEY! WE CAN'T CONTINUE THIS!!
CONTINUED

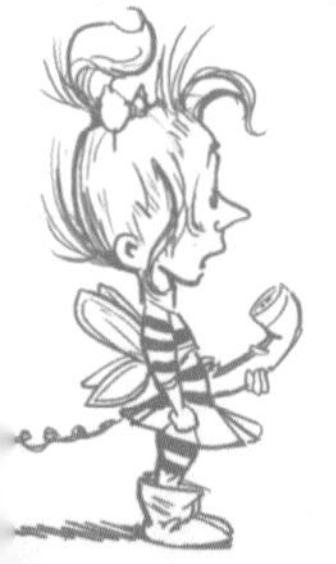

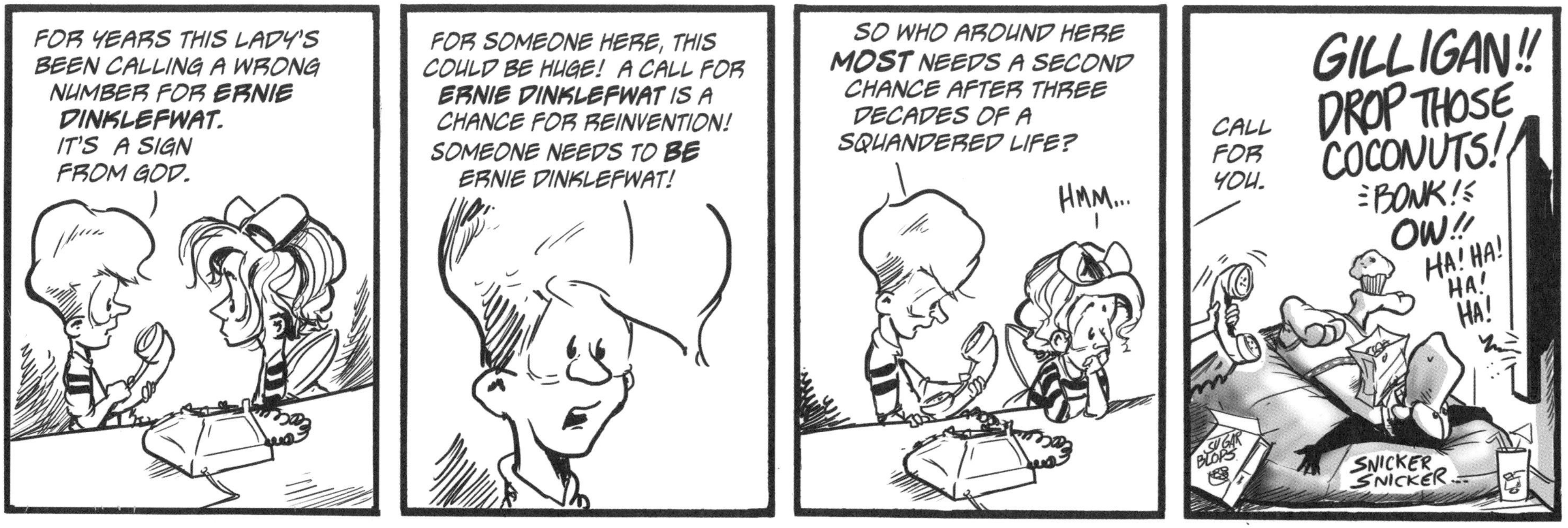
FOR YEARS THIS LADY'S BEEN CALLING A WRONG NUMBER FOR ERNIE DINKLEFWAT. IT'S A SIGN FROM GOD.
FOR SOMEONE HERE, THIS COULD BE HUGE! A CALL FOR ERNIE DINKLEFWAT IS A CHANCE FOR REINVENTION! SOMEONE NEEDS TO BE ERNIE DINKLEFWAT!
SO WHO AROUND HERE MOST NEEDS A SECOND CHANCE AFTER THREE DECADES OF A SQUANDERED LIFE?
HMM...
CALL FOR YOU.
GILLIGAN!! DROP THOSE COCONUTS!
BONK!
OW!!
HA! HA! HA! HA!
SUGAR BLOPS
SNICKER SNICKER...

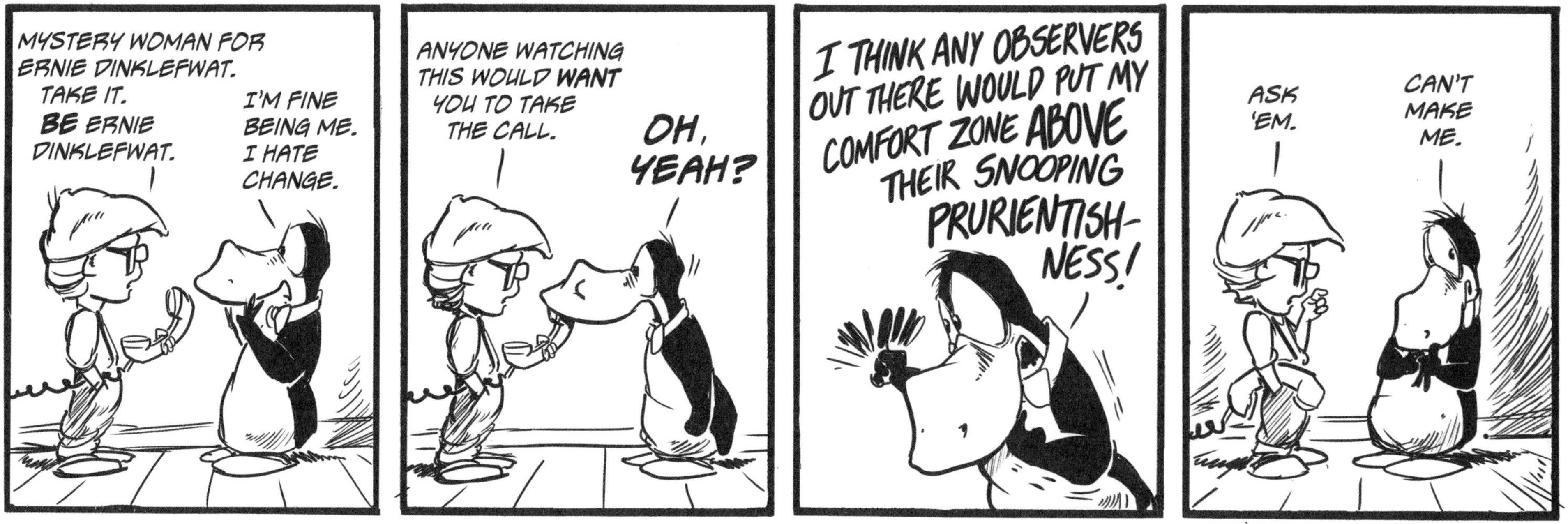
MYSTERY WOMAN FOR ERNIE DINKLEFWAT. TAKE IT. BE ERNIE DINKLEFWAT.
I'M FINE BEING ME. I HATE CHANGE.
ANYONE WATCHING THIS WOULD WANT YOU TO TAKE THE CALL.
OH, YEAH?
I THINK ANY OBSERVERS OUT THERE WOULD PUT MY COMFORT ZONE ABOVE THEIR SNOOPING PRURIENTISH-NESS!
ASK 'EM.
CAN'T MAKE ME.

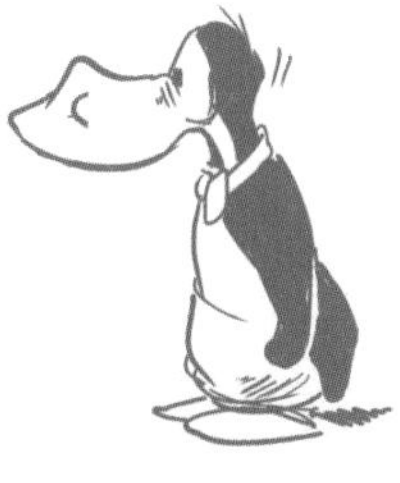

OPUS, THE UNIVERSE IS REACHING OUT WITH JUMPER CABLES FOR YOUR BORING LIFE...

Bloom County
by Berkeley Breathed

... AND THEY'RE HELD BY A LADY WITH A WRONG NUMBER CALLING FOR ERNIE DINKLEFWAT.

TV

OPUS IS BUSY

FOR ONCE, TURN THE TV OFF AND IMAGINE THE POSSIBILITIES.

HOW MANY OF US GET THE CHANCE FOR A RESTART? A REDO? A REBOOT?

RERUNS ARE ENOUGH EXCITEMENT.

REALLY? YOU JUST WANT A TEPID, SPICELESS LIFE WHERE THE ONLY EXCITEMENT IS LIVED ON TV?

YEAH! WELL, NO. I GUESS NOT. NO!

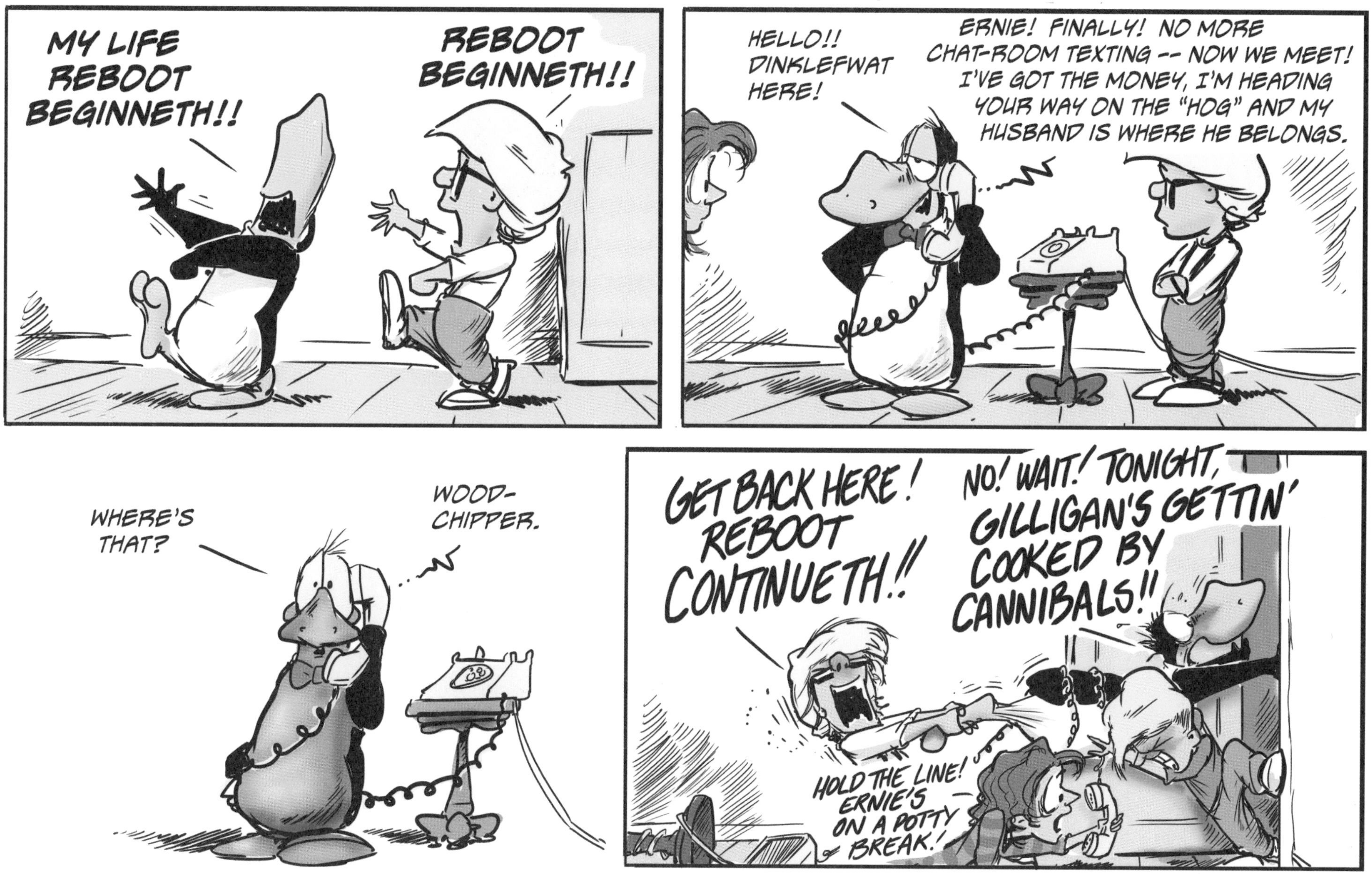
MY LIFE REBOOT BEGINNETH!!
REBOOT BEGINNETH!!
HELLO!! DINKLEFWAT HERE!
ERNIE! FINALLY! NO MORE CHAT-ROOM TEXTING -- NOW WE MEET! I'VE GOT THE MONEY, I'M HEADING YOUR WAY ON THE "HOG" AND MY HUSBAND IS WHERE HE BELONGS.
WHERE'S THAT?
WOOD-CHIPPER.
GET BACK HERE! REBOOT CONTINUETH!!
NO! WAIT! TONIGHT, GILLIGAN'S GETTIN' COOKED BY CANNIBALS!!
HOLD THE LINE! ERNIE'S ON A POTTY BREAK!

Can you imagine if we actually had the city of *Bloom County*, populated by the fans of this comic strip? How freakin' awesome would it be to live there?

—Becky Piazza

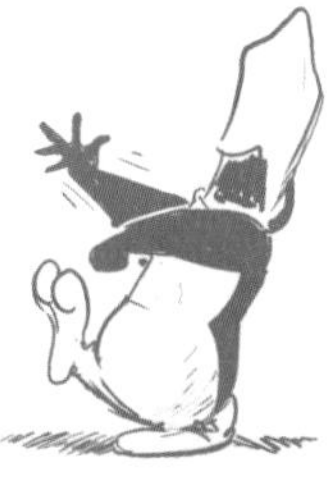

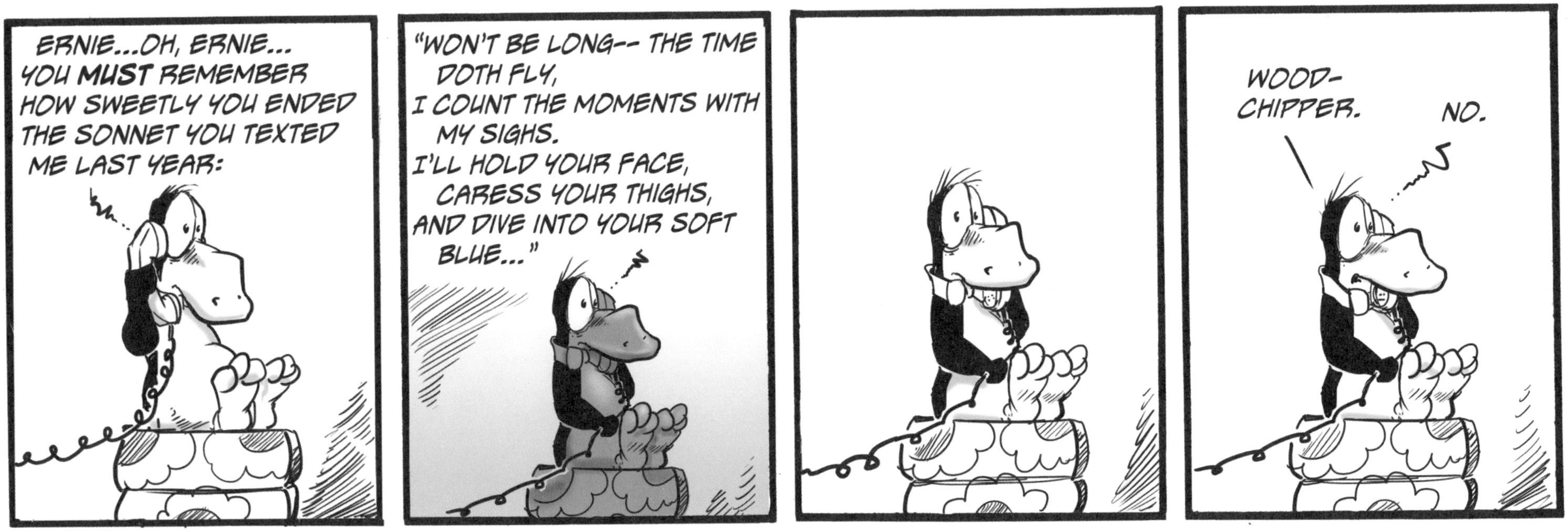
ERNIE...OH, ERNIE... YOU **MUST** REMEMBER HOW SWEETLY YOU ENDED THE SONNET YOU TEXTED ME LAST YEAR:
"WON'T BE LONG-- THE TIME DOTH FLY,
I COUNT THE MOMENTS WITH MY SIGHS.
I'LL HOLD YOUR FACE, CARESS YOUR THIGHS,
AND DIVE INTO YOUR SOFT BLUE..."
WOOD-CHIPPER.
NO.

132

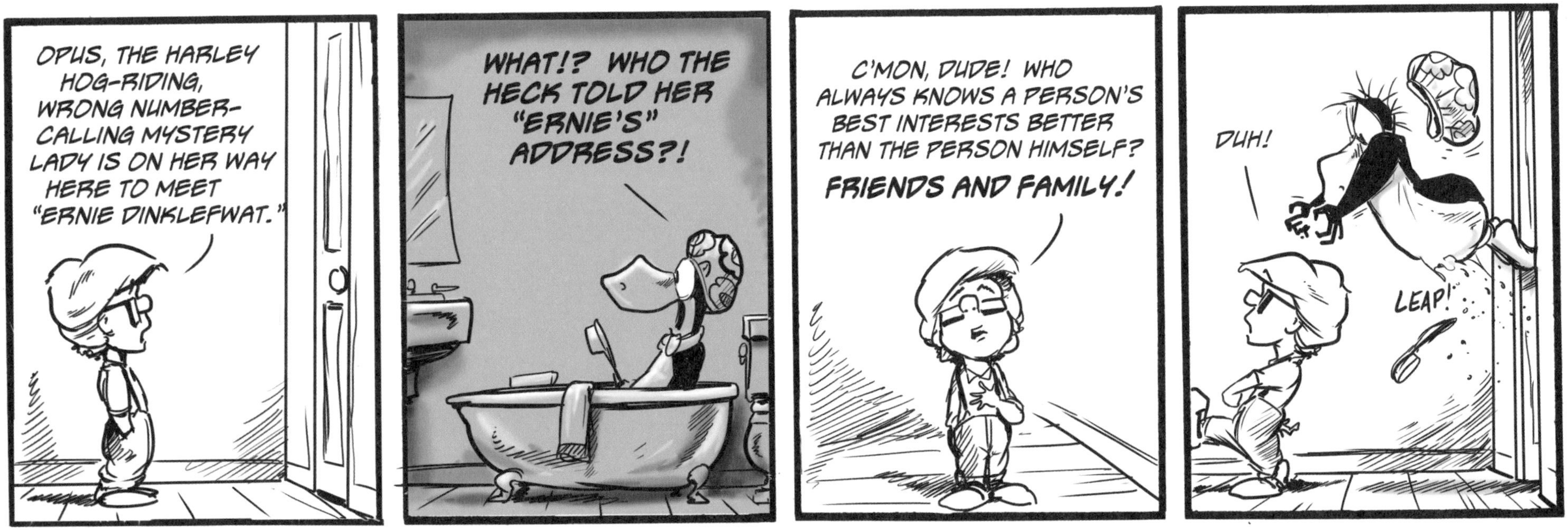
OPUS, THE HARLEY HOG-RIDING, WRONG NUMBER-CALLING MYSTERY LADY IS ON HER WAY HERE TO MEET "ERNIE DINKLEFWAT."
WHAT!? WHO THE HECK TOLD HER "ERNIE'S" ADDRESS?!
C'MON, DUDE! WHO ALWAYS KNOWS A PERSON'S BEST INTERESTS BETTER THAN THE PERSON HIMSELF?
FRIENDS AND FAMILY!
DUH!
LEAP!

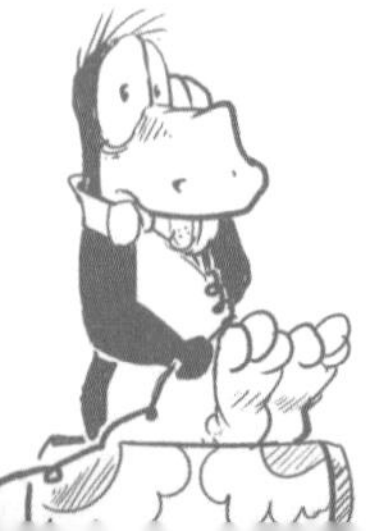

SO THERE IT IS: I TAKE A CALL FROM A SILKY-VOICED NUTCASE WHACK-JOB **WRONG NUMBER** AND NOW I'M SEDOOCLED INTO A COMPLETELY FRAUDULENT WEIRDO REBOOT OF MY NORMAL WORLD!

YOU'VE BEEN DINKLEFWATTED.

ROYALLY DINKLEFWATTED! I WONDER IF THIS EVER HAPPENS TO ANYONE ELSE?!

WHAT.

ELECTION YEAR, DUDE.

OH, YEAH YEAH YEAH YEAH.

TO BE HONEST, I'M A LITTLE NERVOUS THAT WE'RE FINALLY MEETING SOON. I HAVE ONE LAST QUESTION, MADAM...

OH, ERNIE... CALL ME "SWEET CHEEKS" LIKE YOU'VE TEXTED FOR YEARS.

NOT ERNIE

DO YOU LIKE **PENGUINS**, SWEET CHEEKS?

PENGUINS?

YES. TUBBY, LONG-WAISTED LITTLE FELLAS.

THEY'RE WONDERFUL!

WHEW!

WITH SOME FAVA BEANS AND A NICE CHIANTI!

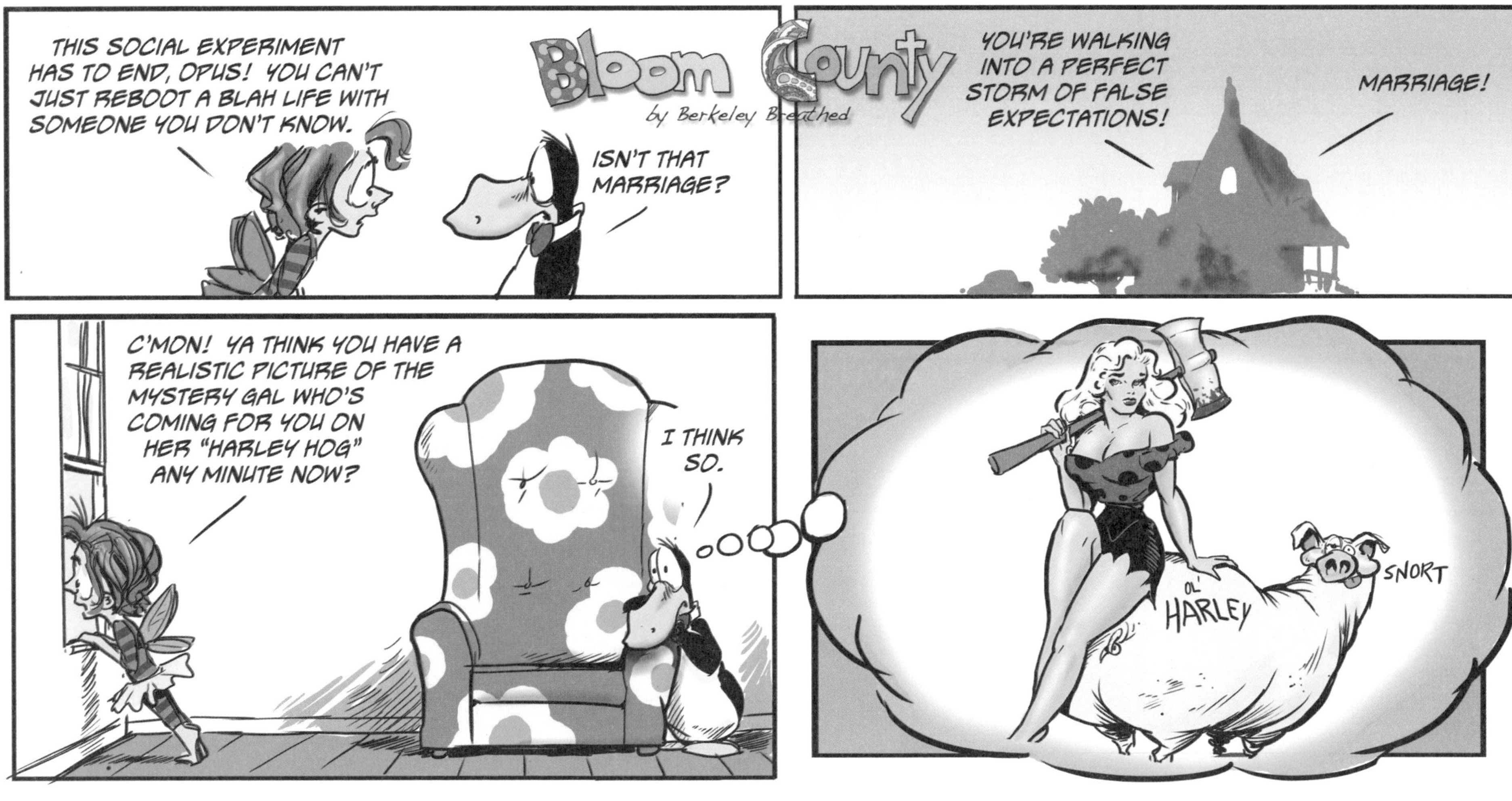
THIS SOCIAL EXPERIMENT HAS TO END, OPUS! YOU CAN'T JUST REBOOT A BLAH LIFE WITH SOMEONE YOU DON'T KNOW.
Bloom County
by Berkeley Breathed
ISN'T THAT MARRIAGE?
YOU'RE WALKING INTO A PERFECT STORM OF FALSE EXPECTATIONS!
MARRIAGE!
C'MON! YA THINK YOU HAVE A REALISTIC PICTURE OF THE MYSTERY GAL WHO'S COMING FOR YOU ON HER "HARLEY HOG" ANY MINUTE NOW?
I THINK SO.
OL' HARLEY
SNORT

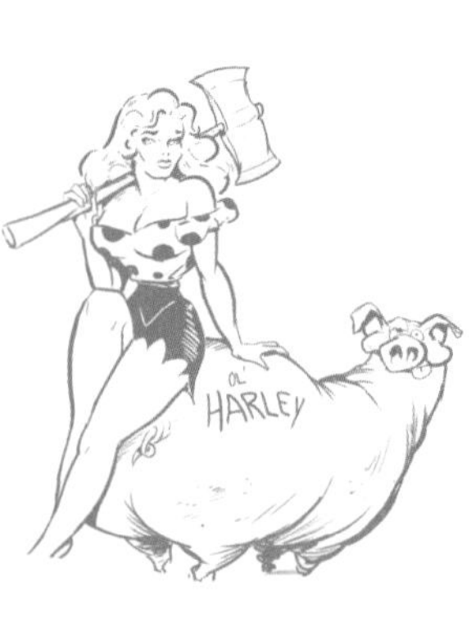
OL' HARLEY

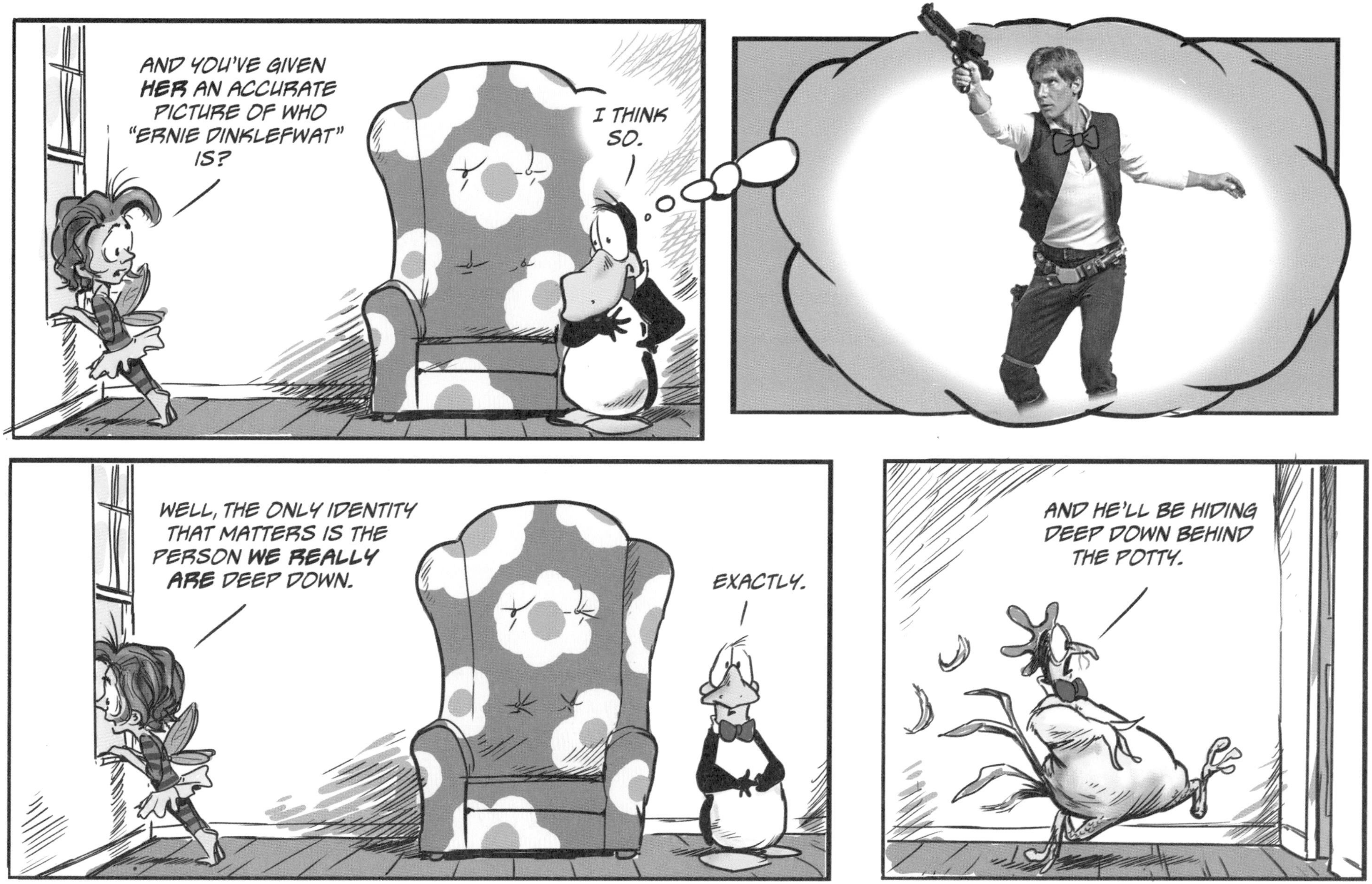
AND YOU'VE GIVEN HER AN ACCURATE PICTURE OF WHO "ERNIE DINKLEFWAT" IS?
I THINK SO.
WELL, THE ONLY IDENTITY THAT MATTERS IS THE PERSON WE REALLY ARE DEEP DOWN.
EXACTLY.
AND HE'LL BE HIDING DEEP DOWN BEHIND THE POTTY.

Only on Facebook can a genius comic strip artist inspire such brilliant armchair comment comedians. Would that be sit-down comedians instead of stand-up comedians?

—Val Mallinson

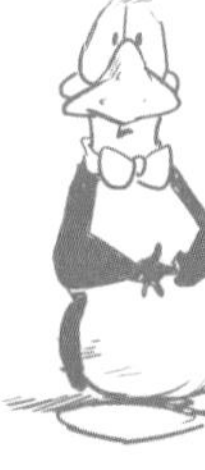

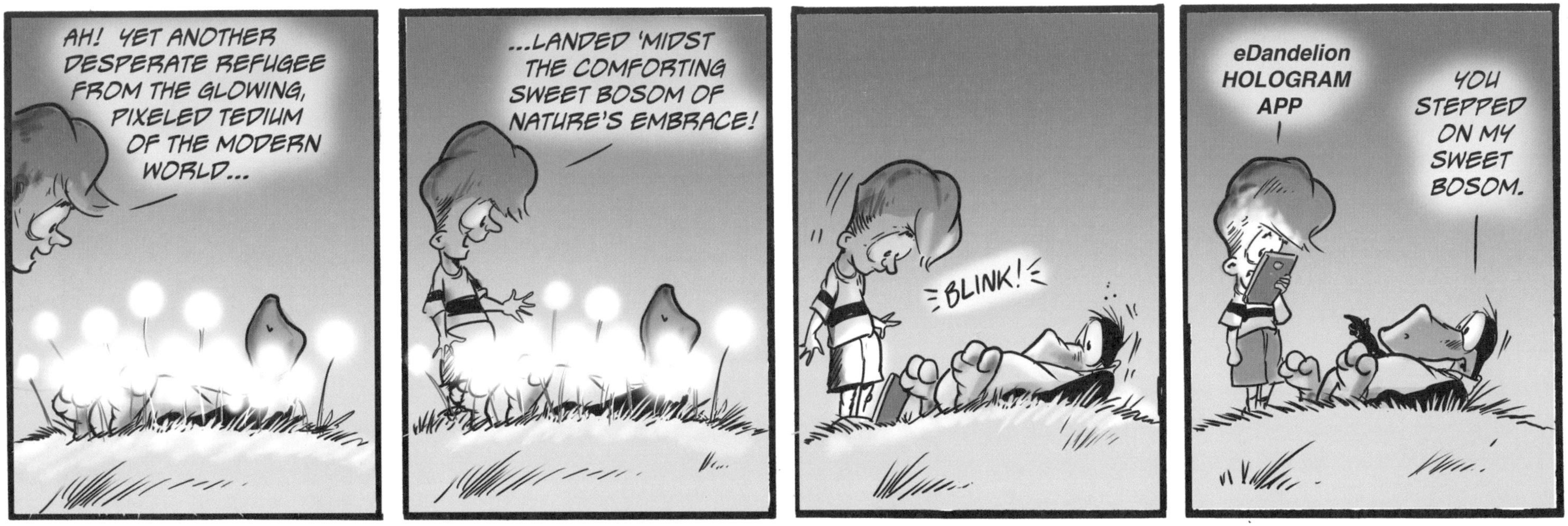
AH! YET ANOTHER DESPERATE REFUGEE FROM THE GLOWING, PIXELED TEDIUM OF THE MODERN WORLD...
...LANDED 'MIDST THE COMFORTING SWEET BOSOM OF NATURE'S EMBRACE!
BLINK!
eDandelion HOLOGRAM APP
YOU STEPPED ON MY SWEET BOSOM.

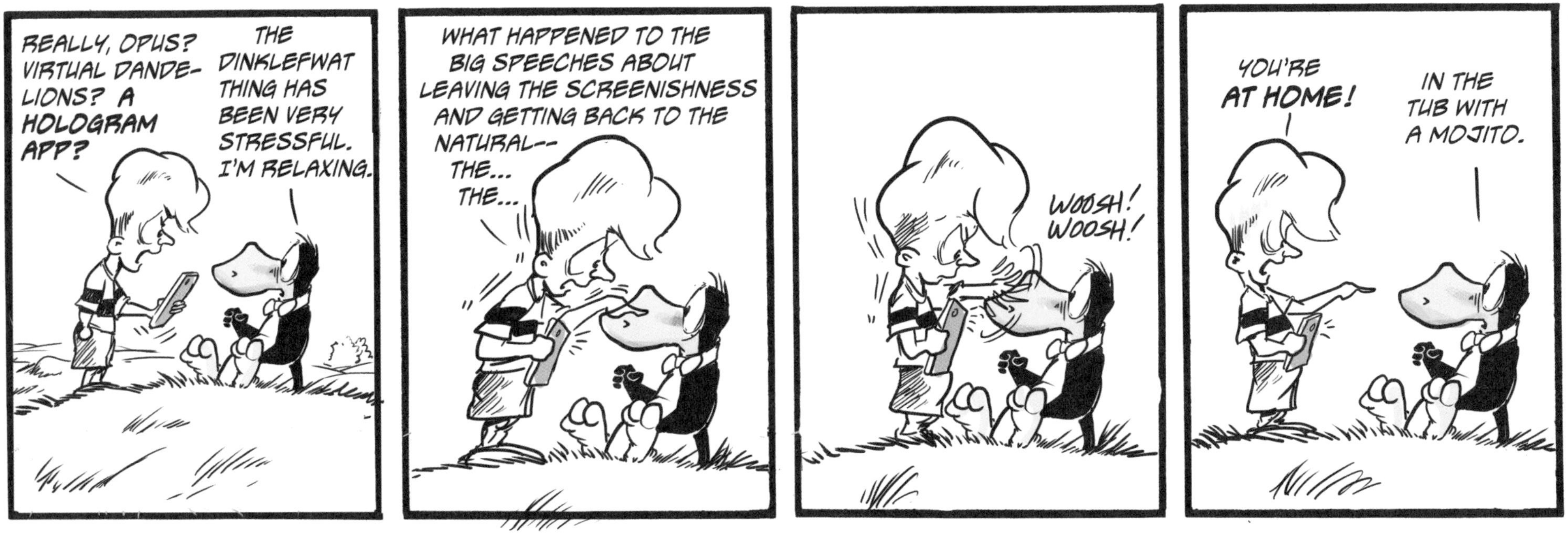
REALLY, OPUS? VIRTUAL DANDE-LIONS? A HOLOGRAM APP?
THE DINKLEFWAT THING HAS BEEN VERY STRESSFUL. I'M RELAXING.
WHAT HAPPENED TO THE BIG SPEECHES ABOUT LEAVING THE SCREENISHNESS AND GETTING BACK TO THE NATURAL--
THE... THE...
WOOSH! WOOSH!
YOU'RE AT HOME!
IN THE TUB WITH A MOJITO.

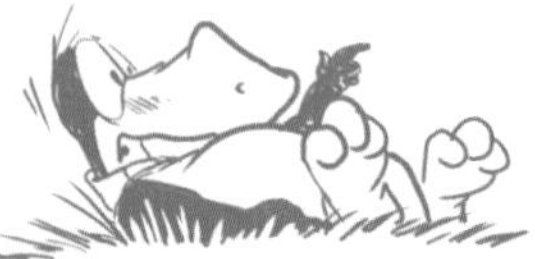

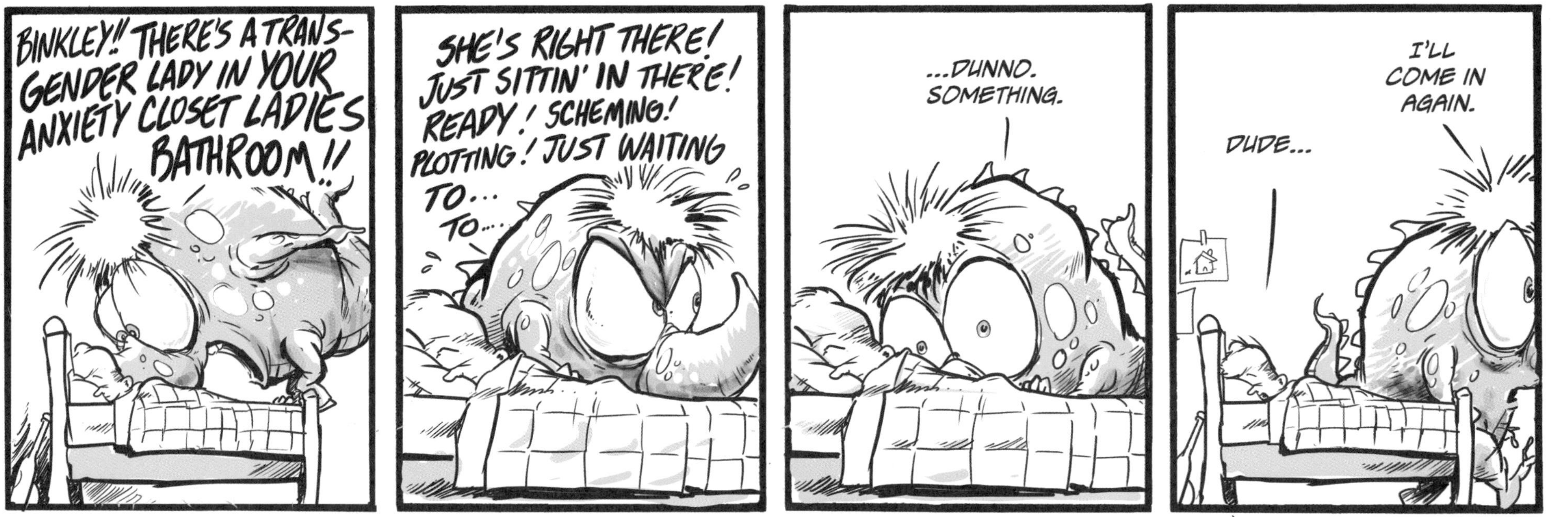
BINKLEY!! THERE'S A TRANS-GENDER LADY IN YOUR ANXIETY CLOSET LADIES BATHROOM!!
SHE'S RIGHT THERE! JUST SITTIN' IN THERE! READY! SCHEMING! PLOTTING! JUST WAITING TO... TO...
...DUNNO. SOMETHING.
DUDE...
I'LL COME IN AGAIN.

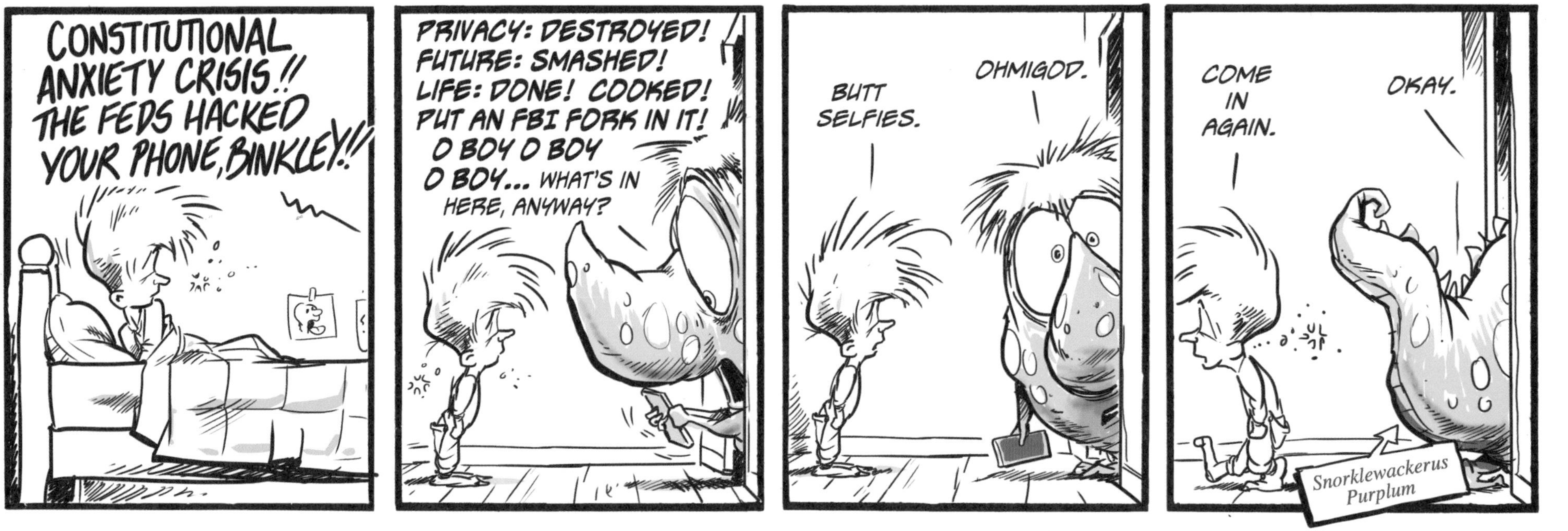
CONSTITUTIONAL ANXIETY CRISIS!! THE FEDS HACKED YOUR PHONE, BINKLEY!!
PRIVACY: DESTROYED! FUTURE: SMASHED! LIFE: DONE! COOKED! PUT AN FBI FORK IN IT! O BOY O BOY O BOY... WHAT'S IN HERE, ANYWAY?
BUTT SELFIES.
OHMIGOD.
COME IN AGAIN.
OKAY.
Snorklewackerus Purplum

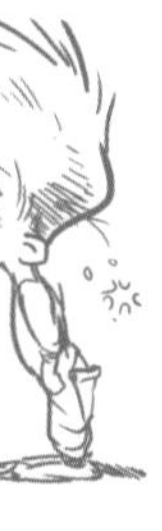

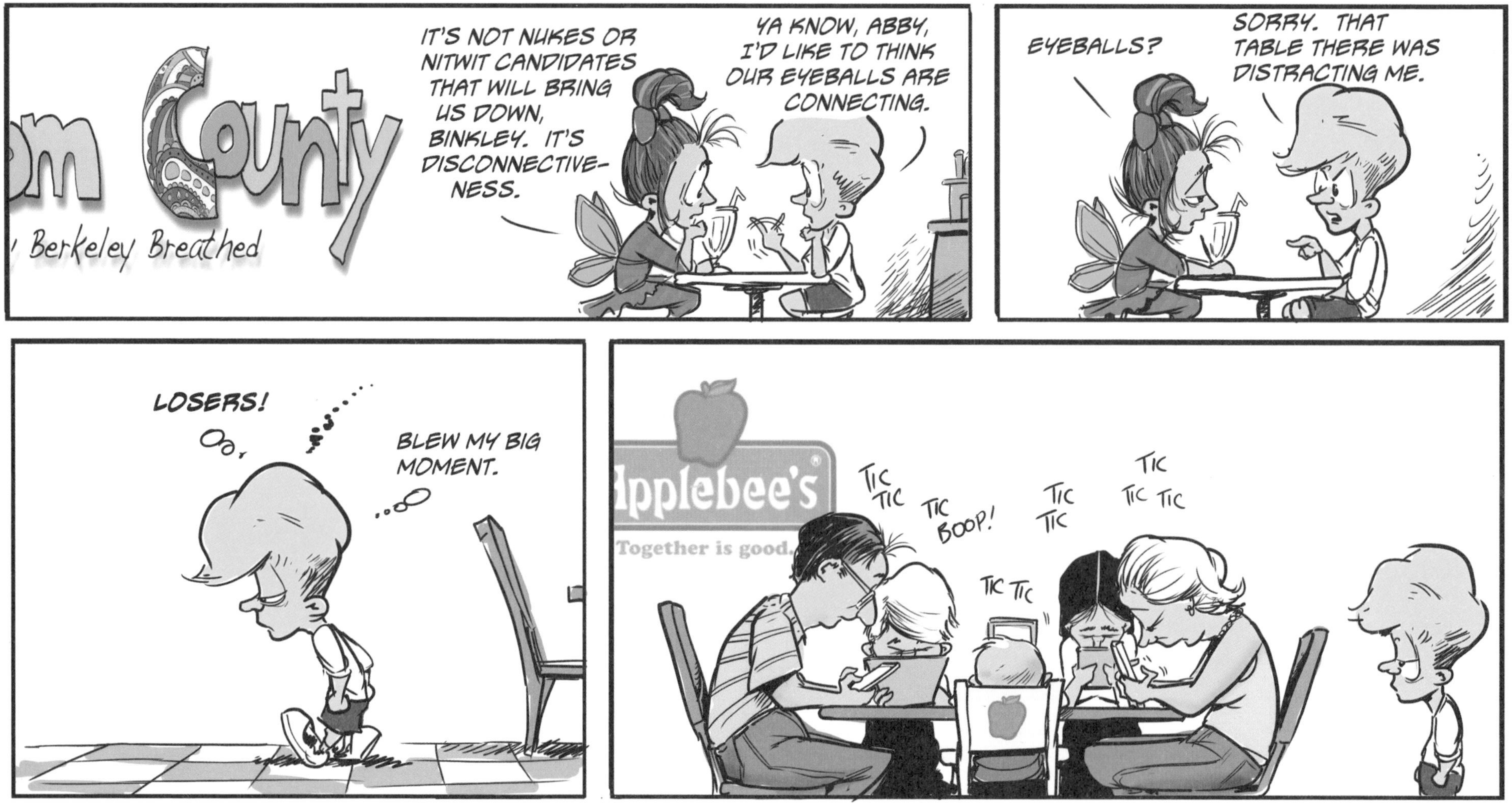

om County
Berkeley Breathed
IT'S NOT NUKES OR NITWIT CANDIDATES THAT WILL BRING US DOWN, BINKLEY. IT'S DISCONNECTIVENESS.
YA KNOW, ABBY, I'D LIKE TO THINK OUR EYEBALLS ARE CONNECTING.
EYEBALLS?
SORRY. THAT TABLE THERE WAS DISTRACTING ME.
LOSERS!
BLEW MY BIG MOMENT.
pplebee's
Together is good.
TIC TIC
TIC BOOP!
TIC TIC
TIC TIC
TIC
TIC TIC
TIC TIC

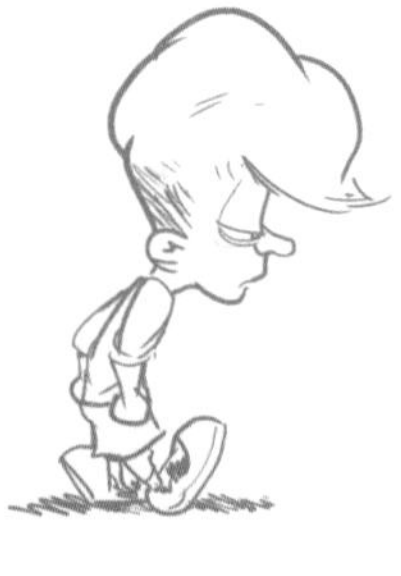

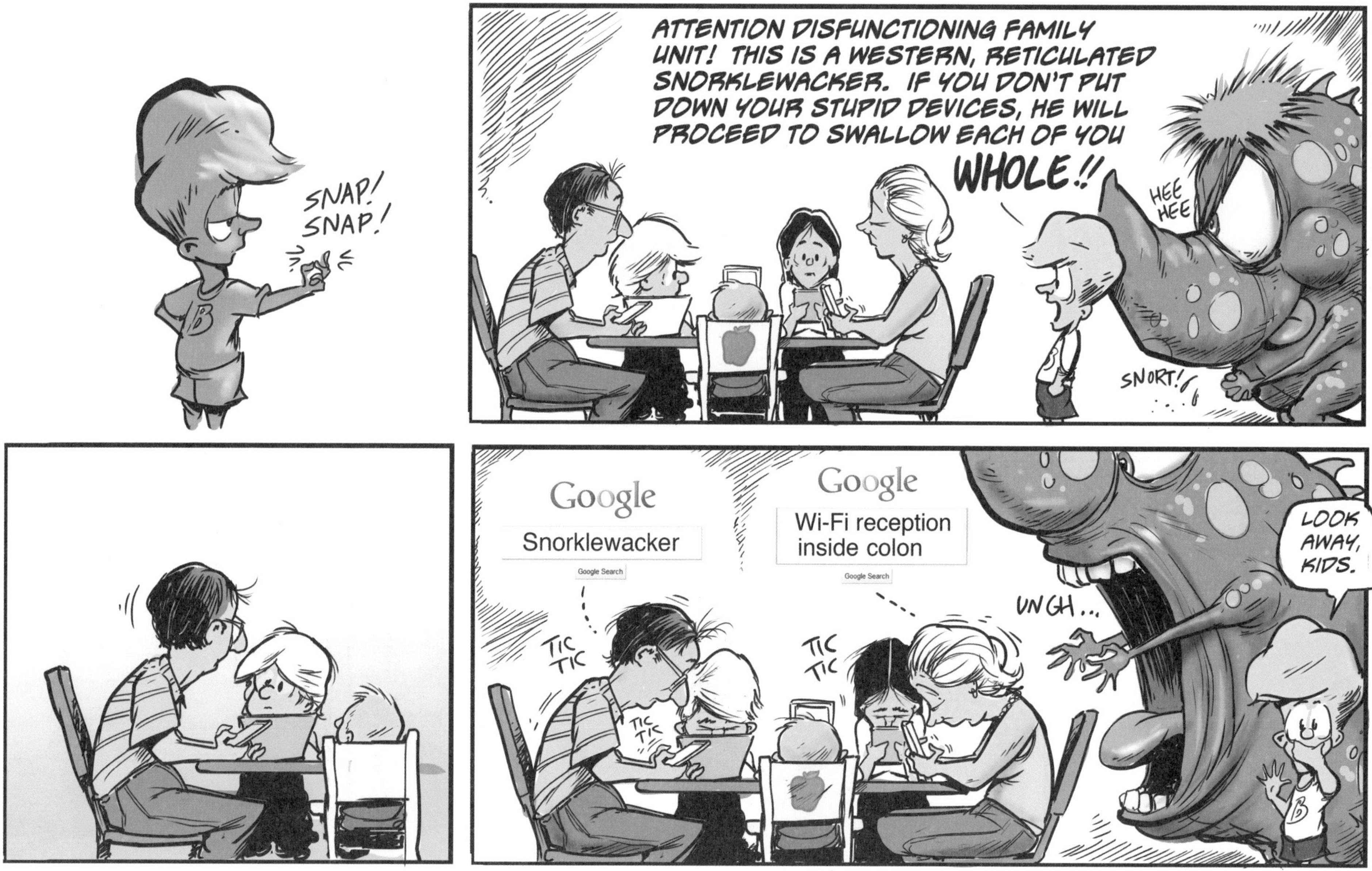
SNAP! SNAP!
ATTENTION DISFUNCTIONING FAMILY UNIT! THIS IS A WESTERN, RETICULATED SNORKLEWACKER. IF YOU DON'T PUT DOWN YOUR STUPID DEVICES, HE WILL PROCEED TO SWALLOW EACH OF YOU WHOLE!!
HEE HEE
SNORT!
Google
Snorklewacker
Google Search
Google
Wi-Fi reception inside colon
Google Search
TIC TIC
TIC TIC
TIC TIC
UNGH...
LOOK AWAY, KIDS.

This comic strip got me from 12 to 14 without killing myself. Not a joke. Thank you.

—Jess Ingalls

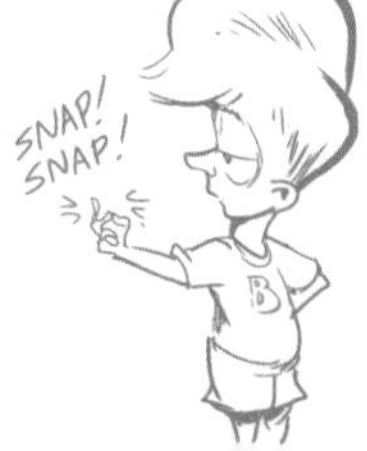
SNAP! SNAP!

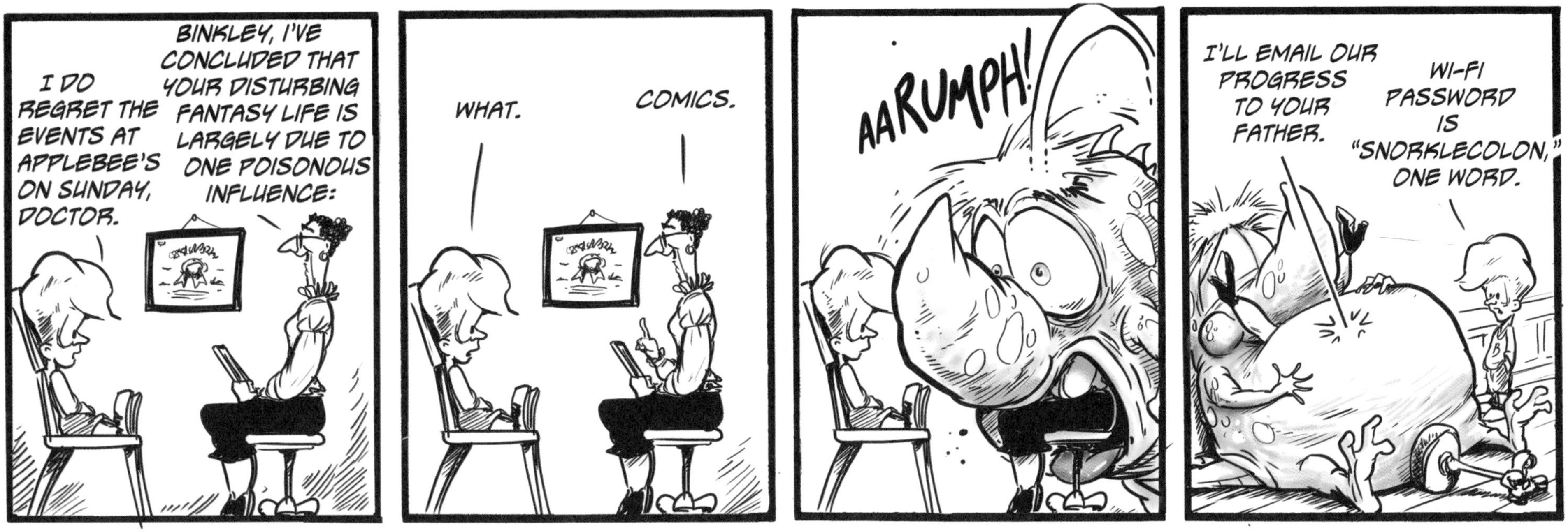
I DO REGRET THE EVENTS AT APPLEBEE'S ON SUNDAY, DOCTOR.
BINKLEY, I'VE CONCLUDED THAT YOUR DISTURBING FANTASY LIFE IS LARGELY DUE TO ONE POISONOUS INFLUENCE:
WHAT.
COMICS.
AARUMPH!
I'LL EMAIL OUR PROGRESS TO YOUR FATHER.
WI-FI PASSWORD IS "SNORKLECOLON," ONE WORD.

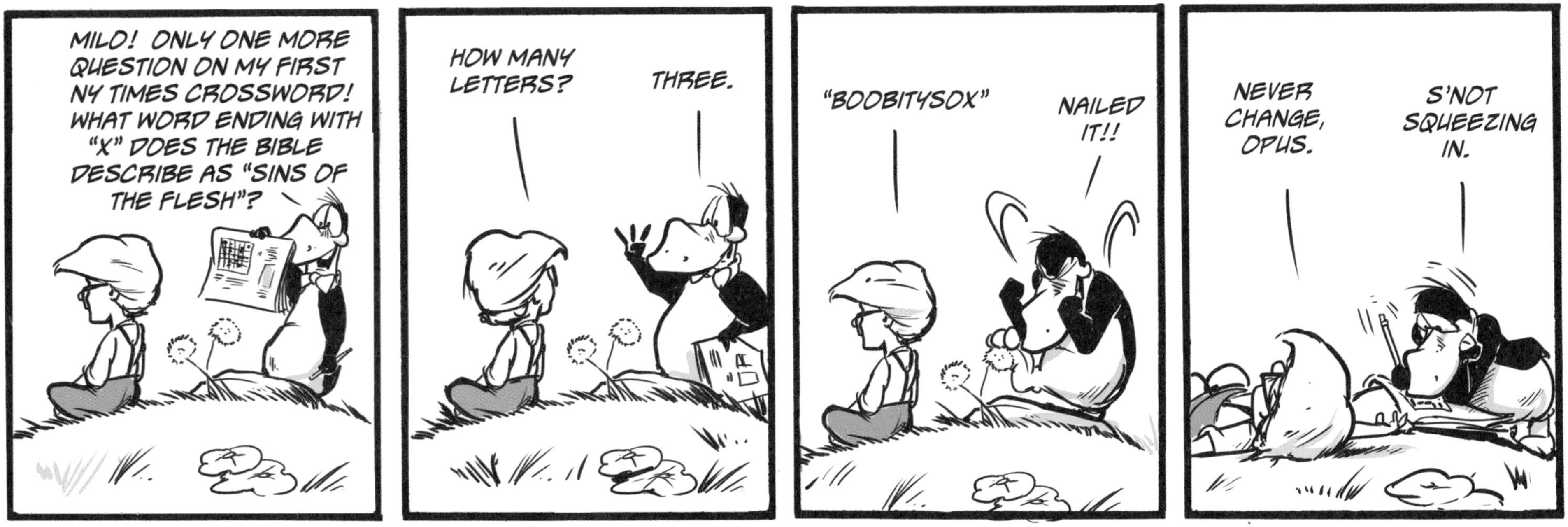
MILO! ONLY ONE MORE QUESTION ON MY FIRST NY TIMES CROSSWORD! WHAT WORD ENDING WITH "X" DOES THE BIBLE DESCRIBE AS "SINS OF THE FLESH"?
HOW MANY LETTERS?
THREE.
"BOOBITYSOX"
NAILED IT!!
NEVER CHANGE, OPUS.
S'NOT SQUEEZING IN.

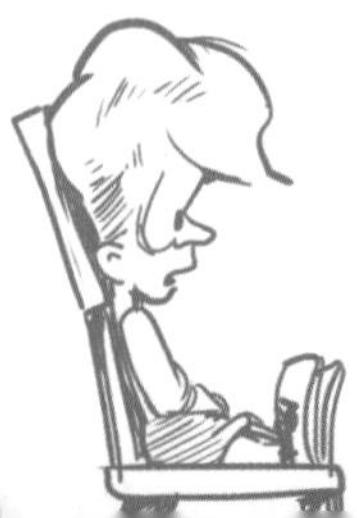

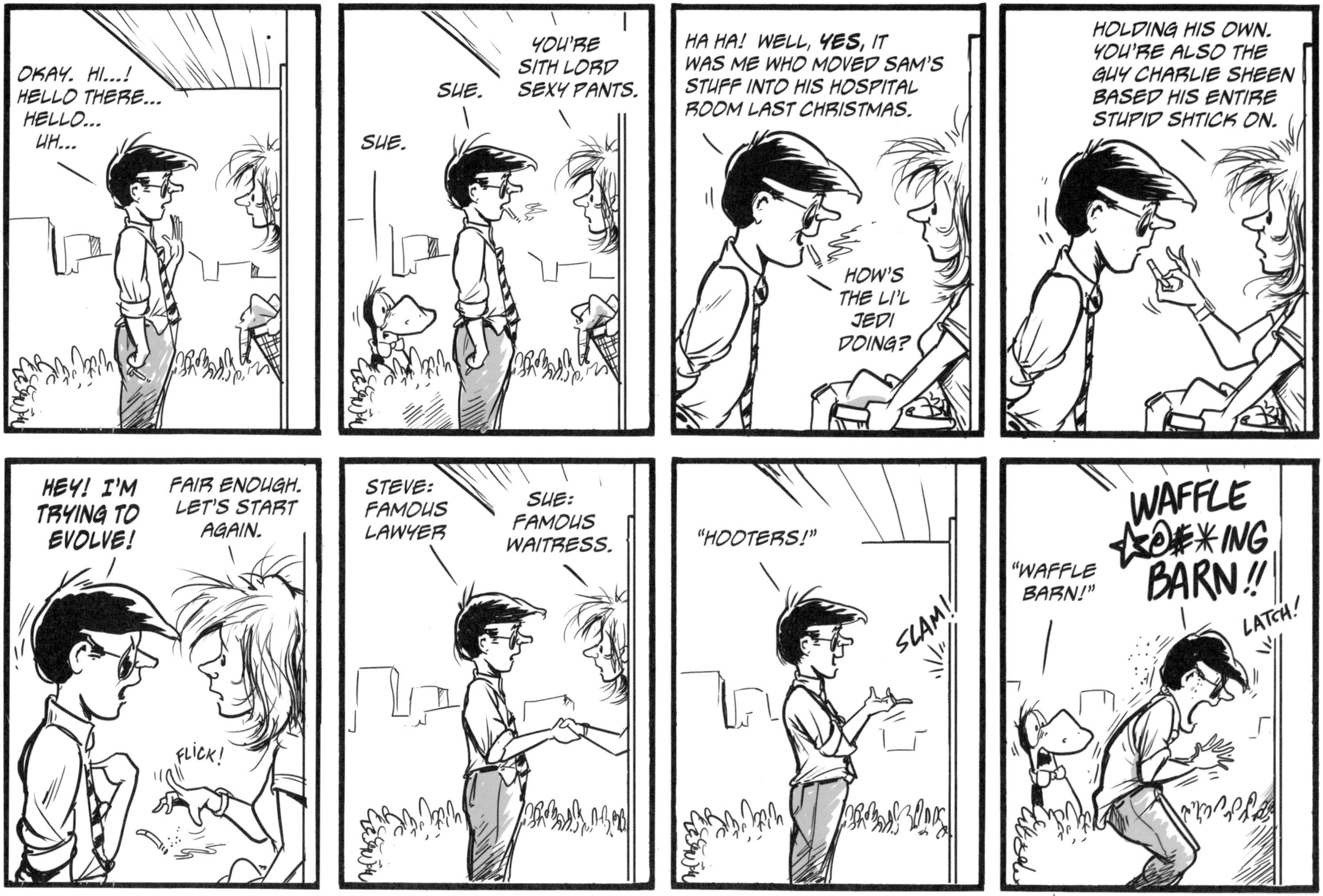
OKAY. HI...! HELLO THERE... HELLO... UH...
SUE.
SUE.
YOU'RE SITH LORD SEXY PANTS.
HA HA! WELL, YES, IT WAS ME WHO MOVED SAM'S STUFF INTO HIS HOSPITAL ROOM LAST CHRISTMAS.
HOW'S THE LI'L JEDI DOING?
HOLDING HIS OWN. YOU'RE ALSO THE GUY CHARLIE SHEEN BASED HIS ENTIRE STUPID SHTICK ON.
HEY! I'M TRYING TO EVOLVE!
FAIR ENOUGH. LET'S START AGAIN.
FLICK!
STEVE: FAMOUS LAWYER
SUE: FAMOUS WAITRESS.
"HOOTERS!"
SLAM!
"WAFFLE BARN!"
WAFFLE ☆@#*ING BARN!!
LATCH!

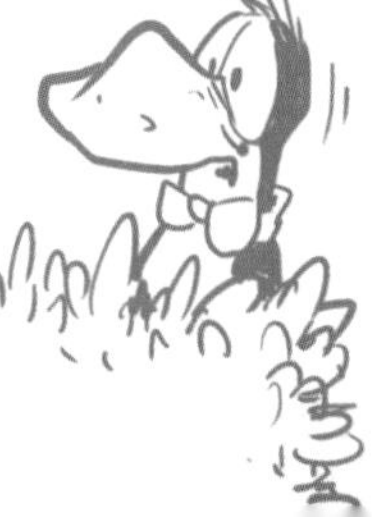

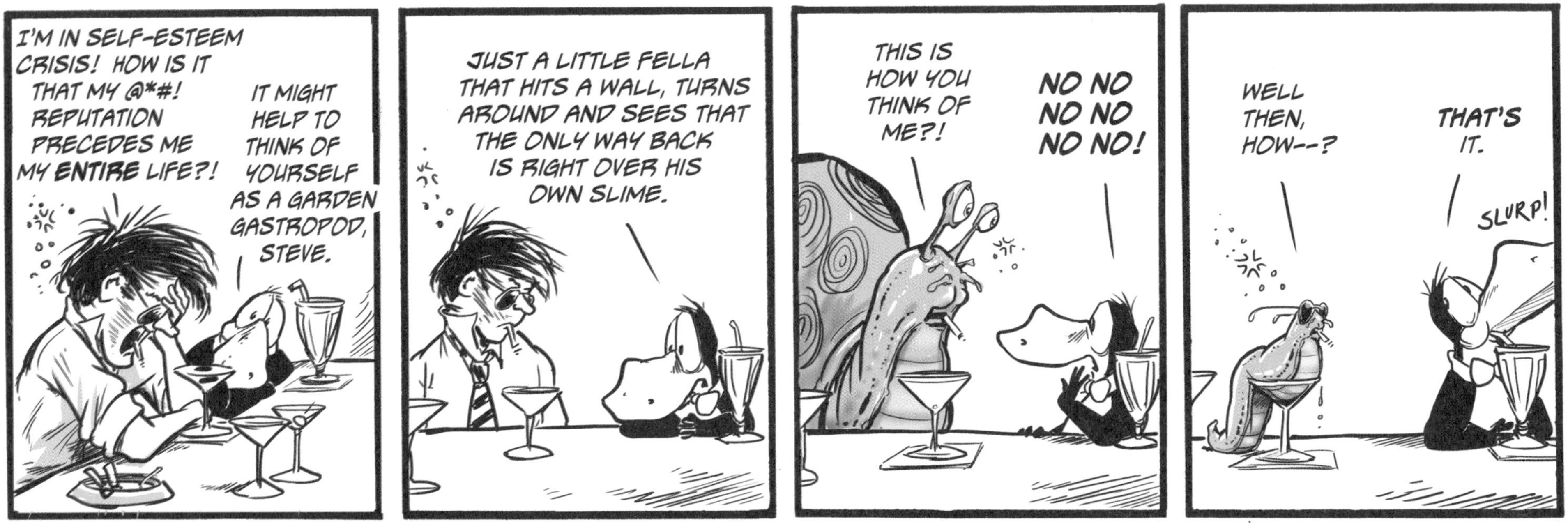
I'M IN SELF-ESTEEM CRISIS! HOW IS IT THAT MY @*#! REPUTATION PRECEDES ME MY **ENTIRE** LIFE?!
IT MIGHT HELP TO THINK OF YOURSELF AS A GARDEN GASTROPOD, STEVE.
JUST A LITTLE FELLA THAT HITS A WALL, TURNS AROUND AND SEES THAT THE ONLY WAY BACK IS RIGHT OVER HIS OWN SLIME.
THIS IS HOW YOU THINK OF ME?!
NO NO NO NO NO NO!
WELL THEN, HOW--?
THAT'S IT.
SLURP!

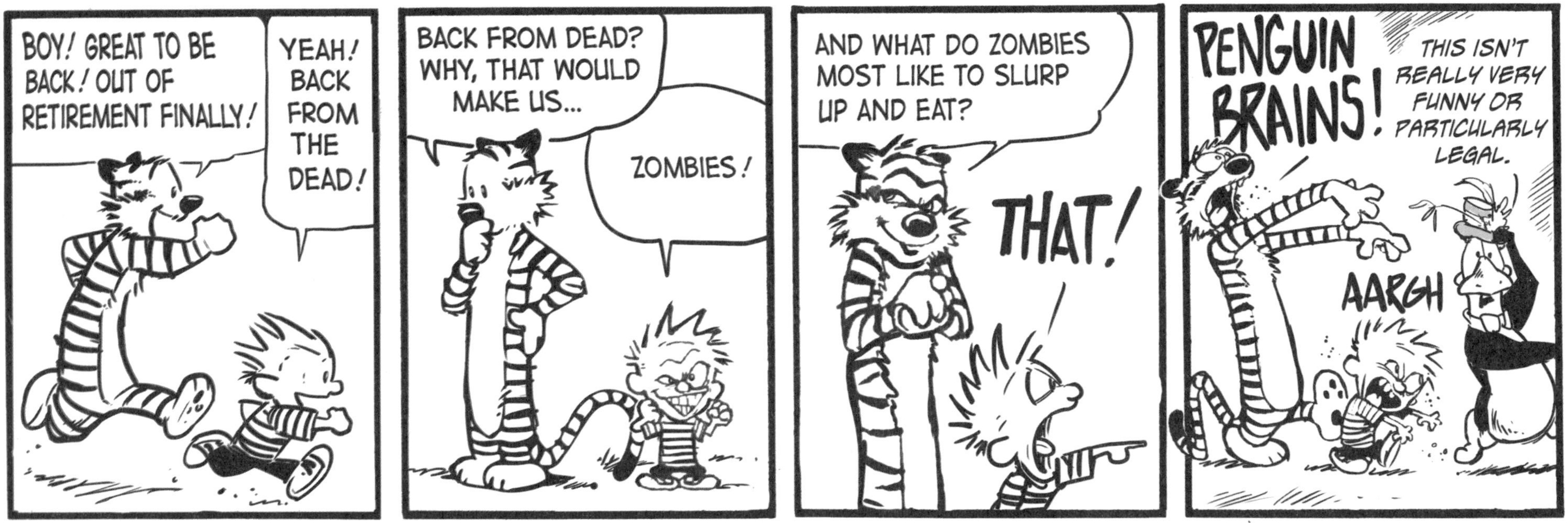
BOY! GREAT TO BE BACK! OUT OF RETIREMENT FINALLY!
YEAH! BACK FROM THE DEAD!
BACK FROM DEAD? WHY, THAT WOULD MAKE US...
ZOMBIES!
AND WHAT DO ZOMBIES MOST LIKE TO SLURP UP AND EAT?
THAT!
PENGUIN BRAINS!
AARGH
THIS ISN'T REALLY VERY FUNNY OR PARTICULARLY LEGAL.

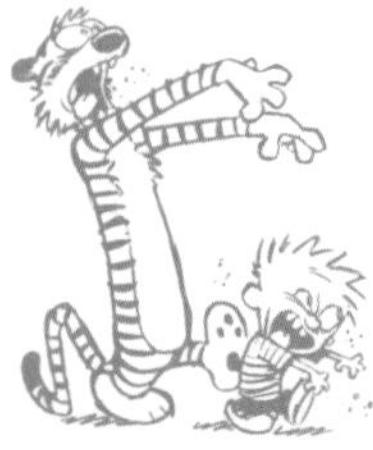

BLOOM COUNTY
WILL RETURN!

Berkeley Breathed is the award-winning cartoonist of *Bloom County*,
Outland and *Opus*. His entire comic strip catalogue has been collected by IDW Publishing
and is available at finer booksellers everywhere.

Follow him on Facebook at:

www.facebook.com/berkeleybreathed

For more on IDW Publishing and their amazingly diverse selection of fine
graphic novels and comic strip collections, visit **www.idwpublishing.com**